INA LOU

THE LEFT SIDE OF WRONG

Pine Lake Books

West Guilford

Ina Louise Jackson (mom ♡)

First printing

Pine Lake Books has allowed this work to remain as the author intended.

All characters in this book are fictitious, and any resemblance to real persons, living or dead, is coincidental.

978-1-926898-56-8

Pine Lake Books

Pine Lake Books

West Guilford

Also available in eBook format

www.pinelakebooks.org

eISBN 978-1-926898-55-1

Prologue

It is easy to tell the difference

Between right and wrong,

What is hard is ...

When wrong is more right.

Dedication

For Evelyn Pauline
My friend ... My mother
1935 - 2010

Who taught me that the journeys
Are just as important
As the destinations.

That there are always lights
At the end of the tunnels.

And ...

The times they are hard to find,
Go in and out all the doors
If that doesn't work,
Try the windows.

Foreword

Pretending domestic abuse or malevolent forces aren't out there is like putting a cheap dollar store Band-Aid on the cut on your arm that requires stitches and going out in the rain. Soon the Band-Aid will unglue and the blood will trickle down your arm and flow into the webbing on your fingers. Though, at first all is as simple as it seems ... A cut with a Band-Aid protecting it from the elements. But soon ... It will uncover becoming the gaping tear that requires a trip to the hospital with four or five stitches. Proving once and again that things are not always as they seem. Take Julie Porter for instance: Nothing in her life is as it seems either.

: The dictionary defines abuse as ... To treat wrongly or improperly.

: The glossary defines malevolent as ... Evil or ill disposed.

: The police define both as ... A bothersome headache.

What do you think Julie defines it as?

Shall we go together and see?

SECTION ONE
THE ABUSE

Chapter 1

"I've been toying round the idea of opening my own restaurant! What'd you think?" Tony Porter said, in a tone of voice borrowed from his childhood. He absent-mindedly rolled his uneaten peas in circles on his dinner plate with his index finger waiting for his wife's response.

"Sweetie, what do you think?" he repeated. He lifted his head and studied her briefly, blowing out a loud long sigh in her direction. It went by unnoticed sucking itself into the silence. He switched from rolling peas to running his hands through his hair, shaking the loose strands down onto the plate. He blew out another sigh. "Sweetie?"

Julie had tried to appear as if she'd been interested in their one sided dinner conversation, but had lost. She quit nodding in all the right places quite a time before the grandiose *'Opening my own restaurant,'* drifting completely off somewhere else.

Tony shook his head drumming his fingernails into the tabletop. "SWEETIE!" he exclaimed. He pivoted his chair sideways with his right foot crossing his ankles, hoisting his legs crane like above the table and dropping them, landing his heels down in a loud thunk bouncing his plate like a rubber ball cross the table. "SWEETIE!" he yelled again.

Julie returned from her somewhere else. "What did you say honey?" Her eyes flicked to his ... To the table ... Back to his ... Back to the table, where a wet beaded ring of oil and sweat was growing about his heels as if it had just been granted a life of its own. The remnants of her somewhere else smile drew itself into a grimace, stiffening and cementing her lips against her teeth, stretching the skin trampoline tight as the first wave of pungent fumes crashed and foamed their way up, curving under then over her chin and quickly bypassing her lips as if it knew her nostrils were open season. It shot through, stopped, hung, then crawled its way into the back of her throat to set up camp.

Tony reached forward ruffling up her hair with one hand. "Anybody in there? ... Earth to Jules! ... Earth to Jules! ... Come in Jules!"

Julie pushed his hand away. She wasn't in the mood to receive the hard knocks on the top of her head that invariably followed this routine. She leaned forward, putting both elbows on the table and resting her chin in her palms. She cupped her nose with her fingers, filtering the slipstream of vile air coming from the growing mass on the table. It was too little too late and she gagged, dry retching. "Wh ... What we ... Were you saying?"

"For Christ's Sake! ... It's not that bad! ... Come on!" He uncrossed his feet wiggling his toes in her face, his controlled smile resembling something not quite human.

She lifted her left palm out of need for air, sucking in then quickly replacing it, her head swimming round in circles from the stink.

Tony tilted his chin skyward. He sniffed up the air in piggy like snorts rocking his shoulders. "Ah," he said. "That's just the sweet smell of hard honest work!" He leaned in to her pulling at her hands. "Take a good long whiff! ... It'll do you the world of good!"

Julie choked on the mouth full of saliva that had pooled under her tongue. "I'll pass," she muffled through her hands.

"So ... Getting back to the subject, what do you think?"

"Of what?"

"The restaurant?" Tony moved his hands from hers.

She bumped his toes with her elbow motioning with stiff head jerks to get his feet down. He gazed at her intensely his half-assed smile freezing, melting, and freezing again, as he ever so slowly obliged.

"Jules?" he questioned, softly almost misplaced.

She studied him finding this indulgent tone out of context and somehow unnerving. It didn't mirror anywhere on his face. She didn't count the frozen smile, which seemed to fit a different definition of unnerving.

"What do you think?" He did not wait for an answer. "Jimmy's not doing so well. He is having a lot of problems. I mean a hell of a lot of problems. He has not filed taxes in six maybe seven years. He owes so much he's screwed. His home life is kaput. He has been sleeping at the restaurant for months now. And business is way, way down. I think he's going to have no choice but to claim bankruptcy. And you know ... I've always wanted to open up my own restaurant. So I was thinking now's my chance. What do you think?"

Her jaw hit the floor as she tried to get a handle on what he'd just all lumped together in one basket. One big basket.

"So?"

"You ... Want ... To ... Open ... A ... Restaurant?" she asked. Shock wedged its self into each word like an extra syllable.

"Thinking about it. What do you think?" Tony bobbed his head side to side like one of those plastic bobble toys.

She couldn't believe her ears. His ready willingness to take advantage of Jimmy's downfall. Jimmy and him were supposed to be friends, you help your friends not stomp them into the dirt and plant lawn seed on their head.

"But ... But," she stammered.

"But what?"

"But you have always wanted Pizza not Chinese!" she exclaimed scrambling for words.

Tony grasped her elbows, "Pizza, Chinese, what's the difference?" he asked.

Julie's eyes grew big. "You can't open a Chinese restaurant, you're, you're ... You're ... Italian for God's sake!"

Tony smiled, bobbing again. "So ... What's your point?"

"An Italian can't run a Chinese restaurant, it's ... It's ... Sacrilege ... It's ... It's ... Just ... Just not right! And ... And besides what about your card shop?"

He chuckled. "An Italian can so! We have the Midas touch! We are good at everything!" Tony lowered his voice to a hush, stroking her palm gently back and forth with his thumb. "Especially when it comes to women aren't we sweetie?" He made slurpy noises sticking out his tongue flicking it provocatively.

Julie's skin crawled off across the table, quickening its pace as droplets of saliva started to glob, dribble and drop from the corners of his mouth as he continued to flip and sway his tongue. If she'd had a knife, she would have hauled off and cut the damn thing off.

He winked at her giving her the once over. "The card shop is a cinch to run, I can hire a kid part-time for some of the days," he said.

"You're going to work all day at the factory with your Dad? Run a card shop part-time and open and run a Chinese restaurant?" Julie asked. She was stunned.

"I'm thinking! ... So? ... Jules, what do you think?"

Julie tried to find something other to say than a repeat of what she'd just said. She stared at him blindly letting her thoughts go. "What do I think? ... What do I think?" She coughed on purpose, stalling, hoping any second her brain would right itself and she'd be able to find the words to say all the things she should be saying.

"Honey come on. You're acting like you've never heard this before!"

"What do I think?" She said it again. All this about Jimmy was news to her. Her husband's unadulterated willingness to take advantage of someone when they were down was something she had never imagined. She was at a loss. She silently rose up her hands in the 'got me pose' to stop another 'What do you think?' coming out. She stayed frozen that way as the vision hit her of Tony full of grease, grunge and oil, stinking of sweat, running his hands constantly through his hair, feeling and jiggling his jewels every couple of minutes cooking Chinese food for people's meals. She shuddered.

Her frozen what do I think raised hands got me pose must have translated into you know best dear. He left the table without so much as another word, whistling as he sauntered off slowly up the stairs, no doubt imaging himself as the next 'Chinese Food Restaurateur King of the World.'

Julie lost herself to her thoughts as she cleared the table and put the dinner dishes in to soak. She just couldn't get all this. She had drifted in so deep, the upstairs bellowing slipped past unnoticed. As the shouting picked up momentum, adjectives and volume bouncing into the dishwater off the back-splash she keyed into the imminent danger circling round in the upper stair well.

"FOR FUCK'S SAKE! ... YOU FUCKING GOD DAMN BITCH! ... FUCKING COME UP HERE! ... NOW!" Tony boomed.

She put down the dishcloth with hands that trembled right up past her elbows. She started to pray, her heart felt like it had just stopped in mid beat. Her throat narrowed, choking itself off as she left the kitchen, her limbs robotically climbing the staircase. By the time she reached the top landing her skin was wearing a beaded blanket of sweat. There was something almost sinister sling shooting around up there. She could feel it. Her tongue stuck to her palate and hung there with no moisture to oil it out. She dragged her feet slowly down the length of hallway, stepping and snapping the eggshells that had grown up through the carpeting. She stopped in the bedroom doorway.

"WHERE IS MY WHITE FUCKING TEE-SHIRT?" Tony screamed. He was way too far the other side of angry.

Julie looked from him to the dresser cabinet full of white tee shirts and back again. She tilted her head side to side dog-like attempting to rationalize what was being said to what she was seeing.

"I ASKED YOU A FUCKING QUESTION!" Tony shouted.

Julie swallowed her cardboard tongue back as it folded down off the roof of her mouth. She hesitantly crept in beside him picking up some of the white tee shirts and offering them up to him.

He stared a cold stare that would have frozen hell over. "I FUCKING ASKED YOU A GOD DAMN FUCKING QUESTION BITCH!"

"All ... All ... All your tee-shirts are white ... I ... I ... I don't understand," she stammered injecting chilled breaths of fear between the words.

"WHAT ARE YOU FUCKING STUPID OR SOMETHING?" He roughed through the shirts with clenched teeth, cursing, picking up handful after handful, shaking them in her face.

"What ... What ... What ... What ... Sh ... Shi ... Shirt are you ... You looking for?" Her tongue was still folded back and did not move when she spoke. Her mouth and throat had dried and was splintering off in all directions. She reached down forcefully pushing her shaking knees together with her hands.

"MY!!! ... FUCKING!!! ... WHITE!!! ... ONE!!!" Tony punctuated each word as if it was a separate living entity spraying beads of saliva into the air as he went.

He lifted his eyes from the tangled mass of tee shirts to hers. She watched helplessly as streams of fire shot out of his sockets landing themselves into hers, boring large holes right clean through her skull. She could feel the after burn sparking off the wall behind her. Her entire body vibrated, bouncing back and forth, side to side, shattering all the eggshells. She searched his face for his soul. It wasn't there. She stepped backward. He moved forward matching step for step. He resembled a half-crazed mutant out of a b-science fiction movie more over than the human being that professed to love her. She was sure at times of her conviction that aliens had tip-toed into their house one night a couple months back while they were sleeping and replaced Tony with another look-a-like Tony. Only this one was really a full-blown out and out prick from planet 'Dickhead.'

"WHERE THE FUCK IS IT?"

"Which? ... Which? ... White ... White ... One?" she stuttered, slurring. She kept telling herself to breathe. It wasn't working. She could not remember how.

11

"MY FUCKING WHITE ONE! ... THE FUCKING ONE I WORE FUCKING YESTERDAY!" He reefed the wooden drawer from the dresser cabinet flinging the shirts at her.

She stepped sideways, her knees quivering so badly her body jolted back and forth into the doorframe as the room snowed with thick clumps of tee shirts. Her open mouth responded. "It's ... It's ... It's in the laundry!"

"IT'S IN THE LAUNDRY!" he retorted. "IT'S IN THE FUCKING LAUNDRY! ... FUCK!!! ... FUCK!!! ... WHAT THE FUCK IS IT DOING IN THERE?"

"It's dirty!" she said. She gulped and swallowed the pooled saliva as split second anger fused and shot through seeding thoughts clicking in her brain. She couldn't believe she had just answered such a stupid question. *'No it's in the laundry because it's clean! ... You stupid, dumb, jackass,'* she mouthed to his turned back. It was what she wanted to say, should have said, could have said. Her life lately seemed to be filled up with a lot of silent talks to his back with the wanted to's, should have's, and could have's. And, she didn't know or understand why?

"WHAT THE FUCKING HELL DO YOU DO WHEN YOU GET HOME FROM WORK? ... I SUPPOSE THE KIDS' CLOTHES ARE ALL CLEAN! ... AREN'T THEY? ... FUCKING AREN'T THEY?"

Julie did not answer. She couldn't, she had clicked off. He was right in front of her, invading her invisible barrier 'safe distance' air space. She opened her mouth then closed it. She couldn't think of anything to say. Her tongue had curled backwards on the roof of her mouth, hanging its self upside down, the tip sliding neatly down her throat.

She stood frozen and lifeless facing him as every fibre of her being fled in terror. She felt them leave. They'd just walked off on their own right on down that there hallway, running full out when they hit the staircase, leaving a gaping hole where they had busted through the front door.

She could hear loud knocking as her body jolted and jostled. But, without her thoughts she had no way of knowing it was her limbs stiffly thumping against themselves. Her eyeballs self-propelled in wide circles round and round, and round watching his every move. Her frigid brow dug into her forehead furrowing itself in horror, fine-tuning and tightening, as required. Seconds seemed like hours, as she stood before him like a plastic doll left out in the sun too long.

Tony rushed the door of the linen closet lifting out the laundry basket and rifling through it. "FUCK ME!" he screeched. He plucked up a single white tee shirt, brutally shaking it at her. "JUST WHAT DO YOU CALL THIS? ... WHAT DO YOU FUCKING CALL THIS?" He cursed an entire sentence made up of fuck, twisting and flinging the shirt into her face. He mashed the tee shirt back into the basket burying it so deep he snapped and popped all the rungs in the plastic base. He jerked the basket off the floor tossing its contents into the staircase, punching at it with both fists as they jetted through the air.

Julie's subconscious sent a subliminal message to her legs to move back into the wall, her palms marking her stop spot with perpetrate perfect half moons.

"WELL? ... WHAT HAVE YOU GOT TO FUCKING SAY FOR YOUR FUCKING SELF NOW? ... WAS THAT NOT MY WHITE FUCKING T-SHIRT?"

Her lips opened and closed in silent rapid secessions. Her palms had cooled, freezing her to the wall. She couldn't move.

Tony glared, examining her in minute detail like she hadn't quite pushed herself into the wall far enough yet to suit him. He leaned into her, feeding off her fear.

She flipped her feet sideways bringing them up horizontal to the baseboard, blending herself further into the nothingness of the paint and plaster. There was pure silence. An unnerving lifeless silence, the kind where you could swear you were dead.

Tony suddenly turned, pounding past her and shattering the air. It snapped and fissured in his wake.

Julie tore herself free, slithering along the wall until he came in view. If she was going to die she wanted to see it coming so she could shut her eyes at the right moment.

He had his back to the doorway. He was still yelling "YOU FUCKING GET HOME WAY BEFORE ME! ... I WORK FUCKING THREE JOBS! ... I DON'T SPEND ONE FUCKING DAMM FUCKING CENT OF MY MONEY! ... I PUT ALL MY FUCKING PAYCHECK IN THE FUCKING BANK! ... AND YOU FUCKING CAN'T EVEN FUCKING WASH A DAMN FUCKING SHIRT?"

Julie's black-holed, open mouthed silence fuelled him further. He lunged at the bed tearing away the comforter and sheets. He kicked at it again and again as if it had been taken over by some kind of diabolical presence that had refused to repute its sins in death and was damned well going to. He repeatedly smashed the sheets together with his fists, twisting and turning them as the ripping material screamed out with unadulterated agony. As suddenly as this round began, it ceased. In the time it took to blink one could almost swear on their mother's grave that none of this had happened. Even the bedding was gently cascading down to the floor.

Tony slowly turned her way giving slow motion brand new meaning, his big dead eyes fixating on hers stealing out every ounce of life she had left.

She didn't know who this was. She didn't want to know. She didn't ever want to know. This was way beyond worse even for the alien counterpart of him she'd come to know. It was getting hard to tell what was and what wasn't. Everything had become too hard, swimming in all together, mixing up the fine lines that define all things. All she really knew was primal right at this moment of place and time. She clamped her eyes shut wishing a wish with all her might. If she could just make herself disappear into the patch of plasterboard, all would be all right. He'd go away because he couldn't see her any more. Her concentration broke as shrill screams shattered the air.

Tony was on his hands and knees swivelling his head side to side, his mouth forming a perfect O as he screamed and howled in piercing guttural gurgles. His tongue flicked in and out, in and out swollen to twice its size gorged with blood. Deep, dark, fresh, red, blood. He raised his fists over his head letting go another set of high-pitched gurgles. It changed half way through to something inhuman. She would have ran and hid in the next town if she could have. He brought his arms down fists first into the middle of the barren mattress. Again and again he beat it, his head whipping side to side and up and down like his neck vertebrae were rubberized.

"FUCK ME!" he squealed. He crashed his hands down breaking below the surface into the coils. He suddenly stilled, turning his attention her way, offering up a toothy smile that had death written all over it. He jerked his body ever so slightly in her direction sticking out his tongue, drooling red as he laughed and laughed seemingly sucking up her fright.

She pushed back into plasterboard denting in.

As if refuelled, he resumed his frenzy, ripping his hands free from inside their lair, his flesh tearing as it caught in the sharp edges. He deliberately, slowly licked the dripping blood from his hands as he moved back from the bed. He whooped then jumped into the air coming down on the mutilated bedding with his feet, stomping it, flattening it out. He clenched his teeth grinding his heels into it with so much force pieces of carpet fibres stuck right through one side and out the other.

Julie welded her eyes shut. She didn't want to see any more if she was next, it might be better and quicker to be surprised. She had stopped praying. There was no prayer for this. Her stomach twisted itself inside out knotting on a kidney, taking it and most of her inner organs with it, sitting them all up inside her in a neat little ball. She waited not breathing, telling herself maybe soon she would feel no more, be no more, then all would be well.

The room all at once silenced. The stillness of silence wormed its way up inside her, inching along eating at her soul. She was beyond scared, she was right up full to the line of insane. She tottered on a thread as she strained listening, listening for something, anything. But there was nothing. She had prayed for silence so long back she had forgotten and now here it was. She had it. She had fear and terror too, in their purest of forms, nothingness. She felt as if she had picked the short straw out of a twisted hand of fate and was cast suddenly into the middle of a horror film by some demented misguided director who wanted realism.

Out of the nothingness came a sweat filled breeze. It pushed past her, trailing itself off on down the hallway. Then there it was again, the voice.

"YOU SHOULD FUCKING TRY DOING FUCKING EVERYTHING I FUCKING DO! ... JUST FOR ONE FUCKING WEEK! ... MAYBE FUCKING THEN YOU'D FUCKING APPRECIATE ME FUCKING MORE! ... AT LEAST I FUCKING WORK! ... IT'S FUCKING MORE THAN YOUR FUCKING OTHER FUCKING HUSBAND FUCKING DID! ... FUCK ME! ... THAT'S FUCKING RIGHT JUST FUCKING FUCK TONY UP THE FUCKING ASS!"

The slamming of the front door echoed in the darkness, mixing in with the 'fuck this fuck that' reverberating in and out of her skull like a lone 'CD' caught forever on a hair line scratch. The squeal of tires resounded in the distance coaxing a shallow stab at reality. She began to breath in real breathes. She counted to one hundred twice just to make double sure before opening her eyes. Then counted again. By five hundred and twenty-three she melted, trickling her way slowly down the wall, pooling at floor level. It took her hours to convince herself she was still alive. It took her longer to believe it.

The telephone had rang many, many times. She rose to her hands and knees squinting through the darkness in the direction of the nightstand hoping for blackness, but the darkness glowed with little sharp red flashes announcing there were messages from hell waiting. *'And why shouldn't there be?'* she thought. *'He'd have to do it! He'd have to put them there! He'd just have to! He isn't finished with me yet. Not by any stretch of the imagination!'*

As time passed her mind regained wattage, switching all but to the 'on' position. She thanked God for the boys not being a party to this latest alien onslaught. Basketball at the neighbours after dinner was starting to look a lot like Christmas. She had been asked to go too but had opted instead for quality time with *it*. The corners of her mouth turned up. *'Yeah right,'* she thought.

Later she tucked both boys into bed, kissing their foreheads a sweet goodnight, revelling and soaking in the beautiful aromas of their hair and skin. The scent that belongs to a child put there for their mothers to love. The scent that says, 'hey I am yours and always will be'. The one and the same, that is just as good with or without the mud. She stood by their bedsides for a long while watching them as they slept and turned into angels as all children do. She traced the outline of their cheekbones with a fingertip. It was the simple things in life that always gave her cause to smile and be thankful for each and every moment. Her cup had been half-empty from this day instead of half-full, now the tables had turned and it was half-full again.

Julie put her hands in her housecoat pockets, sitting on the edge of the bed watching the phone's red warning beacon blink on and off, on and off. She sat for the longest time in no apparent hurry for hell. She counted the blinks out of curiosity. There were twenty-two. She had hoped it would ring just once more so she could get it over with all at once but it hadn't. She dialled his cell phone number hoping to reach him but desiring not too all the same. Being yelled at and pounded once more this night would sure be better than some twenty-two times. But the cup turned back to half-empty. It was turned off. She tried his work, card shop, restaurant, and pager. All were the same ... Off. *'Surprise! Surprise!'* she thought. "Yeah! Really what was I thinking!" She said. "He'd never make it that easy for me now would he?"

Julie took several deep breaths, eleven in fact, before she depressed the buttons to retrieve the messages. They rolled off one by one. Hell might as well have just jumped up and bit her in the face.

"Jules are you there? I fucking know you're there. Pick up!"

"JULES FUCKING ANSWER THE FUCKING PHONE!"

"JULES?"

"SEEING AS YOU WON'T FUCKING ANSWER THE FUCKING PHONE! FUCK YOU!"

"I'm going to the card show. I'll be there a couple hours. There's some stuff I have to pick up from a supplier. If the casino is on tonight I just may go the FUCK THERE FOR AWHILE SEEING AS MY FUCKING WIFE CAN'T EVEN PICK UP THE FUCKING DAMM FUCKING PHONE! WHAT ARE YOU FUCKING TOO BUSY DOING? FUCKING PLAYING WITH YOUR SELF? FUCK YOU! FUCKING FUCK YOU!"

"JULES FOR FUCKING CHRIST'S FUCKING SAKE FUCKING PICK UP THE FUCKING GOD DAMN PHONE! WHAT THE FUCK IS YOUR FUCKING PROBLEM! I FUCKING DON'T ASK FOR FUCKING MUCH! I FUCKING WORK! WORK! WORK! ... AND FUCKING PAY! PAY! PAY! WHAT THE FUCK DO YOU WANT ME TO FUCKING DO? GET FUCKING FIVE MORE FUCKING JOBS SO YOU CAN FUCKING SPEND FUCKING MORE? FUCK ME JULES! I JUST WENT TO THE FUCKING BANK. YOU WROTE ANOTHER FUCKING CHEQUE FOR TWENTY-

FIVE FUCKING DOLLARS. FOR FUCKS SAKE FUCKING MONEY DOESN'T FUCKING GROW ON FUCKING TREES YOU KNOW! WHAT MORE DO YOU FUCKING WANT FROM ME? I FUCKING LOOK AFTER YOU! I FUCKING LOOK AFTER YOUR FUCKING KIDS. YOU HAVE DECIDED NOT TO GIVE ME A FUCKING KID OF MY OWN YET FOR SOME GOD DAMN FUCKING REASON! YOUR KIDS FUCKING FATHER DISAPPEARED OFF THE FACE OF THE FUCKING EARTH AND HAS NEVER YET SENT ONE GOD DAMN FUCKING RED FUCKING CENT FOR THEM EVER! ... NO FUCKING TONY CAN FUCKING FEED THEM AND FUCKING CLOTHE THEM. TONY CAN JUST FUCKING GET IT UP THE FUCKING ASS. FUCK YOU JULIE! FUCKING FUCK YOU!!!!!"

Julie hung her head sighing a ten pointer. She held the receiver out from her ear. She rubbed her temples soothing the hell-a-gram's hits and stabs against her person. She lay down on the bed, placing the receiver under the pillow. She could still hear him screaming, yelling and swearing but it was delightfully muffled making him sound more like '*Alvin the Chipmunk'* than Tony / Husband / Alien.

Fifteen minutes went by as hell's bells seemed to be simmering down to low burn instead of high fuel injected. '*Must have run out of the souls they use for the propane,*' she thought.

"I won't be home till around two a.m ... Okay? I need some time to chill out ... I'm just going to drive around a bit."

"Honey ... Pick up the phone baby ... I'm sorry! ... Okay?"

"You know I love you don't ya? I'm just stressed out. I am Italian! We are high strung! I just need to blow off steam! You know me! I don't mean anything by it! Jules? ... Jules?"

"Jules baby ... A restaurant is my dream! ... A dream for us! ... Our dream! ... Baby?"

"Julie! ... Jules? ... Honey are you there? ... Come on dolly pick up?"

"I just called again to say I'm sorry. Okay? I'm really sorry. I don't want to upset you. See you in a while. Okay?"

"My phone is going dead; it's beeping just so you know in case you try to call me. I'll be home soon sweetie."

Julie dropped the telephone into the cradle slipping into bed, housecoat, slippers, and all. She lay on her side starring blindly at the little roses on the wallpaper. There were no thoughts to be thought. She just lay there until her eyes blurred and closed.

Chapter 2

The dog started to bark waking Julie long before the car door slammed shut in the driveway. She yawned, slowly rubbing the sleep out of her eyes. She turned her head squinting at the clock radio that read a green three-forty-five a.m.

"Hey Stupid, it's just me! Come on Stupid quit barking! Hey want some cookies Stupid?" Tony said. He gave Barkley a ruffled pat on his head, then turned and kicked the front door shut, jamming the dead bolt home. "Come on Stupid. Let's see what mommy's doing. I got your cookies! Come on Stupid. I'll race ya!"

The stair steps heaved and squealed underneath the mad dash to the top. Tony scrambled down the hall on all fours alongside Barkley mimicking his every movement.

Julie rolled over onto her back and heaved a very heavy *'Why me Lord'* sigh. She draped her arms up over her head stretching. *'If he'd just give him the damn cookies in the kitchen I wouldn't have this to go through every night,'* she mused.

She moved her hands shading her eyes in anticipation of the forth-coming light show counting silently to herself. She had gotten to four when the entire room lit up. She covered up her amused smile; he had never once failed to disappoint her.

"Hey Stupid! What to watch some TV with mom and me?" He patted at the bed for the dog to jump up. Barkley quickly obliged wagging and wiggling, a cookie sticking out the side of his mouth.

Tony turned to Julie. "Want to watch TV with Stupid and me?" He picked up the remote channel surfing as

Barkley gleefully hopped to and fro and back and forth from one end of the bed to the other, over top of all and everything including Julie. He pawed and dug in sheer delight, whipping his tail so fast it went round in circles as he fetched and munched down all the cookies Tony had littered the bed with.

Tony tossed a last cookie out and over the end of the bed ditching the remote along with it. He gently rolled Julie over to face him planting a kiss on the top of her head. "Want to watch TV with me and Stupid?" Tony pressed his nose against hers, smothering her in an over abundance of little 'Eskimo' kisses.

"No! ... And his name is Barkley! ... Stupid!" Julie muttered. She rolled back over onto her stomach, shoving her head under the pillow.

Tony grinned, pouncing on her tickling her sides. "Just what was that you said young lady?" he laughed.

"You heard me!" Julie retorted.

She could feel the pain and hurt starting to drain away from her mind and body. She couldn't figure out why it was. But, it was.

"Yeah I did hear you actually. I just wanted to see if you'd say it again!" Tony chuckled. He scooped Julie up holding her tenderly in his arms, searching her eyes for forgiveness or at least a sign that it might be hiding in there. He lovingly stroked her hair back off her face and neck running his fingers through the length of it. He smiled planting a dozen soft, slow kisses about each of her temples. With each kiss, he whispered an accompanying tender *'I'm sorry baby.'* "Jules? ... Do you forgive me?" he asked. He did not wait for her answer before continuing. "Brought you something ... Do you want it?"

"No!"

"No?" He repeated not hiding his amusement. "Are you sure you don't want it?" He kissed her forehead. "You'll like it," he added.

"No!"

Tony reached around underneath the covers wrenching one of Julie's arms free. He unfolded her hand placing a single rose within it. He closed her fingers around it one at a time sealing off each with a delicate kiss. He placed his hand over hers kissing her gently on the lips. "Do you like it?" he whispered.

"No!" she said, the corners of her mouth turned up in a roguish smile that she just could not stop from coming.

Chapter 3

The telephone's insistent ringing fuzzed over changing into acoustic white noise as Julie mindlessly floated somewhere in-between asleep and awake. Her slow yawn fumbled at the humming's concealment, dissolving it, altering it into a more salient component. She shoved her head under the pillows in an attempt to stifle it out. It didn't work. The relentless ringing just kept on and on, nagging, echoing around, and pounding its way in under those pillows. No sooner would it stop then it would start again. She reached out her arm. Thoughts started to form and got at her, she swiftly recoiled.

'What if it was him?' she mused. *'Or worse still! ... What if it was the alien form of him? ... If it were the right Tony, the one she knew and loved over the past five years it would be okay, with an explanation of course, but okay ... But what if it wasn't?* She choked abruptly ingesting a mouthful of squirting saliva. *'If it wasn't?'* She answered her thought. *'He'd be there, yelling and screaming and kicking and mashing! ... Mashing those dirty, greasy, steel toed boots of his right into her skull and out the other side ... And probably through anything else that was still kicking, all for her leaving work early ... It wouldn't matter she was sick with the flu ... It wouldn't matter at all ... Every dollar ads up he would say ... You can't get ahead in life if you're sick and come home early from work ... He works when he's sick ... Everybody he knows works when their sick ... Hell the whole entire world works when they're sick ... Everybody with the exception of her of course!'*

She gulped trying to get rid of the fear lump that had inched its way up her throat attaching itself onto the back of her tongue. It just sat there growing grapes as the phone declared its presence again in a shrill ring that seemed to cry out *'I will ring, forever and ever and ever Julie ... I will just keep on ringing! ... Ringing and ringing around in your little old head, no matter what you do, no matter where you go.'*

She slithered out from under the pillows using the comforter as a backdrop for a telephone peep show and tell. She still had quite a bit of the gray matter fuzz left. She needed more time before she picked up that there thing ... Just in case. She squinted, opening and shutting her eyes as the ringing continued. She yawned, her mouth filling with afternoon twilight. She stretched her body out in stops and starts, resembling a voodoo curse gone all wrong, staying in sync with the pulsations of the machine with the receiver attached to it. She wished right at that moment the blasted thing was never ever invented. *'What-ever was Graham Bell thinking? ... Somebody should have clubbed that man to death!'*

She watched the bedposts willowy ghost like silhouettes dance amongst the rose patterned wallpaper, and all in tune to the ringing, but dancing was dancing all in the same. They swung back and forth bringing the leaves underneath to life. They scrambled and crawled off in all different directions as if scattering from the last rays of light.

She allowed herself another yawn and another thought. *'If Tony, either them, had known she'd come home early he would have phoned hours ago.'* She snatched up the receiver. "Hello?" Julie said in a hoarse voice, her throat dry, her tongue stuck to the spot the lump had left.

"Hello Julie," Jimmy said. "Did I wake you?" he asked.

"No ... No." Julie fibbed, sinking down relaxing in out and out Tony relief.

"You know where Tony is?" Jimmy asked. "He supposed to be in four o'clock today!"

Julie rubbed her eyes with her free hand. The bedside clock had read thirty something. She'd assumed the other part was a four. "Jimmy, he's only a half hour late ... He should be in any time ... Maybe he's stuck in traffic."

"It seven-thirty." Jimmy sounded frantic. "He my only driver tonight! ... I ... I."

Julie's eyes blinked wide. She pressed the receiver tighter to her ear. She'd always been able to understand perfectly through Jimmy's heavy Chinese accent. But she could have sworn he'd just said it was seven-thirty. "What did you say?" she asked.

"Tony! ... He my only driver tonight! ... It seven-thirty. Do you ... "

Julie cut him off. "WHAT?" she exclaimed. She sat up staring down the numbers on the clock in disbelief. It read a frantic Jimmy without Tony the driver seven-thirty p.m.

"Julie!" Jimmy pleaded. "Can you try find him?"

"Yes of course! ... Right away!"

"You call me back? ... Okay?" Jimmy begged sounding desperate.

"I'll call you right back!" Julie dropped backwards into bed receiver in hand. *'You poor, poor shit Jimmy ... God I feel for you,'* she thought.

"Tony! You're such a jerkass!" she said loudly. She propped herself up on the pillows. "Just where in hell are you?" She called each of his toys systematically, one by one like she'd done so many times over the last couple months, always attaining the same end. Off! ... All of them ... Off! ... *'And,'* she began under her breath. *' Why in hell would they not be? ... It's Murphy's Law.'* She got out the phone book as a last resort, calling everywhere else she thought possible and everywhere else she thought impossible. She pursed her lips together. He'd pulled off his magic act again, disappearing into thin air.

She decided to give one last heave-ho dialing his parents number hoping on the off chance they might know where he was. The telephone seemed like it rang longer than forever."Come on Allie ... Answer," she said.

"Hello?"

"Allie? ... It's Julie!" She tried to mask the desperate under currents.

"Yes love ... What's wrong sweetie?"

"Have you seen Tony? ... I ... I ... Mean T.J?" Julie spit it ou too fast, not masking the currents, fumbling, mistakenly calling her Tony, Tony instead of the required much regumented T.J. Tony's dad's name was also Tony. Confusion always prevailed if forethought wasn't right up front in one's mind for the when's, what's and whom's, where names came into play. Julie's stomach was flagging her in waves of pain signalling this flu wasn't quite done yet. She hoped Allie had caught the fast two step fumble and knew she'd meant her son and not her husband.

"Do you mean T.J. or Tone?" Allie asked.

The fumble wasn't fast enough. Allie was confused. Julie had to stop and really think for a minute Tone was a new one here. *'Tone? ... Tone?'* Perspiration beads formed along her forehead. *'Tone? ... Who in the hell was Tone?'* The cramping pain was intensifying, fogging and weighting her head. *'Tone? ... But ... Of course,'* she nodded. *'How stupid of me! ... Tone equals, Tony the husband ... T.J. equals Tony the son ... I get it!'* "T! ... J!" she squealed, like she'd just won a prize.

"No ... I haven't seen him since this morning. Him and his Dad left around ten a.m. or so to go see a customer. His Dad came back about noon ... What's wrong honey? You don't sound too good?"

"Just a bit of flu. But ... But ... "

Allie cut in "Oh hon ... I'm so sorry."

"No! ... No!" Julie shot out. "Well ... No ... I mean ... Thankyou for your concern but that's not why I'm looking for him. Tony ... I mean T.J." She'd done it again. It slipped by. "T.J. was supposed to be in at the restaurant at four today and hasn't showed yet. Poor Jimmy's having a conniption. T.J is the only driver on tonight!" Julie put her hand to her mouth sustaining a ballooning burp. It obeyed as if on cue lodging itself in her chest. She would have felt way beyond embarrassed if she'd belched into Allie's ear, flu or no flu.

"God, I don't know what to tell you here! ... Hold on a second dear ... I'll ask Tone if he knows where he is ... He might have said something to him this morning."

The phone clunked as if dropped on wood. She could hear Allie calling out for Tony's dad and then the padding of footsteps, heavy at first, turning light, then disappearing all together. The burp seemed to sense it was safe and let go rolling her stomach, it's watery contents rising in her mouth. She dropped the receiver, snatching up the pail spewing greenish yellow bile down the sides. She retched three more times then started to dry retch as rows of prickling goosebumps migrated up and over her flesh. Her body swarmed over in cold sweat, racking and shivering her head to toe in the wake of the torment's demise. She hauled the blanket up about her cocooning in the immediate warmth.

"Tone ... Said ... He ... Didn't ... Say ... Say ... Anything to him." Allie puffed in short bursts. "Just ... A ... Sec ... Hon ... I gotta ... Catch my breath ... I ran up the stairs ... Whoo!"

Julie could hear Allie shuffling something, as if papers and the squealing of wood on wood. She could hear Allie's breaths full and laboured like she was sucking air back through a funnel.

"Sorry love ... Boy I gotta lose some ... Weight." Allie paused, coughed, then resumed. "I don't know ... What to say to ya here? ... Did you try his cell? ... Sorry ... Stupid question! ... Of course you did! ... Didn't you?"

"Yes ... And everywhere I could think of!" Julie said.

"Well honey that's about all you can do!" Allie made a ten point sigh into the receiver then chuckled. "Well ... That about says it all ... Doesn't it?"

"Yes and then some!" Julie countered. A smile broke onto her lips. Allie had just summed this whole thing up quite neatly, even tying a bow around it.

"Well honey ... Dinner's cooking away here ... I'd best be getting back to it ... If I hear from him I'll call you and you do likewise okay?"

"Okay I will." Julie replied. She was glad the conversation was over. She'd been having a hard time stopping herself from grilling her mother-in–law like some stupid teenage dipstick on her missing son's where abouts. Not for Jimmy and the waiting deliverys of Chinese food, but for her own personal. Part of her had been off on the sideline, engaged in a silent war. A vigorous silent war! Where emotion had triumphed over reason and she was on the verge of waving the white flag. '*Should I? ... No ... But maybe ... No! ... No! ... No! ... But then and again ... Maybe I should ... Maybe ... Yes.*' She knew if Allie had stayed on that phone one more second she would have blurted it. Blurted the words ... The silly stupid words of young girls. '*Where do you think he is? ... What do you think he's doing?* She shook her head giving herself a mental shot in the mouth. "God! ... Julie!" she said."Just how lame are you becoming?" She didn't answer herself, which she thought all considered was a good thing. She'd heard about those people who ask themselves questions and then answer them.

She placed the receiver into the cradle, studied it, then reluctantly picked it back up punching in the restaurant telephone number.

"Dragon Flower Chinese Food," Anna speaking.

"May I speak to Jimmy please?" Julie was relieved he hadn't answered.

"He not here ... He go on deliverys." The reply was hurried like all hell was breaking lose in there. "Can I take message?"

"Yes! ... Could you please tell Jimmy, Julie called and cannot find Tony!"

"Okay ... I tell him for you," Anna said.

"Thankyou."

"Bye now."

"Bye." Julie hung up the phone. Her stomach was unassuming for the first time in hours. Her eyes were mossed and heavy. She was asleep before retrospect could sneak in ... Where Tony was ... He was.

The phone rang ... Stopped ... Rang ... Stopped ... Went again ... Stopped, then went again.

Julie sleepily pulled at an arm. It didn't budge. She didn't try again, her chest felt heavy like a ton of bricks had been off loaded onto it. If her arm was stuck then it would just have to stay that way. Right now she really didn't care. She'd intentionally mummified herself earlier with all the blankets at hand in an attempt to keep warm. And for some reason it still felt way past good. For the first time since the early morning hours she was pain free and comfortable. She relished the simple pleasure and just lay there. The reason she'd woken slipped on by without so much as a second thought. She sleepily yawned a long yawn.

Barkley on cue wiggled and plastered his tongue end to end with a happy to see you wet slurpy kiss.

"Oh Barkley!" She snapped her mouth shut scraping her teeth backwards over her tongue. "Did you have to do that?"

Barkley started wagging feverishly bouncing her up and down on the bed.

She was now coherent enough to realize why her chest felt heavy and how she had gotten that tongue kiss so lightening quick. Barkley had draped himself over her chest and stomach adding to the mummification prinicples. *'No wonder my arm was stuck!'* she thought. *'It was wrapped up all neat and tidy underneath three blankets, a comforter, and a forty pound dog!'*

The telephone signalled again.

"How am I supposed to get out of this mess Barkley?" she asked.

Barkley took this as his personal cue to wash Julie's face as fast and furiously as possible.

The phone sounded out again. Stopped ... Rang ... Stopped ... Rang.

"Ah!" Julie said. She winked at Barkley knowingly in between his kisses. "We both know who that is! ... Don't we now?" She tilted her head attempting to steer Barkley off course from the other ear he was steaming ahead to. She couldn't be bothered struggling to answer the phone. She knew who it was. Well, one of two anyway, and besides she had no arms. It was a just reason to her. She figured she was probably better off this way right now too. Couldn't do much but ... Better off.

And there it was again.

"There should be some kind of law on how often and how many times a person can call you? ... Don't you agree Barkley?" she asked. "Well my lovey ... Mommy's got to get out of this mess before that dickweed calls again."

Julie rocked her shoulders back and forth a couple times picking up enough momentum to pivot onto her left side, sending Barkley sprawling head first into the pillows. She smiled as he scrambled to his feet picking up the rectangle shape responsible for his head plant, shaking the living daylights out of it. "That's it Barkley you get that thing," she coaxed. Barkley responded by tossing it into the air, refirming his mouth, and giving it what for.

The phone rang again ... Again ... And again.

Julie struggled to free herself from her bindings, grinning, watching Barkley. He'd dropped the pillow and was turning his head side to side examining and studying it. She figured he was surveying the excellent job he'd done. The thing was lifeless, wet, soggy, and bunched up in a heap. It wasn't going anywhere anytime soon. And was injured just enough now, that it wouldn't be able to get him again.

Barkley turned his attention to Julie who had become a wiggling mass. His head bounced to and fro then halted as he lowered his front end and pounced.

"You're a lot of help here. You ... You poo face!" Julie giggled. She pulled her arm out tousling up his hair. He turned over onto his back in delight putting all four feet in the air. Julie played tickle tummy holding her other arm out to the night table counting under her breath. She got to four when she said hello.

"Where were you?" Tony asked.

"ME? ... ME? ... Where were you?" She countered.

"Where were you?" he repeated. His tone gave new meaning to the words 'not very nice'.

She was tempted to keep playing this game just to see how long he would do it. It was pretty hard not too, but then and again, why throw a lit match on gasoline soaked kindling. It would only take a split-second to go up ... She would have to be happy with the thought. "Here," she answered. She wore a smirk he couldn't see.

"If you were there? Then why didn't you get the damm phone? I must have called twenty times," Tony said.

"Really?" she asked, sarscastically."You could have fooled me!" She'd meant to only think it. '*Oh well,*' she thought. '*There goes the match!*'

"JULES ... WHERE IN FUCKING HELL WERE YOU?" he shouted.

"Here," she said. "Where else?" she added. She had the alien again. She glanced at the clock-radio. It read ten-thirty p.m. '*He must have flown back to his planet for something or other he'd be needing.*' Her inner voice countered the thoughts '*Yeah! ... Like the key that turns counter clockwise opening up his brain to allow things like decent and human being to be said about him within the same phrase!*'

"What do you mean? ... You were there, where else?"

"What do you mean? ... What do I mean?" She asked her lips drawing into a smile for the one that snuck right by him. She bent her head, stifling her laughter in Barkley's tummy. He paused the slightest of pauses, just enough to make her worry, *maybe he hadn't missed it after all.*

"If you were there, then why the hell didn't you pick up the fucking phone?" Tony asked.

'*Yep!*' she thought. He missed it! '*One for my side! ... Earthlings one! ... Aliens zero!*'

"JULIE!" he screamed.

"What?"

"I'm not going to ask you again! ... Why didn't you pick up the fucking phone?"

'*He's calling me Julie! ... This can't be good,*' she thought. "I couldn't," she replied.

"What the fuck do you mean you couldn't?"

"You wouldn't believe me if I told you."

"Fucking try me!"

"Okay, then ... I was stuck!"

"Stuck? ... What the fuck are you talking about?"

"See ... I told you you wouldn't believe me!"

"What?"

"Forget me ... Where were you?" She tried to get it in matter of factly before he went off again.

"What?"

"Where were you?" she asked, again.

"What?"

"What time did you get into the restaurant?" She worded it differently this time. That was three what's and she knew a fourth would be coming pretty soon. Hell this what thing could go on for ten, maybe more, 'what's' if she kept pressing for an answer.

"Why?"

He fooled her with a why question just when she'd got to thinking it was going to be the old ... Where? ... What? ... Who? ... And then the bases would have been loaded. She decided that repeating the direct approach, "What time did you get to the restaurant?" was the best.

"Along time ago! ... Why?" he snapped.

She was stunned. She couldn't believe her ears. She'd actually gotten an answer from him. She went for broke.

"'Cause Jimmy called around seven-thirty looking for you," she replied.

"Jimmy? ... Jimmy called around seven-thirty?" His little boy voice joined the conversation. "Couldn't have! ... I might have been a little late ... But not, no seven-thirty! ... Nope! ... No way! ... Me and my dad had a lunch meeting with a customer today and got balled up in traffic on the way back, but seven-thirty? ... You gotta be dreaming here."

Julie let a small too quiet to hear 'oh' escape her parted lips. There was no more point to this. She put the receiver down beside her and sat there. She didn't speak anymore. She couldn't find anything to say or anything even worth saying any more. But she should have ... Should have said lots and lots more ... Like Jimmy's even later call around ten p.m. still looking for him. Or the conversation with his mom. The one where his dad had returned before noon by himself.

"Jules? ... Jules you still there? ... Jules? ... Can you hear me? ... The fucking phone must be breaking up. I can't fucking hear anything! ... Jules?"

The phone picked up static, whirred and went dead with not so much as even a peep or a beep. She was relieved by the silence. She didn't want to hear his voice anymore. Her eyes reddened filling themselves to the brim with moisture. As it spilled forth, it chilled in the night air, dropping down and stinging her cheeks with hundreds of tiny silver slivers.

She lay back down on the bed, her head burrowing into the pillow in such a way her eyes couldn't take leave of the king size blurry black and white flashing teletyped message running back and forth across the ceiling. 'LIAR—LIAR— LIAR— LIAR.'

'There had to be a reasonable explanation for all of this,' she thought. *'Maybe? ... Just maybe ... Everybody, herself included, was just all mixed up ... It could be possible? ... Or everybody's watch was off? ... Or a power failure? ... Or a thunder storm? Or better still this was just all a dream? ... Yes ... That's it.'* She nodded confirming her notion.

'Husbands don't out right lie ... This is all but a dream.' She closed her eyes not allowing the teletype in any more. The words liar had no place to go except fade back off where they had come from.

Chapter 4

"I'll be there in two minutes ... Be ready!" Tony spat gruffly, hostilely. He tossed the cell phone to his other hand, reaffirming his grip on the steering wheel rounding the corner race car fashion.

The road noises from the open car window slung shot, bouncing and reverberating over the miles of invisible air space that lay between them, mixing his words. Julie switched the receiver to her other ear pressing it close, the side of her mouth curled in a half smile. He sounded like he was a chipmunk speaking in a strange foreign tongue. "What did you say?" she asked.

"I'll be there in two! ... That's two! ... Two minutes! ... Be ready!"

Julie lifted an eyebrow studying the kitchen clock. "Be ready in two? ... We can't be ready in two!"

She glanced down at the lumpy hall floor covering. It looked like it had lost a grand battle and was laying there ready to pull out the white flag. There were: three scrambled pairs of soccer shoes, four corner flags, an array of frozen water bottles, shin pads, goalie nets, balls, gloves, knee pads, and one extremely large overstuffed duffel bag, complete with boy bum dents from two kids that had sat and waited for over three quarters of an hour before finally giving up and going outside.

"I said I'd be back around twelve noon. Didn't I?" Tony barked.

"Well it's one! We were ready then, but not now!"

"Then get ready again ... We're late."

The telephone buzzed and went dead. Julie tossed it onto the cradle. "Be ready in two minutes?" she said, mocking him. "I don't damn well think so!" She animated the top half of her body tossing her shoulders side to side as she continued. "God damn asshole! ... Just who does he think he is? He's an hour late picking us up for soccer practice and expects us to be just waiting around like hungry dogs at the door!" Frustration gave way to anger; she dropped kicked one of the soccer balls. It whistled past by barely an inch above Caleb's head, launching out the open screen door. It gained momentum rotating in the air as it flew over top of the walkway, crossing the street in a single bounce.

"Hey! ... Way to go Mom! ... Good shot!" Caleb snorted. He shaded the sun from his eyes watching the ball lodge in the neighbour's hedge.

Julie gave her son a right-handed thumbs up claiming ownership. She smiled to herself thinking. 'Yep ... *He's right, that wasn't too shabby! ... Not too shabby at all!*' She blew on her knuckles, rubbing her tee shirt and sticking out her chest with pride. She looked about the street. "Caleb?" she said. "Have you seen your brother?"

Caleb didn't get the chance to give an audible reply, shrill stiff horn blasts rocketed out beating him to the punch, consuming all available air space, even the air the neighbour's dog was using to pant with. They continued in short swift bursts, resembling a form of dyslectic 'Morse' code, as the car neared.

"Mom ... I was just going to ask where Tony was ... But ... I guess ... I don't need to now." Caleb let his voice trail off not hiding his amusement. He kicked off his runners, bent down and pulled on his soccer shoes.

When the horn sounded again, Julie and Caleb held one another's eyes. Not as mother to son or son to mother but as one person to another when they share the exact same thought. '*Asshole!*'

She hurriedly poked on her other shoe as the horn pierced its way into the house bouncing around in the front hall, up the staircase then back down. She hunched her shoulders cringing at its vehemence. *'Man!'* she thought. *'If it is this intense in the house, it must be deafening outside.'* She could just imagine how many of the nosey neighbours were all ready peering out their windows, shaking heads and pointing. She made her lips disappear into her mouth as she closed out her thoughts with, *'probably all of them on the street and the next one over too!'*

She looked down studying the mounds of soccer equipment. She secretly wished there was some way, any way, for Caleb and herself to disguise themselves in amongst it to get by all the know it all's ... But there wasn't. She picked up the Duffel bag, flags, and as much else as she could manage with the horn blasts serenading her efforts like a stuffed shirt drill sergeant with a whistle cemented between his teeth. As the blasts changed in pitch and viciousness, she took cue and rushed faster but that old expression ... *'The more hurried I go the more behind I get,'* was making a major appearance as things started to fall. "Jesus Christ," she muttered.

"Mom? ... Mom? ... Why doesn't he come and help? ... If he's in that much of a hurry?" Caleb picked up his Mom's overflow hooking things into and around his wrists and fingers. He opened the front door with one foot, booting it backward with the other, slamming it intentionally off the wall. He looked more like an animated equipment stand with a head than a kid.

"I don't know," she replied. "I honestly don't know why he doesn't damn well help!" She tossed the last water bottle into her mouth clamping down on it with her front teeth as she bunted the door open with her rump. The duffel bag caught on the door handle causing it to groan as she squished on through and by.

"Mom I'll go find Cor ..." Caleb stopped in mid word seeing his brother's head pop up from behind the bush across the street. He watched him skilfully study the hedge from three different angles, back up and give a swift back kick with a half twirl, dislodging the ball their mom had hit, and sending it home. Regardless of where it had gone, it was a cool shot. For the first time ever he was actually thankful he was still just twelve and had not started to sprout up. For surely to heck, if he had been a hair taller than what he was right now, he would have been beamed right in the head with that ball. He laughed out loud at the thought, wondering if he would have tasted pavement.

"For Christ's Sake!! ... Put a fucking move on!! ... All your fucking dilly dallying around has made us late!!" Tony said. His impatience was fraying like a too well used tight rope. He jerked open the trunk, knocking the lid off the back window. "GOD DAMN IT!!! ... YOU HAVE FUCKING MADE US LATE!!!!" he screamed, the corners of his mouth had wrinkled in distain. He grabbed and tore the equipment from them like they were lower than the lowest manservant. He threw it into the trunk.

Julie could feel a counting to ten session welling up inside her. She spat the water bottle into the trunk. "ME! ... ME? ... YOU'RE THE ONE THAT'S MADE EVERYBODY LATE! ... DON'T BLAME ME!" she shouted. She'd stopped her count at three, losing to temper. She untwisted Cory's shoelace from her pinky finger, flexing it to make sure it still worked right.

She turned to the boys, silently motioning to the car with her head for them to get in. She followed suit plopping down in the front seat.

Tony was already in the driver's seat, seated sideways, facing her dead on.

She had been waiting for his wrath to let loose on the late thing she had snarled out but he had not bitten on it. He had not even chewed a little. He had not said so much as a

39

single solitary 'God' given word ... He'd just sat there ... Looking at her ... But that said it all. That stare seemed to come right out of the very darkness itself. It made her skin goose-bump and creep off under the seat.

"Mom! ... Mom!" Cory exclaimed. He had flipped down the seat and was searching the trunk.

Julie was relieved to break the foreboding Tony trance.

"Mom! ... I can't find my lucky water bottle! ... You know the one with the red top! ... Mom!" Cory was frantically looking under everything including his brother.

Julie could not remember having it or seeing it. She gave Tony a sheepish 'oops I forgot it' glance not meeting his definitive eyeholes. She did not want to see what ever that was that she just saw ... Again.

"FUCK ME!!!!" Tony yelled. He rammed the car into park. It rocked and jerked half way down the drive, the gears grinding in defiance as it came to a halt whiplashing all of them forward.

Julie flung open her door, jumping out, feet running before they hit the ground.

Cory slapped his hand over his mouth, his eyes widening to the size of pie plates as he realized all the trouble he'd gathered up for his mother. He slunk into the back seat, and then sat back up hastily surveying. He grabbed the back of the headrest pivoting his body forward, throwing his torso halfway into the front seat, frantically checking out the foot wells. He was too consumed in his mission to notice or care about Tony's ... *What the hell are you doing kid'* look. He quickly rolled down his window leaning his body out, almost toppling himself onto the driveway in the process. "MOM! ... MOM!" He yelled knuckling his hands together arching them over his nose. "MOM! ... MOM! ... BARKLEY! ... WE FORGOT HIM! ... HE ALWAYS COMES! ... MOM! ... HE'S OUR MASCOT! ... WE CAN'T PRACTISE WITHOUT HIM! ... MOM! ... MOM! ... CAN YOU GET HIM TOO?"

Julie acknowledged him with a back handed wave as she flew through the front door of the house.

Cory stayed transfixed in his sentinel position; eyes glued forward awaiting the sign of return.

Tony revolved, fixating his death stare onto Cory, mumbling streams and streams. When he got around to the God ... Damn ... Jesus ... Fucking, something or other his murmuring was too audible ... The entire street too audible.

Cory did not divert his attention. He knew Tony was staring him down. He could feel it. He was trying to dish him over and turn him inside out and it was not going to happen ... Not this time! He figured his Mom could handle it when she got back. If she couldn't and he got yelled at in the process of it all, he didn't care much, he would have his lucky water bottle and his dog ... And that is all he wanted right now.

Tony gave him a long cursed look and got out of the car slamming the driver's door shut with so much force it quavered the car back and forth making Cory lose his grip on the window and topple backwards into his brother. Tony stood alongside looking up into the clouds for what seemed like a five-minute endless eternity before he moved around to the trunk.

"I'd bet anything," he muttered. He popped it open. "FUCK ME," he blurted. He left the trunk open, stomping off reclaiming his spot looking skyward more often then he needed too. He whistled the same four notes, over and over and over picking up additional wind currents with each air look.

Julie pulled the front door shut tugging it once to make sure it was locked. It had not been before. She ran down the drive, victoriously waving the red-topped water bottle in one hand and the end of Barkley's leash with a bounding Barkley in the other.

Tony blew out one last air honk watching her approach, drumming and tapping his foot on the black asphalt much like a parent does prior to scolding a very bad child ... A very, very, bad child.

"Okay! ... We've got everything for sure this time," Julie puffed. She hastily poured herself and Barkley into the front seat. "Tony?" she questioned. Puzzle lines formed on her forehead. He was just standing there alongside the car, un-moving, un-anything. It was like adding two and three and coming out with seven. It just did not add up, no matter which way you turned the square. They were late, incredibly late actually ... Yet there he was, out there, taking up air, space, and time. He should have been in the car driving way too fast, a yelling and screaming and cursing ... But ... Nope ... There he was, unmoving, standing along-side the car for all to see. She waited a moment, and then called to him again. "Tony? ... Tony? ... Are you coming? ... Tony?" She wanted to ask him what in the hell he was doing out there and why he was doing it but thought better of it.

"Jules? ... Just where is the case I asked you for?" he asked. He started to sway his body back and forth.

The tone of voice was unnerving. An unnerving dead monotone said by a still life dead person with swaying hips. She thought he had to be dead, because he was still just standing there swinging away, to and fro in the breeze, later than hell for an important soccer practice he should have been at over an hour ago.

"Where is it?" he said.

"Where's what?"

"Where's the case I asked you for?"

"Where's the what?" She totally had no idea of what he was talking about.

He spiked his head forming his mouth into a perfectly rounded O shape. He held the pose, yelling into the air. "YOU KNOW THE CASE! ... THE BLUE ONE! ... THE COOL THING!" Half way through a sway he hauled off and back-kicked the driver's door just below the handle leaving a larger than life imprint of his heel, and then seemed to freeze in place, his leg hanging mid-air.

The resounding sonic boom seemed like it ping-ponged off each and every house on the street.

Then as if the time delay was up, he lowered his leg, completed the sway, returning like before ... Standing, in the drive, dead, swaying away.

Julie's eyes widened ringing themselves. She leaned forward, knowing and aware, she was really seeing what she thought she was seeing. She tried to think ... *'He wants a case? ... A blue case? ... A cool thing?'* Wheels turned, ground, and then clicked. "The cooler? ... You want the cooler?" She blurted, it all suddenly coming together in her head. "You never said you wanted the cooler!"

Julie turned to Caleb and Cory mouthing *'Did he ask for the cooler? ... He didn't ask for the cooler! ... Did he ask for the cooler?'*

Both boys shook their heads no, in perfectly timed unison.

"I specifically said ... I wanted the damn fucking case or cooler as you fucking call it, when I phoned you and said I'd be right here!"

"You did not!" She snapped back.

"For fucks sake Jules! ... I fucking did fucking so! ... I know what I fucking ask for!" He gudgeoned his body around with such finesse, he could have been a retired *'Michael Jackson'* back up dancer. He grasped the metal window frame with both hands twisting and squeezing it as if he was crushing the very life right out of the poor thing. His knuckles whitened, staying that way as he continued to squeeze and squish. "Who the hell cares if we're late! ... I'm only the fucking coach! ... Why be there on time? ... Why fucking damn well go at all?" He released the metal, the tip of his tongue sticking out the side of his open mouth as if he was mentally preparing for another go around with it.

Julie watched him intensely, waiting for more of the onslaught. None of this made any sense. Not in the least. She could hear him breathing in an odd sluggish pattern, in and out in and out. She coughed twice before noticing her left hand had inched its way all on its own, up to and around her throat protecting and covering it. It was in grabbing range. She placed her right hand on top of the left.

He rounded his mouth pulling his gums back from his teeth letting out a stiff breath and then lunged, grasping the metal dab smack in the middle this time. He forcefully pinched it together as if making sure he had done the job right, like kicking a dead body once or twice just to make sure.

Julie watched him with newfound fright and horror. Fear gave way to terror as it quivered back and forth inside her becoming alive, spiralling and tunnelling as it worked its way into the very threads of her being. This was the first time he had done anything in front of a street audience. She stifled back a hard dry swallow, her back coming tight against the passenger door. She checked for signs of boy related life in the back seat via the rear view mirror, but they were much smarter than she was this time. They had both sunk down below vision level, no doubt relying on that 'Out of sight ... Out of mind' theory.

"I don't ask much from you," he said so matter-of-factly it could have fit into almost any conversation ... Except this one. He ever so slowly let go of the window frame allowing his fingers to slip off and disappear down below the edge like a monster returning to its depths. He sauntered off toward the house far too calmly for the whole scenario that had just played out.

She shook her head, and then shook it again. She couldn't figure out how to tie in his calmness, his last statement and the ones before. She mentally went over them. *'I don't ask much from you ... Who the hell cares if I'm late ... I'm only the fucking coach ... Why be there on time? ... Where is the case I asked you for.'* For the life of her, she could not figure out what all this had to do with a case / cooler that he never asked for?

"IT'S IN THE GARAGE!" she yelled after him. She hoped giving him this small but worthy tid-bit of information might speed up things avoiding a return trip to the *'Outer Limits,'* by way of *'The Twilight Zone'*. She crossed her fingers praying for some form of luck. Even just a little borrowed from tomorrow's would be wonderful. She was aware her luck was only doled out in limited rations lately, for whatever reasons, but if God would just let her borrow, just this once, she would take her lumps as they fell the next day or even the next two days.

She watched him disappear in behind the garage then slumped down in her seat. Her mouth was bone dry. The lump from the back of her throat had shifted and was now sitting on the roof of her mouth. She needed a time out ... A breather so to speak ... Before round two came about ... And there was always a round two and three and even four, sometimes. Besides she had picked up on the smidgeon of the something he'd left lying out there in the shadows of the walkway. The feeling he had indirectly called her a liar in a way she did not comprehend. And, all over a damn stupid cooler, which he didn't ask for to begin with. The more she contemplated the more she was sure, the word liar was laying out there, in the shadows wake, whitewashed and partially hidden, but there if you looked at it hard enough and she was a-looking. And ... Of all the things she was, the good and the bad ... A liar she surely was not! ... However, as for him? ... Well, well now ... Mr. out with his Dad, had a lunch meeting, got caught in a bit traffic, wasn't late for work yesterday ... Her God damn ass!

Her thoughts were rakishly intercepted as swearing crashing and banging raced out of the garage spinning around and landing right atop her head, re-writing the cartoon balloons inners. The amount and intensity told her he was having trouble ... A lot of trouble finding the cooler. She drew her lips into a tight grimace, wrinkling her brow prune like, the last noise sounded like china shattering into ten million pieces. She clasp her hands together praying it wasn't her grandmothers English bone china teacups and saucers. She'd had them all down from the storage shelf a few days ago cleaning them. But, they were in a box ... A brown cardboard box ... A brown box sitting way off up and to the side in the garage ... A brown box did not even in the slightest, remotely resemble a vivid blue cooler, even on a bad day!

"Mom ... It's one-thirty! ... We're so late Mom! ... Can you find it for him? ... It doesn't look good if the goalies late!" Cory pleaded. He touched the back of her prayer hand with his fingers.

"Okay ... Okay." She opened the car door stepping out. She'd made up her mind she was going to let him find the damn cooler himself, especially after all his shit, but Cory's pleading had melted away her decision. She hiked off down the walkway towards the garage. '*How hard could a cooler? ... A bright blue one ... Be to find? ... When it is sitting right inside the door? ... Even a two-year-old could find it! ... But,*' she paused peering around the corner of the open door. '*Maybe this Tony had never seen a cooler before or knew what the color blue looked like ... That must be it! ... That must be what's wrong!* ... Nothing else fit in the make sense hole ... *That surely must be it!* ... She then pounded and pounded the square puzzle piece into the round hole, making it make absolute perfect non-sense.

She leaned forward lightly, hesitantly tapping Tony on the shoulder. She silently motioned for him to look down ... Down at the cooler an inch or so beside his left foot.

"YOU COULD HAVE FUCKING TOLD ME WHERE IT FUCKING WAS! ... FUCK!! ... FUCK!! ... FUCK!!" he bellowed, snatching it up. He reefed the garage door, catching it off side, knocking it against itself, snapping the top hinge. It hung cockeyed, the bottom swinging mockingly, as if biting its tongue for all the things that should be said. "THERE'S ANOTHER FUCKING THING ... I'VE GOT TO FIX NOW! ... AND ... IT'S ALL YOUR FUCKING FAULT! ... IF YOU'D GOTTEN THE FUCKING THING OUT WHEN I'D ASKED IN THE FIRST FUCKING PLACE ... NONE OF THIS WOULD HAVE HAPPENED ... WOULD IT?" Tony pounded off towards the car with the cooler ranting and raving and cussing all the way.

Julie followed him silently ... Angrily ... Watching ... Watching the way he stiffly sauntered, as if he hadn't had a good shit in a week.

"JULES!!!! ... PUT A FUCKING MOVE ON! ... YOU'VE MADE ME FUCKING LATER THAN YOU ALREADY HAVE! ... FOR FUCK'S SAKE! ... FUCKING MOVE IT! ... WILL YOU?" He yelled, sternly, boldly, as if staged for all that was listening. And how they were.

Julie's temper took wing. She wanted to run up and kick him in the calves so hard his knees would buckle. This thought delighted her so much she continued. She would then jump onto his back ripping and tearing at his tee shirt, twisting it, choking him with it. Then she would dig her fingernails deep into his black expressionless eye sockets for fun just to hear him squeal. And ... Finally in a move that would make wrestling history, she would throw him to the ground giving extra stomps above and beyond the call to his solar plexus for good measure. Then, she'd roll him over and pin his arm back while twisting his head sideways demanding to know who he really was and just what he'd done with her husband.

She rolled her window the rest of the way down parking out her right arm. Barkley happily took cue and climbed onto her lap sticking his head out the car window. His ears flew around in circles with the air currents as the car accelerated.

Without warning, the car fishtailed amongst a flurry of tire squeals and burning rubber, halting in the middle of an intersection banging Barkley's head and hers off the front window shield. Julie grabbed him back into her lap not realizing the car had been stopped on purpose nor sensing the foreboding stare with her name on it. She checked Barkley for bumps finding none; she rubbed her own head where there were lumps and bumps.

Out of nowhere the air seemed sucked out of the car ... Her lips dried ... She ran her tongue along them moistening them ... They dried again ... She could feel the hotness of a lurking presence off to the side. Him ... Him, waiting for her ... Waiting for her to lift her head ... She didn't.

"Just what the fucking hell are you smiling at?" Tony demanded like she was three and had a hidden piece of bubblegum under her tongue.

Julie buried her face into Barkley's hair; she'd not realized she had been smiling. If she had of, she wouldn't of. Not outwardly anyway. *'But then and again ... Why not smile?'* she thought. *'After all ... She had just declared herself the winner of the "Twilight Zones" first unofficial wrestling match.'*

"WELL? ... WHAT THE FUCK WERE YOU SMILING ABOUT?" he screeched.

"Nothing," she replied.

"Yeah right ... We all smile at fucking nothing, now don't we?"

"Since when is it a crime to smile, anyway?" She retorted through Barkley's hair.

Tony completely ignored her question. "I suppose ... It's a stupid question to even ask you, if you brought a bag of ice?"

She separated her lips, starting to answer then stopped herself. She gazed at him out of the corner of one eye. *'Well but of course dear ... Of course ... I brought a bag of ice for the damn cooler ... I didn't know you wanted ... Why wouldn't I? ... I always bring ice! ... I carry it with me wherever I go! ... One never knows when one will need a bag of ice ... Now do they? ... Asshole!'* She smiled again.

"I guess not!" He answered his own question and then muttered something indistinguishable. He heavy footed the gas pedal whipping the car out of the intersection in a one sixty crossing the red light as if it was green. They drove a long two blocks to his parents in silence. He pulled into their drive slamming the gearshift into park. He plucked the cooler from the trunk disappearing and reappearing in minutes, tossing it back into the trunk, dumping a box of popsicles into it. He jerked the car into reverse, squealing the tires. They puffed out little bits of themselves, freshly sealing his parent's driveway with chunky burnt rubber.

Julie watched Allie's tea towel float to the ground unnoticed as Allie clasp both her hands over her mouth, eyes like saucers, standing half in and half out of the front doorway. She couldn't tell if it was appal or horror or both wrinkling across Allie's brow. She gave Allie a timid overhead good-bye wave out the window.

"What the hell are you waving at?" Tony said.

"I'm waving to your Mom! ... Is there something wrong with that?"

"Whatever!" he snarled.

"You bought popsicles for the practice?" She asked, keeping her tone light and stupid. She knew he had, she'd seen him dump them into the cooler he didn't ask for through the rear-view window. She sighed heavily, diffusion was greatly needed here ... It was greatly needed a long time ago.

"YES!" Tony yelled, sarcastically. "Why in hell did you think I wanted the fucking cooler? ... For the good of my health?"

She could have picked from the dozen or so answers that immediately came to mind. "That's really nice," she finally replied, which was not even in amongst the top one hundred.

"I thought I'd get a surprise for the team for after practice! ... And no one! ... I repeat no one tell! ... I thought I would do something nice for the guys! ... Anything wrong with that?" He said harsh and demandingly.

"No ... No ... Of course, not ... They'll really like that," she replied. *'Is there anything wrong with you doing something nice Tony?'* She silently asked, then answered. *'Yes ... Most definitely ... You nice? ... There's a hell of a lot wrong with that!'*

Tony sprinted off across the soccer field to the team leaving Julie and the boys to fetch all the equipment. She could hear realms of distorted laughter on the incoming breeze as each and every head turned their way. Tony no doubt blaming her, blaming the kids, maybe even blaming the damn dog as he delivered one of the many excuses he used as to why they were so late. She wondered how far he'd have to reach down into his bag of tricks for this one. Nevertheless, she could rest assured in amongst it all, there would be the old standbys as to how long he'd waited for her and the kids to get ready. How she had been in the shower when he'd arrived home not realizing it was a practice afternoon. And how even one of the kids had to be hunted down from the corner store ... Yet again! This one was a constant. It always happened.

She opened the trunk loading up herself, Caleb, and Cory. She couldn't get over how so many supposedly intelligent people could buy into all this crap time and time again. But, they appeared to. It showed on their faces. *'That guy must have a magic wand stuck up his ass,'* she mused. She tried to shake his bullshit off as she started across the soccer field, but it remained in a place way down deep inside ... The place, where no one ever sees the truth. She however, did not have a magic wand or even a toy magic stick and did not get off lucky in the ways Tony and his undeniable bull-crap-shit always did. She suffered some stern wayward glances and stiff scowls as she neared the halfway point. She tried not to let it bother her, but lost. That deep place that she hid things inside was starting to choke her with all the clutter she had been gathering up in there lately.

Tony grinned, grins that almost looked real as he glanced her way now and then. But ... There was just something ... About the timing. It was as if they'd been carefully orchestrated to fit in between the breaks in the giggles and laughter. His latest saying when out and about, *'Well what can you do? ... Women ... You can't live with them and you can't live without them,'* fanned overhead.

She tried to pretend she didn't hear it ... But ... That ... That particular one always seemed to get to her ... Maybe, because it was such a sexist remark ... Or maybe because it rubbed her the wrong way ... Either way ... It bugged the living hell out of her.

At the three-quarter mark, Tony excused himself, jogging over to her and the boys as if he did not have a care in the world. He wore a smooth smile for the team and parents when they could see, erasing it when they could not. He didn't say a single word as he grabbed the duffel bag from Julie ... Only the duffel bag. He flung it up effortlessly over his shoulder as if it contained aerated duck down; walking a good ten paces ahead of them, never looking back once.

Julie wondered if he did this to show off or to ram home, how much of a loser and total out and out wimp she was. And that she ... They ... Were not even good enough to walk with. After all, her day was now about not bringing a cooler and ice he didn't ask for, about being late which she hadn't been, and probably currently about wimping out and not being the new and improved female version of *'King-Kong!'* ... Whatever else this day was to bring about didn't matter anymore, right this minute anyway ... All that mattered was having one less thing to tote across the rest of the damn field!

One of Cory's teammates flew down off the slide as the three of them came into his line of vision. He ran full tilt at them arms a waving, motioning to throw him some of the equipment. "How are you Bud?" Steve asked. He gave Cory a fist thump on the back before plucking some of the equipment from each of them.

"I'm great!" Cory retorted, kneeing Steve in the butt getting him back for the thump.

Steve had the weekly paper tucked under his right arm. "Hey Bud, there's something I wanna read to ya?" He dropped the equipment with a smirk, hurriedly opening the newspaper to the page he had marked with his gum wrapper.

"Okay shoot!" Cory edged.

"Last week the undefeated famed 'Red Devils'," Steve motioned with an arm to himself, Cory, and the team. "That's us," he continued, adjusting the paper. "The undefeated 'Red Devils' did it again this week. Winning a sure fire twenty-two to nothing jolt against the 'Blue Knights.' Much of this winning streak can be attribulated ... Attribulatated?" Steve looked helplessly up at Julie.

"Attributed," she softly corrected.

Steve gazed at her helplessly puzzled.

"Attributed means to be accredited to, to be given to," Julie said.

Steve appeared deep in thought, his brow lined and wrinkled in-between the longish bangs. "Oh! ... I got ya now! ... Gee thanks!" He exclaimed. He tossed his head whipping his hair from his eyes as he continued reading the article. "Can be attributed to Cory Parker, the 'Red Devils' powerhouse of a goalie. That's you!" Steve butted Cory with his shoulder. "Who since the start of the season has not had one single goal scored on him. We will be watching this team! Though I think, it is safe to assume with only three games left in the season that this team may all but have the first place trophy in the bag. They stand in the charts with a whopping fifty-nine point lead. The second place team is the famed 'Black Angels' who the 'Red Devils' play next week." Steve slipped the paper in under Cory's armpit. "You can have it powerhouse. I've got another one at home."

"Thanks Steve!" Cory beamed. "Hey!" He leaned over swinging the cooler back and forth in front of Steve. "Bet you can't guess what we've got in here?"

"What?" Steve asked.

"It's a surprise!" Cory said, teasing Steve, rapping the cooler up and down in the air.

"Come on! ... Tell me! ... Tell me! ... Tell me!" Steve pleaded.

None of them had so much as given a single moments thought to Tony ... Nor had they sensed the need to compute how far a conversation just might carry over and across a breeze ... Or ... Who might hear it! ... The four of them had been walking along bantering back and forth, happy and carefree.

Julie had been especially enjoying the playfulness of the boys and did not realize she should have allowed her brain to give way more significance to the thud and the dust cloud.

Dirt devils swirled in all directions running along the ground like escaped convicts. The duffel bag sunk in the middle settling into the grass. Tony's feet anchored and burrowed themselves into the ground as he stood motionless, shoulders tensed, back bristled. He did not turn to face them; he did not remove himself from the line-up either. He just stood, ready, and waiting in full camouflage, gun loaded and cocked.

"WATCH OUT MOM!" Caleb yelled, too late.

Julie looked over at Caleb. "Wha ... t?" She thundered into Tony's back, bouncing backward. "Tony! ... For Christ's Sake! ... What the hell are you doing just standing here? ... That hurt! ... You could have said something or warned me or." She abruptly broke off in mid sentence as he pivoted coming face to face.

The afternoon sun backlit his outline, casting his front side into greyed darkness. His silhouette seemed as if elongated, exaggerating his height giant-like. He didn't move so much as a muscle. He didn't even twitch. It was as if he had been suddenly, cast in stone. His chest didn't even rise and fall with breath. His eyes were recessed and replaced by two pooled black holes. His teeth were the only things of color. They appeared like a thin *Rolaid* line of white against the dark gray backdrop. His lips were masterly stretched in a horrid grimace. He looked like the epitome of evil.

If she could have gotten her lead filled feet to move she would have ran for miles never looking back once. But she couldn't. She couldn't get anything to move. She took a dry breath that hurt. She felt vulnerable, lost, not in control and following his lead, her body without permission arched to stone. She could feel it inside her as if he was casting a silent spell upon her, into her. She took another dry breath; this one burnt all the way down. She stood, cast into his shadow, waiting ... Waiting for him ... To speak ... To walk ... To shatter into pieces ... To anything.

He just stood, silent, motionless, mocking her, owning time, boring little holes into her forehead with no eyes. She felt like she should ask for mercy. She might well have if she had been able to get her mouth open. But she couldn't seem to do that either. She couldn't do anything but wait for the wrath of the Plutonic God before her.

After seconds, minutes, or hours, it was hard to tell how much time had passed everything was going on by in a slow motion movie. Tony took a single step forward. He lunged at the cooler not breaking the no-eye to eye tractor beam he had constructed. He swept it out of Cory's grasp, swinging it up above his head, violently shaking it. "THIS WAS SUPPOSED TO BE A FUCKING SURPRISE!" he yelled. He rammed the cooler into the ground with so much force puffs of grass and dirt bounced up onto the lid. "NO ONE WAS SUPPOSED TO KNOW ABOUT IT!" He checked over his shoulder to see if anyone was watching. He smiled, no one was. "NOW YOU'VE FUCKED UP EVERYTHING!" He was yelling in controlled anger just loud enough for her to hear.

Julie's forehead broke out into pea size beads of perspiration where he had bored the holes. "What ... Do ... Do you ... You ... Mean? ... I ... I ... Have gone and ruined ...

Ruined every ... Everything?" She stuttered in stops and starts in tune with her knocking knees.

He arched into her barely an inch from her face. "IT'S YOUR DAMN FUCKING KID ISN'T IT?" he bellowed.

She stepped backward. "Well yes ... But ... But ... He didn't ruin ... Ruin ... Ruin anything ... He just said we had a ... A surprise." She lifted one foot then the other attempting to get rid of the shaking.

"HOW IN THE FUCK CAN IT BE A SURPRISE? ... IF YOU SAY IT'S A SURPRISE!" He latched onto her wrist, grasping harshly, twisting the skin round in circles.

"For God's Sake! ... He didn't do anything! ... I didn't do anything! ... He's just a kid! ... He was happy! ... All he said was we had a surprise! ... He didn't say we had popsicles." She defended, forcefully prying her arm from his grasp, her flesh instantaneously welting in bright red rings.

"I FUCKING TOLD YOUS NOT TO SAY A FUCKING WORD! ... DIDN'T I? ... FUCKING DIDN'T I?" He slowly swivelled his head gazing in succession from Julie to Cory.

"LEAVE MY MOM ALONE!" Cory piped. He squished in between them. "SHE DIDN'T DO ANYTHING! ... I DID IT! ... I WAS THE ONE THAT SAID IT!" he yelled.

Julie dropped the equipment. She hadn't realized she was still holding it. She put her arm around Cory's shoulders and neck corralling him backwards, landing him tightly up against her. His body was racking and shaking in feverish torrents. She wrenched him closer, welding, form fitting him to her body. She fretfully looked about for Caleb. He was there, frozen to her left side, his hand glued to her jeans, his sweating palms speaking volumes. She glanced down at Cory. "It's okay Cor," she soothed. She squeezed him in a one armed hug. "You didn't do anything wrong honey."

"WHY IN THE FUCK ARE YOU TELLING HIM THAT? ... NO WONDER YOUR KIDS ARE ALL FUCKED UP! ... HE DID DO SOMETHING WRONG!" Tony yelled hissing out hot air. "HE FUCKED UP THE SURPRISE!" He knocked his glare down a few notches fitting it to Cory.

Cory jumped in behind his mother, the scare lines stretching his lips thin. He turned sideways, crunching down trying to become invisible. His entire being trembled and vibrated right into and through her own protective layers sending them flying off out of reach. She began quivering and shaking right along with him.

Cory wrapped his arms around her waist patterning her tee shirt with little wet prints as his hands lifted on and off with the juddering.

"FOR CHRIST'S SAKE! ... YOU'RE FRIGHTENING THE HELL OUT OF HIM! ... HE IS ONLY TEN YEARS OLD! ... WHAT ON EARTH IS WRONG WITH YOU?" She shouted mother-bear like. She started to back away appearing like one large and two small synchronized swimmers in the final heat.

Tony marched forward, matching her stride for stride. "WATCH YOUR FUCKING YELLING!! ... THEY'LL HEAR YOU!!"

He was right up in her God Damn face again. "I DON'T CARE IF THEY HEAR ME!" She looked over his shoulder at the team.

"WELL YOU SHOULD! ... YOU ARE THE ONE WHO IS GOING TO LOOK LIKE THE STUPID BITCH!" He paused, clenched his fists, unclenched them then re-clenched. "YELLING AT ME FOR NO FUCKING REASON!"

"NO REASON? ... NO REASON? ... YOU'RE THE DAMN ONE YELLING AT ME!" She shot back.

"I'M NOT YELLING AT YOU, IF NO ONE ELSE CAN HEAR IT!" he retorted.

He was so close his heated breath was stinging her skin. "What?" She lowered her voice; the yelling was making her hoarse. "What did you just say?" She didn't understand the logic in how a person, who was yelling, wasn't, if no one could hear it ... Except her.

"DON'T PLAY GAMES! ... YOU DAMN WELL HEARD ME!" He was closer still, so close, too close, touching close.

Julie shoved his chest making him step backward. "You're not making any God Damn sense! ... What the living hell is wrong with you?"

"YOU!! ... YOU!!" he screamed. He drew his hand across his lips wiping off excess saliva. "You," he said again. "That's what's fucking wrong with me! ... You! ... You and your fucking damn fucking kids! ... Is that fucking clear enough for your fucking pea brain?" His red-faced anger boiled over. He booted the cooler sending its top flying off into outer space. The air snowed ice and popsicles, coming back to earth coating the grass in pastel coloured wrappers and melting bits. "I can't even give my fucking team, a fucking surprise, without it getting fucked over! ... You and your fucking kids just continually fuck up everything!"

Julie 's eyes widened and bulged, ringing themselves in white as she gawked from Tony to the cooler, to the heaps of torn paper, ice and broken popsicles and back. Born and bred instincts took hold. Without thought, she covered Cory's hands with one of hers. She grabbed Caleb from her side with her other hand whipping him in behind her with his brother and Barkley, shielding them, protecting them with her body. She then took a step forward ... Then another ... And another ... Right at Tony. Her eyes rimmed with tears of hurt and anger. "You're a God Damn asshole!" she began. "No-body forgot anything! ... No-body was late! ... No-body ruined anything! ... No-body did anything! ... You've got problems!"

Tony forced a laugh pointing his index fingers inward tapping his chest. "Me? ... I've got problems?" He poked her hard in the shoulder. "You're the fucking one, with the fucking kid, that can't keep his fucking mouth shut! ... Aren't you now?" He poked her hard again, giving new meaning to the word cruel.

"I've had enough of your shit! ... I'm going home!" Julie took both boys by the hands, turned her back, and started walking.

"Jules! ... Jules? ... Julie! ... For Christ's sake quit making a fucking scene!"

She did not honour him with a reply, nor did she stop walking.

"Just where in the fuck do you think you're fucking going?"

"HOME! ... ASSHOLE!" she yelled, without turning around.

"Fine! ... To fucking hell with you! ... But ... I'll be dammed if you're taking fucking Cory!" Tony switched on a smile to the team holding up his index and middle finger signalling he would be two minutes. He bounded around her blocking them. "You're not taking fucking Cory! ... Didn't you hear me?"

"Cory's coming with me ... After all ... What was it you said?" She put her finger to her temple. "Oh yes! ... I remember now ... He's my damn fucking kid that just continually fucks up everything!" She pushed past him.

"HE'S THE FUCKING GOALIE! ... WE CAN'T HAVE A PRACTISE WITHOUT THE FUCKING GOALIE! ... YOU AND CALEB CAN FUCKING GO! ... BUT ... YOU'RE LEAVING CORY HERE!" he yelled.

She stopped and turned. "I DON'T FUCKING THINK SO!" she fired back then started walking again.

"For fucking Christ's, fucking sake! ... Whatever then! ... Be a fucking bitch! ... You can at least pick up the popsicles before you fucking leave!"

A slight smile drew across her lips as she halted again, turned and glared. It was her turn to burn some of those holes into him he had been burning into her. "Pick them up? ... Not on your life!" she said quietly.

"Fuck! ... What am I supposed to do with them, then?"

"Jam them up your ass, for all I care." They started walking again.

"I'm not going to buy the fucking kids a treat ever fucking again! ... And ... It will be all your fucking fault! ... So live with that one!"

Julie ran her thumbs down the back of her son's hands, stroking them gently. None of them said a word.

Tony watched, shaking his head, cursing under his breath. He opened and shut his fists, digging his nails into the flesh of his palms carving half-moon shapes into them that bled. He clicked back on his smile, turned and trotted off towards the team. He talked up a storm with a dimpled aren't I a nice guy smile, explaining to all the parents that the kids had come down with the flu the night before which was why they'd all been late today and they just weren't well enough to stay and practice. He told the team something entirely different, forgetting what he'd said in his parent speech. He then turned back to Julie and the boys giving a fake wave. "Call me on my cell when you get home to let me know how the kids are," he yelled knowing they were out of earshot.

"Mom?" Cory said, finally breaking the silence.

"Yes honey."

"Do you think anyone will be mad at me for not practicing today?" Cory mindlessly swung the end of Barkley's leash in circles.

"No sweetheart ... Not at all."

"Mom?" Caleb said.

"Uh huh," she replied.

"What do you think is wrong with Tony?" Caleb questioned. He seemed like he really, honestly wanted to know.

She gazed into his bright blue eyes. She didn't have an answer for him. She didn't know what on earth was wrong with Tony. Allie had said work at the factory was very busy and stressful lately and that Tony's dad was very grumpy too, but all this crap and shit did not fall into the definition of grumpy, as she knew it to be. It fell more into the something else category that she really didn't want to go to, when a husband starts to find fault with everything and anything and lie. "I really don't know my love," she finally said. She was choked to the brim with the tears she'd been battling to stop. They flooded down her face.

"He used to be so nice and now he's not ... I don't like him anymore mom ... And he makes you cry a lot ... Like now ... And I don't like that either." Caleb went up on his tippy-toes, partially climbing her, brushing the tears away from her cheek.

"I'll be okay," she reassured. "You'll see ... Tony will be nice again real soon ... And everything will back to normal ... Everybody will be happy again, just like before."

"Really Mom?" Caleb's eyes filled with the hope of innocence.

"Of course ... My love." She glanced into both sets of blue eyes fixated upon her. "My love's," she corrected. "Would I lie to my two most favourite people in the whole wide world?"

Caleb and Cory smiled up at her, believing in her words. They slipped out of her hands running off ahead laughing and playing with Barkley.

She strolled along the path towards the house, wrapping her arms around her middle; she so needed a hug. Sometimes, being alone with her thoughts was not all it was supposedly cracked up to be. She did not like the things she thought lately. And, above all else mixed in with all those thoughts, the last thing she never ever wanted to do was lie to her sons. She prayed she wasn't.

Chapter 5

Julie awoke to the soft glow of candlelight dancing across her face from the nightstand. Off to one side sat a steaming mug of her favourite raspberry tea. She propped herself up on one elbow, only to be pulled back down, strong arms enveloping her.

"I don't want to talk to you," she said.

"I don't want to talk to you either," Tony whispered. He kissed her ear lobe.

"And I don't want to make love with you," she added.

He didn't say anything. He gently rolled her over into him. He smiled, tracing her cheekbones lightly with the back of his index finger. He shifted her closer, pressing the full length of his hard muscled body against hers.

He felt so good. She wanted to get lost in him. But, she just couldn't let go of the pain and hurt she had cried herself to sleep with. She buried her head into his chest. He moved a hand to her head gently stoking her hair.

She pressed harder against him, mentally fighting off his provocative touch. She didn't want his warmth infiltrating inside her head mixing her all up again.

"Come on honey," he coaxed. He tilted her chin up with his thumb and forefinger. "You know I'm sorry don't you?"

"No," she said. She closed her eyes. He looked way too sexy basked in candlelight.

He kissed one eyelid then the other allowing his hot breath to filter slowly over her face, kicking her pulse up a notch. He ran his palms wantonly down the length of her body pausing in all the right spots. "Have I told you lately how beautiful you are?' he whispered. He kissed her lips softly.

"No!"

"Well then, I'll tell you now. You're beautiful. And when you're mad at me your even more beautiful. You know that?'

"No."

He chuckled. "Can you say anything else but no?"

"No!"

"Will you open your eyes and look at me please?"

"No."

"Come on sweetie," he pleaded. "Come on ... Look at me please honey?"

Julie took her sweet time opening her eyes. Ever so slowly, she opened one and then the other. His dimpled smile was there ... Waiting for her. His brown eyes so incredibly soft and warm; inviting her to a place only they could share.

He searched her depths for the answer, his smile widening. Masses of thick dark hair hung about his face catching and trailing itself in his day's growth of beard.

'No doubt about it,' she thought. 'This guy is a real looker ... A prick but man oh man what a looker and he knows it, which makes it all worse.'

He was much too close to her for her own good and she knew he could sense it. He slipped his hands down to her waist. She shoved her head under the covers.

"Oh! ... Okay! ... I'm up for that!" he said. He playfully pushed her head down the bed.

Julie swam out from under the blankets arms flaying. "You're a bastard you know!"

"I know," he cooed, his voice husky.

"Stop this right now!" Julie demanded. She really was losing here.

"Stop what? Is something wrong?" He ran his tongue gently across her parted lips.

"You! ... You know very well," she whispered.

"Let me make love to you and show you how sorry I am!"

"How is that going to show me how sorry you are?"

"Let me and you'll find out."

"No."

"Honey?"

"No!"

"Okay baby have it your way, well at least for now." He gave her a boyish wink reaching over top of her. "At least have your tea then. I made it special just for you." He held the mug out for her to grasp. When she went for it, he moved it just out of reach. "It'll cost you a kiss." He moved it back and forth fanning her nose. "One little kiss won't hurt now will it baby?"

"Yes."

He moved his arm away.

"Okay! Just one," she said. She sat up quickly planting a kiss on his cheek. She motioned with both index fingers for the mug to be returned to her pronto like.

Tony shook his head, his eyes flashing with wicked amusement. "You're such a little brat!"

Julie grabbed the tea spilling it on herself.

"Here let me get that for you," he snickered. He snatched the tea back off her. He pinned her arms down with his hands and proceeded to lick the tea off her neck and chest with his tongue ever so slowly.

"I hate you," she said.

His body came down onto top of hers.

"I know you do, but you will love me again soon, I promise you!"

"Promise with all your heart?"

"Yes baby, I promise."

Julie turned her head, arching her back surrendering herself to his compelling kisses. She opened her eyes. The bedside clock blinked from five-thirty-one a.m. to five-thirty-two a.m. She stared at the clock repeating the time under her breath until it registered. "FIVE- THIRTY-TWO!" she burst out. She pushed his chest lifting him up off her. "Where in the hell have you been?" She demanded, the spell he'd cast upon her breaking into tiny pieces.

"With you," he murmured.

"What time did you get home?" She pushed him again.

"Baby not now please. I don't want to talk to you!" He cradled her flipping her over on top of him.

"I want to talk to you and now!" she commanded.

"For Christ's Sake ... Honey ... Now?"

She sat up on top of him straddling his hips. "Now!" She repeated, forcefully poking him in the ribs.

He reached grasping her waist. He lifted her placing her back down a few inches from where she was. She hastily squiggled back up, backhanding him lightly in the head.

"Can't blame me for trying now can you?" he asked. He playfully rolled his eyes blowing her a kiss. "Okay! ... Okay! ... Let's get this over with then! ... What do you want to know?" He rested his hands on her hips stroking her sides with his thumbs.

"No hands ... I don't trust you." She shoved his arms down pinning his hands to his sides with hers.

"Hey baby ... I'm not doing nothing ... Trying ... But not doing nothing." He winked at her showing his incredible dimples again.

"Will you just stop it," she ordered.

He sighed a ten pointer. "All right my love ... Let's get this over with then ... Ask away." He blew up at the hair in his eyes. It came back down bringing double with it.

"What time did you get home?" She rapid fired.

"I don't know ... A while ago ... Why?"

"What time is awhile ago?"

"Christ! ... I don't know exactly what time it was." He propped himself up on his elbows almost toppling her backward, spreading her legs in the process. "Hum ... That looked nice!" He raised his knees for her to lean against. "Sorry." He sighed a real sigh. "I know I'm supposed to be answering questions here." He bit his bottom lip giving her a slow sexy once over. "Even though my gorgeous, incredibly seductive wife who I want to make love to right now ... I might add ... Is straddling me wearing only a tee shirt, making it hard for me to think of anything else."

He rolled her off him cuddling up face to face. "There that's better," he said. "There's just no way in hell I could answer anything with you sitting on me looking like that." He lowered his voice whispering into her ear. "And you had no idea of how good you looked and how crazy that was making me did you?" He stroked her hair back from her face. "God you smell so good!" He kissed her gently darting the tip his tongue through her lips. He pressed himself against her allowing her to feel what she was missing at this moment. "Tell you what," he said. "Ask me all your questions at once and I'll answer them ... That is if I can keep myself from throwing you down on the floor and having my way with you! ... I'm having a hell of a lot of difficulty here trying to contain myself, just in case you didn't notice honey." He put his finger to her lips. "Wait a sec, before you start!" He got out of bed, rolled himself tightly up in the blanket and climbed back in facing her. "That should help where my head is or at least slow me down some," he sexily chuckled. "Okay Babe! ... Shoot!"

She took the cue. "What time do you think you got in? ... What time did you get off work? ... Where in the hell were you all afternoon? ... Why didn't you say you were sorry earlier? ... What the hell was wrong with you this afternoon? ... Why were you so damn mean? ... And who in the hell are you anyway?" She had been so dead serious at the start but he had done it again to her. She couldn't even keep a straight face. She sounded like some deranged psycho on way too much medication or not near enough. Either way it seesawed back and forth on the thin line of ridiculous and hilarious. She comically cupped her hand over her mouth, wrestled herself to the bed with the other, gagging and choking. She peddled her feet in the air, stiffened out, and played dead dog. She checked him out giving him a slow erotic once over. She laughed and crawled off collapsing on her stomach chucking her head under the tablecloth from the nightstand.

His outburst of laughter brought her head back out. She tossed her hair out of her eyes provocatively licking her lips.

He immediately unwrapped himself from his make shift prison. Once free, he got up on his hands and knees crawling towards her in animated slow motion. He talked up a whirlwind keeping his promise to her. "I think, I got in about three a.m. ... I did not come to bed right away ... I watched TV for a bit, well maybe a long bit ... Then I made you a tea, grabbed all the candles I picked up in the afternoon when I was driving around like a teenage jackass cursing and swearing at you for something I did ... Then I came upstairs and lit them ... I then put the phone back on the hook that I assumed you took off so you wouldn't have to put up with my ... What is it you call it? ... 'Asinine bullshit?' ... There are probably at least thirty dozen messages on the other answering machine from me to you ... But of course, you would have no way of knowing that ... The first ten dozen or so are swearing and cursing ... The rest are made up of a lot of I'm sorrys with the odd grovel thrown in for good measure ... Why am I so mean? ... I don't know why? ... I wish I did ... And ... You little girl are about to find out who I am!"

He pounced on her laughing and tickling anywhere he could get a hold of. When he got down to her foot she pleaded with him to stop. "And just what will you give me if I stop?" He flashed her a wicked smile. "Come on speak Babe! Wc both know you can!"

"What do you want?" Julie asked. Tears of laughter rolled from her eyes. She pushed with her free foot at his hands in a failed attempt to break lose.

He seized the opportunity, grabbing it as well, tickling both. "Ah ... I really got you now!"

Julie bucked and flapped her feet. But, she was done. She couldn't break free.

"So little girl ... Just what will you give me if I stop?" He held up her feet running his tongue up and down the soles, sending her completely insane.

"ANYTHING ... ANYTHING," she screamed.

"I'll take that!" He collapsed on top of her rolling them over and over. They landed on the floor in a heap.

"You okay?" he whispered.

Julie nodded yes.

"Good," he cooed. "I love you Jules. You know that don't you?"

She nodded again weaving her fingers into his dark hair.

He lowered his head stringing a slow line of kisses along her stomach. "Let's see how much I can make you sweat shall we?"

Chapter 6

"Come sit." Tony patted his thigh.

Julie took the offer. She stretched her legs out curling her toes in the warm sand, leaning back against him and making herself comfortable.

He wrapped his arms around her waist sitting his chin on her shoulder.

Julie closed her eyes in utter contentment. She tilted her head drenching her face in the summer sunshine. There was just enough of a breeze coming in off the lake to cool the eighty-five degree heat. If she could have picked a moment in time to freeze, it would have been this one.

"Hey it's Barkley!" Cory squealed. He smacked the water with his open palms churning ripple waves. "Come on boy," he called.

Barkley paced back and forth at the water's edge.

Caleb coaxed him further. "Come on Barkley! ... You can do it!" He patted the water's surface.

Barkley danced along the beach skipping in and out of the shallow waves. He lowered his front end, ruffed twice and bounded into the water dog-paddling straight at them.

"Good boy Barkley," Cory said.

"Why did you let go of his leash?" Julie said, without opening her eyes.

"Why not? ... Poor Stupid needs to have some fun too, doesn't he?" Tony said.

"But, I just combed him all out and gave him a bath."

"Well, now he's had another one! Speaking of which maybe you should have one too!" He all at once grabbed her, shooting his legs out to a stand, lifting her up off his lap. He chuckled as he slowly walked towards the lake with her in his arms.

"TONY! ... NO!" She screamed, it too quickly sinking in what he was about to do. "I have a dress on!"

"And you'll still have a dress on ... Just a wet dress," he snickered.

"YOU CAN'T DO THIS!" She screeched kicking and flailing trying to escape him.

He tossed her up into the air as if she was a feather, catching her effortlessly and holding her to his chest as he entered the water. "Oh I can't ... Can I?" He was waist deep. He had been debating whether to really throw her in, but he would just have to now. He waded in chest level raising her above his head. "So long sweetie," he chuckled. He let go of her.

She hit the water butt first going completely under.

He made sure she was all right before turning, hopping and running for shore. He figured beating it the hell out of there and fast was a good plan.

Julie popped her head out of the water, got her bearings, took a deep breath then re-submerged swimming after him in a straight line.

The distance between them closed much more rapidly than he had anticipated. He abruptly splattered face first into the water as his feet jerked out from under him. "You little bitch!" He quipped in fun. "Now you're really in trouble! ... Just wait till I get my hands on you!" He rose, set his sights, and then dove back down into the water. Two could play this game.

Julie looked back and forth not knowing which way to go, he was coming up on her like greased lightning. She sucked in a quick breath and went straight down onto her knees, disappearing into the water. She probably would have opted for a plan 'B' if she had known he was standing but a foot from her watching her hair submerge.

He shot his arms under the water lifting her up and out. "Thought you could hide on me? ... Did you now?" He laughed, placing her on his shoulders. "You thought wrong!" He wrapped his arms around her shins twirling her in circles.

She grabbed hold of his neck as he whirled and whirled her round. He all at once let go of her legs, playfully choking and hacking. He then dropped backwards sending them both down and under in a kaleidoscope of bubbles.

"Had enough?" Tony settled his feet into the sand. He gave a head toss flipping his shoulder length hair from his face and grinning to beat all hell at her. She could have gotten a job as 'Cousin It's' double right about now without an audition. He reached out grasping her arm keeping her from floating off. He wiped the hair back off her face, attempting to stifle his laughter and losing. "Had enough yet babes?" he chortled.

She smiled moving up close and personal. She stood up placing her hands delicately on his hips guiding him closer still. When his body came up against hers, she winked broadening her smile then all at once launched her mouthful of water at him.

He roared with laughter. "You just don't know when to quit! ... Do you?" He picked her up hurling her over his head backward into the water. "I can keep this up all day if you like?" he teased. He plucked her from the water launching her again. "That is ..." He paused placing his hands under her arms mocking a lifeguard save routine. "That is unless you'd rather have an ice cream from that cart over there instead?" He motioned with his head back behind him.

She nodded, grabbing onto his arm with both hands and floating her body.

"Thought so!" He bounced backwards towards the shore towing her with him.

"Well fuck me!" He shot out. He mouthed sorry to Julie realizing he'd sworn in public. "Jules ... I can't get my damn hand in my pocket!" He motioned with his head for her to come, his eyes flicking back and forth to the edge of his pocket. He was dripping water from everywhere and anywhere he could drip water from, making himself a most worthwhile spectacle.

She flashed him a much too amused grin settling herself back against the rail fence. She was enjoying watching him trying to get his hand into his skin tight wet jeans pocket, wiggling and wriggling his butt around. But then, so were the two elderly women behind him who had stopped walking and were just standing there smirking in approval to beat all hell. One of them gave Tony an obvious once over, raising her eyebrows and fanning at her chest, mouthing 'My ... My,' at Julie. The women were her final straw and she burst into torrents of laughter.

"A lot of help you are," he exclaimed. "Do you think you can tear yourself away and come over here and help?"

She could barely shake her head no.

He held up his middle finger posed in the 'up yours' sign.

It backfired.

She laughed harder.

He attempted once more jumping up and down and trying to ram his fingers in. It didn't work. He flashed Julie an 'I will get you for this grin' then whistled at the boys, motioning for them to come in to shore.

"What Tony?" Cory asked.

"Cor? ... Could you do me a favour? ... Can you get your hand in my pocket and grab my wallet?"

"But you're all wet," he protested.

"So are you," Tony whispered back at him

"But ... But." Cory was taking stock of his skin tight jeans. They didn't look like they had any pockets. He couldn't figure out how Tony got his wallet in there in the first place.

"Come on Cor ... Your hands are a lot smaller than mine," he coaxed. "I'll get you two ice creams instead of one, if you can get my wallet out in the next ten seconds!"

71

Cory pulled it out in two.

Tony called to Julie over his shoulder asking her what she wanted off the cart.

She almost said a popsicle, stopping herself dead, remembering the happenings of the day before. "Surprise me," she said.

He wandered off towards the cart with the boys. He returned with two cones and a dish of ice cream, both boys following behind happily working on their two double cones.

Julie gave him a questioning look.

"Ah what the hell! ... They're good kids!" He sat down beside her, sliding the dish through the sand towards Barkley.

"We're going to sit in the water and eat ours ... Okay Mom? ... Tony?" Caleb asked.

"Sure guys ... But don't go back in till you're all done, all right?" Tony said. "Right?" he said again, quietly gazing at Julie for confirmation.

"Right!" She agreed. "Honey?" she said, her tone slow, serious.

"What?" He replied looking out over the water, hoping he could find a way to side step what lay in between the letters.

She linked her arm through his. "What's wrong with you lately honey?"

"What do you mean?" He said, initiating stage one of the side step.

"You know what I mean." Julie edged not wanting to let go of it, this time. She really needed to know, as did her heart.

"No I don't babes," he said. He had decided to go with the stage-two, matter of fact approach.

"Yes you do! ... You're like a *Jekyll and Hyde* lately."

"Who's that?"

"Come on!" Julie sighed.

He propped himself up, studying her. There was no sweet smile coming off her lips or in her eyes. She'd gone serious on him. "I thought we cleared all this up last night? ... Didn't we honey?"

"No."

"But?" His tone was more of a plea than anything else.

"NO!" She said, loud, sternly. She was not about to let him worm his way out of it again.

"You know it's hard for me to talk about stuff. I've always had trouble talking. And I think ... I have talked to you more since we met seven years ago than anyone ever in my life ... And I do really try to talk." He looked down at his wedding ring twirling it round his finger.

"Yes, sometimes you do ... I guess but," she paused stroking his face.

"But ... What then?" He didn't seem to have a ready grab and go stage-three. He tried to slough her off. He didn't want to have this conversation. He could see where it was heading and he did not want to go to that place. He didn't even want to visit it. He did not want to talk about anything unless its overtone was nothing. He took a brief look into the vivid blue eyes searching his. There were way, way too many questions he did not want to answer in there. He fidgeted with his watchband, flopping back in the sand. He clasped his hands knitting them together under his head. "Oh babes ... I don't want to do this ... Everything is so nice ... Do we have to do this?" he asked.

"Tony please." Her voice held a soft tremble.

She was pleading. Hanging on to the moment. Waiting for him. He couldn't even find a smile to force out for her. That always softened her edges. But it wasn't there. He had no ammunition to fire at her. It was a long time before he figured out any words. "Sweetie," he began. "Honey ... Man ... Honey I'm ... I'm just having a lot of problems lately ... I don't know how to put them all from inside here to out there for you and I am tired too sweetie ... I'm just so damn tired."

Julie broke in. "You don't need to work so much. We don't need the money that bad, do we?"

"Babes ... We've got your two kids to raise, all on our own. I know their dad's never going to help us out with them. He just seemed to vanish off the face of the earth after he got out of jail. He hasn't called them for years even to wish them a happy birthday. Has he?"

Julie shook her head no.

"See ... It's all up to you and me. I want us to get ahead and I want them to have a good education and that takes a lot of money."

"You haven't answered what I asked you?"

"But I did baby ... I said I'm having a lot of problems."

"What are they then?" She asked softly, barely above a whisper. She was hoping he'd open up, even just a little, like he used to.

"If I knew how to explain it to you, I would honey."

"Can't you try ... Please ... For me?"

"Sweetie," he said. He ran his fingertips up and down her arm. "I'm afraid to. If I try and it comes out wrong in any way then you'll get hurt and cry. And I don't want you to cry. I hate it when you cry when I know it's been my fault. I've never ever meant to hurt you honey. You know that don't you?"

She nodded.

"Is it my kids?" she asked. She didn't look up at him, now fidgeting herself, drawing circles in the sand.

"No, it's not the kids. I do admit they are a handful at times. But when I met you, I knew you had them. God ... Do you know they were only three and five when I met you? Shit. Time goes fast. I remember when we moved you from the country to the city. Remember that?"

Julie smiled. She remembered.

"None of you could sleep at night for the first while from all the noise. And the first week we had to go out and drive around in the car each night for hours and hours until the kids finally fell asleep. That was what a month or so before our wedding. Wasn't it?"

"I think so."

He picked up her hand kissing the back of it. "Do you still think you did the right thing coming here to be with me, marrying me five years ago?"

"Yes ... You know I do," she replied.

"Do you still feel lost here?"

"Yes."

"Don't you like the city?"

"No ... Not ... Really ... Not really much at all ... To be honest."

"I guess I don't spend as much time with you as I should. Do I?" He didn't wait for her to shake her head back and forth in a no before continuing. "I'll have to do something about that."

She looked at him searching to see if he meant it or if it was just something he was saying to appease her and squirm out of all this. He was masked. She couldn't read him at all.

"What's so different about here? ... As opposed to where you came from anyway? A town is a town. This one is just bigger, so they call it a city?"

"I came from a place where the moon and the fire flies light up the sky at night, not street lamps." She dug her toes into the sand remembering. "Where the sky is blue with crimson sunrises and sunsets not just a permanent gray with or without a haze. Where a highway is two lanes, one going each way, not sixteen with eight going each way and still people drive the wrong way. Where people are courteous and friendly, ask you how you are, and mean it. I'm not used to people cutting me off in traffic, giving me the finger, swearing at my kids and myself or kicking my car door in at Christmas time because I pulled in a parking spot they say they saw first when they weren't even there. Everybody here is too busy to see all that is important in life, like going for a walk when the spring flowers are blooming or giving someone a hand when they really need it and when they don't. I feel like I might as well have stepped off the moon."

"I guess, maybe looking back in hindsight you should have probably thought twice and not been so quick to offer your help when I was broken down on the highway that day huh?"

"No I shouldn't have thought twice about it ... No ... Not at all ... If the truth were known, I fell in love with you the moment I saw you. Even if you were all covered head to foot in oil and grease. And I was glad you stole my telephone number off my cell phone and started calling me long distance every day."

"But baby ... Look what I'm doing to you ... I'm breaking your heart ... Am I not?" He sandwiched her hands between his.

"You are not breaking my heart. You aren't doing anything to me. I left where I was willingly to be with you. It would take something entirely different for you to break my heart. Like if you died or had an affair or left me. Those things would break my heart. I love you totally, completely. I put all my faith, trust, hope and love in you with everything that I am or ever will be. I am just having a tremendous amount of difficulty understanding you lately. It's like one morning you got up, kissed me goodbye, went off to work, and came home an entirely different person who I should be calling Tom, Dick or Harry or something."

He grinned. "Tom, Dick or Harry?" He repeated, his grin becoming broader and broader by the second.

"You know what I mean!" she retorted.

"Tom, Dick or Harry?' His body was jiggling. He put his hand over his mouth trying to stop his laughter.

"Cut it out!' She said, swiping at his head, intentionally missing.

"Sorry," he snorted. He wiped the tears from the corners of his eyes. He could not contain himself any longer and roared with laughter. "You never cease to amaze me with all these cute little expressions you have." He pounded the sand with his fists in between fits of snorting and chuckles. "God

... I ... I ... Don't mean to laugh at you, but I just can't help it ... I'm so sorry honey. It was just the look on your face when you said it. You were so serious and I never heard anything like that before. I was pretty good up until then wasn't I at least?'

"Yes," she replied. The furrow in her brow softened. *'Good God,'* she thought. *'He has the attention span of a two-year-old.'*

He pointed his index finger at her "Bet you ... I know what you're thinking right now!"

"Okay what?"

"I'm nothing but an over grown kid, right? ... Am I close? ... I bet I am ... You're smiling ... Honey? ... There's something I've been meaning to ask you?"

"What?"

"Do you love me as much as I love you?"

"No."

He squeezed her hand making a pouty face. "No?"

"No! ... I love you more," she said.

"Think so ... Do you?"

"Nope ... I know so," she said.

"I bet you're wrong."

"Nope." She shook her head affirming her nope.

"How so?"

"Cause you're an asshole and I still love you and I'm not an asshole and you love me so all thing being equal ... I love you more cause I still love you even though you're an asshole!'

"Bet you can't say that all again." He smiled through his boyish dimples.

"Probably not," she laughed.

"Want to try?"

"No!"

"Ah come on," he coaxed.

"No! ... Why further perfection or duplicate it?"

"Hum." He stood dusting the sand off. He offered Julie a hand up. "Come on old lady we've got to get going, or I will be late for work."

"Old lady my butt! ... I am only a year older than you are! ... You ass!"

"So," he smirked.

"I wouldn't finish that statement if I were you!" She pulled the corner of her dress up thigh high, showing off leg. She ran both her hands slowly up her body pausing at her hips and breasts. She shook a finger at him mouthing not for you later. She dropped her dress back down and slipped into the front seat of the car

"I think I got the point!" He stroked her thigh.

"Thought you would," Julie said smugly, moving his hand onto the car seat.

"Come over here." He pulled her across the seat draping his arm around her shoulder giving her a squeeze. "You're a very bad girl you know!" He gave her a once over putting his hand back onto her thigh.

Cory tapped Tony's shoulder from the back seat. "Can we stop on the way home and get some chips?"

"Cor ... I don't have time or I will be late for work. But I'll bring you some home okay?"

"'Kay ... But ... You're always home after I'm asleep," Cory said.

"I'll be home really early tonight if I have to damn well quit to do it."

"Really? ... For sure?" Cory questioned.

"Yep!" Tony turned and winked at Julie. "Really! ... Really! ... For sure! ... For sure! ... You can count on it!"

Chapter 7

"Come on answer," Julie said.

The ringing seemed to go on for an eternity, which this day measured a long two minutes. She hung up and dialled the number again.

"Good morning 'Stefon's Bakery' Sherry speaking."

"Sherry," Julie started in. "I ... I"

Sherry cut her off. "Did you just call love?" she asked. "I had my arms full of day olds, and couldn't get to the phone."

Julie nodded yes. "I won't be in this morning," she said.

"Still not feeling too good yet, huh?"

"No." Julie replied, collapsing into her pillow, pulling the blankets into a turtleneck.

"Okay hon ... I'll tell Stefon for you. Ya really got a mean one their kid. How long ya had it now? Three or four days at best?"

"I ... I think so ... I thought I'd have it beat by not coming in Friday and staying in bed all weekend, but it's still here," Julie answered.

"You know what they say about that stuff love?" Sherry didn't wait for the what question before continuing. "Three days coming, three days here, three days going."

"Thanks for sharing that," Julie muttered.

"Well someone's gotta make your day for ya now. Might as well be me," Sherry snickered. "Well sweets ... You hurry up and get better now ya hear? I miss ya! It's not the same here without you! Take care. Bye ... Bye now"

"I will. Bye." Julie smiled, she missed her too. Sherry was a good friend. She closed her eyes and left the world.

She slept deep, way-way down and far away. Far away, enough that the telephone's ringing had swept on by over the last couple of hours without even so much as the slightest twitch of an eyebrow. If she had heard the telephone, she might have spared herself the calling card from hell that had just arrived and hoofed the front door open.

Tony punched his fists into the bed two inches from her face. "JULIE!" he screamed. "I CALLED YOU AT FUCKING WORK AND THEY SAID YOU WEREN'T FUCKING IN TODAY!" His fury had put a white froth to the corners of his mouth. He punched the bed again catapulting Barkley to the floor.

"Whaf?" She said, thoroughly dazed, thoroughly confused. She'd heard the screaming but not the words. He had so abruptly awakened her; she felt as if the bottom part of her jaw had fallen off and gotten lost in the bedding. "Whaf," she muttered again.

"WHAT THE HELL! ... JUST WHAT THE FUCK ARE YOU TRYING TO PULL HERE?" He ripped the covers from her, balling them in a heap at the foot of the bed.

She instantaneously curled into the fetal position, the smaller the better. She shut her eyes hoping this was just another one of those bad dreams that she'd been having lately, where Tony swore and screamed and swore and screamed some more.

"WHAT THE FUCK ARE YOU FUCKING PULLING HERE YOU BITCH?" he hollered.

It wasn't a dream.

He crushed the mattress down beside her chest.

She stuck out her arm stopping herself from rolling into him. She did not want to be any closer than she already was. Her body started to shiver uncontrollably. She didn't know if it was because she had a fever or if it was because she had reached the outer edge of frightened. She kept her eyes closed not wanting to see the things in his eyes that she often did. Inhuman dark things ... Things that haunted her long after he was gone. She straightened out one leg, groping with her toes for the covers. Finding them, she kicked at them, tossing them within arm's reach. She rolled herself up like a sausage cocooning in the instant warmth.

"I ASKED YOU A FUCKING QUESTION! ... NOW ANSWER IT!" Tony spat.

The breath from his words stung her flesh like battery acid. She hid her head under the crook of her forearm borrowing Barkley's favourite logic. *'I can't see you, so therefore you can't see me.'* She lay there as still as the dead, in total silence, hoping and hoping with a lot of praying thrown in.

"WHY THE FUCK AREN'T YOU AT WORK?" he screamed.

"Because I'm sick," she murmured into her arm. "And ... Stop yelling ... You're hurting my head." She was disappointed Barkley's hiding trick hadn't worked. She would have to perfect it, for next time.

"Why the fuck? ... Are you still sick? ... You've been sick all fucking weekend!"

"So?" she countered. *'Oh my god,'* she thought. *'I asked and I received ... He actually stopped yelling.'*

"So? ... So! ... Why in the fuck are you still sick?"

"I don't know! I just am!"

"Why didn't you fucking phone me and tell me?"

"I did."

"When?" He grabbed her arm.

"This morning," she answered.

"When this morning?"

"Before I called into work. I left a message. You were in the back."

"I didn't get the message!"

"Who'd you give it to?" he added.

"For God's Sake! ... Stop this!"

"I damn well asked you a fucking question! And I want an answer! Fucking answer me!" He tightened his fingers, firming his grip on her arm and jerking it sideways knowing full well he was causing her pain.

"Answer what?" She grimaced, trying to pry his fingers from her reddened skin.

"Who'd you give it too? For fuck's sake, open your eyes and look at me when I'm talking to you! My patience is wearing thin!"

"I can talk to you without my eyes open." *'His patience is wearing thin,'* she thought. *'My arm is burning like hell on fire ... You God Damn bastard!'*

"JULIE!" he screamed.

She rolled onto her side opening her eyes, her arm still in his clutches. "What the hell!" She jerked her arm trying to free it. "What is it you want?" She jerked her arm again. "Let go of my damn arm! ... You're hurting me!"

He slid his fingers down to her wrist relenting just a little on the tightness. "Why the fuck didn't you go to work?"

"I already told you!" *'Jesus Christ,'* she thought. *'What'd he do? ... Down a whole bottle of stupid pills this morning?'*

"Then fucking tell me again!"

"Because I'm sick! ... Is that plain enough for you?"

"Don't fucking fuck with me!"

"Just stop all this! Will you please! I'm sick! I have a bad flu! And you know all this! And I told you yesterday that I might not go in today if I was still this sick!"

He glared at her allowing her to see he was drawing back in his steeds of anger ... But showing her, they were just behind a gate ... An unlocked gate. He slowly released her wrist, rubbing at the red welts with his thumb and forefinger.

She couldn't figure out if he was trying to erase them or burrow them in further.

"I always go in when I'm sick ... Always," he stated.

"I guess that makes you a better person than I am. Doesn't it now?" She drew her arm away from him stuffing it under the covers.

He'd barely gotten his mouth posed for the comeback when his back pocket boldly ended the interrogation with whirling and beeping. He scowled a *'You'd better not move Bitch ... If you know what's good for you ... I'm not done with you yet,'* at Julie. He tilted his left ass cheek fetching the pager flipping it open with his thumb. His eyes sparked, flashing with amusement before he caught himself and readjusted his facemask back into the wrath of hell.

But ... The split second reprieve might well have been a yearlong. That sudden flash had lit up the whole entire sky, even lingering on after it was gone. It was as if she had just not been looking in the right direction for that lighthouse beacon as the tidal wave from hurricane Tony was sticking its clawed fingers out and around her neck. All she had seen was the island of purgatory off in the distance as her lungs filled with salt and water, making her decide to go down with the ship. But now ... She could actually jump free and surf her way to the 'Bahamas' on a piece of the wreckage.

She gripped his hand tilting her tiny saviour to the light, half expecting to see something much more incredible like a digital version of *'Mother Theresa'* than just a mere mortal seven digits. "Who's that?" she asked, not recognizing the number.

Tony lowered his eyebrows growing them together. He snapped himself away from the light, his fingers furiously pounding the tiny machine's face pad.

Julie's mouth gaped open, her eyelids blinked once, as he slung shot back into place like a too stretched elastic band, even pinging when he thudded up against her shoulder.

He lowered the pager. "It's just the restaurant calling ... See." He tilted it back and forth in the light for her to get a good look. "They must have a delivery or something." He added.

Her eyes bulged from their sockets as she stared at the pager. Her gearshift seemed to have slipped. What she'd thought she had just seen was not going around right in the gray matter. It just kept skidding, grinding, and skidding some more, until it finally stalled out leaving her sitting there, mouth gaping, staring, eyes bulging. "This," she put herself in neutral so she wouldn't stall or have to shift. "This ... This ... This ... Isn't the number. It ... It ... Just showed. You ... You ... Changed it. I watched you ... You." She broke off, opening and closing her mouth, attempting to rid herself of the nervous stutter. She shook her head. This all passed over the line and went into '*Ripley's Believe It Or Not.*' Her mind was not at all wrapping around it. She thought she knew what she saw was real. But if it was, she didn't recognize the number at first ... But now she did. She looked at the number again. She felt like the room had just fuzzed over.

"This is so the number!" Tony declared.

"No ... It's ... It's ... Not."

"It fucking is so the number!" he said. His voice held the smug air of 'I am right and you are wrong.'

He was going through a lot of shit to prove his point, instead of getting up and walking off yelling and cursing like he usually did. She knew deep down she must have seen what she thought she did. "No it isn't," she muttered. She grabbed onto the bedding, kneading it in her fingers and forcefully ramming herself into first.

"If this fucking isn't the fucking number ... What was it then?"

"I don't know!" she replied.

"That's what I fucking thought," he snapped. "This is the fucking number! ... And If you don't fucking know what the fucking number was ... How in fucking hell can you sit there and tell me this isn't fucking it then? ... Jules? ... Are you calling me a fucking liar?"

Her open gaping mouth dropped further consuming her chin. It grew hinges, swung back and forth, as disbelief spelled itself out across her forehead in capital letters. She swivelled her eyes looping from the pager to him and back again. She used both her hands to push her mouth shut. Her tongue felt sticky. Her mind had left and was floating above in a cloud. She tried to pull it back. The cord snapped. She sat there silent, motionless, staring at the glinting silver in his hand. The letters scrawled upon her forehead had started to smell foul and seemed as if oozing down her temples.

She went over what she thought she knew. *'She was sick at home with flu. Tony had come home yelling ... A given. His pager had gone off. But ... This is where it started to get tricky. She thought she had not ever seen the number it showed when it went off but now she did. She thought she saw him turn away from her and punch in numbers. He was accusing her of calling him a liar, saying he did not do what she thought she just saw him do ... There was something wrong here ... Really, really wrong ... She could not get this ... It was like she'd just been handed a puzzle to complete in one minute for a psych test by a group of grinning psychologists who full well knew that when she opened the box all the pieces were square and the holes were round.'*

"Why in the fuck didn't you go to work today?" he said.

There it was again, that question. She didn't answer. She swung her legs over the side of the bed and walked towards the bathroom.

"FOR FUCKS SAKE! ... ANSWER ME!" Tony shouted.

She closed the door, sat on the edge of the bathtub, and hung her head. She thought she could hear the beeping of the pager again.

"Jules?" His voice was suddenly soft, warm. "You all right, honey?" He rapped the door with his knuckles. "I'll make you a cup of tea, okay baby? You go on and get yourself back into bed. I'll bring it to you."

Something nagged and pulled at her as she stepped through the bedroom doorway to turn about and go the other direction. She did. She stopped at the railing. She could hear faint conversation climbing its way up the staircase and as it closed in, it became clearer and clearer as if something wanted her to be a party to it. So much so, she actually had to look about herself for her own piece of mind, it was as if she was suddenly standing right there beside him. She could hear him. Hear him talking and laughing. It was the laughing part that perked her really up.

"Me too ... Yeah ... Yeah ... Of course ... Later okay? ... I can't really talk right now ... There's lots of people around at work here ... Yep ... For sure ... Of course ... You know I do."

Then, as if the something figured she had heard all she needed to, the conversation faded back down the stairs trailing off into inaudible whispers. She stood with her back to the railing, straining, listening to see if he was still on the telephone. She couldn't tell.

"What are you doing out here?" he whispered.

He was so close she could feel the words on the back of her neck. Her heart stopped, starting again ten feet from where she was standing. "I ... I ... I," she stammered. She opened the linen closet door. "I ... I ... Just ... Just was getting another blanket."

He put his mouth tight to her ear. "Is that all you were just ... Just ... Doing?"

She nodded a lie filled yes, not meeting his eyes.

"Here's your tea ... Get back into bed like a good girl now."

She sat holding the mug of tea. She had felt him kiss her forehead good-bye and heard the front door bang shut and lock. It all seemed like an eternity ago. She looked over at the clock, it was just nine a.m. He had been gone five ... Maybe ten minutes at most. She took a long slow sip of the tea allowing it to filter its way down her throat. It was beyond dry.

'Funny,' she thought. 'The restaurant doesn't open until noon. I wonder why they'd be calling for a delivery when they weren't open?' She shrugged off her thought. It wasn't making much sense. She turned to the other thoughts filled with disappearing numbers. But, they too didn't make any sense. She suddenly smiled, everything coming together. She had it now. It was way too early for all of this to have happened this morning. Everything had to be a dream. This was another one of those bad dreams. None of this was real. How could it be? Things mostly made sense in real life and never did in dreams, especially the ones she kept having lately.

She closed her eyes content in her convictions, falling off to sleep clutching the mug that could not be there because it was all a dream. But ... It did not matter anyway, by the time her mind rejoined her it wouldn't be in her hands. It would just be in the bed or on the floor and she would have another good excuse for how it got there.

Chapter 8

Tony flew in and out of the house in record time. Readying and leaving within five minutes taking boys, soccer equipment, and his plastic wrapped foam plated dinner.

Tonight was the be all and end all ... The final game of the season.

He had for the first time Julie could ever remember, arrived home when he said he would. She had informed him earlier that she would walk over to the park a little later with Barkley. His mom was to be dropping by any time now, to pick up trays for the big birthday dinner tomorrow.

There was certainly one thing you could say about Tony's mom; she had a heart of gold when it came down to all show. And, show necessitated the need for Julie's grandmother's antique sterling silver trays.

Tony's dad's birthday was the big event of the year, always fussed and fretted over for months and in great detail.

Julie and the dad had never seen eye to eye, nor had they bonded together like Tony's brother, Troy's girlfriend and him had. There had always been this invisible, thick impenetrable wall standing between them. She supposed part of it was because she had almost every type of blood flowing through her veins including American, Canadian, German, French, and the like except for of course the all-important, Italian. He had referred to her once as a white cocktail, to which she'd countered with a damn good retort. Come to think of it, he had never really spoken to her too much since that time, unless of course he couldn't get out of it. After all, she was a mutt and a woman to boot and the only one in his whole entire life that had stood up to him. He was old school Italian where women should be 'Seen and not heard.' Allie had told her once, while her husband did not like her, he did respect her ... And that worked for her. Yep ... Tone as he was called was sure one class 'A' asshole! They say the apple does not fall far from the tree, which probably explains everything about the son, right there, in that one sentence.

She glanced at the kitchen clock. It read six p.m. Game time was seven. She went upstairs fetching the laundry, deciding to save time later. As the water gushed in, a shrill beeping circled out from the machine stopping and starting in short intervals. She checked the washer out top to bottom worried something was wrong or caught or coming apart, but nothing seemed amiss. Dumping in the soap she heard it again, only this time it was hollow. She swished around the clothing, suddenly smiling, coming hand to hand with Tony's pager. She gave the number a quick glance then shut it off shaking it, placing it on a towel to dry.

It was now six-thirty p.m. with no sign of Tony's mom. She leashed Barkley, detouring off to Allie's to drop off the trays on her way to the park. Tony gave her the aren't you a bad little kid, tapping foot, one hand on the hip, other pointing to the watch routine. She plopped herself down on the sidelines ignoring his demeaning gestures, holding up her hands in the 'What you want me to do about it' pose, mouthing his mom was late. She smiled thinking of his water soaked pager sitting at home in the laundry room, laughing outright as he continued to throw her scowls. 'What goes around comes around,' she thought and began to laugh so hard tears formed and ran.

The game went by faster than fast with the team winning fifteen to zero. They had beaten all the odds, ending the season as they'd started, in a conquering victory and shutout. The final three whistle blows were drowned into the earth under shouts and screams of happy kids and parents as

Cory's entire team leaped in the air firing their hats skyward and doing the victory dance. It looked like it was snowing red baseball hats. And it was!

They hooted, hollered, and kicked sideways, bee lining it right down the field, converging and tumbling into the goalie net on top of Cory. They looked like a heaping mass of red wiggling, giggling ten-year old boy bodies, intertwined and woven together. They were sweaty, dirty, grimy, bruised, bleeding, and happier than any pigs in shit.

She shifted her glance to Tony, shaking her head watching him walk round and round the field in tight circles holding up his clenched fisted arms, jerking them up and down hooting like he'd just won it all himself. Julie rolled her eyes "And I married this idiot! What was I ever thinking?" she muttered.

Tony packed up the car half way through the pizza, chips and pop celebration, handing Julie the games register to be filed away. She had been watching him check his watch every thirty seconds for the last ten minutes. She had convinced herself he must have a big surprise in store, like maybe an ice-cream cake or movie tickets or something equally grand. She could barley wait to see what it was.

He checked out the field over his shoulder as he walked towards her. "Look babe ... I got to go," he said.

Julie's happiness faded to black. Her lips tore and pulled at the corners of her mouth as she listened to him in disbelief, having him repeat he had to go.

He planted a half-assed kiss atop her head. "I'm sorry to leave in the middle of this, but," he paused ruffling up her hair with his fingers. "There's a card show tonight and I have to go. I have customers breathing down my neck for rare cards and those dealers will be there. Don't wait up for me I'll probably be late." He turned and jogged towards the car.

She was stunned. He had said what he needed and left. Left like the kids and the win meant absolutely nothing. She pasted on a smile she found left over from the triumph laying on the field. She didn't have one of her own to wear. She stood and watched him leave. She could not be positive, but he'd looked like he was talking up a storm smiling and laughing on his cell phone as he pulled away. He didn't wave goodbye or even look back. He just drove off as if he hadn't even been there at all.

As four-thirty a.m. came and went turning its self into five-thirty a.m. Julie had no conscious recollection of the words, sentences and paragraphs that had passed back and forth over the telephone line, as to why her husband was just now on his way home. Or, the why and how of his accidentally falling asleep in the car after the card show. It was all there though, explained right down to the minutest of details. It was all summed up and in there somewhere, just lingering around under and below the surface.

The front door opened softly, re-closing the same way as the mantle clock sang, welcoming in the half-passed hour of seven-thirty a.m.

Chapter 9

"Just a minute while I find a pen and paper." Julie sat the telephone receiver down scrounging about the kitchen looking for something to write on, coming up empty she ripped off a piece of paper towel. "Okay shoot, what is it?"

"Five-five-five—three-seven-two-three ... Got it?" Allie asked.

"Yep ... I got it," Julie answered.

"Oh I almost forgot!" Allie blurted. "Troy was supposed to bring you the trays I borrowed on his way to work but he forgot. How the kid could forget in just two blocks is beyond me, but he did. Anyway, he put them in the back seat of T.J's car. Hope this is okay with you?"

"Sure, that's fine." Julie screwed her face up, mouthing why me lord looking up at the ceiling. 'Well that's just great,' she thought. 'Maybe I'll see them again sometime, or not.'

"Oh honey ... Did I give you the name for that number?"

"No."

"Gosh sweets ... I was hoping I did, I didn't write it down ... Wait a minute let me think ... Well if that doesn't beat all hell it's left me ... No wait ... Anderson ... Something Anderson."

"Okay thanks. I'll give it to him when he gets in." Julie paused ever so slightly then added. "When-ever that is."

"What did you say honey, I didn't hear the last bit there? I'm doing the dishes. I guess I was rattling."

"I'll give it to him when he comes home," Julie repeated, not adding the last bit Allie asked for. Some things were better off, left unsaid.

"Take care sweets and tell him sorry about being so late with his message. It came into the card shop a day or two ago and I put it in my pocket and forgot all about it ... Till now that is." Allie chuckled. "Oh well, that's what you get when you hire family, total incompetence."

"Take care. Talk to you later," Julie said.

"Bye honey."

She scrawled the name down beside the telephone number. She absent-mindedly pinned it to the bulletin board, returning to the stove, making sure things were on course for supper. She sang along to the tunes on the radio while setting the table, all at once whirling round to the bulletin board. The bulletin board with a single piece of paper towel pinned to it. She suddenly had the strangest feeling. She stepped forward, studying the number, the feeling growing stronger, like sideways *'Déjà vu'*. She plucked the paper from the board turning it round in her fingers. She was sure she had seen this number before ... But where?

She grinned a toothy grin holding the tip of her tongue between her front teeth. "I got it," she said. "I'll just bet!" She tore off downstairs to the laundry room. She clicked the pager on, hit the retrieve button, and there it was five-five-five—three-seven-two-three. She walked over to the telephone and punched in the number. It rang four times before an answering machine snatched it. She cradled the receiver between her shoulder and ear trying to act as nonchalant as possible, tossing wet laundry from washer to dryer, her stomach whirling in somersaults.

'Hi ... You've reached the voice mail of Nancy Anderson ... Sorry I'm not available to take your call right now ... Please leave a detailed message with your ...'

Julie cut the message off hanging up the receiver. "This is silly," she said. She felt lower than lowest telephoning that number, though not a soul other than herself and Barkley knew. She'd just out done herself. Accomplished the impossible, humiliating herself, to herself and the dog. It made her feel like crap. Worse, even. *'He always gets lots of calls, always, always. What makes me think this one's different from all the rest?'* She was talking to herself inside her head where the dog couldn't hear. She didn't allow herself any answers; she was bordering on ridiculous and insanity if she answered herself. Only crazy people ask themselves questions and then answer them. Her stomach was the only one that disagreed as it kept up its circling and nagging. She finished off the laundry figuring her insides were flip-flopping because she had gone and telephoned. It was payback. She pursed her lips, biting down on them, shaking her head at her childish stupidity. Her own phone rang and she galloped up the stairs answering it in the kitchen, leaving the pager, the paper, the woman named Nancy Anderson, her knotting stomach and her thoughts behind.

"Hello?" she said.

"Hey you? ... How you keeping?" Sherry asked.

"I'm good and you?" Julie countered.

"Okay, well kind of." Sherry's voice trailed off into serious.

"What's up?" Julie asked.

"They've called a special meeting at the bakery Monday morning for ten a.m.," Sherry announced.

"They have?" That was news to Julie.

"They just phoned me," Sherry reaffirmed.

"No one called me," Julie stated. She pulled a kitchen chair over and sat down.

"They will. They said all staff was being called in for it. They have never ever done anything like this before. And, Monday's our day off. What do you think is going on?"

"I don't know ... Not unless," Julie paused placing her feet up on the phone stand tipping her chair back on two legs. "Not unless it's about moving again? Remember last year, they called a mini meeting after work about expanding and moving a few streets over? Maybe they have found

94

somewhere and we're going to be moving at the end of the month or something?"

"Well ... Yeah ... That makes sense ... Maybe you're right? ... I was just a little worried you know ... But I always make mountains out of molehills ... Now don't I? ... But God Damn it! ... Monday is our day off and to have to go in for a damn meeting ... It's just not right, you know?"

"Yes ... I know what you're saying." Julie agreed with a nod Sherry could not see.

"Well I guess I'd better let you go. You're probably next on the phone tree to call."

"Okay then," Julie said.

"Let me know if they say anything different to you than they did me? ... Will ya girlfriend?" Sherry asked.

"For sure I will."

"So I guess I'll be seeing you Monday at ten then?" She lowered her voice to a whisper. "And you won't let on I called ya? ... Will ya?" Sherry asked.

"You know me better than that," Julie said. She had been trying to sound dead on serious, but lost.

"I know!" Sherry laughed. "You're biding your time waiting till I really screw up big so you can get me good aren't ya?"

"But of course! ... This is just chicken feed! ... Only worth an honourable mention, if that," Julie chuckled.

"See ya!"

"Ditto," Julie said.

No sooner had Julie hung up the telephone, then the bakery called informing her of the meeting. When done, she decided to give Sherry a quick call to lay her mind at ease. She had been informed of the same, almost word for word. They gabbed on for a good hour before saying their goodbyes.

Julie gave dinner a quick stir as the phone rang again.

"Hello?" she said.

"I'll be a bit late. I've got to work late at the factory, then go out with my dad to see a piece of machinery he's thinking of buying. I should be home by eight. Can you keep my supper warm for me?" Tony asked.

"Sure," she answered. This was the second time she had used the sure word over the telephone in the last hour ... Once to Allie and now once to him. She hadn't meant it either time.

She sighed looking over at the dinner table. The boys had asked to stay over at a friend's for the night; giving her the incentive to prepare the beginnings of what she'd envisioned becoming a very romantic evening. She had slipped into something sexy and made his favourite meal for starters. She had pulled out all the stops, setting the table using the dozen long stemmed yellow roses that had arrived late afternoon as the theme. This was a total first for him, he always sent her red, and only on 'Valentine's Day', but maybe yellow was a sign he had turned a new leaf. She figured this was his silent apology for being so out of sorts. And, she was going to accept and make it a night to remember.

"I'll phone you later honey. I've got to get going. See you in a bit." Tony's voice trailed off with a bye babes, the telephone disconnecting before she could say thanks for the roses, a so long, bye, or anything else.

Eight p.m. came and went. As did nine, ten, eleven, twelve, one, two, and three, before she got the call telling her he was on his way home. As she went to hang up the receiver her thumb slid off the number pad accidentally hitting the retrieval button, a telephone number shooting out before she knew what had happened.

'You have reached five-five-five—nine-eight-six-four. This number is equipped for outgoing calls only. Should you need further assistance please hold and an operator with be with *you shortly.'*

Julie fumbled with the receiver. It slipped and hit the floor bouncing on the carpeting.

"Operator ... Can I help you?" a voice said.

Julie stared at it as if it was some foreign being. She slowly plucked it from the floor with her thumb and middle finger.

"Operator, can I help you?" the voice repeated

"I ... I," Julie stuttered.

"Can I be of assistance ma'am?"

"Hum ... I," Julie paused not knowing where to go with this.

"Yes ma'am?"

"The number that just rang in here ... Called me ... I was just trying to call it back ... Call my husband back and I ... I." She stumbled out words that did not make any sense. She hadn't been trying to call him back. She hadn't been trying to do anything but put the telephone back. She felt like a complete fool ... A complete dumb fool.

"I'll check that for you ma'am." The line hummed then clicked. "Five-five-five—nine-eight-six-four is a phone booth number in the 'High Park' area. It is equipped for outgoing calls only. Is there anything else I can do for you ma'am?"

"No thanks, that's all right. You have done more than enough. Thank you." Julie replaced the receiver. *'A phone booth in High Park?'* she thought. *'This does not make any sense. He has a cell phone. His dad has a cell phone. Why would he call from a phone booth? And what was he doing way down in that area? It was residential. She thought he had said they were going to look at a machine.'*

She got out of bed, pulled on her housecoat, planting herself down in the middle of the front staircase. She just couldn't wait for that front door to open. Another hour passed and still she waited. As brightness reflected, Barkley roused and barked, continuing as it faded back into darkness and a car door slammed shut. She knitted her fingers together, watching in silence as he entered the house, whispered to Barkley and went into the kitchen.

He picked up the kitchen phone, depressed the redial button and listened, jotting down the number it spit out. He gave the dinner table set for romance a quick once over. He opened the oven door lifting a corner of the tin foil and peeking at his dinner. "Not bad," he muttered. He hauled the tray out grabbing a fork while mindlessly walking toward the stairs.

Julie waited in utter stillness like a hunter in no hurry to let its prey know it's there. She didn't speak until he was on the foot of the staircase. "Hi," she said.

He jumped backward assuming the appearance of that old saying 'Almost jumping out of your skin.' "Shit! ... You startled me! ... I almost dumped my dinner! ... What the hell are you doing there?"

"Waiting for you!" she said.

"On the fucking stairs?"

"Well," she countered. "Whatever works!"

"What the hell you still doing up?"

"Waiting ... For ... You ... Tony!" She dragged her words out slow and deliberate.

"Why?"

She didn't answer, just smiled. He looked like he was about to come unglued.

"Why?" He said, again. He cleared his throat. He sounded like something was stuck in there, like a stick or a log.

She broadened her smile.

"Fuck! ... Why?" He repeated, thumping his throat with his fist trying to swallow.

"Why? ... Why don't you tell me why?" she said, nonchalantly.

"Tell you what?"

"Why," she said.

"You're making no fucking sense!"

"Really ... Now." She stared right into his eyes.

He looked down at his plate. "It's late ... I just want to eat this and go to bed!"

"Yes it is late, isn't it?" she said.

"Fucking! ... Jesus Christ!"

She pulled up her knees, crossing her arms on them.

"Can't me and my Dad go out for fucks sake?"

"I didn't say a word about that, did I now?"

"Fuck, are you accusing me of fucking something here?"

"Not going to answer me are you?" she asked, ignoring his sideways question. She wasn't going there. She was staying right where she was.

"Answer what?"

"Why I'm waiting for you?"

"You're starting to really piss me the fuck off here! ... Can't I go out with my fucking father without you making a scene and accusing me of all kinds of shit?"

Julie got up off the steps and walked over to the telephone snapping up the receiver putting her back to him pretending to dial. "Shall we see what time your dad got in seeing as its past four a.m. and he gets up about now?" She knew she shouldn't have done it, but she just had to call his bluff. She knew he was not out with his dad and he knew she knew it. She could see it in his eyes.

Tony rushed the telephone, ripping the cord from the wall.

"You going to do that to all the telephones in the house? ... Well no matter ... I can always go out and use a pay phone!" She hit his eyes dead on. She grabbed her housecoat belt tying it tighter, covering her legs. She didn't want him to see how bad they were shaking.

"What the fuck does that mean?" He grabbed her shoulders giving her a shake.

"Take your damn hands off me!" She pushed him backwards.

"For Christ Sake! ... What the fuck is wrong with you?"

"You! ... You are what the fuck is wrong with me!" She picked up his car keys backing up to the front door. She unlocked it, banging it open, turned and ran off toward the driveway in the rain. She did not want him to see even one single tear, let alone the stream running down her face. Tonight, she would cry in solitude far away from him.

She ended up at the plaza six blocks over. That was about as far away as she could manage. She pulled up alongside the bank, turned the key off, put her head down on the steering wheel, and cried a million tears. She cried for herself, for Tony, for their marriage, and lastly for the dreams, her dreams, which seemed to be lying there along with her whole entire life in that puddle outside the car.

She turned her head sideways wiping her nose on her sleeve. She turned back looking out the front window at a man approaching her. She gathered herself together as best she could, which wasn't at all even close to together, and rolled the window down a crack squinting from the flashlight pointed at her.

"Oh sorry ma'am," the police office said, apologetically. "I didn't mean to hurt your eyes."

Julie watched him give her a concerned once over. From her bare feet, to her nightgown, to her housecoat, to her tear soaked face. He rifled through his pockets pulling out a tissue and offering it.

"You all right ma'am?" he asked. He motioned her to roll the window down further, handing her the package of tissues.

She took it mouthing a silent thank you.

"Ma'am," he started in. "I can see you're upset, but you can't stay here."

"Why?" she asked. She didn't think she was bothering anything.

"Well ma'am." He placed his fingers on the edge of the window bending down face to face. "Normally, you could stay here as long as you liked but tonight you can't. There has been a break in at the bank. We just came from around back, and you are out front. And ma'am," He lowered his voice to just above a whisper. "It looks about to me that you've had more than enough upset for the night. You don't need a bunch of us coming up and asking you questions about why you're right out front here when there's been a robbery. Now do you?"

Julie shook her head no. "Can I go over there then?" She pointed across the parking lot. "I don't think I can drive home yet. I don't think I want to either. Would that be okay?"

The officer smiled and nodded yes, resisting the temptation to ask just what the bastard she was crying over did to her?

"Thank you," she said softly. She turned the key in the ignition drove across the lot and parked.

She watched the police cars and officers gather about the bank. She stayed until her tears stopped and her breath came easy. She felt as if someone had just stabbed her in the heart. But maybe that's what had happened? She wasn't sure.

She pulled at her housecoat trying to wrap it round her. It did not budge. She glanced down. It was stuck in the door. *'Why not?'* she mouthed. *'Why shouldn't it be?'* She opened the door jerking it free. Something hit the ground with a thunk. She blindly felt about the pavement splaying her fingers under the edge of the car. The thing that thunked was something folded and leather. She pulled her hand back tumbling a black wallet ... Tony's black wallet over and over in her fingers. She looked up nervously surveying the parking lot. She flipped it open. Then shut it. She put her head back on the headrest mentally kicking herself right in the butt for opening it. How could she do such a thing? She sat back up. "Piss on it!" she said, "I'm looking through this baby!"

She slowly, methodically went through the wallet taking out examining and replacing everything just as she found it. There were credit cards with 'Taco Bell' receipts wrapped around them ... Their dinner outings ... Gas receipts and more credit cards. Reaching the last slider, she peeled back a thick wad of receipts wrapped round a credit card held by an elastic band. She carefully undid it, her mouth dropping open. The receipts were from all the fine restaurants in town. She examined them, the over the top expenses, the bar tabs, the meals, all in multiples of two, meaning two people had dined at these places. She felt sick. The receipts went back over a couple months. She came upon two dated tonight. One for two dinners and bar tab amounting over the two hundred dollar mark plus a gas fill up receipt from High Park Imperial gas station time stamped at three-fifty-five a.m. Telephone number five-five-five-seven-eight-nine-zero. She crushed the receipts in her hands. Somewhere in between the *'God Damn You to Hells'* and the *'Why Oh Whys?'* She noticed ink scribbles. She picked it up unfolding it carefully as if it was made out of rice paper. She put it on her knee smoothing out the wrinkles. It was a hand written list. It read ...

'To Do List'

Get haircut.

Get new pants.

Get new shoes.

Get book 'Older Women – Younger Men Having Babies'.

Get haircut.

Take etiquette classes.

Get haircut.

Julie rolled down the window suddenly unable to breathe. She opened the car door, stumbling out, her legs buckling as if they were made of matchsticks and rubber. She hit the wet ground crawling onto the grass. She twisted onto her side curling up into a tight little ball, crying for all she was worth.

As dawn started to break, dissolving the evening sky, she crawled from the grass into the car. She sat staring straight ahead watching the rain droplets hit and run down the windshield until it turned into a blurred mass of little tiny rivers going nowhere. She turned the key and drove home. She dropped the wallet down in between the driver's-' seat and door, where she assumed it had been in order to fall out like that. She unlocked the front door, climbed the stairs, and slipped into bed without so much as even making a single sound. She smiled to herself. *'Her husband should have taken lessons from her on how to come home late, unnoticed.'*

She pulled the gas receipt and to do list from her housecoat pocket, folding them together in half and half again, shoving them far under her side of the mattress, breathing life into that old saying *'Something to sleep on.'*

Chapter 10

Julie watched the sunrise creep across the wall. It had been a long time coming. It was like the watched pot not boiling over into seven a.m. so that the alarm would sound and he would be gone. She closed her eyes praying that when she looked again an hour would have passed ... It hadn't. Time seemed to be mocking her, sticking and standing still.

She played this is the church and this is the steeple with her fingers until they ached. She counted all the flowers on the wallpaper. As a last resort, she played peek-a-boo with the clock as the seconds methodically, slowly, ticked by.

When it flipped over to six-fifty-nine a.m. elation set in. She counted down the seconds one through sixty clenching her hand making a fist, punching her arms into the air mouthing a triumphed yes. She snapped her eyes shut and covered herself head to foot, giving off the appearance of someone who hadn't been up all night thinking all kinds of thoughts waiting for that alarm clock to go off in the morning. She held her breath ... Nothing happened ... Nothing at all. She exhaled and took another breath holding it once more ... Still nothing. She grabbed the clock depressing the alarm button her mouth dropping open, it read eight a.m. not seven.

She buckled her lips into her mouth. "So! ... You want to play games do you honey?" she whispered, asking more so for herself than him. She turned to the motionless bulge beside her raising the clock, placing him in the line of fire. For a split second she just wanted to drop the damn thing on his skull making up whatever excuse came to mind after he was done swearing. She smiled fingering it, thinking it. It could slip now, couldn't it? Just one little slip and it would be all said and done. She wondered how big the bump would be. Before temptation got the better of her, she lowered it to her chest changing the setting from eight a.m. to seven-zero-five a.m. She grinned, adjusting the volume control to maximum. She reached over propping it in the pillows against his head, her *'I got you now sucker,'* smile broadening.

"WHAT THE FUCK?" Tony exclaimed. He batted the alarm clock with his fist smashing it onto the floor. "How the hell did that get here?"

Julie was back to the pretend sleep no breath thing. As his swearing turned a good blue streak, she pulled the covers up over her face rolling over into the pillow. She had to; laughter had gurgled up and was right there trying to get out.

Tony plucked the clock from the floor. "Jesus Christ," he muttered, turning it round in his hands. "I thought I set it for eight! It says seven-zero-five! Did you fucking change it?" He poked her in the ribs. "Jules! ... Wake up!" He poked her harder. "Fuck! ... Fuck! ... Fuck!" He slammed the clock down on the nightstand. "JULIE! ... WAKE THE FUCK UP!"

She didn't move a muscle.

He leaned over ripping the covers from her, shaking her arm up and down. "Did you fucking change the alarm?"

"No," she mumbled. She blindly groped for the covers, not lifting her head from the pillow.

"Well if you didn't. Who in the fucking hell did?" he demanded.

"Don't know."

"What?"

"Don't know," she repeated.

"How could you not know?"

Julie buried her head deeper into the pillow, she was prepared to keep this up all day if need be. She gave herself a pat on the back for doing so well. As long as she did not have to look at him she would be okay until he left. If she looked at him, she knew she would haul off and hit him with that radio just for starters. "Don't know," she said again.

"You don't know how you don't know?"

"No."

"You're not making any fucking sense!"

"No?" she questioned.

"Fuck this! ... I'm having a shower!"

"Thanks for telling me."

"Just fuck off okay? ... Just fuck right off!" Tony slammed the bathroom door, showering and leaving in the shortest five minutes she had ever seen.

When the front door banged shut, she jumped out of bed sticking her arm between the mattresses. She lay down on the bed unfolding the 'to do' list and receipt. She read them over and over and over dog earring the corners. Then read them some more.

She got off the bed going down to the laundry room fetching the pager and returning, flashing the retrieve button on and off showing the five-five-five—three-seven-two-three. She folded then unfolded the to do list setting creases, making the paper look ancient.

She snatched the telephone and dialled.

"Hello?"

"Is this Nancy Anderson?" Julie asked. She held the receiver with two wobbly hands that suddenly seemed made of cheap wet cardboard.

"Yes."

"Do you know a Tony Porter?" she asked. She closed her eyes not wanting the answer.

"Yes."

"How do you know him?" Julie pulled her knees up to her elbows, resting her telephone receiver arm on top of one knee, she was having terrible trouble holding it still with her whole body vibrating and shaking the way it was.

There was a long pause. "Who wants to know?"

"Julie Porter."

"As in Mrs. Tony Porter?" Nancy Anderson asked.

"Yes," Julie answered. Tears formed and dropped, sliding the telephone receiver down her face.

There was a long period of silence ... Too long.

"May I ask how you know him?" Julie sniffed.

"He is a friend."

"A friend? ... Nothing more?"

"No ... Just a friend." Nancy replied.

"Did you write him a note with a to do list on it?" Julie questioned.

"Yes," Nancy answered

"Last night?"

"Yes."

Julie did not utter another word. She just sat there ... Sat for a long time ... An endless time... Staring off in the middle of nowhere with no thoughts, the telephone receiver with the disconnected call cupped within her sweating cold dead hand.

As tears and time passed, she found herself lying back on the bed unfolding and folding the list again. She read and re-read it as Nancy's words echoed around in circles.

She rifled through the bedding searching for the receiver.

"May I speak to T.J. please?" Julie said. There were no shaking hands. She was cool. So cool and matter of fact she could have sworn she was someone else.

"What?"

"Is that any way to answer a phone?" she questioned. She smoothed the list out in her hands.

"What the fuck do you want? ... I'm fucking busy here!"

"Okay then," she said. She paused, ever so slightly. "I have something to read to you."

"You fucking phoned me at work to read to me?"

"Yes ... Yes I did."

"I'm fucking busy read it to me later ... Bye."

Julie cut him off. "No bye ... I want to read it to you now."

"Then hurry the fuck up! ... I'm fucking busy!"

"Okay ... I promise you ... I won't take long ... It's quite short actually."

"Well? ... I'm waiting!"

"I bet you are honey," she whispered. It was too soft and low for him to hear.

"Well?" He said again.

"To do list," she began. "1) Get haircut. 2) Get new pants. 3) Get new shoes. 4) Get book 'Older Women Younger Men Having Babies.' 5) Get haircut. 6) Take etiquette classes. 7) Get haircut." She smiled, there was nothing from the other end of the telephone. Not even a breath. If she didn't know, better she would have sworn he was dead. "Interesting ... Don't you think ... Honey?" she said.

Julie replaced the receiver.

The telephone rang over and over and over and over.

She didn't need to answer, she knew who it was and why he was calling and she had said all she had to say. Besides ... Something had come along when she was on the telephone. Sneaking and stealing its way closer and closer until it got itself near enough to jump into her mouth and slide right on down her throat, closing off part of her windpipe, making her unable to catch her breath. She bent her head wheezing and sputtering, feeling the something squirming and biting and clawing its way up her throat losing its grip and slipping back down as she swallowed. She became afraid, fearing she would choke to death with it. But, then and again ... Maybe that might be the lesser of two evils. The telephone had stopped ringing. And ... She knew all too well ... What that meant.

Chapter 11

'Soon,' Julie thought. 'Soon ... The wolf will come wearing its sheep's clothing.'

She watched out the window, waiting, hoping, and praying for something other than the inevitable. The waiting part was easy. She had done it a million times, now it was just a million and one. But ... The hoping? ... The praying? ... She could not get a handle on why that was in there sharing the same space ... Hoping and praying for exactly what? ... Answers to questions she already knew the answers to ... But soon ... Would be so upside down and twisted and bent out of shape they would not be recognizable. Wolves were slippery little suckers ... Tricky too! 'Maybe ... Just maybe,' she thought. 'The hoping and praying was for her ... She so needed something.'

She pursed her dry lips together biting off a piece of skin on the bottom left corner. She closed her eyes tilting her head back, resting it against the wall above the window seat. The wolf had cast anchor.

"Jules? ... Baby? ... You up there, honey?" Tony bounded up the stairs three at a time. "Honey? ... Baby? ... Where are you sweetie?"

Julie did not answer. She did not move. She did not open her eyes. She just remained as she was, as if someone had come along and clicked her on pause while they went and made a sandwich.

"Sweetie? ... Baby? ... Come on honey? ... Where are you? ... I got something for you."

She could hear the creaks and thuds of the doors opening and closing as he worked his way nearer and nearer.

The twenty minute drive from his work, if one was lucky enough to hit all the green lights, had been made in less than ten. And ... He even had something for her? ... She bet he must have really glued that sheep's costume on even adding in extra whiskers for effect ... He'd probably had his makeup done too, changing his slanted amber eyes into soft innocent round brown.

The bedroom door opened.

"Ah ... There you are! ... I finally found you!" He gently unfolded her knotted hands, placing a takeout specialty coffee in one and a yellow rose in the other.

Julie glanced down at the rose; it was freshly broken off. This was the third time in a matter of days he had given her roses. Ever since a little girl she had never liked yellow ones, never, ever, ever ... And now here he was giving them to her.

"Why," slipped from her mouth before she could stop it. 'Why,' had to be the most dumbest outright stupidest thing to say at this moment. But ... There it was in her voice floating overhead in the bubble complete with 'You're a stupid ass Julie' written in small letters underneath, all under scored twice in bright red. She felt like hauling off and shooting herself in the head. She had just put herself number one on the stupidest things to say list in the lame hall of fame. Her thoughts broke off as her eyes trailed his over to the bed where the pager, the note and the receipt lay all neatly a lined as if props to a play.

"Why?" he said, pasting on a cartoon like smile.

He had repeated her number one top ten stupid question of all time. She studied the seat cushion wishing she could just crawl in under there and hide forever or at least until someone else topped that list.

He picked the simplest to answer. "Because I thought you'd like the rose." He stroked her hair delicately. "Honey?"

She lifted her head, searching his eyes for any telltale signs of preludes to truth. She could not tell what he was at present a wolf, a sheep, an alien, or her husband. She needed time to look around in there. Eyes never lied if one could dig around underneath the masks. And he had many.

He dropped his glance out of range. "Jules? ... Baby?" he cooed. He went to place his arms around her.

She blew him off, shaking her head back and forth no.

The hurt of the refusal showed on his face. His lips went slack, trembling, making the corners of his mouth droop down. He resembled some kind of storybook creature that just had every bit of life sucked and drained from it and wasn't long for the world. He swallowed hard making dull thudding noises in his throat as he repeatedly glanced to the bed and back. He traced her cheek with the tip of his index finger, his eyes brimming over with huge tear droplets. "I ... I ... I ... Wanted to hold you," he said. He started to sob. He dropped to his knees resting his head in her lap.

Julie unconsciously raised a hand to soothe him. She caught herself, halting, hanging her arm mid-air ... He didn't deserve compassion ... He didn't deserve anything ... She was the one that deserved something ... And it was a hell of a lot more than a coffee and a damn yellow rose he swiped from someone'--s garden. She placed her hands deep under her thighs so neither of them could wiggle free and dare attempt any more foolishness.

He gathered his arms about her waist crying uncontrollably. "Baby ... I ... I ... I," he broke off too choked to speak.

Julie watched him with moistened eyes, the hurt and pain tugging at her heart. She could feel his stringers in there too ... His deceit ... His falsehood ... His dishonesty. She had not seen him cry since their puppy had died a few years back. But ... This was different ... He was losing it ... And why was he? ... She hadn't even said anything yet, and there was much to say.

He huddled into her seeking comfort, needing her touch as much as he needed the air to breath. When it did not come, he collapsed on her like a rag doll that had not been played with in years.

She looked away unable to watch any longer. Her love for him was stronger than the pain. She searched for the pull cord to switch herself off, finding it seconds before she would have laid her head atop his and wept for all she was worth too.

It seemed like his tears were going to span time and space before he finally cleared his throat and spoke. "Honey," he began. "I ... I."

She locked her fingers together.

"Baby ... I ... I ... Never ever meant to hurt you ... It's just a silly old note I carry around in my wallet ... I've had it a long time and ... I."

'Why was he stuttering? ... Nerves maybe? ... Or was it a wolf tactic?' She cut him off. "A long time is yesterday to you ... Is it?" she said. She lowered her voice to a whisper. "The date on the paper is yesterday."

"Baby ... I ... I ... Mean ... Well ... I."

"Just what is it? ... You mean?" she asked. Mixed emotion tears took hold of her eyes. They dropped down onto her cheekbones, chilling, turning to daggers all at once pivoting and aiming, shooting directly at her heart. She could feel them tearing through her chest, feel them surrounded in blood. Her hands still underneath, snarled as one, grew still and lifeless, like a pile of old dead rotting flesh about to fall away from the bones.

"Oh baby," he said childlike. "I ... I'm all mixed up now ... I didn't mean a long time ... I meant." He stopped mid-sentence, raising himself up, coming face to face, showing her his misty fawn-like brown eyes. "Baby ... I don't want to lose you ... I love you so."

"Why would you lose me?" She was almost sure she could smell damp wolf hair.

"Cause of what you're thinking right now."

"And just what is that?" She said in a tone as dead as her hands.

"I don't need to say it do I?"

"I think you do ... I think you need to say a lot ... And ... Right now ... Don't you?" 'Yes,' she affirmed. 'That is damp wolf hair.'

"Baby ... I ... Don't know what to say ... But that, I love you with all my heart and soul."

"Did you love me with all your heart and soul when you were out with Nancy last night too?"

"Baby ... I."

She leaned over nose to nose. "Well?" She stared directly into his eyes. They seemed off color as if dark-brown and a mix of amber. 'The makeup must be coming off,' she thought.

"No, baby it's not like that ... She's ... She is ... Just a friend ... She's been a friend of mine for a long time, sweetie ... Before I knew you. We've always gotten together once in a while and have dinner."

"You get together once in awhile and have two hundred dollar dinners on our credit cards? ... Really?" She smiled, pausing excessively long before continuing. "So why haven't I ever met her, or been told about her?"

He hung his head.

"Look at me." Julie tilted his chin up with her middle and index fingers. "Well?"

"I can't talk to you with you looking at me like that baby ... You're breaking my heart sweetie ... I ... I."

"Let's not go there with whose breaking whose heart here."

"Baby, don't do this to me."

"Don't do this to you? ... What is it I am doing to you? ... If you ask me ... I am the one that is being done to ... Not you!"

"Baby, honey, sweetie ... Please."

Julie could not play into this any longer. She dropped her shoulders slinking down in the window seat. She wanted her husband back, her real husband, not who or what this was.

He gathered her in his arms. "Honey ... You got it all wrong baby" He picked her up and walked over to the bed laying her down gently. He stroked her hair. "Baby ... You know in your heart I love you and would never do anything to hurt you ... Don't you?"

She laid her head against his chest wrapping her arms about him, feeling maybe she actually did have the man she loved so. He reciprocated, cuddling her tightly moulding her into his warmth. He was saying everything she needed and wanted to hear complete with the violins and she was soaking it in like a dry sponge. He rocked her gently as he reaffirmed all this, was not at all, what it seemed. It could not be so therefore it was not; she had just jumped to the wrong conclusion. Even Nancy herself had said on the phone that they were just friends. She had not said for how long but she hadn't thought that far ahead to ask either.

"Feel better?" he whispered. He kissed her ear lobe tenderly allowing his fingertips to wander down her neck, along her collarbone and down, tracing out the outline of each of her breasts.

She attempted to pull back, not quite ready to surrender, but she was deadlocked, held and snuggled into the soft fluff of the sheep costume.

"Baby ... I love you more than anything on this earth ... You know that don't you?"

"Then why are you out with someone else? ... And why the note?"

"She is just an old friend from school that I've kept in touch with. About twice a year we get together for dinner or a drink and talk," he smiled combing his fingers through her hair. "She was just saying last night how much of a mess I was and that I should take better care of myself for you and wrote some things down on the back of a receipt we found for a joke ... We just get together and talk about how our lives are going and stuff."

'We just get together and talk ... Opening and closing statement virtually the same ... They ... As in they, together ... Wrote things on the back of a receipt ... They ... As in they, together ... Found? ... The receipt with yesterday's date ... The receipt with the credit card that said Porter along the bottom ... Okay! ... Right!' She thought she saw a wolf hair floating in the air. "But, what about the book?" she said. She rolled her eyes; she was definitely still in the lame hall of fame.

"What book honey?"

"Older women younger men having babies?" She watched the wolf hair she thought she saw floating in the air, land on her arm.

"Oh that ... Her husband is a lot younger than she is and she has been trying to find that book to give him and just added it to the note in case I should happen upon it," he replied. He could feel her body starting to relax. "That's all baby," he said.

"Why didn't you tell me about her ... I don't understand why you would keep it from me ... I wouldn't have cared ... I." She broke off. 'I am going to be forever in this lame hall of fame, no-one will ever deliver lines of such stupidity, but the sheep wool was just so soft and fluffy.' She bit her lip, thinking she saw yet another wolf hair.

"I guess, I stupidly just didn't think you would understand about me having a female friend and I didn't want you upset and I know now that was so very wrong. I should have told you about her. Well actually, I should have brought you along. I always talk about you so much she is always saying that anyway."

She looked deep into his golden eyes. She so wanted to believe every single solitary word was the sheep's God's honest truth or strike him down dead. "Swear to me on our love for one another that she is nothing but a friend to you," she whispered.

He rolled her onto her back gently coming down on top of her. "I swear," he said. He held her eyes, allowing her to search the surface mask for signs of the something that was not there.

She had asked him to swear to her and he had obliged. He waited until he saw the dark blue start to glint and spark; lightening into the velvety blue eyes, he loved so. Her body softened underneath him. He moved slightly to the side, allowing his hands to roam up and under her nightgown. "I love you baby. Only you," he whispered. "Want to go out with your husband for lunch and a movie then go out somewhere really nice for dinner? We will even go shopping after the movie and pick you out a dynamite dress to wear. Okay?"

She nodded.

His sheep's costume and dimpled smile had won. Her thoughts had gone off onto other things where they should not have been.

He cupped her hands in his turning them over and planting soft kisses in her palms, slowly inching his way up her arm lingering at her ear lobe. "Sit up for a second baby this night gown of yours is suddenly in the way here."

"What about work?" she murmured. "It's mid morning. Won't your dad be wondering what on earth happened to you?"

"Fuck him! He'll see me tomorrow! You are all that's important to me." He laid her back down throwing both their clothes in a heap on the floor. "You are all that's ever been important to me. You and only you. I love you baby." He rolled her on top of him his hands tracing her outline seductively, pausing ever so slightly at her inner thighs. "I love you darling. Please forgive my stupidity? I'll never ever do it again. I can't bear to hurt you." He whispered sweet nothings repeatedly, as he attempted to smolder her thoughts engulfing her in red-hot flames, infusing her senses with all that he was.

Too bad he hadn't seen that newly shed clump of wolf hair on the sheets, the one she was staring directly at.

Chapter 12

Julie and Sherry sat across from one another in a copycat pose so exact they could have been dubbed dollar store bookends complete with tags. Their elbows were splayed identical in slant and depth, crooked chins were resting in their palms with off side grins, left legs crossed over top of the right and both piss drunk as the bar clock hit high noon.

Sherry leaned over to Julie her one elbow slipping out from under her. "So!"

"So?" Julie repeated. She started to giggle.

"Sooo!" Sherry slurred. She cocked her right hand index finger wiggling it naughtily, back and forth in front of Julie's face starting to laugh.

"Sooo!" Julie mimicked. She motioned with her hands for Sherry to come on out with it.

"So!" Sherry cemented her lips together trying to appear serious, gulped then fell into full-blown out and out laughter.

"Will you quit with the so?" Julie blurted. She bunted Sherry in the shoulder with her palm.

"SO!" Sherry belted out. Her entire body jerked and jiggled in roller waves of laughter. "Look ... I just gotta say ... So ... First all right? ... It just goes well there," she snorted.

"Okay ... Here ... I'll say it for you this time ... You know, save you the trouble ... SO," she blurted loudly.

Sherry fist hammered the table hooting so hard tears rolled down her cheeks. "Will you quit! ... You're going to make me pee myself!" She took a half hearted swipe at Julie's head, hitting her by accident.

Julie dropped her head to the table banging it twice, playing dead. She knew it should have hurt, but it hadn't.

She reversed the criss-cross of her legs almost falling off the bar stool, feeling as if she too was going to piss herself any minute if all this didn't stop.

Sherry sunk the top half of her body to tabletop level, resting her chin on the wood, it was too damn hard to hold her chest and head up any longer.

"Ah shit!" Julie reached over and grasped Sherry's free hand intertwining her fingers through hers.

"So?" Sherry grinned devilishly. "The bakery's toast! ... Over! ... Kaput! ... Defunct! ... Busted! ... Slam-dunked! ... Finite! ... Ka-bonked! ... Done like dinner!" She chortled starting to laugh.

They both busted a gut laughing, stamping the floor with their feet.

"So?" Sherry gulped, swigging in air between the laughter. "Tell me girlfriend! Anything else new in your life? ... Other than being unemployed, as of this morning?"

"Well now that you're asking ... Yes in-deedy do ... There is."

"Well what?"

"Well," Julie said. She grinned to beat all hell wrapping both her arms around herself, swivelling her stool back and forth.

"Come on ... Spit it out girlfriend, before I forget what we're talking about! ... I am seriously drunk you know!"

"Well, I think," Julie started to giggle again.

"You think ... What?"

"I think Tony's having an affair ... And I think I'm pregnant."

Sherry snapped her fingers in the air. "Bartender doubles!"

Chapter 13

"So?"

"Don't start that again." Julie chuckled, switching the receiver to the other ear.

"It just keeps damn well coming out," Sherry giggled. "So ... Ya told your old man you lost your job yet?"

"Nope."

"Haven't gotten up the nerve huh?"

"Nope."

"Me either love ... Me either," Sherry said.

"I can't figure out how, you know? ... Like, what am I supposed to say? ... Honey how was your day? ... Oh by the way, the bakery shut down a couple days ago and I kind of on purpose forgot to mention it to you... Pass the potatoes will you?"

"Hey, that's better than what I've been coming up with, do you mind if I use it?" Sherry snorted.

"Be my guest!" Julie chuckled.

"I don't know why we're laughing here?"

"Well, maybe cause ... Oh I don't know!" Julie retorted.

"So ... And don't you dare laugh at me again ... Hey! ... You're doing it ... I can hear you!"

"I'm sorry, but it's funny!"

"So ... When you going to tell Tony?"

"I guess I'd better after we get off here actually."

"So."

"Yeah I agree ... So?"

"Well sweets ... I'll let you go, my old man is coming through the door, so I think I'll do likewise and get it the hell over with."

"Okay. Good luck," Julie said.

"You too ... And call me after okay?"

"Will do."

"Bye love."

Julie depressed the receiver, and then ever so slowly poked in Tony's work number, hoping he was still in the suck up mode. The joy ride had been long lasting making life, hers, as smooth as silk. If luck was still on her side, this small snag should fly. If not well ... She would take it as it came.

"Hey honey how's your day going?" She fidgeted with the bed sheets twisting them round in her fingers.

"What?"

"How's your day?" she repeated.

"You called to ask me how my day is," he countered flatly.

"Yes, and to talk to you a bit?"

"You called to ask me how my day is and to talk with me a bit."

"Yes." Julie pulled the elastic edge off the corner of the mattress bunching the sheet in her fist.

"I'm having one bitch of a day ... But, thanks for asking ... And I'd really love to chat with you baby but I'm really, really busy right now."

It was now or never. "Tony?"

"What?"

"I have something to tell you and it's not good and I don't know how and you're not going to be happy and I just can't and I should have but I didn't and ... Oh brother." Julie blurted the words so fast she sounded like a chipmunk with a mouth full of peanuts.

"What?"

"Oh Tony ... I have something to tell you and I just can't!" She let go of the sheets, twisting the phone cord through her fingers.

"Just tell me."

"Remember Monday when I had to go to that meeting at work?"

"Yeah, what about it?"

"Well."

"Well, what?"

"They told us the bakery was shutting down." There she had said it. It was out ... Over ... Done.

"What did you just say?"

"The bakery's shutting down." She repeated half the sentence feeling her shoulders hunching and knotting.

"When is this happening?"

"Monday."

"Next Monday?"

"No ... This past Monday." The conversation halted in mid air.

"Fuck Jules! ... Why in hell didn't you tell me?"

"I guess ... I was afraid to ... I thought you'd get angry with me and I." She halted not having any words to place in after I.

"Fuck! ... Fuck! ... Fuck!"

"See you're mad ... I knew you would ... "

He cut her off. "You lose your job and don't fucking tell me until almost a week later?"

"It's not a whole week," she interjected. "Just a couple, three or four days."

"Fuck honey ... I just went and ... Shit ... Never mind." His voice trailed off into nothingness. He looked up in the air shaking his head.

Silence was golden so they say. She figured she would give it a test run and there was no better time like the present.

"Why the hell didn't you tell me?" he asked, quietly.

"I was kind of waiting till the right time and ..."

He picked up where she left off. "And you didn't find it, right?"

"Right," she tossed back.

"Fuck! ... We are going to have a long talk when I get home ... Fuck!"

"Okay," she agreed. She would have agreed to anything at this moment. The kindling was not getting gasoline. She mouthed thank you to the ceiling, clasping her hands together smiling.

"Jules?"

"Yes."

"Be up when I get home tonight."

"Okay."

"And Jules?"

"Yes?"

"Can you at least do something about the fucking basement today seeing as you're off? We moved over a year ago and there are still God damn boxes all over down there? I can't find nothing. Think you can do this?"

"Sure," she replied.

"You should have fucking told me at the time you know. What did you think I was going to do? Bite your head off and stuff it under the mattress?"

"Yes ... I ... Mean no." The yes was honest, the no a lie. He did not say goodbye but under the circumstances, she figured his response to the whole thing was five star for him.

She dialled Sherry's number.

"Hello you," Sherry said.

"How'd you know it was me?"

"Just the way it rang love ... And that thing named call-display helps."

"Can't get away with nothing, can I?

"Speaking of which ... How'd it go with the Italian hothead?"

"Minimal collateral damage I'd say!"

"Minimal? Well ... Well," Sherry laughed.

"Yeah," Julie nodded her head starting to laugh along with Sherry.

"What'd you do hog tie him with barbwire, chain him to the car and drag him around the block bouncing his head off the curbs or something?"

"Nope."

"He's still sucking up then huh?"

"Yep, somewhat," Julie giggled. "But I have this feeling it'll be soon over."

"Really?" Sherry snickered. "Well you're one lucky shit aren't you girl?"

"I'll say ... But I did get the," she made her voice husky mimicking Tony. "Fuck! ... We are going to have a long talk when I get home ... Fuck!"

"Hey you do a pretty mean Tony."

"Gee thanks ... So how about you? ... How'd you do?" Julie said.

"Mine tossed a few grenades at me for not telling him sooner but all in all ... I'd say you got off better than me, mine wasn't sucking up for nothing."

"Grenades huh?" Julie snickered.

"Yep the pins were pulled out too!"

"Well I guess I'd better love you and leave you. I have a penance to perform." Julie said quietly, hoping it would sneak on past Sherry.

"A penance? ... Hey, wait a minute! ... I think you accidentally on purpose left that tidbit out ... Didn't you?"

"Well excuse me! ... And like you don't have one chained to your ankles too there?"

Sherry burst out laughing. "No I don't ... I'm just standing here making a homemade apple pie from scratch for something to do ... And don't you dare go there girl."

Julie grinned. "Okay I won't touch it, but it's awfully tempting. I think I'd best be getting off before it gets the better of me."

"Talk at ya later girlfriend ... Hey Jules ... Before you go?"

"Yeah?"

"Still think you're ... You know?" Sherry whispered.
"Yeah."
"Bye hon."
"Bye."

Chapter 14

The basement door latch caught on the outer edge of Julie's sweater pulling it taunt as she passed through the opening. The latch nub distended as if bloating, giving leave of the yarn, and freeing the door. It abruptly whipped backward, then rebounded sling shooting forward, slamming shut in a thunderous whack that reverberated down into the basement and back.

The four-second process plummeted Julie into complete, utter blackness ... Total ... Complete ... Utter ... Blackness. She instinctively struck out her arms, setting herself off balance. She lurched forward. Her legs pivoted and tangled, going over top of one another causing her to lose her footing, sliding her downwards on her heels. She bumped and banged off the wood, coming to a rocky teeter-totter halt on the outer edge of one of the stair.

"HOLY SHIT!" she exclaimed. "That was close!" She thanked her lucky stars she was not laying ass over teakettle broken and twisted at the bottom ... At the bottom in the dark ... In the total, complete, utter, dark. She drew her feet back against the riser. She squinted into the murkiness, her eyes not in the least acclimatizing. She swivelled her neck round in disjointed owl-like circles hoping it would help ... It didn't. She had no idea how many stairs she'd succumbed to, or whether she was closer to the top or the bottom. The obscurity surrounding her seemed closed off, not unlike the insides of a sealed coffin ... It was way past dark ... It was unholy.

She groped for the banister ... It wasn't there ... It did not seem to be anywhere. She gulped in short breaths, swallowing them down whole, sounding like a car, overheating and about to give up the ghost. The air seemed thick and heavy, like a swamp just before a rain.

She stretched out her arms searching blindly for the wall. Chilled air swept through her fingers making them feel numb. "OH COME ON!" she exclaimed. "A wall can't move! ... Maybe a banister! ... But not a wall!" She trailed her arms lower feeling for the constants that did not seem to be there. "FOR GOD'S SAKE!" she screeched. Her words echoed round in circles as if mocking her. Her outstretched arms flailed and flopped clumsily through the darkness as the twinges of panic frost bit her fingertips. She folded them into her palms.

She could feel dewy steam rising from her breath. She hunched her shoulders bunching them into a ball. She did up the top buttons of her sweater as more and more frigid air silently crept in and under, latching onto her skin, travelling back and forth in spurts and starts leaving an array of goose bumps in its wake.

Threads of fear spiralled unseen through the blackness behind her, landing and tangling into the hairs on the back of her neck, standing it at attention, slithering down between the shafts plopping onto her flesh, opening wide, biting clean through.

She began to tremble uncontrollably. Her knees following suit, banging and knocking on and off one another making a strange hollow eerie clacking that resonated about her feet, before taking leave and trailing off into dark corners, nesting and festering there, to return as something else.

She suddenly wanted to get the hell out of there ... And ... Now!

Performing penance was rapidly losing ground, to something irrational, she could not even begin to get a handle on ... Nor did she want to.

She slowly pivoted on the step, poking with her toe, putting out feelers for something ... Anything ... But cold dead air. She abruptly halted, her mind jumping over the clog starting the wheels, reminding her why she was, where she was ... The suck up was over ... Tony the alien, no doubt, would fly home by dinnertime ... He'd be in fine soaring form tonight if she didn't do this ... She weighed them both carefully ... Penance – Alien ... Penance in the dark ... Alien from the planet asshole ... She opted for the penance.

She reluctantly slid out a foot carefully inching and worming it forward until she felt the stairs edge. There was a light switch at the bottom of the staircase. *'It can't be that many more steps,'* she thought, shaking off another cold shudder before it got hold and would not let go. "For Christ's sake ... Get a grip here," she said. Her legs suddenly wobbled, bending in directions they were not designed for as if made of cheap rubber. She clutched at her chest with both hands, she felt like her heart was going to pound right on out and run for cover. "Come on ... Pull it together ... Get a grip," she said again.

She hesitantly started to descend the staircase, which seemed to sprout three more steps in place of each one she took. She moved pathetically slow, her feet slipping and sliding over the damp painted wood. She counted as she went. "One ... Two ... Three ... Four ... Five." She suddenly halted, her entire body going into spastic quivers, jarring and tossing her side to side as if she'd become possessed by an evil entity. She wrapped her chest with her arms squeezing tight, comforting herself. "It's just a staircase ... It's just a basement ... Nothing to be afraid of ... I'm okay ... The bottom's soon ... Steady as she goes ... It's okay Julie ... It's okay," she whispered.

She pushed her leg forward with her hands making it take a step. "See ... It's not so bad." She pushed the other leg. "There you go ... Good job ... Now let's try it on your own." She took a single step, then another then another. She resumed her counting. "Six ... Seven ... JESUS CHRIST!" She screamed into the hollow like blackness, stopping, her breaths suddenly coming hard and fast. Her fright had pivoted sideways and was making its way into terror, inch by inch propelling its self along the frayed thin tightrope stretched out between the words. She felt as if she was stepping along a broken down escalator, going the wrong direction, in a twisted fun house after dark where monsters stood behind two-way glass watching and plotting.

"How long is this thing?" She leaned the top half of her torso forward. "Don't answer yourself Julie ... All this is bad enough without asking yourself questions and answering them ... That's called crazy ... Let's just go back to being scared." She scraped her lips with her teeth drawing them backwards into her mouth as she continued talking to herself. "Being scared is okay ... Lots of people get scared."

Her body felt beyond numb, as if ice molecules had escaped the air and penetrated into her pores. She pulled her hands up into her sleeves. She ran inner commentary, reassuring herself, repeating it and repeating it. *'The basement has a floor ... All basements have floors ... Even the ones in horror movies have floors ... Mine has to be out there ... Just a few more steps ... And it will be there ... Just a few more ... Just a few more steps.'*

She went back to counting. "Seven ... Nine ... Eight," she said.

"NI ... NE!" She yelled her voice pitching into a sharp squeal, the tip of her runner catching and hooking the carpet catapulting her up onto her tippy-toes. Both her big toes bent and went under, making her resemble an awkward wanna-be ballerina dancing to a macabre waltz. She sidestepped lurching forward, losing her balance, banging the raw flesh of her ankles into something rock hard ... Something rock hard and immovable. She rocked back and forth unable to stabilize her weight, belted over like a drunk going down for the count, slamming into and against the cold cement wall, rebounding, toppling head over heels landing in a heap on the floor.

"GOD DAMN IT!" she cursed. She rose to her knees, the skin of her ankles burning and stinging and wet ... She needed light and she needed it now. She crawled her hands up the wall dipping and trailing her fingers over and in every crack and crevice. "Where the hell is it?" she said. "It's got to be here ... It's just got to be." She feverishly ran her fingers back and forth, back and forth. "I know it's here," she continued. "I've seen it here ... Just ... Calm down," she said. "Yeah right!" she answered fear reversing from terror opting for crazy ... Crazy was good ... Fear and terror was not good ... Terrible things always happened to scared people alone in basements in the dark ... Once they found the basement, that is ... She had seen it on television way too many times ... But nothing ever seemed to happen to crazies ... Crazy was good. She dragged the tips of her fingers slowly across the damp clammy cement searching for the one thing that would be the end all. She rose to her feet, her thumbs sliding, splaying her fingers sideways, stretching the webbing, making her lose her place.

"Please ... Please God ... Help me," she begged, huffing out short breaths of rising steam.

God answered her prayer.

"OWE!" she screamed. "SHIT! ... OWE!" She repeated, drowning out the crack her pinky finger had resonated in protest as it doubled backward striking a protrusion jutting from the wall. She doused her finger in warm saliva, wincing in pain.

"Hey! ... Wait a second!" She cocked her head to the side. "Was? ... That? ... It?" She circled her palm over it. "YES! ... YES! ... YES!" she screeched. She stamped her feet in swift short bursts as if she had just won the lottery and then flipped the light-switch.

Julie stepped backward ... The thing that had caused this whole mess ... At the bottom of the stairs ... Getting her again ... Landing her on her ass ... The score ... Thing two ... Julie nothing. "What in living hell?" she said, picking up the ten- inch by ten-inch box laying aside her left knee. It was wrapped tightly in a heavy Menlo brown paper. She rested the box in her lap rolling it over and right siding it.

"What on earth is in this thing?" she said. "Bricks?" She turned it round reading the red express post label. "To: Mrs. Pauline James care of Mrs. Julie Porter 1497 Thomasview Crescent. From: Peaceful Acres Funeral Parlor 963 Evendon Road." Her eyes widened like goose eggs. "OH!! ... MY!! ... GOOD!! ... GOD!!" she screamed her voice pitching and shrilling, turning hysterical. She threw it, kicking feverishly scrambling onto her hands and knees crawling toward the stairs, propelling up to the top landing.

She hit the door with her shoulder reefing the doorknob with both hands. The knob gave way, bouncing one by one down the stairs, somersaulting at the base, twirling and spinning like a top across the floor, coming to an abrupt halt alongside the brown-papered carton.

Julie stared with her goose egg eyes, her mouth dried and open, her limbs feeling as if made of cracked brittle plastic pipe. The round part of the knob was turned her way ... Looking like it had her name on it ... Looking like it was grinning up at her. She was sure it was going to open its grinning mouth and start to whisper any second ... Whisper the words ... *'You're next Julie ... You are the next to bounce down these stairs ... You're next Julie.'*

Terror glued and fired up her plastic limbs. She turned towards the door in one fluid motion booting it open with her left foot, her right running before it hit the floor. She flew through the living room and on out the patio door right through the screen.

She doubled over in half, gasping and choking unable to breathe. She wrapped her fingers in back of her knees. Her head dangled loose and free. Blood started to hammer through her temples; thickening as it went, turning from blue to stark black. It started to thunder inside her, coursing throughout, beating that old primitive rhythm that she never, ever, ever thought she would hear again, in this lifetime.

She collapsed on the back porch.

The devil had landed ...

The Devil had landed ...

'Definition'

Dev-il (dev'al)
:The supreme spirit of Satan.

:A subordinate evil spirit.

:An atrociously wicked person.

:A person of great cleverness, energy or recklessness.

SECTION TWO
THE PASSAGE

Chapter 15

"What the fuck are you doing out here, on the back porch?"
    "Nothing," Julie said.
    "It's fucking late!"
    "I know."

"How long you been out here Jules?" Tony asked.

"I don't know."

"Where are the kids?"

"At their friends."

"Why the fuck didn't you do the basement?"

"I can't."

"You can't?"

"No," Julie replied.

Tony offered her a hand up.

She just sat there as if she'd been super glued to the back porch.

"Why can't you?" he said.

"Cause."

"Cause? ... Cause? ... For fucks sake, what the hell is wrong with you?"

"Nothing."

He kneeled down brushing the clumped hair from the sides of her cheeks. It came away stiffly, leaving dark brown imprints on her skin. "Christ, you've been bleeding ... What the hell happened?"

"I think ... I hit my head on the porch."

"For fucks sake," he muttered more for himself than anything. He scooped her up in his arms, carrying her upstairs. He laid her out on the bed disappearing and reappearing with a washcloth.

"Ouch!" she complained.

"Hold still." He wiped the blood from her forehead and cheeks. "Jules? ... Are you okay?" he whispered.

She did not respond, only stared straight ahead as if she had been suspended in space and time.

"What the fuck is wrong with you? ... You see a ghost or something?" he asked.

"No ... Worse ... Much worse," she said. She had answered far too quickly for her mannequin like demeanour.

"Fuck honey." He shook his head. "You're not making any sense ... Just get in bed will you? ... We'll talk tomorrow."

"If it comes," she said.

"What?"

"Nothing."

He picked up the remote and channel surfed as if all this was as ordinary and commonplace as hot apple pie.

"Did you put a box in the basement?" she asked. Her voice was cold, a dead monotone. She stared straight ahead.

"What the hell are you talking about? ... I've put lots of boxes in the basement?"

"A small, heavy, express post box?"

"Not that I can think of ... Oh wait ... Yeah I did ... Shit ... That was at least a month ago ... Why?"

She ignored his question. "Where are you getting the yellow roses you're giving me?"

"From a bush."

"From what bush?" she asked.

"Fuck! ... What the hell is this? ... The Spanish inquisition?"

"From what bush?" she repeated flatly.

"The bush outside." He sunk down in the bed pulling the covers up to his chest watching reruns.

"There's no bush outside," she countered.

"There is too."

"Where?"

"Fuck! ... I'm trying to watch this."

"Where?" she pushed. The last thing in the world she would ever do was to own a yellow rose bush.

"You're really starting to fucking piss me off!"

"Where is the bush?" she persisted.

"Fuck!" He purposefully drew in a deep breath. "I already told you ... Outside."

"Exactly where outside?"

"Outside ... You know ... Outside in the front near the fucking tree, where you God damn well planted it!"

"I didn't plant a rose bush by the tree."

"Well it didn't just get up off somebody else's lawn and walk over to ours ... Now did it?"

"No," she said. *'It couldn't have walked,'* she thought. *'Someone or something had to have put it there'* ... Roses didn't have feet and if they did she certainly did not want to know. "I have to go see my mother tomorrow morning."

"What?"

"I have to go see my mother tomorrow morning," she repeated verbatim.

"What the hell do you have to go and see that crazy old broad for?" he asked. He did not wait for an answer, nor did he want one. "Half the time she doesn't even know who the hell you are."

"So ... She's still my mother."

"A loony tune if you ask me?" He twirled his index finger around in circles at his temple sticking his tongue out the corner of his mouth.

"I didn't ask you."

He gave her a look.

"Could you put a new knob on the basement door?" she said. "One with a lock," she added.

"Why?"

"Cause it fell off today."

"Well ... Jules," he paused smiling. "If it fell off, then it fell back on. It was there when I got home."

She glared at him, her eyes widening to the point they felt like they were going to flip over inside out.

He glanced up from the television. "What?"

"Nothing," she said too quiet to hear. She tugged the covers up over her nose nervously looking about the room.

He narrowed his brows watching her; she was giving new meaning to the word weird.

"Can you change places with me for the night?" she muffled through the coverlets.

"I thought you liked sleeping by the door?"

"Not anymore."

Chapter 16

Julie threw the hedge clippers into the garage. They skidded across the floor smashing into the wall up ending themselves. The front lawn looked like a scene out of a low budget sci-fi movie where a lawn and a bush had battled for their lives. The wounded and dying lay strewn about the decapitated. Clear rose sap oozed and dripped like blood from the few remaining root tops, spilling out and over darkening the brown earth black. However ... She figured three or four bottles of weed kill should take care of that.

She climbed in the car.

The two-hour drive to the nursing home had been a welcoming distraction, totally devoid of thought, the radio purposefully too loud, the windows all the way down.

Julie entered her mother's room, finding her fretfully working away on a knitted blanket the size of a lap warmer. She pulled up a chair alongside the bed draping her jacket over top, sitting down in silence watching her mother knit with pretend needles, stop, knit, stop, turning the blanket this way and that, examining it. She remembered when her mother had first made it. It was the most beautiful blanket she had ever seen; all in jewel tone patchwork squares, no two alike. Whoever the dumb ass was that had thrown it in the hot water wash should have been shot on the spot.

The doctor had talked to Julie at length on her last visit about her mother's 'Alzheimer's.' The words, *I know Pauline is barely past sixty, but the disease has advanced rapidly during the past two years, causing such profound intellectual decline and degeneration, that for all intents and purposes she might as well be viewed as an eighty year old,'* echoed around inside her head.

Julie grasped one of her mother's hands in hers, lovingly stroking the back of it with her thumb. Her mother continued her incessant work on the blanket, knitting with one hand seemingly unaware of her daughter.

"Mom? ... Mom? ... I miss you so ... You know that don't you?" Julie said. She waited for a sign of life from her mother ... There was nothing, just the one handed knitting. Tears sprouted in Julie's eyes. "I know you weren't expecting me today but I had to come ... I really have to talk to you ... No, that's a lie ... I really *need* to talk to you." Julie moved her mother's hand up to her face gently rubbing her cheek back and forth on it. "Mom? ... Mom? ... Do you know I'm here?"

Her mother's eyes momentarily flickered over Julie's face then returned to the blanket.

"I need to talk to you ... Please come and be here with me? ... Please?"

Her mother nodded.

Why or at what the nod was for? ... Julie didn't know, didn't care ... She leaped at it, latching on, seizing it as if a golden opportunity had just landed in her lap. "Do you remember the long talk we had when Dad died?" She paused hoping for another nod, hoping the first nod had been for her and not the blanket ... There was no sign of life ... It had been for the blanket. "Do you remember?" she continued. "Do you?" she repeated.

"Look dearie ... I've done four rows while you were sitting here with me." She held out the blanket for Julie to admire.

"That's wonderful." Julie smiled; her mother was somewhat present, at least she knew someone was there. She put her hands over both of her mother's lowering them and the blanket into her mother's lap. "Mom?" she said. She hoped and prayed she would soon come to earth. She sighed deeply. They had always been the best of friends, along with

140

being mother and daughter, and she so desperately needed her mother and her best friend.

Her mother smiled shyly.

"Mom?" Julie said. Her voice quivered, her control slipping.

Her mother offered up the same smile. "Why are you calling me mom dearie?"

Her mother had asked so matter of fact it just did not fit in. "Because you're my mother," Julie replied. She shook her head. Her mother had not come to earth yet.

"I am?"

"Yes," Julie said. She sighed again. "You are."

"Are you sure dear?"

"Yes ... I'm sure."

"What a nice surprise! ... I didn't know I had a daughter! ... That is just so nice! ... What's your name honey?"

"Julie ... My name is Julie."

"Well ... Julie ... Pleased to meet you ... That's a very pretty name ... Julie." Her mother pressed the blanket out flat with her palms, starting to fuss over it again.

Julie pulled herself in closer. "I need to talk to you."

"Yes child ... Susie isn't it?"

"Julie."

"Julie? ... Not Susie?"

"Yes ... Julie not Susie ... Mom? ... Do you remember when dad died?"

"Oh good heavens child! ... My dad's not dead, is he?"

"No ... No ... Not your dad ... My dad." Julie became exasperated, pitching herself forward, flopping her head onto the bed.

"Something wrong child?"

"Yes."

"Well dearie you can talk to me if you like ... I don't mind if you don't."

"No, I don't mind," Julie slowly replied, starting to weep.

"There ... There ... Dearie." Her mother combed Julie's hair with her fingers.

"Mom?"

Her mother looked around hesitantly. She lowered her voice to a whisper. "You know ... It's really nice of you to keep calling me mom ... I get a great big giggle out of it ... But ... You do realize ... I am all but thirteen ... Folk's say that I do look a might older than that though, don't you know ... But good golly ... To be called mom ... I hope I am one someday ... There's this boy I really like ... And ..."

Julie cut her off. "Will you please get a grip? ... I really need to talk to you!" she said sharply.

Her mother put down the knitting ... Sat up straight ... Clasp her hands together ... Stared ahead. "Honest Mrs. Martin, it wasn't my gum. I found it stuck under the book." She gave Julie a cute wink.

"MOM! ... FOR CHRIST'S SAKE!" Julie yelled.

Her mother's forehead furrowed.

"Please ... Please ... Please ... I'm begging you, just pay attention to me for a minute ... One single minute ... Will you?"

"Okay," her mother replied almost too quiet to hear. She hunched her shoulders, then rounded them drawing them forward, making herself look small and meek.

Julie took her mother's hands in hers. "When dad died ... My dad ... Your husband ..." She spoke slow and purposeful, pausing often, clarifying the whose-who as she went. "When dad died, we had a long, long talk ... Do you remember?" She turned her mother's hands palms up placing them one on top of the other and covering them with her own. "Do you remember?"

Her mother stared blankly ahead, sitting straight as a board.

"We talked and firmly agreed that the funeral home, Peaceful Acres ... Would keep the urn until the time arose that both ... Yours and his, urns could be taken to the cemetery together ... Do you remember?"

Her mother glanced at her out the corner of her eye like a scolded child while the shit is hitting the fan.

"Why oh why? ... Just ... Out of the blue? ... Would you change things without telling me? ... And ... Have dad's ashes delivered to my house? ... Why?"

Her mother opened and closed her mouth as if to speak ... But didn't.

"Mom? ... Mom? ... Are you in there? ... Are you hearing any of this?"

Her mother folded her hands inside out.

"God damn it!" Julie said, harshly.

Her mother gulped, swallowing, sputtering and hacking pretending she had something stuck in her throat.

Julie gave up the ghost, bending her head, sobbing out of control.

Her mother poked the tissue box towards her using the thumb of her left hand.

"My whole damn life is falling apart ... I need you ... I need you so much right now." Julie rested her head on her mother's shoulder. "Mom ... I lost my job ... My marriage is going down the tubes, for reasons I don't even know ... I'm pretty sure I'm pregnant." Julie blew her nose. "And," she blew her nose again. "And ... Now I have dad's ashes in my house ... This is all way more than I can deal with ... Why in hell is God doing all this to me?"

"Whoever said it was God ... Julie?" Her mother whispered, slow, deliberate and disconcert.

Julie's jaw dropped, hitching itself to her collarbone ... Her skin rippled, then froze as if she had just been shoved alive, into a morgue's deep freeze with nothing but a thin sheet. She could feel the cold numbing her. Feel it worming and weaving up through her layers. Feel it burrowing, right into her bones. She slumped herself back from her mother's shoulder, fumbling with lead weighted arms and hands that did not function. She tried to push herself from the bed with feet that slithered and slipped on the tile flooring, rotating and flopping to and fro like cold dead fish washed up on shore.

"What? ... What? ... Did? ... Did? ... You just say?" Julie's tongue seemed thick and weighted making it difficult to speak. She couldn't have heard, what she thought she head ... What she thought she heard was totally beyond the scope of words.

Her mother smiled a grin that was not at all God like. "You heard me," she said.

Julie's eyes widened, bulging, swelling out from the sockets. She pushed away from the bed, rapidly jerking to a stand, flinging the chair backwards. It skidded across the floor on two legs, slapping into the wall. She scrambled for the door on limbs that refused to move in one direction. She sidestepped, tangling her feet, banging her shoulder and hip into the doorframe, bouncing backwards then sideways into the wall. She clawed her way along the wallboard and out the opening, leaving tiny half-moon dents from her fingernails.

Her mother was as she had been ... Bolt upright ... Sitting in the bed ... Hands clasped neatly in her lap. She did not even need to swivel so much as her head, to watch her daughter through the window running wildly through the parking lot.

She smiled, catching the reflection of the chair where her daughter had been sitting in the mirror. The jacket still draped across the back.

She pulled her lips back from her teeth, her smile changing into a horrid grimace. She got out of bed ... Walked across the room ... Straightened the chair ... Put on the jacket ... Not once taking leave of her daughter's disappearing taillights.

Her room door opened.

"Did you have a nice visit with your daughter Mrs. James?" the nurse asked. The nurse placed a vase of freshly cut yellow roses on her bedside table. She fluffed the pillows offering her an arm to steady herself back into bed.

"Very nice," she replied. She picked up her knitting, replacing the grimace with two thin drawn out lines, that only the mirror saw.

"Oh! ... Mrs. James!" the nurse cooed. "What a lovely new jacket, you got there!"

"Yes it is ... Isn't it? ... My daughter bought it for me."

"Would you like your lunch now?"

"Oh yes ... Please and thank you."

As the room door closed, the toothy smile reopened, accompanied and serenaded by gulps and wheezes of hoarse guttural laughter that echoed throughout the room.

Chapter 17

Julie moulded her body into a tight ball, fitting herself neatly into the overstuffed armchair. The home pregnancy test kit with the two positive wavy blue lines lay on the chair arm beside her. She had been relatively sure but now the 'I's were dotted and the 'T's crossed.

She sat dangling the telephone receiver cord by her teeth, swinging it, debating what to do. She nodded ... Deciding ... If it stopped on the right, it was tell him now ... If it stopped on the left, it was tell him later. It swung round in circles stopping in the middle every time. She decided to have another go later dropping the receiver into the cradle.

It rang instantaneously startling her, making her insides hop and vault in a colossal hiccup. Before she could fetch the receiver, the answering machine snatched it. She waited for the flashing message light. There was none.

It rang again.

"Hello?"

"Hi Julie ... It's Nancy Anderson ... Do you remember me?"

"Yes," she answered. *'How could I forget?'* she thought.

"We spoke a couple weeks ago," Nancy said.

"I remember."

"I've been thinking a lot about you."

"You have? ... Why?" Julie asked.

"Because ..." Nancy hesitated, and then started over. "Because ... I lied to you."

"You lied to me?" Julie grabbed the corners of the armchair turning sideways on the edge of the cushion almost toppling onto the floor.

"Yes ... I did." Nancy's voice was low, solemn. "I know we don't one other, but I need to tell you the truth."

Julie's head started to spin, vomit burped in her throat.

"You still there?" Nancy asked.

Julie nodded, the flesh of her cheek making a dull rubbing noise into the receiver.

"I don't know how to say this."

"Just say it," Julie's hands had started to shake. She dropped the receiver, retrieved it, fumbled with it, and dropped it again.

"I'm so sorry ... I ... I." Nancy paused, loudly clearing the lump from her throat against the receiver.

"You're sorry?" Julie questioned. "Why are you saying, you're sorry? ... He told me all about you ... You're old friends ... And ..." She shut down mid sentence cupping her free hand over her mouth her body tensing, her mind dictating out words of that old standby called 'Intuition.' Her body felt as if it had tensed into petrified wood. *'Please ... Please don't say what I think you're going to ... Please don't say it ... Please don't ... Don't do this to me.'* She dropped her head hearing the dry earthy swallows from the other end of the telephone.

"No ... We aren't old friends," Nancy said, her voice drawing raspy and thin as if she was in need of oxygen.

"Please don't ... Oh please ... God please ... No."

"I'm sorry ... With all my heart ... I am so sorry ... I would never have gone out with him, if I'd known he was married."

"No ... Please ... No," Julie cried out.

"I'm sorry." Nancy said ... Again.

Julie felt like her heart and soul had been ripped from her chest ... It hurt to breathe. The room circled in slow motion, tears rolled down her cheeks, pooling in her open mouth. She threw up in the garbage can somewhere in between ... 'We've been going out for six months ... Her daughter catching the two of them going at it on the living room floor ... Having her tubes untied so they could try and

147

have a baby together.' Julie pulled the receiver from her ear as Nancy continued to recount detail after detail after detail, she did not want to hear. She threw up again.

"Are you okay?" Nancy whispered.

"No."

"Julie?"

Julie dry retched into the pail. "What?"

"You do believe me don't you?"

"As in what?"

"That I never would have gone out with him if I'd known he was married. I ... I ... Could not do that to someone ... I." Nancy started to cry. "Please believe me?" she sobbed.

Julie heard the word yes quietly escape her lips ... Whether she actually believed Nancy or not didn't much matter ... Nothing mattered right then ... Not even breathing.

"Is there anything else you want to know?" Nancy asked.

"No ... I think you have said about enough ... More than enough," Julie added.

Nancy's voice shook. "I ... I."

"How did you meet?" Julie blurted, out of nowhere before she could stop herself. She looked up in the air. She had gone back in through the doors of that lame hall of fame again. Nevertheless, for some hidden reason she'd discover and yell at herself later for, she just had to know how.

"We met on a chat line." Nancy said.

"A ... Chat ... Line?" Julie countered.

"Yes."

"I don't understand chat line. What do you mean?"

"You know a chat line ... It's a paid service for singles ... You place a voice-ad saying what you're looking for in someone and people leave one another messages and then you talk one on one and if you click, you meet."

"Oh my God!" Julie gasped. "It's like a dating service?"

"Yes, somewhat," Nancy said.

"JESUS CHRIST!" Julie shouted. Her throat closed off, shrilling her voice. "Oh my God! ... I don't believe this! ... You met through a God damn dating service ... A DATING SERVICE? ... OH GOOD GOD!" Julie's breathing laboured. She collapsed down into the chair knocking the test kit with her elbow. It fell onto the floor landing face up showing off its 'yes you're pregnant' two blue wavy lines. She felt like her head was about to blow off. '*A dating service? ... A dating service?*' Repeated round and round until it sunk in.

"We were supposed to move in together next month," Nancy said her tone seemed comparable to the ass end of a donkey. "We were supposed to start painting the house this coming weekend. He was ... "

Julie let go of the receiver. She had already heard way ... Way too much. Why was this person still going on so? She would have asked but fear got in the way, in case there were more juicy tid-bits not yet disclosed that would make her throw up again. She could hear Nancy calling out her name repeatedly in between sobbing and wailing and apologizing for her actions. She bunted the telephone with the heel of her foot to within arm's reach, unexpectedly finding herself feeling sorry for this person on the other end of the line that had just ripped her heart out.

"Nancy? ... Nancy ... Shhhh ... Shhhh there," Julie soothed. "It's okay."

"No it's not ... I'm so stupid ... I didn't know he was married ... I didn't know ... I thought I'd really found someone to have a future with ... I am so stupid ... And now I've hurt someone and ... "

Julie cut her off. "You didn't hurt me, he did," Julie said stunned. She actually held a form of rational compassion ... Compassion for a woman who had been sleeping with her husband.

"But ... Buf." Nancy stuttered, slurring her words.

"You didn't do anything wrong."

"Yes I have ... Oh my God! ... Oh my God!" Nancy cried. "What in hell have I done?"

Julie looked down at the test kit. She could have given her a really good answer to that particular question.

"Are you okay?" Nancy asked.

"No, are you?" Julie mirrored.

"No."

"Well then," Julie said. "That seems yet another thing we now have in common doesn't it?" Julie closed her eyes, as all the things they indeed had in common swirled round her like a cyclone with Tony's smiling poster perfect face smack dab in the middle. "God damn him to hell!" Julie booted the test kit under the bed.

"Would you mind if I call you again?" Nancy said. "Just to see how you're doing?" she added.

"I guess it would be okay," Julie said. It was definitely a for sure thing now. Her poster had been framed and put up in the entrance of the lame hall of fame. What was wrong with her? Why had she lied? She never wanted to hear Nancy's voice or her name again.

"Are you sure?" Nancy's voice was snuffled.

"Yes," she answered. Another lie ... But ... Lies seemed to be in abundance all around in her life. *So what did it matter if she bounced out a few of her own?* she thought.

"Talk to you soon?"

"Yes ... Okay." Julie hung up the telephone without a goodbye, wishing she had never said hello. She slithered out of the chair to the floor crawling on her hands and knees fishing the test kit out from under the bed. She flattened herself out ... Rolled onto her back ... Held the kit to her chest sobbing and weeping for all she was ... Until ... Hate crept around the corner, landed and seeped in ... Travelling slowly at first then like lightening whirling and turning inside out, reappearing as unadulterated anger ... She stood, threw the test kit to the floor, stomping it until it turned into little ruptured pieces of nothingness.

She bent over picking up a piece of the test kit. The two blue wavy lines were still there. Nancy Anderson was still there. Her lying cheating asshole of a husband was still there too.

She sank back to the floor, curling into a fetal position, rocking back and forth gently. She remained so, as hours passed, allowing for enough tears to fill an ocean. There was no comfort to be found, it had run off and hid itself in one of the paperbacks on the shelf within pages that read *in the blackest of nights at the end of an endless day.*

She applied warm tea bags to her swollen eyes that felt as if metal needles had been embedded within them. She held the bags in place with one hand blindly groping for the telephone with the other. She punched in the number, without looking. Her fingers knew it all too well.

Tony answered on the first ring.

"I just spoke with Nancy Anderson," she said quietly, calmly. "It would appear your definition of a friend and mine are slightly different." She drew her lips inward.

There was dead silence. The air seemed sucked from the line, leaving it lifeless and defunct, like space.

"I'll be right home," he said.

She threw down the receiver. '*Of course you will,*' she thought. '*Your den has fallen in ... Yet again ... Will it be the same sheep costume? ... Or a brand new one? ... I wonder?*'

Chapter 18

"I love you," Tony said.

"You have a unique way of showing it," Julie countered.

"Come on Jules ... I said she was a mistake."

"Interesting mistake!"

"Why are you being like this?"

"Oh I don't know ... Why don't you tell me?"

"Honey ... Baby ... You seemed fine after we went out for dinner and had that long talk last night."

"Seemed fine? ... Really?"

"I thought you were fine. I know you didn't eat much at dinner but I just assumed the food was too rich and you'd drank too much."

"I didn't drink near enough!" Julie proclaimed.

"Honey ... You said you forgave me?"

"God ... Maybe I did drink too much!"

"I love you. You know I love you, don't you?"

"So you keep saying ... Look ... I really don't want to talk to you anymore right now."

"But sweetie," Tony's tone was cute and pleading.

"Don't but sweetie me!"

"Don't do this honey ... I just called to see how you are and tell you that I love you."

"You have called thirteen times all ready this morning to see how I am and say you love me."

"Thirteen," he chuckled. "You're counting?"

"Yes."

"Well, maybe by lunch I can get in another thirteen."

"I wouldn't!'

"I wouldn't? ... Threatening me now are you?" he snickered.

"If that's what it's going to take get you to stop this!"

"What wife would want to stop her husband from telling her how much he loves her?"

"This one!"

"Want to go out again for dinner tonight?"

"No!"

"I'll take you to that fancy new place."

"No!"

"I'll pick you up at five okay?"

"No!"

"I love you baby."

"Yeah ... Whatever."

"Oh honey ... Before I forget to tell you, I really like what you've done with the front yard."

"What?"

"You know ... The front yard ... It looks nice."

"What the hell are you talking about?" she questioned, puzzled.

"The rose bushes."

Julie threw the telephone over her shoulder, whipping out through the screen door, beating it down the walkway to the front lawn.

Two yellow rose bushes, heavily laden with blooms flanked the tree.

She ran into the garage, flinging and booting everything that was not nailed down out of the way searching for the hedge clippers ... They weren't there.

"Is that a new way of gardening?" the neighbour from across the street asked. He placed a hand on Julie's shoulder, leaning over in order to get a closer look.

Julie offered him up a quick glance, plunking down the empty can of gasoline, lighting a match. "Yep," she said. "Totally works for me!" She stepped back and threw the match on the bushes.

Chapter 19

"Did the cell phone bill come in the mail yet honey?" Tony asked.

"I don't know. I haven't checked today," Julie said.

"Can you please baby?"

"I'll do it in a bit, okay?"

"Could you do it now sweetie?"

"What's with you? You've had me looking every day this damn week for the thing. What's it matter?"

"Last month I didn't pay the whole amount and I just want to catch it up before there's too much interest on it. Can you go look honey?"

"All right."

"I'll just hold okay?"

"Fine ... I'll be right back," Julie said. She sighed. looking outside at the heavy rain. She clunked the receiver down and ran for the box fetching all inside.

"Is it there baby?" he asked.

"Hold on for Christ's sake will you?" She cradled the telephone against her neck and shoulder freeing up both hands. "We definitely need a new mail box everything is soaked," she said prying it apart.

"Okay honey ... I'll pick one up tomorrow for you. Is it there sweetie?"

"Just wait will you?" She rifled through the letters. "Nope, it's not here."

"Okay honey thanks. It will probably show up tomorrow."

"Tomorrow is Saturday," Julie announced.

"Monday's then. Pick you up for lunch?"

"Let's skip it today."

"How come honey? I thought you were enjoying going out just the two of us?"

"We've been out every day for the past couple weeks. I'd like to stay home today."

"Okay baby, whatever you like. How about I bring it then?"

"Whatever."

"Ah honey, don't be like that."

"Sure ... Fine ... Bring lunch ... Is that better?"

"I love you. Going to tell me you love me yet?"

"No ... Bye." Julie hung up the receiver, grabbed a knife, inserted it into the side of the cell phone bill envelope, and slit it open.

Chapter 20

Tony whistled sauntering down the drive towards the house. He had knocked off work early to surprise her. He carried all the fixings to make chicken Caesar salads for lunch in a brown paper bag. It was her favourite. He stopped at the walkway kneeling down in front of the tree drawing his pocketknife and clipping off a baker's dozen of yellow roses from the three bushes. He checked to make sure he couldn't be seen ducking into the garage through the side door. He searched through her craft tub for a binding to tie the roses. He smiled, finding a length of red velvet ribbon.

He hoped all his efforts would let the by-gones be by-gones and he'd hear the soft whispers of 'I love you too,' leave her lips. She had not said it in weeks. He never thought he would miss such a thing, but he did. He longed for life to be back the way it was before. He missed the warmth of her love, not to mention having her every night. He hoped soon all would be forgiven and forgotten. The one thing he had learned over the years was how to work her ... And work her ... He would.

He turned the door handle pressing his shoulder against the door. It didn't budge. The door was locked. "SHIT!" he exclaimed, annoyed. He fumbled through his pockets for the keys.

He tucked the bouquet and the bag behind his back stepping into the entrance.

"Sweetie ... I have a surprise for you! ... Honey? ... Where are you baby?" There was no reply other than the silence. "Baby? ... Honey? ... Dolly?" he called. He climbed the stairs stopping at the landing, cocking his head and listening for movement. He called out again, coming up empty.

'Maybe she's in the basement,' he thought. He reefed the door open, the noise of it echoing down the steps, pinging and ponging, returning to him as something else. It was way past dark down there. The words 'Pitch Black' did not even do it justice and it was cold. Black and cold like nothing he had ever experienced before. He was sure steam was rising from his breath. He felt a twinge of something ominous ... Something ... Down in there ... In the blackness. He slammed the door shut. He stood on the other side of the door, drew his fingers across his lips, turned, and walked away.

A thunderclap roared. Rain poured.

He moved through the house talking to himself. "Where the hell is she? ... She has to be here ... Her car is in the drive." He snapped his fingers. "Of course ... She's out back with Barkley." He went into the living room, avoiding the basement door. He pressed his nose against the glass squinting into the rain. It was coming down in buckets making the lawn furniture resemble oddly shaped gray blurry blobs. *'She wouldn't stay out there, not in this,'* he thought.

He ruffled his hair with his hand scratching his head, sauntering into the kitchen. "She must have popped out to the store," he said. He flipped on the light switch.

"OH FUCK! ... NO! ... NO!" he shouted.

The roses and bag hit the floor with a loud thud. The walls picked it up, ricocheting it about the room. He stared at the kitchen table in disbelief. "FUCK NO! ... FUCK NO!" he screamed. He pressed his hands against his ribcage, rubbing in circles, trying to halt the flip-flopping his stomach was into. It didn't work. He doubled over as his stomach knotted, double knotted, squishing and dividing it in half. His head swam in circles. Vomit boiled in his throat. He groped for a chair, screeching it across the floor, slopping down into it.

The pages of his cell phone bill were separated and all neatly laid out and duct taped in a horizontal row to the kitchen tabletop. Four separate colors of highlighter lit up blocks of telephone numbers. Bright red marker encircled the numbers, one, two, three and four, which inter connected with a barrage of black arrows. Directly underneath the bill lay a huge charted graph on stark white Bristol board.

It read:

Number One: Nancy Anderson. Code Green. Seventy calls. Not including the seven to Florida. Forty-two years old. One hundred and forty-five lbs. No condom used. Six-month affair. Met = Dating service. Moving in together. Trying to have a baby.

Number Two: Nancy Smith. A.K.A. Dawn the Dominatrix. Code Yellow. Forty-seven calls. Sixty-four years old. Two hundred fifty-one lbs. No condom used. Eleven-month affair. Met = Answered her ad in newspaper for a slave. Currently seeking donor eggs to try and have a baby.

Number Three: Sylvie Northingham. Code Blue. Twenty-eight calls. Forty-nine years old. One hundred thirty-four lbs. No condom used. One-month affair. Met = Escort Service Date. Considering having fertility testing to try to have a baby.

Number Four: Susan Brakaus. Code Pink. Seventeen calls. Thirty-nine years old. One hundred sixty lbs. (Said she could not remember you at all. I personally figured she must have been the last one of the day, judging by the number of phone calls and the time of day they were made. But then again, you were probably getting pretty worn out by then, I would assume.)

Under each name was a point form columned account of intimate details. How many times a week they saw one another. The time of day. The day of the week. How many times a day they made out. What position was used. Where they went. What they ate. What they did.

The very bottom of the page contained an over sized asterisk marking the words; added note. 'I thought I would help you out and introduce all your friends to one another. The word 'Friends' was underlined in all four colors. So ... I took the liberty of providing each one with a set of three names, other than their own of course and the appropriate corresponding telephone numbers. 'HAVE A NICE DAY NOW!'

Tony dropped his chest banging his head off the table on purpose. "You God-Damn Fucking Son Of A Bitch!" he said, quietly. He reached round his back pocket turning off his cell phone and pager. "Have a nice day now, my ass," he muttered. He laid his face on the table. "FUCK! ... FUCK! ... FUCK!"

Chapter 21

Julie climbed the stoop and leaned on the doorbell.

The front door opened. "Hey you!" Sherry exclaimed.

"What's up with the for sale sign?" Julie pointed to it over her shoulder.

"I told ya a week or so ago we were putting it up for sale. You forget?"

"Must of."

Sherry looked past Julie. "Where's your car?"

"At home."

"How'd you get here?"

'Walked."

"You walked? ... It's pouring! ... Are you crazy or something?" Sherry put a hand on Julie's shoulder. "Jesus Christ Girlfriend ... you're drenched right through to the hide ... You're going catch a death of cold ... Get in here."

"No I won't!" Julie laughed, waving an empty wine bottle inches from Sherry's face. "I have this." Julie tipped the bottle closely examining the contents, shutting one eye then the other. "Hum," she muttered. "Correction ... I had this."

Sherry grabbed Julie by the front of her jacket flinging her inside.

She stumbled losing her footing and bouncing off the closet door. She held up both arms seeing Sherry's look of alarm. "All's okay! ... Don't worry none! ... Didn't feel a damn thing!" Julie snickered.

"Shit girlfriend ... You're damn well pissed," Sherry said.

Julie slipped her arms out of her backpack. It rattled and clanged as she dropped it down.

"What the hell you doing with a backpack?" Sherry looked from Julie to the backpack and back.

"My purse wouldn't hold enough bottles," Julie said matter-of-factly. She peeled off her wet jacket, booting it into the corner.

"How much did you bring?"

"Lots ... I drank one on the way here ... Should have drank two ... But we can always go to the store if we run out ... Right?"

Sherry tucked her arm through Julie's starting to walk her into the living room.

"Wait a sec." Julie hooked her foot into the strap of the knapsack dragging it behind her as they headed for the sofa.

"Anything ... You want to tell me?" Sherry laughed.

"Yeah! ... But you better have some of this first!" Julie plunked down a wine bottle on the coffee table.

"I'll get us glasses."

"To hell with that!" Julie exclaimed. She fumbled with the top, unscrewing it pushing it directly in front of Sherry. "That one's yours." Julie drew out another bottle, unscrewed it, taking a big swig and wiping her mouth with her sleeve.

"Hey girl ... You okay?" Sherry took a sip of her wine resting the bottle between her knees.

Julie shook her head back and forth in a slow no.

"What the hell is up? ... Spill it."

"You haven't drunk enough yet."

Sherry slanted the bottle back downing a quarter. "Now?"

"Better go again," Julie said.

Sherry drank again. She sat the bottle on the coffee table studying her friend's eyes; there was something very unsettling in there.

Julie slammed another bottle down in front of Sherry. "Trust me ... Your gonna need it after you've heard what I'm about to say." She reached in the backpack yanking out three more bottles. "These are for safe measure," she said.

"What in the hell has happened?"

"Before I tell you, will you promise me something?"

"Sure love ... Anything."

"Good ... That's all settled then."

"What?"

Julie finished her bottle.

Sherry grinned. "Well? ... What?"

"Well ... Whaf ... What?" Julie slurred.

"What did I just promise you? ... You idiot."

"Oh that ... Hey this wine is working ... I feelin fretty sood." Julie laughed waving a finger back and forth at Sherry. "I mean ... Ah the hell with it ... You know whaf I faying."

"Shit girlfriend ... I was wrong! ... You're way past pissed!" Sherry said.

Julie cleared her throat holding up both her hands. "Well," she said. She spoke slow and deliberate so as not to tangle her words. "The one I drank before I left home did nothing ... Anf ... The one on the way over was a kind of ... The empty stomach helped however it ... ."

Sherry cut her off, laughing. "Okay I get ya ... So, before I totally forget ... What something, did I just promise ya? ... Just so I know."

"That you'll drive me to my appointment in a week. They want somebody to bring me and take me home ... Dumb huh?"

"So where are we going that you have to have a ride?"

"The Scottsdale Abortion Clinic, downtown."

Sherry downed the rest of the bottle, unscrewing one of her reserves, gulping in more, setting the bottle on the table and burping loudly.

"I think you're about ready now ... Want to hear my story?" Julie asked.

Sherry's tongue wiggled back and forth dancing about her mouth cheek to cheek, heavily coated in wine fuzz, which right at this moment seemed to match her brain ... Fuzzed.

She searched inside her friend's drunken silly half-crooked grin, waiting for the telltale signs to let her know the whammy she'd just let lose about an abortion was all but an odd sideways joke. There wasn't any.

Julie pulled herself close to Sherry "Just bear with me, Okay?"

Sherry nodded grasping Julie's hands in hers.

Julie dropped her head in a heavy sigh fighting off tears, losing. "Sherry ... Remember when ... When ... I."

Sherry broke in. "Oh love ... Whatever is so wrong?"

Julie locked her fingers through Sherry's. "Remember when I told you about the Nancy Anderson thing?"

"Yeah ... How could I not? ... You change your mind and decide not to try and work it through with him?"

Julie shook her head no, flinging tears onto Sherry's shirt. "No ... That's not it."

"Even if it was girlfriend ... Hell ... I wouldn't blame you one Damn bit ... It is hard enough to deal with a man on a daily basis, but one that has cheated? ... My God! ... Lordy! ... Lordy! ... So, what is it then? ... Is something wrong with the baby?"

"No ... That's not it either."

"No?"

"No."

"What then? ... You're killing me here."

"Oh Sherry." Julie rested her head on Sherry's shoulder hooking her arm in around Sherry's waist.

"Did you go out and have an affair to get back at him?" Sherry shot out.

"No ... No."

"Then what could be so bad love?" Julie had her completely puzzled.

"There's three more of them," Julie blurted. She raised her head looking Sherry dead square in the eyes.

"Three more of what?"

"Women."

"What?" Sherry couldn't believe her ears. "Say again?"

"There's three more," Julie said.

"He's had three affairs?"

"No ... There's three more of them in addition to the one he had with Nancy and one of them is a two-hundred-fifty pound, sixty-four-year-old dominatrix."

Sherry's mouth dropped. "There's three more?" She could not get a grip on all this. She had to be hearing wrong. She repeated herself. "Three more? ... Three more?"

Julie nodded.

"And one's a what?"

"An old fat dominatrix!"

"A what?"

"A dominatrix ... You know, whips and chains and ..." Julie stopped in mid sentence watching Sherry's oars starting to paddle.

Sherry snatched all the wine bottles from the table, hers, and Julie's guzzling one right after the other.

Julie winked. "See ... I told you ... You'd need more."

"A dominatrix? ... Three more? ... Oh fucking Jesus! ... This can't be? ... This just can't be?"

"It is," Julie said. She dug in her backpack pulling out two more bottles.

"How ... How did ... Did you?"

Julie finished the question for her. "How did I find out? ... He wanted that God Damn cell phone bill, way too much. The sucker had me looking every day for it. But today ... Today ... When he had me go out in the pouring rain after it ... Well, I added two and two and low and behold it equalled four."

"OH JESUS!" Sherry exclaimed

"Oh Jesus! ... Damn right! ... And ... I called every one of them too! ... They were quite obliging, actually ... After they got over the shock that is ... Every one of them thought he was single and they were his one and only true love."

"OH MY GOD IN HEAVEN!"

"That's not even close to what I said." Julie downed the last of the wine in the bottle between her knees, scooting the two reserves across the table in front of them.

"Oh girlfriend! ... Oh my God! ... Four of them! ... Oh my God! ... And one's a Dom!" Sherry popped the top off her wine bottle with her teeth, spitting it onto the floor.

"I think I'm going to need therapy for the Dom one. I just can't seem to wrap my head around that one ... You know what I mean?"

"Jesus Fucking Christ!" Sherry leaned over, grabbing Julie, pulling her tight up against her body, cocooning her within her arms. "What can I do for ya love? ... What can I do?" she whispered.

"You're already doing it," Julie said. She melted into her. "Just don't let go," she said. She wrapped her arms tight around Sherry. "Just don't ever let go."

"I won't love ... You know I won't ... I love you girlfriend ... And I'll always be here for you ... Always ... Always."

"I love you too, Sherry. You're the closest to a sister I've ever had."

"You too love ... You too ... Fucking hell! ... I don't damn well believe this!"

"I still don't."

"How could he do this to you?"

"I don't know."

"Why he would he do this?"

"I don't know that either."

Sherry tightened her hold on Julie rocking her back and forth gently. She planted little kisses along the top of Julie's head, patting her back. "It's okay love ... I'm here ... I'm here ... Just let it go," she whispered.

Julie's floodgates burst. She knotted her fingers into the front of Sherry's shirt crying for all she was worth.

Sherry dropped her head onto Julie's crying right along with her. They stayed that way for hours finding comfort and solace in their kindred as their hearts melded becoming one.

Sharing and feeling the pain of the lies ... The betrayals ... The malice and deceit ... The loss of futures ... The dying of love that was supposed to outlast forever. She hung onto Julie's limp body as the two drifted on the waves of tears in and out of the dead dreams that were supposed to be the essence of one's life force. She sang gently, soothing and coaxing her friend's spirit back to life, she'd felt it slip and go, getting lost in the truth that Tony the faithful loving husband was none of the above. She, for the first time ever in her adult life needn't no soul searching, or moral commentaries, to know an abortion was the right thing here. She would do the same if Tony were her husband.

"Want to stay for the night?" Sherry whispered.

"No I can't. The kids."

"You sure?"

"Yeah I'm sure."

"If you change your mind, you know where my key is?"

Julie nodded. "Thanks," she said. She forced a smile, and then stood grabbing onto Sherry's hand, towing her over with her to the far side of the sofa and the backpack. She pulled out the last two bottles. "More wine?"

"Yeah," Sherry said.

Chapter 22

"Is that you Mom?" Cory pushed his chair from the kitchen table, leaning it up on its back two legs.

"No ... It's me," Tony said

"Oh ... We thought you were Mom. She said she'd be home in a while when she phoned."

"She phoned? ... What time did she phone?"

"I don't know," Cory said.

"Where is she? I've been out looking for her all afternoon."

"She didn't say."

Tony stepped into the kitchen. The boys were gulping down pizza. His eyeballs zoomed to the table. The cell phone bill and chart were being used as a tablemat for dinner. He studied them to see if their eyes had followed his to the tabletop. He couldn't tell. He carried on as if it was all perfectly normal to have a cell phone bill and a charted four women affair duck taped to a kitchen table.

He walked across the kitchen picking up the telephone receiver turning his back to them, coding in the symbols and numbers to retrieve the last number that had called. It came up as private number. He smiled. She was one smart-ass bitch today. She had caused him all kinds of problems. She'd went out without her car. She had call blocked when calling home. It seemed like she didn't want him to find her ... But he was going to.

He scooped up a piece of pizza joining the boys at the table. "This is good pizza," he said.

"Yeah," Cory answered

"Where did it come from?"

"Pizzaville," Caleb said, taking over for Cory.

He tried again. "Who brought it?"

"The driver," Caleb said.

Tony smiled. "When did it come?"

"Just a bit before you got home," Caleb said.

Tony turned his attention to Cory. He would be easier ... He was younger. "Did mom say she was sending it?"

"No," Cory answered. He flashed his eyes to Caleb.

"No?" Tony questioned, leaning in his face.

"No ... But." He glanced nervously at his brother.

He had him. "But ... What Cory?"

"But ... But she did say Sherry was sending us a surprise."

Caleb fist punched Cory in the forearm. "You ass! ... Mom told us not to tell."

Tony smirked, "She did, did she?"

They both nodded in unison.

"Let's just let it be our little secret then ... I won't tell her you told me ... Okay? ... Mum's the word." He held his finger up to his lips pretending to zip them shut. He dug into his pocket pulling out two twenty dollar bills. "Here ... This is for you guys." He handed them each one. "Enjoy your pizza. I'll be right back."

"Where you going?" Caleb asked. He threw a piece of pizza on the floor for Barkley.

"Sherry's."

As soon as the front door closed, the boys moved the pizza box back to the kitchen counter, where they'd had it before he came in. They picked up reading where they'd left off.

"Do you think mom made this for Tony?" Cory said.

"Yeah," Caleb said.

"Do you think it's a joke or something?"

"I hope so Cory ... Because if it ain't ... Tony's in a whole shit load of trouble," Caleb answered.

168

Chapter 23

A flash of light glinted off the back wall.

"Oh! ... Oh!" Sherry said. She got up off the sofa, drawing back the drape.

"Oh? ... Oh? ... Why the oh, oh?" Julie asked. She had not associated the flash with headlight glare.

Sherry turned to Julie. "You ready?" she asked.

"Ready for what?"

"Your asshole just pulled up!"

"Ah shit! ... I was hoping it would take him a lot longer to figure out where I was."

"Want me to get the door?" Sherry peeked out from behind the drape, watching him get out of the car. "Or not ... We can ignore him if you like?" she added, grinning.

"He's hard to ignore ... But we can try." Julie snickered. "Or ... You can find out what he wants, if you like."

"Okay ... It's your call." Sherry opened the front door a crack. She pushed her face up to the opening glaring at him one eyed. "What do you want asshole?"

"Is Jules here?"

"Yes," she said. She slammed the door shut in his face and headed back to the sofa. "He didn't ask to speak with you," she laughed. "He just asked if you were here, true?"

"That's true." Julie smirked. "That's very true." She found this whole scenario, most amusing.

The doorbell rang.

"Want me to answer it?"

The doorbell chimed a second time.

"Sure ... Well ... Only if you like, that is ... After all, it is your house."

"Now that you put it that way." Sherry laughed, "I just don't know if I should."

It rang again.

"Think he'll give up eventually and go away?"

The corners of Julie's eyes wrinkled and grinned as she shook her head back and forth in a no.

"Me neither." Sherry got back up re-opening the door a hair. "Yes?" she said.

"Is Jules here?"

"I already told you yes," Sherry answered. She wiped off her beaming grin. She slammed the door shut leaning on the back of it sticking both hands in the front pockets of her jeans whistling. She gave Julie a wink. "Saves me getting up again."

Tony knocked loud and heavy.

Sherry opened the door, peering through an even smaller crack. "Yes?"

"May I speak with her please?" he asked.

"Who?" Sherry questioned, putting on an innocent air, as if she didn't know who her was.

"Jules."

"Oh ... Just a minute then." She kicked the door shut almost taking his face with it.

"The asshole wishes to speak with you. Do you wish to speak to the asshole?"

"Depends," Julie said. She was having trouble keeping from bursting out laughing. "What does the asshole want?"

Sherry re-opened the door. "She wants to know what it is you want asshole."

"Sherry for Christ's Sake! ... Just let me talk to her ... Please? ... Please?" He moved forward slipping his fingers in between the door and frame.

Sherry raised her eyebrows staring directly into his eyes, then at his fingers, then back to his eyes. "I wouldn't if I were you," she warned, her eyes sparkling with the *'You better believe I will buster.'*

170

He drew his hand back.

Sherry smiled, she was loving this. "Just a minute." She closed the door again. "Well?" She turned to Julie. "Do you wish to speak with the asshole?"

"Nah."

Sherry again opened the front door. "She doesn't wish to speak with you asshole! ... Good bye!" She banged the door shut doubling over with laughter. She peered out the side window. "Do you want him to suffer?"

Julie nodded.

Sherry opened the door. "Hey asshole, get off my front porch!" she yelled. She slammed the door shut just as he pointed upwards at the pouring rain wearing the most pleading of looks.

"Did he?" Julie asked, grinning, amused as hell at Sherry's antics.

"Let me have a look see." Sherry pressed her face to the glass. "Yep ... He's standing on the walkway ... Shit girlfriend ... Is it ever pouring ... Hear that?" Sherry cocked her head sideways, smirking. "I think it's starting to hail." Sherry's giggle turned to full-blown laughter as dime sized ice balls pelted off everything outside, including the asshole in the middle of the walkway. "Do him good it will! ... He needs a few good pelts on the noggin ... The more the better! ... I'd say! ... More wine?" She retrieved a bottle from her own wine rack, popping the plastic cork into the air.

"Don't mind if I do." Julie took a long drink passing the bottle to Sherry, who did the same passing it back. They replaced it twice over, as an hour and a half ticked by.

"Like I said before ... You can stay you know," Sherry said.

"Yeah, I know." Julie held the wine bottle to the light tilting it one way and then another. "Shit we're out! ... Now we're both out!" she exclaimed. She shook the last drops onto her tongue. Disappointment lined the sides of her mouth. "I have to go home sometime. Might as well be now I suppose." Julie stood, walking into the entranceway.

"Want your jacket?"

Julie glanced down at the dark ball with the puddle oozing from it. "Nah ... It's still soaked," she said.

"Backpack?"

"Yeah ... I might need it again." She gave Sherry a slow wink.

"Hug?" Sherry asked, holding out her arms wide and full.

"How about two?"

Sherry wrapped her arms snugly around Julie. "I got as many as you need love." She peeped out the sidelight. "Man is he wet ... He's waiting for you ... You know that, don't you?" She chuckled.

"Yeah ... I figured as much."

Sherry opened the door holding up her index and middle fingers waving them back and forth at Tony silently warning him not to move from where he was.

He heeded her, not coming forward, remaining where he was leaning on the lamppost.

"If you need me girlfriend, just call," Sherry said. She gave Julie's hand a squeeze that said much more than words ever could.

Julie smiled and nodded stepping out into the front porch. She pulled her sweatshirt hood up turning to face her drowned rat of a husband

Tony held out his hand. "Going home with me?"

"I'm going home, but not with you." She walked past him.

He ran up beside her. "Baby ... Come on ... Honey please ... Get in the car."

"Nope."

"Honey ... Please ... How are you going to get home then?" He followed along behind her.

172

"Same way I got here." She tightened the strings on her hood knotting them, heading down the driveway out onto the street.

Tony jogged, catching up, side stepping, crossing over in front of her. "Come on honey ... Just get in the car ... Please? ... I'll go get it ... You're going to catch your death of cold."

She grinned a toothy smile at hearing the same words Sherry had used when she'd first arrived.

"Why you smiling baby?"

"Don't call me baby!"

"Why you smiling honey?"

Julie glared at him. "Don't call me honey, either!"

"Okay sweetie ... But why are you smiling? ... Everything's okay?"

Julie rolled her eyes. "No! ... And ... No! ... Everything's not okay! ... What a dumb-ass stupid question! ... You're such an asshole!" She smiled wickedly, thinking of all the things that she would like to do to him. A slow painful death topped the list.

"If everything's not okay ... Then why you smiling baby?"

"Didn't I just tell you not to call me that?"

"Sorry baby ... I mean sweetie."

She rolled her eyes. "Since you just, have to know, why I am smiling I will tell you. It's the second time today I've heard the exact same words?"

"What words?"

"You're going to catch your death of cold," she said, slow and pained.

"Well its true ... You are honey." He placed a hand gently on her shoulder attempting to turn her in the direction of the car. "I don't want you to get sick."

"I'm already sick," she said, sarcastically. "And don't you dare touch me!"

"Sweetie ... Just let me get the car."

"I'm not stopping you."

"Come with me to get it?"

"Nope!"

"Please baby?"

"Nope!"

"Honey, please?"

"No ... And stop the honey, baby, sweetie shit!"

"If you won't come with me to get it, will you at least wait? ... I'll run ... And you are going to catch your death of cold ... Look at you ... You're shivering."

Julie's Cheshire cat smile broadened. She stepped toward him putting her hands up into his wet hair knotting her fingers through it, pulling his face to hers. "If I get in that damn car with you right now," she paused. She gave him a look of sheer evil. "It will not be me that catches my D ... E ... A ... T ... H!" She punctuated the word death loudly. "Do you catch my drift?" She paused, again, giving his hair a hard tug. "Now ... Would you like me to repeat this four times over for you, seeing as that seems to be your number of choice?" She knocked him hard in the chest with her fists shoving him backwards and making him lose his footing. She turned and walked off, crossing the road and heading for the pathway through the forest.

"Baby ... Please," he begged in a little boy voice. "At least let me walk with you?"

She stopped and turned. He was right behind her. "Go fuck yourself!" She poked him hard in the shoulder. "But, I bet you've already tried that one too," she said.

Tony did not say a word. He hung his head kicking at the grass, sniffing loudly. He slipped off his jacket placing it on her shoulders.

She flung it off her launching it into a puddle. "You touch me again and I'll punch you right in the mouth ... You got that asshole?" She looked him dead in the eye.

"I love you."

"Fuck off! ... Just fuck the hell off and leave me alone!" Julie walked the rest of the way home in silence; he followed one pace behind. She opened the front door of the house quickly slamming it shut, locking it, leaving him outside in the rain.

He searched his pockets coming up empty. "Shit!" he muttered. He knocked on the front door. "Jules? ... Honey? ... Please open the door? ... My keys are in the car."

She slid the side window open a hair. "Well, well, now," she said. "That's your problem, not mine. Isn't it?" She shut the window, locking it, grabbed another bottle of wine, and went upstairs.

Chapter 24

"Man Oh Man ... Is it ever pouring!" Sherry exclaimed. She rounded the on ramp, merging the car out into the highway traffic. "You know what they say about the rain, don't ya?" she offered up, softly, glancing over at her friend.

Julie was slinked down in the passenger seat like an old used up rag doll, head down, torso cockeyed. She had spoken little if anything since arriving at Sherry's that morning. Except for the odd sniffle and nose wipe one would not have known whether she was alive or dead.

Sherry continued. "They say rain is the angels crying ... They cry for us and with us." She reached across the seat gently squeezing Julie's limp hand.

"It's been raining steady for over a week. I don't think they would cry that long for somebody like me," Julie said, slowly without movement.

"Somebody like you? ... What does that mean?" Sherry coaxed.

"You know what it means."

"You think you're undeserving of some heavenly tears?"

"Yes."

"Well ... My love ... I don't know anybody more deserving than you for an angel or two or three for that matter, to be crying for."

"It's not angels crying," Julie broke in. "It's god pissing ... He's been watching me and knows what I am about to do and he is pissing down all over my head, kind of like that cold commercial on television. You just watch ... No matter what I do or where I go there will be a cloud above my head, pissing down on me."

"Oh love ... Don't you for one minute think that."

"I'm not thinking that. I know it," Julie said. She wiped the tears from her cheeks.

"Come on now."

Julie's weeping over took her, consuming her, tears rampaged in torrents down her face and neck.

"Oh love ... Don't cry. Everything is going to be okay. It will be, you'll see."

Julie grabbed another tissue wiping off her face and neck. "How? ... How is everything ever going to be okay? ... My life is so far removed from okay ... I don't even remember what okay is anymore."

Sherry glanced over at her friend again. She wanted to tell her she would find okay again. She was sure of it; sometimes it just takes a little longer than we think it should. God never gives anyone more than one can handle. She wanted to say all this and more, but she couldn't, the words kept breaking apart in her throat almost taking her with them. She knew Julie needed way beyond what she was offering at this moment. She'd been trying to hold it together, to be strong, to show all would be right again and okay just like she'd said, all that was needed was to get this next few hours over with and a bit of time. She made a silent promise to herself that she would find the words of wisdom and courage for her after all this was behind them. She wiped her silent tears from her cheeks on her driving arm sleeve soaking it through.

Julie's head was down again.

Sherry wove her fingers into Julie's stroking the back of her hand with her thumb. The lump in her throat had doubled making it hard to swallow. She looked back at the road, tears abruptly streaming in rivers down her face.

Sherry let go of Julie blindly groping for a tissue, smiling as one poked into her hand. She turned her tear stained face, meeting and holding onto the same, their eyes locking and cradling one another's fragility.

Julie glided her fingertips over the back of Sherry's hand drawing circles in delicate wisps expressing more than any mere word ever could on this earth. In the middle of all of this, Julie had sensed her need and was coming through.

Sherry gave herself a mental kick for suddenly being so needy. It should have been the reverse. This girl didn't need angels by her side, she was one. She picked up Julie's hand touching it to her face, caressing it gently back and forth with her cheek. "Oh God love," she sniffled. "I ... I," Sherry broke into pieces, sobbing.

Julie's lips quivered as she forced a smile. "It's okay to cry ... Tears are the soul's way of cleansing itself," she said. She searched Sherry's eyes for the spark, the one that said yes I know. "Isn't that what you keep saying to me?"

"Yes."

"Well, then?" Julie asked.

"Jesus, I ... I." Sherry stuttered. She couldn't remember what she was going to say. Sadness had drowned her and sunk her to the bottom.

Julie brought Sherry's hand down into her lap cupping it with hers. Neither spoke a word the rest of the way ... They did not have to.

"Well ... We made it," Sherry said. She parked in the clinic lot opening the driver's door.

"Yes, we did," Julie said.

Sherry slowly walked round to the passenger door, bending down to open it. She delicately stroked Julie's hair back off her face planting a single kiss on her forehead. She stretched out her hand palm up. "Shall we?"

Julie placed her hand within Sherry's. "Yeah."

Julie went through the motions, the check in, the counselling session, the ultra sound. She nodded in all the right and wrong places with no one noticing. Sherry had stayed by her side through it all never once letting go of her hand, ignoring each time she was asked to leave like it was said in some strange foreign language she didn't understand

and wasn't about to. She helped Julie change into the nothing but hospital gown and thick socks, right siding the gown when she noticed they had gotten it inside out and backward.

Sherry's hand was the be-all and end-all to Julie providing the lifeline she needed to pull through this cold place she had come to with the pale blue walls and pale blue floor that matched. She held on to the embrace as if it was going to be the very last form of human touch in her existence.

When Julie's name was called she linked Sherry's hand to her lips, kissed it softly and mouthed thank you. She rose and silently followed the nurse down the hall.

"Hop up here honey," the nurse patted the operating table.

Julie obliged.

"Okay hon, lay down. I am going to start an intravenous in your right hand. It's going to pinch a little." The nurse inserted the needle into the vein on the top of her hand taping it in place.

It pinched way more than a little. Julie slammed her teeth together wincing, stiffening.

"The doctor will be here in a minute. I am going to give you a bit of medicine now. It will make you a little drowsy. Okay Hon?" The nurse said more so than asked.

Julie nodded.

Minutes later the doctor was by her side explaining the process in detail. The only thing Julie could remember was her saying it would all be over in about five or ten minutes.

Julie turned her head wiping off her wet cheek on the sheet as she was asked to squiggle down the table and place her feet in the oven-mitted grey metal stirrups. She felt a hand slide into hers offering something other than sheets to hang on to. Julie wrapped her fingers around the flesh and cried.

The nurse pulled a tissue from the box. "It's okay to cry hon ... You ... Go right ahead ... Everybody has their own reasons for doing ... And it's all okay." She dabbed at Julie's tears with her free hand giving her an extra squeeze with the other.

The doctor moved into position between Julie's legs. She told her there would be slight cramping and pain. She placed a hand on the inside of Julie's thigh, patting lightly signalling it was time to commence. She pulled a tray of instruments alongside picking one up.

Julie lay on her back staring into the glaring lights. The room was cold. The steel table with the plastic padding and plastic over-lay was cold. The nurse's hand was cold. If hell had been depicted as cold then she was certainly in the right place. For this, was no doubt a piece of hell placed on earth with a porthole for the dead and doomed to pop up through and poke the living in the ribs.

The nurse spoke to Julie gently and softly explaining through non-technical language what the doctor was performing each step of the way. The slight cramping she had been foretold about, hit her no sooner than the words left the nurse's lips. She had been warned ... She had not been ready. The slight cramping was out and out agony, escalating out and out agony. She felt like someone was sawing through her belly from the inside out with a dull hacksaw blade. She grabbed the sides of the table as it intensified further. She couldn't breathe. Her head swam in circles, taking the pale blue ceiling round with it. The pain skipped steps, heightening, becoming a red-hot searing poker, blinding her in torture as it zoomed in and out, in and out of one single area deep inside her. The place deep inside where her baby lay. She clamped her eyes shut, a crucial part of herself dying. She couldn't have done it any better if she had taken a gun and blown her own brains out. Her baby was dying inside of her, of her own hand.

"It's almost over hon, just a couple more minutes," the nurse soothed. She inserted her hand back within Julie's.

Julie's entire body broke into a beaded sweet as she opened her mouth screaming with physical and mental pain. She wished she could just die, then and there. She didn't.

She sobbed and wailed uncontrollable as a cold steel pan was shoved tight between her upper thighs. There was one more intense dagger of indescribable pain, then a gush of warm liquid, containing a singular lump of jelly. It rushed from her body plopping into the pan splattering the flesh of her thighs in warm blood, cooling instantly on contact. She turned her head pressing her face into the nurse's uniform sobbing as her dead baby lay between her legs in a pan. The baby she had prayed and longed for, from the man she had loved so much she would have freely given her life without even a seconds' thought. The man, who had been her whole world ... The man that came home and made love to her every night ... The same man that before coming home to her, made love to four other women. Coming down on top of them with the weight of his naked body, all the while whispering sweet nothings into their ears, kissing and caressing them, entering them, taking them as he did her.

She all at once felt like she was going to vomit her guts up.

"It's all over hon. You alright?" the nurse asked. She touched the back of Julie's head patting it gently with her fingers as the doctor and steel pan moved from the table.

Julie shook her head no. "I think I'm going to be sick."

The nurse pulled a tray from the drawer holding it under Julie's chin with one hand placing the other on her forehead. Within seconds, Julie's head was bobbing up and down violently spewing yellow bile all over its sides.

"It's alright hon," the nurse said. "It's alright," she said, again. She pressed at Julie's forehead with a damp compress. "Feel a little better?"

"I think so."

The nurse guided Julie's feet out of the stirrups moving her up the table and covering her with a warm blanket. "Would you like me to go and get your friend for you?"

Julie pulled the blanket up past her neck rolling onto her side. "Please."

The nurse disappeared.

Julie folded her hands on top of her aching empty womb as more tears glided down onto her cheeks. She was so sorry. Sorry for herself and for the life she had just taken. She had not told her baby that it wasn't going to live to see another day - Or why. She'd just went on as if nothing was out of the ordinary this day; they were both just going for a car ride. She was all at once filled with regret wishing she had taken the time to talk to her baby as any good mother would have and should. Now it was too late. She knew somewhere inside she was now marked for hell. She knew this as surely as she knew her name. She curled up into a tight little ball drawing her knees up to her chest.

"Hey girlfriend." Sherry traced the outline of Julie's cheekbone with her index finger. Sherry's voice was soft and soothing, backing away Julie's thoughts.

They both stretched out their arms to one another, at the exact same moment embracing and crying for what now would never be.

The nurse softly closed the door behind her, writing on Julie's chart stopping dead; pen in hand, eyes skimming the one sentence reason Mrs. Julie Porter had darkened their door. She read it over wishing she had not taken the baseball bat out of her car after the game last night. If she hadn't she would have been up at the head nurse's desk about now making up an excuse to leave for an hour, so she could go and beat the living piss out of that asshole herself just for starters. She had heard and seen a lot but my God, this one took the prize, actually four prizes. No wonder the woman had never told her husband she was pregnant. This was the first time since working at the clinic she had ever broken down and cried her heart out for a patient.

Chapter 25

Julie awoke, gagging.

A foul dense odour hung about the room, curdling the air into thick chunks. It smelled sickening sweet, as if something rotted crawling with white from the inside out. It stuck to the hairs of her nose, clung to the roof of her mouth, stung and ran her eyes. She cupped her nose with her hand, breathing in and out through bridged fingers.

Tony rolled in his sleep landing his right side tight against her back, snuggling, placing his left arm round her chest.

The pain medication had long since worn off, her belly was pitching and cramping in wavy spasms. She moved her hand from her face, pressing it to her underbelly. She dry retched from the pungency, the vile air seemingly getting thicker and thicker by the second. She dry retched again.

It reminded her of the kind of stench that had emanated from the garage last summer after two tomcats had been spatting during the night. The one was dead on the porch in the morning. She had buried it not giving a second thought to the other until a few days later, when she had opened all the kitchen windows and was knocked over by an ungodly reek. She had not noticed the moving chalk line of maggots coming from the side lawn to the garage and back until then.

She attempted to wiggle free from Tony without disturbing him. She did not feel capable of creating a good enough tale as to where she had been all day. That lie could wait until morning. She pushed his arm with her elbow. She really had to get up and out of the bed. The rankness was flip-flopping round in circles inside her stomach making her throat convulse. The pain lower down was way the other side of intolerable, forcing her to hold her breath with each stab.

She shoved hard at the dead weight of his arm. It seemed full of lead, welded in place. She heaved at him again as something warm, wet, goopy, hit the side of her neck and slid underneath her night-gown. She gagged into her hand throwing up a mouthful of vomit, swallowing the sticky remains on the top of her tongue back down.

"Why did you kill our baby?" Tony murmured in words so barely audible, if one had breathed right at that second, it would have went on by and been missed.

But ... She hadn't breathed.

He ran the tip of his tongue along her ear lobe. "Why ... Julie?" He whispered, slowly drawing out the words, his voice off key, hollow, full of gravel, and not at all like his.

Julie froze, freezer burn solid, her mind whirling in circles. *'He couldn't possibly know,'* she thought. *'How could he know?'* ... *She hadn't told him anything about anything* ... *She had not even said she was going out that morning* ... *She had never said a single solitary word about nothing* ... *Not ever* ... *How could he know?* She climbed aboard one of the circles in her mind riding it round and round. She hopped off answering her questions. *'He couldn't possibility know* ... *To him, her monthly cycle was just a heavy one this month* ... *That was all* ... *But* ... *How would he even know that?* ... *It had to be all the drugs the clinic had given her and the painkillers she had taken at home playing tricks with her mind.'*

She thawed out the edges of the freezer burn, her skin flaking off into the bed sheets.

Behind her in the dark, a tongue jutted in and out of a salivating mouth, wiggling and waggling, swishing like a dog's tail. It stretched out, elongating doubling in length as it commenced twirling drill-like as if it was a separate living entity. It made contact with the flesh of her neck, licking, wriggling, dabbing on and off as it traced along her jaw-line.

She felt as if her skin was going to rip itself free and bail. This ... This ... Teetered on the outer edge of disgusting and repulsive. The trail of saliva stuck to her skin, gooping in balls then pooling into bulbous clumps in the hollow of her neck. As it cooled, it thickened and stung, giving off fumes much like a reeking two day old road kill laying out in the burning sun, split open and ravaged by vultures. The stench mingled with the rank air already in the room making it worse than putrid. She retched again folding over in half, drawing her knees up to her chest.

She had to get up out of that bed and into the bathroom ... Before the stench, the pain, and whatever he was doing, did her in totally.

"Why Julie? ... Why did you kill our baby?" He whispered again so hollow it echoed. He flicked the tip of his tongue in and out of her ear. The excess saliva rolled off the edges, dropping onto her hair sticking and matting it together.

She turned, facing him, telling herself this was by far, a too realistic nightmare. It needed to end and now. She peered at him unable to focus through the darkness. The room seemed all of a sudden so black. She moved close to his face needing reassurance of reality. She needed to see the shut eyes, the day's growth of beard, the tousled hair.

She pressed nose to nose.

The sealed eyes fluttered, then popped open.

The black darkness swirled as if paving a pathway.

She jerked her head backwards. The scream choking off in her throat before it even got a chance to rise.

Huge, round, blood streaked, amber, eyes ... Non-blinking eyes, stared profusely at her, into her like a ... A ... A ... There were no words for it. The mouth beneath was malformed and contorted into a toothy half smile. The kind one only saw when you were seconds away from meeting your maker. The end of the tongue was black, pointed, and rolled at the sides. It hung limp, dangling out and down the right hand side of the mouth. Thick, foul smelling mucus like drool gobbed up at its tip, over flowing, staining the pillowcase. The hair clumped in thick sections resembling more so overturned grass. It smelled like damp decaying earth, the kind you would find in a cemetery at nightfall.

Julie watched frozen with horror as the head ever so slowly cocked sideways, the half smile widening, pulling back, exposing black-green rotting gums.

Her scream un-choked, uploading, shrilling, blasting into the walls. She thudded both fists into its neck and collarbone breaking free.

It lurched forward grabbing her by the shoulders.

Sheer terror took over all her senses. She had to get away; even if it meant diving through the second story plate glass window.

She beat its chest wildly to no avail.

The hold stood fast.

She arched her back, brought up her feet and booted its groin full force, her knees rebounding thundering up against its gut knocking the wind from it.

The jolt snapped Julie off the bed backward into the wall whip-lashing her head into the drywall, creasing and cracking it. Dazed she shook her head as warm dark liquid bubbled and sprouted, leaking through her hair and down the back of her neck.

"Why Julie?" Came the same voice, with the same question, from the same thing in the bed.

She scrambled onto her knees, then feet, using her hands, bending her fingers backward as her body swayed and feet stumbled. She ran out of the bedroom her legs liquidating as she jumped onto the landing. She slid down the staircase on her stomach, stood then fell, and then stood again, her flipper-like feet trying to run with dead legs towards the front door. She slammed into the doorframe, fumbling at the lock with hands that did not seem to be attached to her body or anyone else's. She pulled and twisted at the knob leaving streams of bloody whip marks from her hair on the back of the door and the walls.

When the lock let go she flew outside into the night not daring to look back.

She tore down the walkway, the flesh of her bare feet ripping and tearing on the razor like edges of the patio stones. She wasn't breathing. She had forgotten how. And it didn't matter. All that mattered was her legs had remembered how to run like the devil himself was after her. Or worse. She didn't know what the hell that was in her bed. And she did not want to ever find out in this lifetime or any other.

She hauled up her flannel nightgown to her hips nearing the end of the walkway, tipping onto the balls of her feet and leaping into the air over top of the bushes under the tree. Stems shot up winding themselves round her ankles and calves, strategically embedding thorns deep within her skin using muscle tissue for anchors. She came down as if on cue, hitting hard. She could hear hysterical screams in the air. She had no means of digesting them as hers. She clawed at the earth with her hands, rolling side to side on her stomach trying to break loose. It was like the bushes had known she'd be coming and had laid in wait, reaching up and plucking her out of the air at the precise moment she launched.

She flayed her arms backwards pulling and yanking at the stems as her hands painted themselves in deep rich red. She hauled, pulling with all she was worth as they wound tighter and tighter, making her gasp out in sheer agony as her lungs filled above capacity in the sweet scent of roses. She collapsed motionless into the dirt, her vision circling round and round, taking her with it. She raised her hands to her head, she felt like she was going to pass out and throw up all at the same time.

Her one fingertip knocked something hard. She dropped her hands to the earth snapping two of her fingers back at the knuckle and tearing the nails down to the quick. She squinted at the blurred black shape, straining, focusing as it changed from black to brown. She arched her head, digging her toes into the earth, sling shooting her torso forward, flinging out her arms and hooking her fingers into the tree root. She dug under the root grasping it with both hands, dragging herself forward as the hooked barbs bent and pulled, giving way as they tore her flesh leaving holes that hot new red liquid instantly pooled into and ran out of.

She rose to her knees using a bottom branch as a crutch. She reached up into the tree grasping another branch and pulling herself to a wobbling stand, her chest heaving up and down so heavily it hurt. Her nightgown fell loosely back into place about her knees as bits of dirt, rose petals, stems, flesh, and blood made their way silently unnoticed to the ground becoming part of it.

She bent over trying to catch her breath, resting her hands on her thighs, looking at the house upside down through her open legs. It was pitch black like someone had tried to magic marker it out of existence forgetting about the edges. There was no sign of life. It was as if everything alive had been wiped out. Even the birds and bugs were gone. There was just utter complete dark stillness, the kind where you could hear your own blood course through your veins as you look over your shoulder for something you know is out there lying just out of range waiting for you to make the one single mistake ... and then ...

She collapsed, sinking down into the lawn lying full out flat on her stomach. The darkness hiding just a hair's breathe behind her. She turned her head instantly catching the ass end of a breeze winding its way through the grass carrying the tell tale scent of roses. She throated a squeal, clambering onto her hands and knees crossing the lawn onto the drive, bee-ling for the car. She yanked the back door open using the seat belt to pull herself in, passing out just as the car door re-closed, catching and snapping off the rose vine that had crawled along with her unnoticed.

She had no recollection of being carried from the car, up the stairs, washed or changed. Nor did she remember much else of the night. Not even the telltale signs of ghoulish events one could call a nightmare so real the script had her name on every page. But, that could not possibly be. Still ... if possibility could be, then it would be lurking and sulking around as most real nightmares do just under the surface, ready and laying in wait for the slightest of rips to pop itself back through.

"Hey you," Tony soothed. He put his hands under her armpits raising her up against the pillows. He placed a mug of hot tea within her hands. "You okay?" he asked stroking her hair with the flat of his palm.

"Yes ... Why?"

"Just thought I'd ask if you were okay?"

"Why?"

"Double checking."

"But, why?"

"Just concerned," he said.

"Concerned? What-ever about?"

"Just you. Okay? Well I'm off to work. I'll talk to you later." He bent over and kissed her forehead lightly, bending and fetching something off the floor.

"What's that?" she asked.

"This?" He opened his hand exposing a tattered blood stained cloth.

"Yes that."

"It's a piece of your nightgown."

"My nightgown?"

"Yes."

"Why do you have a piece of one of my nightgowns?"

"I used it as a rag to clean up."

"You did what?"

"I used it as a rag," he repeated. "I didn't think you'd mind."

"I wouldn't mind? Why wouldn't I mind? I don't have that many you know! ... God! Couldn't you have used something else?"

He sat down on the bed beside her. "Honey ...When I found you out in the car last night and ..."

She cut him off her voice shrilling, the nightmare just under the surface waking up and readying itself to pounce. "You found me in the car last night? I was out in the car last night? ... Oh my God! ... No!" Her head fogged and swirled as the nightmare popped its head out wearing the toothy 'I got you now' grin, running its own private movie inside her head. "Was I in the back seat?" she shrieked. "Please don't tell me I was in the back seat? ... Was I? ...Was I?" Her tone was on the verge of hysteria. She gulped almost swallowing her dried tongue asking again. "Was I?"

"Yes ... but ..." Tony did not finish the sentence he was too busy catching the mug as it fell from her grasp.

She slumped and quieted leaving this world for a little. Passing out abruptly as the 'yes' word left Tony's lips, sending the nightmare fussing and fuming back to where it had come, leaving it with no other recourse but to retreat and stop the room's rotations.

She lay at peace, blurring and erasing the lines of nightmare versus reality like they had never really existed in the first place.

Chapter 26

"I need to talk to you!" Julie exclaimed, not waiting for the hello. She gripped onto the receiver whitening her knuckles so much so, her hand appeared clawed and dead.

"What is it love?" Sherry asked.

"You're not going to believe me!"

"Of course I will. Why wouldn't I?"

"You sure?"

"Yep! So what's up?"

"I have these three yellow rose bushes outside," Julie said. She was talking so fast the words all ran into one. "Now there's four but that doesn't matter! It is just that ..." Julie's voice trailed off as she leaned back peering out the kitchen window at them biting her bottom lip.

"Just what?" Sherry asked. She rubbed her chin, wondering what on earth had her friends tail tied in such a tight knot.

"I don't know how to say all this without you thinking I've gone off my rocker." Julie whispered, slow and steady. She studied the rose bushes outside counting and re-counting them, still coming up with four.

"Just spit it out! I have never thought you were off your rocker before. And ... I don't think I am about to start now ... well of course unless you keep acting like this," Sherry laughed. "However ... I ..."

Julie cut her off. "Okay," she said. She sucked in a deeper than usual breath totally ignoring the comment. "I have these rose bushes out front and I hack them off right to the ground and pour weed kill on them. Hell ... I've even torched them. But within hours they're right back, just like nothing happened and there is more and more of them all the time!"

Sherry's mouth opened and closed. She furrowed her brow. She knew what Julie had just said but it was not computing properly inside her head.

"Are you still there?" Julie asked. She didn't know how Sherry would take to all this but she sure was going to try to explain the unexplainable and hopefully maybe in the middle of it all come to some form of conclusion herself. They say two heads are better than one. She was determined to test this theory.

"Are you okay Hon?" Sherry asked. Her laugh lines drew out and formed a solid serious ridge.

"No!" Julie shot back. "But that doesn't matter!" She said quickly.

"Hon ... Can I ask you something?" Sherry pulled out a kitchen chair and sat.

"Sure."

"You taking something? Like too much medication or not enough?"

Julie ignored the question. "I knew you wouldn't believe me," she said.

"But Hon, just tell me ... are you?"

"No! ... I don't take anything!" Julie could feel her insides flipping around like someone bouncing a ball too hard up against a wall.

"Truth?" Sherry asked. She knew in her heart her friend didn't take anything except save the odd bit of fruit wine, but then again, she was always there too right alongside her with both feet.

"Truth!" Julie affirmed.

"This is just too weird! You cut them off and within hours, you say they're back? How can bushes grow back that fast?" Sherry asked. She pulled her fingers through her hair, settling into the conversation. Julie was dead serious and not pulling her leg.

"You tell me, cause it's got me beat."

"Are you sure you're really cutting them off?"

"Sherry!"

"Sorry girlfriend ... I just ..."

Julie cut in. "Truth ...You're really having trouble believing me aren't you?"

"Well ... I ... I..." Sherry stopped mid sentence. She did not know what to say. Julie was coming across so real and firm that she was actually cutting down these things and they were growing right back. She had gone through one hell of a lot in the past month, more than most probably go through in an entire lifetime. But she had never known her to tell tales or fabricate things. Not ever. She had to say it once more. She was sure she would be able to tell by the tone of Julie's voice. "Shit girl! Are you dead sure?" she whispered.

"I'm as dead sure as I'm alive and breathing and talking to you on this God damn telephone!"

Sherry pursed her lips together, running her tongue back and forth around the hollows inside her mouth thinking all this over. She knew way down inside that as bizarre as it sounded Julie believed what she was saying, so there had to be something to this. "There's gotta be an explanation then! ... Maybe Tony?" She said. She suddenly wondered why she had not thought of this. She would not put it past him to do something like this to her. Look what he had done already. She continued aloud with her thoughts. "The more I think about it ... It makes sense ... Maybe it is Tony ... You know ... He's sneaking in and planting new ones every time you cut them down to try and creep you out or something?"

"That's too much like work for him!" Julie threw out on the plate.

"Yeah! ... I get your point! But ... Just, hear me out! Okay?"

"Okay."

"Let's just suppose he's planting them back for revenge, to get at you for stuff you've done to him?"

"But ... What stuff have I ever done to him? I've never even made him dog food sandwiches, but believe you me it's next on my to do list!"

Sherry smiled in amusement. Tony did deserve that one. As for the rest. Julie was a good soul. She had done nothing wrong in her eyes. "Nothing," Sherry replied. "You' re right ... you've done nothing to him."

"But? ... Revenge? You really think that?" Julie asked. She bit at the inside of her lip.

"I don't know! ... No! ... This is too messed up even for him," Sherry said.

Julie broke down, crying into the receiver.

"Oh Hon ... Don't cry ... There's gotta be something we're missing."

"You believe me then?"

"Girlfriend ... If you say this is so ...Then it is so!"

"It is so."

"Then yes ... Of course ... I believe you."

Julie plucked the tattered remnant of her blood stained nightgown back out of the garbage, placing it off to the side of the table. "Sherry?"

"Yeah love?"

"Last night I had the worst nightmare I have ever had in my whole entire life, but I don't think it was a nightmare. I think it really happened!" She sucked her lips into her mouth staring directly at the dark red stained material.

Sherry's hand froze on the telephone receiver. "Say that again love?" She needed Julie to repeat herself. She thought she had just heard her say she had a nightmare that was real.

"Last night I had a terrible nightmare and I forgot all about it till this morning when I saw something in Tony's hand that jerked my memory and what he had was in the nightmare, but he had it."

"What did he have?"

"A torn piece of my flannel night gown. It was blood stained."

"You're not fooling here are you girl?"

"No!"

"Go on ..."

"In the nightmare there was this ... this creature ... this thing and it knew I had an abortion and I ran out of the house and fell near the old tree and got all tangled up in the rose bushes that I hacked down hours before with my machete and ..."

Sherry cut her off, her eyes growing wide as pie plates. "You have a God damn machete?" she questioned, hastily. Her mouth dropped open.

"Yeah! ... It goes faster that way!"

Sherry got up pulling her car keys from the hook. "Oh! ... My! ... God!"

"God has nothing to do with it," she said. Her body started trembling and chilling, as she remembered the day not so long ago her mother had whispered something similar to her.

Sherry grabbed her jacket and runners from the hall closet.

"I can prove all this to you! I can show you the piece of nightgown and all the blood on the rose bushes I cut down this morning and threw in the garage. And I can cut down the new ones that have grown back in their place and in the time it takes for us to have a tea we can go back out and cut them down again, cause as sure as I know my name they will be back. I can even show you the trail of blood I left when I crawled to the car and I ..."

"LORD FUCKING CHRIST!" Sherry screamed.

"Can you come over? Can you please come over Sherry?" Julie begged. She stared wide-eyed at the five rose bushes out front.

"I was already on my way!" Sherry threw the receiver on the table running out the back door.

Chapter 27

Julie waited for hours and hours by the front door for the friend that did not come. As the afternoon slipped away into evening bringing with it darkness, the telephone rang.

"Hello?"

"Is this Julie Porter?"

"Yes."

"This is Stan, Sherry's brother. Norm asked me to call you."

"Norm? Sherry's husband? Asked you to call me?" Julie asked. She was puzzled.

"I don't know how to tell you this."

"Tell me what?" Julie asked, puzzlement trading for concern.

"There was an accident this afternoon."

"An accident?"

"Yes," Stan reaffirmed.

Julie put her hand to her throat swallowing so hard it hurt. "There ... there was a ... an ... accident?" she repeated. Her voice started to shake.

"Yes ... Sher ... Sherry," Stan said. His voice cracked and stuttered, losing its composure. He cleared his throat and blew his nose. "Sherry ... Sherry was in an accident."

Julie's flesh goose-bumped in slow motion. Again, she found herself repeating Stan. "Sherry ... was ... was in an accident?"

"Y ... Yes," Stan cleared his throat again.

"Is ... Is ... Sh ... Sh ... She ... Okay?" Julie stuttered. She felt like she had been clicked on pause and squeezed through a keyhole.

"No ... She isn't ... She ... She didn't make it ... Sh ... She was killed." Stan replied. His words jumbled at the same time his voice faltered. He broke down sobbing.

Julie's legs wobbled and buckled, folding her down into neat little sections like an 'Origami' doll. She sank to the floor gasping and holding her chest. "No! ... God! ... No!" she pleaded. Her breath pelted in short rapid bursts.

There were no more words from the other end of the receiver.

"Oh my God," she whispered. "Oh my God ... Oh dear God."

"I'm ... I'm ... sorry ... to have to be the one to tell you ... I ..." Stan stuttered breaking in half, his emotions too raw. The pain welled inside becoming so unbearable it hurt to breathe. He wiped his face soaking the paper towel through and through like he'd just held it under a faucet.

"What ... What ... happe ..." Julie halted mid-sentence, unable to say anything more. She laid herself out flat on the cold kitchen floor sobbing for all she was worth.

Stan finished her question gulping and slurring his words, heartache and despair stabbing at his soul making him double over in half. "If ... it ... was an ... a ... hit and ... ruf ... run," he said. He put his head in his hands cradling his fragility.

'She was on her way here,' Julie said to herself. *'She was on her way here,'* she repeated. "She was on her way here," she said, softly. The lump at the back of her throat doubled in size making it impossible to swallow the tears that had pooled in her mouth.

"I ... I," Stan said. He sniffed, succumbing to another round of tears. He felt like his throat had closed, rendering him helpless, unable to continue.

Julie curled up in a tight little ball wrapping her arms around her knees, cradling the telephone between her shoulder and neck. She rocked herself gently back and forth weeping.

Stan and Julie clung to one another through the telephone wires, sorrow and anguish mixing and melding them together as grief coursed back and forth between them. Both unable to gather themselves back together. The little talk holes in their receivers filled and over flowed with tears.

Somewhere ... Stan had tried to mumble something audible, but had lost. He was too far past the other side of his break point. He had crumbled and fell to pieces quite a time back as had Julie. He could not cope any longer. He depressed the off button sliding the telephone across the living room floor. He promised himself he would call her back later, if and when he got a hold of himself.

Julie lay alone on the cold kitchen floor clutching the lifeless receiver with no one on the other end. Her heart felt like a land mine full of shrapnel had just exploded sending sharp daggered pieces into every part of her being, ripping and tearing at her. It hurt to move. It hurt to draw breath. It hurt to think. It just plain hurt.

Sherry and herself had been better than best friends. They had been sisters by choice. Kindred spirits that could finish one another's sentences without thought. She would have died for her. She still would.

Julie slunk onto her side, the chill of the tile floor numbing her limbs, making her movements cumbersome and slow as she dropped the telephone receiver. *'Why God why? ... Why her?... Why not me?'* she scoffed. Something inside her picked it up. She silently moved her lips, repeating it over and over like a record player stuck in a deep scratch with no one to turn it off. She pawed at the floor rolling herself onto her back.

"WHY IN HELL DID YOU TAKE HER? WHY HER? IT SHOULD HAVE BEEN ME! WHY DID'T YOU TAKE ME? TELL ME WHY ... RIGHT NOW! ... TELL ME!" she screamed at the top of her lungs. She stared down the white stark ceiling. "WHY, WHY?" she cried. "Why did you take her from me?" she demanded. She held her hands up to the ceiling. "Why? ... You have no damn right!" Julie brought her knees up to her chest kicking her feet. "Why? ... Tell me right now ... Why? ... TELL ME GOD DAMN YOU!" she insisted. Her words tunnelled and echoed through the walls.

There was no reply.

God wasn't there.

And what was decided to be silent.

For now!

God was not there

God was not there ...

And what was, decided to be silent.

For now ...

'Definition'

God (god)

:The creator and ruler of the universe, regarded as almighty

:One of several deities especially a male deity.

:Any deified person or object.

'Definition'

Silent (si'lant)

:Making no sound.
:Refraining from speech.
:Speechless or mute
:Unspoken or tacit.

SECTION THREE
THE HAUNTING

Chapter 28

The early morning fog had mutated the street lamps into huge yellowish fuzz balls that changed in shape and color as they spiralled down and around the lamp posts hanging masses of creamy white, evenly spaced ribbons a hairs breath above the pavement.

Julie stared out into the nothingness. Her heart barely alive. Barely beating. She wrapped her shins with both arms pulling her knees tight up against her chest. Sleep had eluded her these past few nights, as had all the answers to the finality of her friend's death.

A cold chill ran up her spine making the hairs on the back of her neck prickle. The greyness of the nothing seemed to have her name on it, looming and reaching up with tarred pavement fingers that had come alive, worming and inching its way into the very fabric of the place within one's conscious that governs that fine line, that life cord. The one that arms us all with the abilities, the logic, to distinguish illusions from reality. The protectors of our inner sanctums. The keepers that restrain all the stuff that lies on the fringes in the in between.

Julie pivoted her head resting her cheek on her knee caps, gazing at the black under garments, the black dress, the black heels aligned upon the dresser. Her chest heaved and laboured as tears rose, fell and left. Her eyes stung, swelling then closed of their own accord.

"J ... u ... l ... i ...e," whispered through the air, low, gravelly, barely there.

It went on by unnoticed.

"J ... u ... l ... i ...e."

She opened her eyes into tiny slits squinting about the room. There was but her. Without so much as a single thought, she re-closed her eyes her head heavy on her knee. It slipped off and flopped down, hanging loosely as sleep found her.

"J ... u ... l ... i ...e," something called.

She was gone.

Gone without the protectors of consciousness into the greyness of the nothing, the in between, where reality and nightmarish illusions don masks and inter-mingle.

Death had a way of doing that.

Chapter 29

The funeral was long. Much too long for hearts to bear. The scripted words referring to the recently dearly departed read from the bible provided little if any comfort. The pain of Sherry's sudden loss over shadowed all the uplifting hymns and psalms declaring it was her time to be called by God to commence his teachings and work and all should rejoice in her life.

Hearts longing for some form of solace were not about to find it in that wooden pew lined church in front of her closed coffin, singing hymns. There was no solace, nor any comfort, nor much of anything else ... Just like standing in the middle of an intersection amongst slivers of glass and car parts clutching a broken headlight from the offending vehicle ... There was no solace, nor any comfort, nor much of anything else.

Julie stood alongside Norm hand in hand. They had entered the church together that way and had stayed that way. Stan had been hospitalized a day before the funeral adding more worrisome burden to the heartache.

Norm and Julie squeezed one another's hands locking their fingers together. The parts of Sherry that lived within them crossing currents, meeting someplace on a higher plane, joining them as one through the delicate lifeline of their touch.

As the service closed, the flowers were layered in bunches upon the coffin making ready for transport to the burial site. The one exception, four over-large bundles containing dozens and dozens of yellow roses each individually tied with black lace ribbon. They had arrived along with explicit instructions that they were to accompany the limousine en route to the burial plot, and then given to each in attendance at the conclusion of the ceremony.

The limousine ride seemed longer than the service, if that was at all possible, and apparently, it was. There was little to say, and when either thought they should attempt, pain and tears welled and took hold, rendering words impossible. All that mattered was being there together, sometimes saying nothing was saying a whole lot of everything. They stayed content in the silence and the offering of solitude that came with it. Their clasped hands still clinging to the threads of a life before memories took hold.

As they reached the town's outskirts, Norm mustered up the courage to give Julie's hand an extra squeeze. He'd planned on calling in on her in person and thanking her that morning after the florist had dropped off the delivery at his home, but he'd become so overwhelmed he just couldn't. She truly was an angel, as Sherry had often referred to her. She had said Julie was very special and that God was looking down on her, adjusting her wings. Sherry had not elaborated any further. Norm was now seeing firsthand what his wife meant.

All Sherry had talked about lately was Julie. Just before she left the house the day God had intervened, Sherry had mentioned something about yellow roses. For Julie to have the forethought to provide a single yellow rose wrapped with a ribbon for each person attending the funeral to take home with them in remembrance of Sherry's life was just ... just beyond all words. The floral company had not said whom they were from, only that they were a gift. When he saw they were all yellow he knew all he needed. Yes he could see it ... as Sherry had said she was an angel.

Norm turned looking directly into Julie's eyes trying to ... wanting to express his gratitude but a lump had jumped onto the back of his tongue, rendering his lips silent. Her kindness was more than he could bear. He turned and looked out the window wiping his sorrow from his cheeks, promising himself after all this was behind him that he would find a way to thank her. But ... somewhere ... something way deep down inside him was not content. It kept circling and nagging, demanding him to tell her. Tell her now. Soon, he could think of nothing else. He turned to her, separating his lips, letting what had to come out come out. "You are wonderful you know," Norm said.

"Don't be silly. You needn't say such a thing," Julie whispered. She met his eyes.

"I do need to say such a thing. You are wonderful ... Just so wonderful."

Julie shook her head back and forth no.

"I really mean it. I do."

"Oh Norm ... It's kind of you, but I'm ..."

"I'm not being kind ... I really, really mean it from the bottom of my heart ... I do."

Norm's words affected her deep down inside stabbing at her heart; her eyes filled and over flowed. "I loved her like a sister." Julie placed her free hand on Norms, gently stroking it with her thumb. "This is where I should be," she said quietly.

"Oh you ... You are just so kind. I am truly at a loss for words. Really I am. It's ... It's just so wonderful of you." Norm cemented their lifeline, clasping his free hand over top of the others.

"You don't need to thank me. Really you don't." Julie could not figure out why Norm was thanking her so over the top for attending the funeral. It was where she should be as she had said. He was oozing and gushing with such deep seeded emotion she felt like pulling her hands away and sliding them into her pockets, not wanting to partake. She suddenly felt awkward. She looked down then back up; his eyes were brimmed with tears. She all at once felt foolish. He was just like her, over come with grief and needing someone to hang onto.

"I am starting to see now why she loved you ... so ... so much," Norm said. His voice skipped, faltering and cracking. He moved in alongside Julie laying his head into the crook of her neck and shoulder, sobbing and weeping.

"I haven't done, didn't do anything anyone else that cared and loved her wouldn't have done." Julie glanced down at Norm. She was having trouble holding herself together as well. She rested her head against his, her eyes overflowing with little rivers of tears. Neither of them should have been dealt this card, they both needed Sherry so very much.

"Oh Julie," he cried. "Oh Julie," he sobbed. "Oh Julie," he whispered. "Oh ... Julie," he cooed. He repeated it over and over slowly allowing his breath to trace and warm the skin along the nape of her neck. She all of a sudden smelled so wonderful, so beautiful, her skin so warm and soft. He closed his eyes as if on cue, lapsing, drifting off forgetting where he was and why.

"Norm? ... Norm? ... Are you all right?" She lifted her head off his.

"Oh ... Julie," he cooed again. "J ... u ... l ... i ... e." he whispered, like a long lost lover. He kissed the back of her neck softly.

Every part of her stiffened. Even her eyes balls and lids stiffened. She tried to give herself an inner shake but nothing budged. She swallowed hard. *'Okay ... Okay ... It's okay,'* she told herself. *'Norm ... Norm is ...Is very distraught.'* Her brain was stuttering with the thoughts, almost as if it was covering up something. *'Okay,'* she started in again. *'It's ... It's ... It's nothing ... Doesn't mean nothing ... It's okay ... It's all okay.'* She was halfway to convincing herself when her name, in Norm's voice, echoed around the flesh of her neck again, turning the *'It's okays'* into *'Oh my God's! ... Norm! ... What on earth do you think you are doing?'* The third *'Oh my God'* rolled itself into a ball, grew feet and nice long teeth as it jumped from Norm's shoulder to hers, chomping down taking out a great big bite of her flesh, chewing and swallowing it slowly. She re-wound her inner tape hitting the stop button and instant replay at the same time. She told herself again and again that *It was okay ... All was fine ... It's just a form of endearment ... It meant nothing ... Absolutely nothing, just nothing from nothing about nothing, meaning nothing ... It was no more than any other distraught grieving husband would do. They all cling onto the wife's best friend for the pieces of her held within.* There was a small white sheet covering something else in her mind but she dared not lift the corner.

It had started to work ... the repeating of things over and over, over and over until belief surfaced and almost took hold ... But ... Then ... The soft words ... *'Oh Julie'* broke in, shooting through the stilled air like a poisoned arrow.

Her mouth fell open. The bally thing on her shoulder smiled, dipping its head, chewing up a storm. The word rationalization took wing and flew off somewhere. She tried to net it but it was out of reach. Norm was just ... Just ... Too overboard, or too close, or too something. It was the or too something that kept flashing in her eyes balls without reprieve and there didn't seem to be any switch to shut it off.

The filtration system in the limousine was clicking on and off. The air seemed heavy and dense with a sickening sweet undertone she knew she recognized, but just could not put a finger on. She glanced down at Norm. He was motionless and slumped up against her like a rag-doll. His head was folded down obscuring his face. It was as if he had suddenly fallen into a deep sleep.

Her open mouth dried, taking her throat along for the ride. She couldn't swallow. She couldn't breathe. She needed air. Needed to feel air. If she could just get some fresh air ... Feel fresh air on her face before they pulled into the cemetery. This would help her make sense of all the things she currently could not make sense of. And they seemed in abundance.

She scanned the door for the window crank. There was none. There wasn't any on either side. She leaned forward tapping the tinted glass between herself and the driver; Norm towed limply along for the ride like someone had crazy glued them together when she wasn't looking. She tapped and tapped, desperation set in as she thudded the window with her fists.

It opened a crack. "Yes miss?" the driver said.

Julie's nostrils blew in and out filling themselves up with a horrid pungent, sickening-sweet odour. In her haste to speak it got into her mouth lodging itself up under her tongue. She cupped her mouth with her hands one over top of the other almost tossing the contents of her stomach onto Norm's head.

The stench seemed to circle almost like it was drifting back and forth in front of her face, worsening and growing in intensity by the second. She moved one of her hands covering her nose, motioning the driver to open the window with a series of jerky one-armed elbow gestures.

"Is something wrong miss?" the driver asked. He spoke without taking his eyes from the road.

"I ... Need ... Air," Julie muffled in bursts. "Please ... Roll ... Down ... The ... Window." Her stomach and head had joined forces swimming and doing the backstroke in circles, the stench making her gag in between each stroke.

"You need ... Some air ... Do you ... Now?" the driver said. He added in her name drawling it out slow and deliberate. "J ... U ... L ... I ... E?"

"Yes ... Yes," Julie answered. She did not pay the slightest bit of attention to being called by name. It had went up and over.

"Well then ... Have some air," he replied in a dead monotone.

Both rear windows shot down then back up thundering with a hollow metal sonic boom as they hit and locked at the top of the window frame.

Julie's face stung and burned from the mini tornado her hair had all at once turned into. She could feel the welts rising on her cheeks.

She pried the hair from her face as the welted streaks drew in terror mixing and melding in horror, painting the reddened flesh. Her heart started to race, then thump. She felt like it was going to pound right out of her chest and inject itself deep into Norm's lifeless head.

Julie's eyeballs popped, swivelling back and forth from the window to the top of the driver's head ... To the window ... To the driver ... To the window ... Then stayed stuck on the driver having no more moisture for mobility. She opened and closed her mouth, her bottom jaw hinging not quite into place, hanging off side catching her tongue thickening and fuzzing it over. She gulped, ingesting the hot saliva that was squirting in all directions from under her tongue, almost puking in the process.

Without warning, Norm's head abruptly dropped down from her shoulder bobbing and dangling onto her chest like it had two feet of excess neck. She pushed him off her. He slithered down her body his shoulders pivoting landing face up in her lap. His right arm dangled loosely, his hand flopped about the floor like a dying fish. His eyes were wide open, almost too wide open showing the whites all the way round. His mouth was open and contorted in a ghoulish half grin with one side up, the other down. His teeth seemed somehow not there.

The tinted window in front of her slithered down a hairs breath. "J ... U ... L ... I ... E," called a gravel-filled voice from the front seat.

Julie immoblized as if she'd been preserved inside a box of mothballs then dumped out on the leather seat where bits of her flaked off and embedded.

The partition creaked as it slowly started to inch its way down. She stared, watching in horror, as the window went lower and lower, swirling the foul fog like air that was so thick she swore she could see it. The putrid air burnt her nose and mouth, coating the membranes in thick goopy mucus as it worked down her throat and settled in her lungs.

She glanced down at Norm. He was as he was; face up, eyes wide, hand flopping, except the grimace had traded itself off for a sneer.

"He's ... Okay ... Julie. He's just having a moment on me," the driver said. He slurred his wording, speaking slowly and matter-of-factly, interjecting a Cajun accent. The window between them was all but down. He lethargically hooked his right arm over the back of the seat, turning to her.

Julie started to scream. And scream and scream and scream.

But ... No one could hear.

The limousine was top of the line. A bomb could have gone off in there and no one would hear. So ... How would anyone ever hear such a simple little thing as a scream or two or three?

The driver smiled in amusement.

Julie grabbed onto the edge of the seat, wildly thumping and banging Norm's lifeless body with her legs until it fell into the foot-well. She lunged sideways grasping onto the door latch with both hands, unlatching it just as the lock pin closed catching onto nothing but air.

The door sprung backwards whipping Julie out onto the pavement, dragging her some twenty feet before she pried her hand free of the latch. The limousine door free of her weight whipped backwards lodging and carving itself into the side panel. Julie flew up into the air that she'd needed so badly, coming down tumbling in a backwards somersault, toppling up and over the median banging her head hard off the last of the cement curbs as the road-way turned from black top to gravel.

No one in the funeral prossession, or anyone else for that matter, noticed a body laying alongside the shoulder of the roadway. It was as if she'd been left out there on purpose to be cold and alone, bleeding from the head like she was some twisted low budget government ad on the perils of getting out of a moving automobile.

Her head had stopped bleeding quite a time before she came to in a half dry sticky pool of her own blood; wondering what in hell had happened to her on the way over to Norm's that morning? ... And how in God had she gotten to be where on earth she was?

But ... For ... Now ... She quietly rested, allowed to be totally free from all thought and rationalization; Where something other than God's angels slithered through and around her stilled body sending all memories of the last few hours deep into the dark crevices of oblivion, within her very own personal storage tank.

Chapter 30

Tony shouldered the doorframe watching Julie feverishly sweeping inside the bathtub.

The bathroom looked like a rose petal hurricane had blown through. There were wet rose petals stuck everywhere. Even Barkley who was lying alongside the tub was covered head to tail, resembling more so one of those cheap yellow pinatas one could purchase at a discount store than anything else.

Julie's back was turned to him. He presumed she was totally unaware of his presence as he stood silently in observation. He did not get her at all lately. Her and all these God damn yellow roses. Every time he came home, there were more and more. And when he'd comment she'd come unglued acting like she didn't know they were out there, going off half cocked, like a loose cannon, running outside, hacking the living shit out of them with some big-assed machete. He'd been wanting to ask her just what in the hell was up with that but ... maybe it was just one of those things better off not to be asking about. How on earth she came by a machete was right up there with why she'd chop them to bits and within hours plant them all back and more. *'Best just left be ... Best left be,'* he mused to himself, *at least until he found out where she kept the damn machete!* He watched her awhile longer, re-adjusting his weight leaning into the room as he spoke. "How was the funeral?" he asked. He smiled seeing he had startled her.

Julie jumped knocking her head on the shower bar, his question not registering. She had not realized he was there. He'd been doing that a lot lately, all of a sudden appearing out of nowhere close up behind her making her jump out of her skin. It was starting to alarm her more than she cared to admit. She wondered if this tactic of scaring the living daylights out of her was a new tool he was trying to keep her off kilter. The reason he would do such a thing eluded her, just like a lot of the other things he had been doing lately. Like today, for the life of her she couldn't figure how on earth he'd known when she'd be home and why he would have the forethought to run a candle lined bubble bath for her filled with fresh picked rose petals. This just was not any of the Tony's she knew, the alien, the dick-head or any other one. All this was way too offside.

"So?" he asked.

"So ... What?" She figured there had to be more to this sentence, unless it was another one of his guessing games, where she was supposed to guess the correct answer to something that she couldn't possibly guess it to, because one could never know the full question to begin with. She frowned, trying hard to ignore him and hoping he would go away.

"Well?"

"Well ... What?" There it was again, different but still the same.

"So ... Well?"

She stopped sweeping, turned, and studied him. There was a half-assed grin on his face. She mirrored him back adding the what word yet again. "So ... Well ... What?"

"How was the funeral?"

"How was the what?" she retorted. She could have sworn he had just asked her how the funeral was like she'd just come home from some damn party or something. She furrowed her brow in disgust, opened her mouth to answer, thought better opting instead for the wide-eyed stare hoping he would not just go but go away.

"So?" he asked, again.

No such luck. He was still there. She put down the broom. He really did expect her to answer.

"So ... how was it?"

"It was just great," she said. She studied his eyes. "We had cake, ice-cream, watched a movie and everything," she said. She waited for a glint or a spark from his eyes. There was nothing. They seemed lifeless like he had no soul. *'Who in their right mind asks anyone how a funeral was?'* she thought. She was still staring at those eyes. *'Even aliens must have some sort of funerals.'* She looked away from him.

"That's nice," he replied. He sauntered down the hall towards the stairs.

She could not believe her ears. First; he'd stood behind her for God knows how long, then spoke startling her on purpose, asked how the funeral was, to which she'd given the most ridiculous reply she could muster. Then he'd said *'That's nice,'* disappearing down the stairs whistling like this whole scenario was as normal as homemade peach pie hot out of the oven. The only thing wrong here was all the peaches were carrot tops and it hadn't ever been put in the oven.

She leaned over the railing watching him pluck his keys from the hall stand.

"Oh ...Before I forget," he yelled. "I put the rose you brought home from the funeral in a vase alongside the bed stand for you." He opened the front door gleaming; he hadn't done it, but thought he would take credit anyway. Who was to know? It was not there when he'd come in. He figured one of the boys must have found it, putting it there for her while he had been watching her. They were little shits like that, always upstaging him; thoughtful so she called it.

"You ... You what?" she said. She started gasping in huge breaths. She did not have any goddamn rose with her when she'd come home. She had been in the bedroom several times and there was no rose on any nightstand. What the hell was he talking about?

He opened the front door. The scent of roses filled him. Both sides of the front walkway were laden with rose bushes heavy in bloom. They boughed up and down over the cobble stones in the sweet summer breeze.

Julie flew down the stairs shredding the rose into the kitchen garbage, throwing the vase, water, and all in on top. She glanced out the window. She had assumed Tony was gone, but there he was, bent down, kind of crouching or something part way down the front walkway. It was the looming *'Or something,'* that drew her in for a closer look. She pressed her nose tight up against the windowpane, staring.

Julie's vision fuzzed over in a total over glow of gold. She rubbed her eyes, stopping, squinting back out the glass in disbelief. She fell against the glass pressing with her palms attempting to steady her weight, her legs wobbling like they were made of springs that had just been pinged by a giant finger. Her head spun and swam in circles not allowing her to get past anything but the visualization that roses were very plentiful out there.

She watched Tony squat taking in over-sized deep breaths, stuffing his nose directly into the center of a rose. He drew back plucking it, turning in her direction, tilting his head like his neck was disjointed, fixating upon her. His eyes gleamed like the yellow glow as they slowly darkened down into black pools of tar the yellow ringing the outsides. His nostrils flared in and out, sniffing and snorting, seemingly of their own accord. He fingered the rose idly starting to turn it round and round as he drew out his lips in a hideous smile, stretching it until it looked like it had been hooked onto his ears.

She watched, unable to look away, transfixed and drawn in.

He turned the rose faster and faster twirling it like a top as the flesh of his fingers began to turn ripe red, dripping and spewing blood onto the walk.

Her palms chilled, un-sticking themselves from the glass, sliding leaving two wavy trails of perspiration in their wake. Her head was swimming like it had never had a lesson in its life. She closed her eyes, reopening them slowly. Everything had blurred over like a dense fog had just rolled in. But ... all that was there ... was still there. Tony was there, as he was, crouched, and head bent, tilted off side, fingers dripping and spewing blood, twirling and spinning that single rose.

Without warning, he suddenly opened his mouth, sucking the rose inside, snapping his teeth together dead heading it. He rolled it around in his mouth then spat it out onto the cobblestones.

No more swimming lessons were in need. The water had just swallowed her up making nothing real. Tony was not in the middle of the walk half bent down or something. He was not staring at her with black lifeless pools of tar. He did not just bite the head off a yellow rose that could not possibly be there. She had hacked them all to bits when she got home earlier. Better, yet ... his fingers couldn't be dripping blood which he couldn't possibly be winding his tongue around and licking, smearing the outside of his lips in deep dark red.

Two perspiration trails marked the way much like a wet roadmap to the kitchen floor where Julie had taken up new residence. She lay still, slumped over to one side. By the time she came back around it had been raining for a spell. A soft gentle rain but still enough of a rain to wash away the blood that an hour or so earlier had dotted the cobblestones. She had looked for it too ... But forgot to look for the deadheaded rose. It had been kicked off the walkway and was laying not quite in view. Almost ... But not quite.

Nightmares were funny things. She thought to herself as she pushed herself up from the floor. *They seem to be able to happen anytime ... anywhere one falls asleep. ...* She didn't complete the thought or add even if it is up against your kitchen plate glass window in the middle of the afternoon.

She just put her jacket on and went back outside looking for something that she kept telling herself couldn't possibly be there.

Chapter 31

"You ready?" Tony yelled. He banged the screen door shut.

"Ready?" Julie questioned.

"Yes! ... Ready!" he retorted.

"Ready for what?"

"I left you a message!"

Julie turned the knobs lowering the heat under the pots on the stove. "I didn't get any message," she said. She checked the vegetables.

"Well I left one! ... Come on Jules let's get a move on!"

"Get a move on for where?"

He eyeballed the answering machine. It was flashing away like a stoplight at a railway crossing. He walked over depressing the retrieve button. "Don't you ever check the damn machine?" he asked. He left no room for an answer. "Here's the message you did not get. *This is a follow up for Julie Porter please call Mary from the Royal Bank at 553-76 ...'* Tony zapped off it off paying no regard. "Not that one! ...This!" *'Don't make dinner I have a surprise for you. I will be home early to pick you up. My Mom's going to get the kids at school and take them out for a burger and a movie. Hey ... Wear something sexy for once will you?'* He leaned on the counter smiling like the cat that just ate the canary, pointing from the answering machine to his chest, to her, back to the answering machine.

"I don't want to go out anywhere," she replied.

"For Christ's sake! I have it all arranged!" He drummed the counter-top with his fingers.

"It would have been nice if you'd asked me first," she said, quietly.

"Ask you first? ... When I want to surprise you? ... That makes as much sense as ..." He stopped mid-sentence staring out the kitchen window at the lack of rose bushes again. Thought about it. Almost said it. But didn't. He ran his tongue over his lips. "You always say no when I ask you to go out lately! ... You ... fucking hold grudges forever you know! ... You always say to forgive people their mistakes. Doesn't that fucking include me? The past is gone! Over! Done! Get over it will you?"

Julie glared at him, his words echoing in her head. '*The past is gone? Over? Done? Get over it?*' She repeated silently as hate, anger, and a whole heap of other emotions welled up inside her sticking like a gob of glue mid way up her throat. She did not know just which part of the equation he was so boldly referring to, *Being an out and out asshole? Taking tens of thousands out of her mother's trust account, draining it over the last couple of weeks without telling her, if the bank hadn't called today about a N.S.F. check she still wouldn't have been any the wiser. The four affairs that she knew of. And God only knew whatever else he'd been up to. And here he was saying she held grudges forever, the past was gone, done, get over it. Like all this was so perfectly okay and normal. It happened to everybody, always. Get over it! ... Yeah right! She'd get right on that*! She didn't answer.

He inched himself along the counter reaching up taking the wooden spoon from her hand. "You haven't been out of the house in weeks." He pasted on a smile trying a different approach. "You haven't been out since your ... friend died." He pulled his words omitting goddamn and all the other adjectives he wanted to say. He cleared his throat continuing. "I thought it would be nice to surprise you. Wouldn't it be pleasant for just the two of us to go out?" He gave her a demeaning once over behind her back, sticking his finger in his mouth gagging, rolling his eyes scanning her jeans and tee shirt. He'd felt like adding, '*I see you wore something sexy!*' ... But how in hell would she know that's what he

222

wanted, when she doesn't answer the telephone or pick up the messages? He turned his back walking over to the table pulling out a chair. "Well ... Come on.... Let's go! ... I'm waiting!"

Julie held up her middle fingers, in the screw you pose, as she turned and rested her back against the stove. She had caught his once over with his finger stuck in his mouth out the corner of her eye. She did not bother with a reply; he had been carrying on this whole conversation perfectly fine all by himself. She placed her hands deep into her pockets, if she didn't she was sure they were going to take control of this situation for her and slap him right across the face for all the terrible things he was doing and mouthing behind her back and still doing. She could see him twirling his fingers in circles poking at his temples. The words *'Just the who in hell do you think you are? How dare you!'* Were already at the tip of her tongue and would have popped out, if her mouth had have been open. But it wasn't. She shook her head in disgust looking down at the floor. He had sure become a piece of work and not in a good way.

Tony turned sideways in his chair softening his tone. "Ah ... Come on, let's go out," he said. He held out his hand to her. Handling her with kid gloves seemed to work when all else failed. "Honey ... Let's go out just the two of us ... Hum? ... What do you say?" he asked. He smiled showing his dimples.

He was taking her out whether she wanted to go or not. She damn well had to go. He needed her. Needed her with him to be able to go where he wanted to go tonight. "Come on Baby, humour me this once and go out with me. It will be fun ... You'll see." He stood facing her, putting a finger under her chin and lifting it gently to greet the cute little mask he'd put on with the painted expression of plea mixed with a side order of boyish mischief.

She searched his eyes, so brown, so nothing else, watching and studying, looking for that sudden flash that would tell her the hint of nothing else was something she would all too soon be putting a finger too. He widened his impish grin relishing how tightly he had affixed the mask. She looked away.

"Sweetie ... Come with me," Tony begged. He dropped his hand to the small of her back gently turning her in the direction of the doorway.

Julie sighed a loud sigh on purpose looking up in the air. Going out with him for a surprise was the last thing she wanted to do. If she had a choice between going out with him or being with a bunch of sharks in the open water with a bleeding wound, she would have opted for the sharks.

"Come on Dolly ... We'll have fun ... You'll see," he coaxed further. He gave her a wink.

She caved. She knew he was not about to give this up, it would be midnight, and he would still be at it. She nodded her head yes, moving it slow as alarms rang deep inside. Many ... Many alarms. She turned off dinner, fetched her purse, pulled on her sneakers, and followed him out the front door.

"Where are we going?" She rolled down the car window.

"Well I actually have two surprises for you not one! I lied to you." He chuckled.

Julie skipped the two surprises word sticking herself onto the lie word flypaper. "You lied to me? Really now? You don't lie do you?" she asked, mockingly. She looked up in the sky for the lightning bolt about to hit the car.

"What?" Tony had been fluffing his hair in the rearview mirror and checking his teeth for God knows what, paying total attention to himself.

She clamped her teeth tightly together talking through them barely moving her lips. "I didn't say anything." It was a lie. *'But ... Well,'* she thought. *'Lying a little doesn't matter any. When that there lightning bolt hits the car, it will all be over but the crying.'* So ... *Really now, what would it hurt for her to get her nickels worth?*

"You said something before you said you didn't ... Didn't you?"

"Nope," she said. She tried to keep the corners of her mouth from turning up.

"Are you sure?" he asked. He stuck out his tongue examining it in the mirror.

"Yep!" She was not going to give up what she had said. 'Is he crazy?' she thought. She lost herself to the smile answering in a silent nod.

"Are you sure, you're sure?" Tony questioned.

"Yep." Julie erased her smirk giving him the 'knock it off, I have had about enough of this shit' stare.

"You're not very playful any more, you know."

'I wonder why ... Asshole,' she answered, under her breath. She watched him fluff again in the mirror "Where are we going?" she asked, for the second time.

"Where? ... You're asking me where?" he kidded. He gave her a wink with one eye and then the other.

"I am not in the mood for this dribble! Where is it we are going?"

"Dribble? ... Dribble! ... I just love how you talk Babes."

"Tony! ... Cut the crap! ... Where are we going?" she demanded.

"You'll soon see! ... Close your eyes! ... We're almost there!"

Julie didn't close her eyes. They pulled into an outdoor mall and parked.

"Come on Honey!" He hopped out of the car prancing over to her, opening the door and grabbing onto her hand, tugging with a child's delight.

She trailed with him through the rows of parked cars. As they reached the sidewalk he cupped a hand over her eyes sealing them inside a flesh coloured blind.

"Well?" he asked. His voice pitched turning high and squealy.

"Well? ... What?" She reached up at his hand pulling and prying at it. She did not want to play this game.

"Guess?" he giggled.

"Guess!" she retorted. She let her anger show through. She'd had enough. "Guess what?" she demanded.

He uncovered her eyes. "Look up Honey! ... Look! ... Look up!" he said. He clasped his hands together bouncing himself up and down on his heels.

She slowly looked up taking in all before her. The storefront with the brilliant red painted door. The paper covered windows. The small handwritten 'Opening Soon' sign stuck in the left bottom corner. The lighted sign atop flashing *'WOK-A-WAY CHINESE FOOD AND WINGS.'*

Her lips hadn't even started to form the words ... *'What in hell are we doing here? ... I don't feel like Chinese ... Take me back home ...'* When he jerked the door open yelling surprise. The surprise word echoing in abundance from inside. In front of her stood his entire family, complete with girlfriends, friends, and the mother that was supposed to be picking up the boys from school and taking them out for a burger and movie. The smell of greasy Chinese grill wafted and lodged into her nostrils sticking the little hairs together in a clump.

Julie stood ... stunned, wide-eyed, none if this was soaking in. A feather could have bowled her over.

Tony put his hands on the edges of her shoulders like two training wheels turning her back and forth. "You surprised sweetie?" he whispered.

'Surprised? ... AM I SURPRISED? ... SURPRISED?' she repeated, inside her head. *'Am ... I ... Surprised?'* she asked herself, slower. There wasn't an answer. He was still pivoting her back and forth. Her mouth hinged open. It was as if her hands had been greased and placed on a leather-covered steering wheel on a hot day. She couldn't get a grip on the what or the why? Or ... How to process this information once attaining it. No one had said anything but *'SURPRISE!'*

There was no point made. Why was she supposed to be surprised? She didn't feel in the least bit surprised. Now if one wanted to talk angry, well ... well now that was a different story. She could run with that one.

"Are you surprised baby?" Tony said. He repeated the question cooing like a dove, right into her ear.

Her brow wrinkled, there was that word again. She had been brought to and was standing in what looked like to be a Chinese food take out place. All freshly painted and tiled in red and white. His family, all of it was smiling in two neat little rows in front of her, waiting for her to? ... To? ... To? ... What? ... Be surprised she was there? Surprised they were there? Their stuck on smiling faces were straining and starting to droop at the corners, altering and turning them almost clown-like. All eyes were on her. Hers were on them. It was like a smile fest standoff at a 'Mexican Burrito House'.

Allie stepped forward giving Julie a hug. "So what do you think sweets?" she asked. She gave her a tighter squeeze. "Overwhelming isn't it?" She did not wait for a reply. "When we found out your and TJ's secret dream was to have a restaurant and he'd came across this place and wanted to surprise you. We all chipped in with the work ... Man oh man have we all been working. And hard. The last couple weeks we've all been here almost round the clock," she paused. She felt Julie's body starting to tremble and quake against her. "Doesn't it look great?" Allie grabbed onto her hand swinging it back and forth between them...

The words mixed in together swirled then floated up to the ceiling hanging around the light fixtures before shooting back down and landing on her head. She slowly picked at them, sifting and filtering as the leftovers pivoted and pointed to the 'x marks the spot'. Which, just happened to be right beneath her runners. She let out a loud gasp, exiting the front door and doubling over in half her hands on her knees. All of the air seemed to be sucked from her lungs *'OH*

MY GOOD GOD IN HELL!' she thought. She moved her lips, silently mouthing it in little puffs over and over.

Tony smiled excusing himself, making sure he'd shut the front door tight before erasing the smile. He caught her by the elbow jerking her up straight. "Jules! Fucking hell!" He was standing way to close for comfort. Her face was drawn and pale, like she had been hit full force in the stomach with a slap shot. "This isn't what I expected of you! I thought you'd be happy! What in fuck is wrong with you?"

"Wrong? What is wrong?" she retorted. Her voice cracked and wheezed as she spoke. She felt like she was going to faint. Her knees weakened, wobbled, and then slammed against one another, vibrating back and forth like a broken hand mixer.

"What the fuck is with you?" He swung her around in front of him wrapping his arms about her middle encasing hers.

"Look up ... Look up!" He moved one arm tilting her head back. "What do you think?"

"I ... I don't understand," she said. Her voice wavering and tilting.

"What's not to understand? What the fuck? What don't you get? This is ours! Our restaurant! The one we always wanted! You know!"

"Say ... Say that again? ... Ours?" She suddenly clicked on. This was no dream. It was real life. Right up close and personal like. "Where was I in the ours?" she asked. She rewound, racing her thoughts backward then forward watching the re-runs of the last half-hour.

"This is all ours! ... Mine! ... Yours! ... Ours!" he stated. He jiggled them both up and down.

Julie trolled her eyes back and forth over the flashing sign, there but not there searching her archives for the opening a restaurant together conversation. She paused finding a piece on Jimmy his friend, the friend who had a restaurant. It had gone on from there, but was so badly torn and mashed she could not make any sense of it. As a faded white tee-shirt floated by her face catching and sticking on her eye-lashes, her skin goose-bumped instantaneously chilling her, sending her body into waves of shuddering limb knocking convulsions. She stopped thinking.

Tony pushed her towards the door, opening it. shoving her back inside. His toothy smile gleaming and sparkling like an ad for a new toothpaste against the overhead lights for all a looking to see. "She's so happy and overwhelmed," he said. He gave the skin on her lower back a sharp pinch. "We had a little happy tears crying session out there. All's okay now. She's still a bit speechless though! Women huh?" He grabbed onto her hand before anyone could move in for conversation, giving her a forced tour of the back of the restaurant cooking areas. She towed along blindly dragging her feet which, seemed suddenly like two concrete blocks.

No one noticed how pallid Julie was as they returned to the make shift buffet out front. Tony picked up two paper plates filled with food, handing her one.

"DIG IN," he proclaimed, loudly. "First meals free!" He raised his hand rubbing his fingers together. "Then it's pay time," he laughed.

"Why aren't you eating?" someone asked. Julie had no idea who they were. She had never laid eyes on them before.

"I'm … I'm … I'm not hungry," she replied.

"Eat something for fuck's sake!" Tony said. His demeanour was low and dead calm. Almost, an unnerving dead calm. He pressed his mouth against her left ear. "Eat! … You're embarrassing me in front of my family!"

She gave herself a shake, sidestepped turning, staring him down, mirroring what he'd said. "Eat? … Embarrassing you?" She watched his body stiffen in controlled anger. "Are you out of your mind?" she blurted. *That's a stupid question,'* she thought. *'Of course, he is! And has been for months now!'* She moved toward him. "You did all this? … Didn't tell me? Hid it all till today? Then … Announce it in front of all these

Goddamn people? ... Pretending it is a surprise? ... How could you do this? ... How in hell could you do this to me?"

"YEP!" he belted out. He nodded and grinned.

"You did all this behind my back? ... With what money? ... We don't have money like this," she shot out.

"Knock it off, will you?" he said. He contorted his mouth talking out one side of it.

"Knock it off?" she repeated. Her voice shrilled.

He bent speaking low, a hairs breath from her ear. "Your acting like it's the first time you've heard this. Remember ... I told you a while back I wanted to open my own restaurant?" He sounded smooth like a well-educated con man about to close the deal on a pay up front vacuum cleaner that was mail order. He smiled a tight smile through clenched teeth. "Well ... I did didn't I?" he added.

"Tell me this Mr. Big Wig! ... Just where did you get the money from? ... Oops! ... Sorry! ... Let me rephrase that," she said. She cleared her throat lining her voice box with steel and ice. "Just where did we get the money from?" She poked his chest with her plate snapping it in two. "Tell me that! ... Will you?"

"Not now! ... Don't you fucking dare do this to me in front of my fucking family! ... Or I'll ... I'll ..." Tony all at once silenced, mouth open and posed. He glanced down at the plate smashed into his chest.

She was out the door in a flash pasting her picture under the word expeditious in the dictionary, leaving him to deal with the remnants of his *'Surprise'* dripping from his tee shirt. He replaced her picture with his, excusing himself saying she had accidentally bumped up against him.

She had made it half way through the parking lot before he caught up stepping in front of her. "For fuck's sake! ... You just fucking wreck everything! ... Don't you? ... I thought you'd be fucking surprised! ... Happy! ... We have a fucking restaurant! ... It's our dream!"

Julie stopped walking. "You have a restaurant! ... We don't have a restaurant! ... It's not my damn dream! ... Not at all! ... And Tony..." She poked him hard in the ribs. "You'd damn well better take out a loan tomorrow and put all that money you stole from my mother's bank account back! I know you took it!"

He caught her by the elbows digging his fingers into the hollows on each side. "I didn't steal it!" he said. He jerked her forward, making her come up tight. "If anyone did, honey ... You did! ... I gave the bank a withdrawal slip with your signature on it." He swung his head side to side making a low scoffing tutting sound. "Remember the one you were going to take in a while ago but didn't?" He smiled a sinful smile; her light bulb had not clicked on yet. He lowered his voice to a whisper deciding to offer her up the switch. "The slip you filled in for the extra the nursing home said it was owed?" He bent his free hand into a fist looking at it, polishing his shirt. "The arrears? ... The one in the same they phoned a day or so later about saying, it was an account mix up and it was not needed after all? Well! ... Dear ... You forgot to take it out of the book and destroy it. ... And ... Well ... what's that saying of yours? ... Oh yes! ... Don't look a gift horse in the face! ... All I did was find it, adjust the date, add a few more zeros, and *Voilà*! ... A restaurant!" He stepped back tugging her with him, lodging them between two parked cars. "It would seem to me all things considered here ... You are the one that needs to take that loan out tomorrow! ... Not me!"

Julie could not believe her ears. This was so far from right, wrong did not even fit. She could not be hearing him properly. She couldn't be. All this just ... Just was not possible. It couldn't be. This thing in front of her pretending to be her husband had looked her right smack dab in the eye while admitting to stealing from her mother and pinning it on her. And to make matters worse it was so well done! So well done she had to shake her head to loosen all the shit it had just been shot.

Her mother had given her power of attorney on her accounts years before she had ever met Tony. She had invested them doubling the principle, and had then blended them into one. This had guaranteed that her mom would always have the best of care with all the perks thrown in like the spa treatments, hairdressing, manicures, and the trips she'd come to enjoy once a week.

Tony bent his head, kissing her neck, tracing words on her flesh. "Lighten up ... All's not lost! ... You can work for me and maybe if you're lucky, earn it back over the next ..." He pulled back scrunching his mouth up like he was in deep thought. "Say ... Twenty or thirty years," he chuckled. "Of course there'll be interest on it. You can't pay that, you'll have to work that part off."

Julie felt like frozen mud. Everything seemed thick and out of sorts. She openly stared at him, through him, moving her feet back, waiting for the earth to open and swallow him up. But it didn't. It did not even give off a rumble. The phrase the devil looks after his own crawled out from where ever it comes from and wound itself around his ankles.

He stroked the skin on her arm smiling a hollow smile. She stood before him lifeless, feeling as hollow as that smile. Tony tip-toed her backward towards the car, leaning her up against the passenger door, holding up a finger and telling her to stay he had to get a clean shirt from the restaurant. He might as well of said sit, stay, for all it was worth.

"Come on Hon," he said. He puffed in bursts, out of breath from running across the lot. But he could have walked; the dog had obeyed and was as he had left her. "Let's go on to surprise number two, shall we?" He opened the car door.

Julie got in. Her mind had grown long fuzz. This was out there ... Beyond thought. There was nothing to come up with. And ... If she could? ... Or did? ... What was she to do with it? Her attempt at threatening had been made into something feeble, backfiring into her face, scorching and leaving little burnt bits. If anything, things were worse than ever. Things that should not be going wrong kept on going wrong. That 'Never Say Never' cliché was getting much worn and dogged eared. She was long tired of all the square puzzle pieces and round holes.

She sat silently watching him survey his teeth in the mirror, squeezing saliva in between them and swishing it back and forth in his mouth. The more she watched, the more the feeling came over her of wanting to reach over, grab him by the back of the head and punch his teeth down his throat. She slipped her hands underneath her body; they were itching way too much.

He turned, smiling like they were long lost lovers about to pull into a sleazy motel for an hour at lunchtime.

That did it. "TAKE ME HOME!" Julie blurted. It had no effect. "I WANT TO GO HOME," she shouted. She tugged at his sleeve.

"Nope! ... Not on your life! ... Surprise number two coming up!"

"I've had all the surprises I can handle for one day! ... Take me home! ... Take me home right now!"

"Nope! ... A promise is a promise!"

"You didn't promise! ... Take me home." She cleared her throat. Her voice was breaking into dry, raspy pieces.

"Your right! ... I must have over looked that little detail! .... Thanks for bringing it to my attention!" He reached under the seat pulling out a bottle of wine twisting the top free, offering it. "Want a drink?"

"A drink?" She lowered her eyebrows scowling for all she was worth. "No! I don't want a drink!"

"We both know you like wine! ... Now don't we?" he teased.

"Go to hell!"

"Feisty little thing aren't you?" He padded the seat beside him motioning her to move close.

Her dirty look answered him.

"You sure you don't want some wine? You never know, you might thank me later!" He tipped the bottle back, drinking like it was soda pop.

"I don't want any God damn wine!"

"Okay. Suit yourself. Don't say I didn't ask!" he said. He smacked his lips checking her over. "I thought it might loosen you up some! You do look pretty tense there! ... Here we go! ... Surprise number two!" He pulled into another outdoor plaza and parked.

Her eyes grew gigantic, almost popping like popcorn over an open fire. "NOT ANOTHER RESTAURANT? ... DON'T TELL ME YOU'VE GOT ANOTHER DAMN RESTAURANT! ... NOT TWO OF THEM?" she shrieked. She bounded out of the car looking for another flashing WOK-A-WAY sign.

"Nah! Better! ... MUCH BETTER!" he laughed. He pulled the bottle from between his knees untwisting and throwing away the top. "Don't get me wrong though." He kicked the door shut. "There isn't much better in this world than money. But I think this here surprise just might be!" He grasped her by the hand pulling her into a dark lit, smoke filled bar packed with people with the small sign lodged in the top corner of the window that read 'Private Party.' "Here Hon," he said. He slugged back a gurgle of wine wiping his mouth off on his arm digging in his pocket. "Put my wallet and car keys in your purse so I don't lose them."

She was about to ask why he would lose them, but stopped. She really did not care. She would have liked to lose him though. He was acting bizarre, even for him. She squinted into the noisy darkness coming up with only dense gray moving blobs. People she presumed, she hoped.

"Drink Babes?" He held out the bottle to her.

"No! ... I already said no! ... Where are we?" she asked, rudely. If this was the surprise? Okay she had seen it. It was time to go home. "I want to go home!"

He ignored her. He wasn't about to take her home any time soon. "You'll soon see where we are ..." He went behind her placing his hands on her hips swaying himself back and forth tight up across her butt. He guided her up through the crowd towards the dance floor.

"What in the hell is this place?" she asked. She glanced around. Men and women were standing in clumps about the room openly fondling, rubbing, and kissing one another. "I don't like this! I want to go home," she protested. She looked away.

He cuddled her tight, her back to his front, clasping both her hands in his one, provocatively rubbing himself to and fro on her backside as his free hand took to wandering across her breasts. "I want you to watch this," he whispered. He clamped tightly onto her wrists. "Now ... Shush ... Watch."

Julie felt like a fish netted and held high above the water. She squirmed and tugged as he did things to her, up against her, that should only have been done in their bedroom. He tightened his hold coughing on purpose, whispering a warning to knock it off or else. The or else followed as he slowly started twisting the skin of her wrists round, tightening and pulling as he went. "If you stop fighting me I won't have to hurt you," he said. He bit her ear lobe.

Julie's wrists were burning beyond measure, she felt like she was going to throw-up any second. She stilled.

He smiled, loosening his death grip but not quite enough to let it all together fade. If it faded she would try again to break free, he knew her. She could be stuck in her ways sometimes. Her sense of right and wrong needed altering. So ... he figured a little pain might go a long way.

The announcer interrupted the music calling a '*Ladies only dance! ... Ladies only dance!*' The lights dimmed to black, all at once shooting back on in the form of coloured spotlights, which circled and swirled about the dance floor. The crowed room converged, surrounding the floor like ants to a picnic, packing themselves in tight. Within seconds the dance floor was filled with half dressed women.

All eyes were upon them, like they were privy to some naughty peep show.

Julie almost backed right through him in her attempt to turn and run, forgetting her wrists had been held prisoner.

"Jules," he tutted. "What did I say?" He twisted hard digging in his nails and grinning as she winced and bent her knees. "Quiet down. Stay still and watch."

The pain had spooned itself into a bowl mixing with it her empty stomach and the two surprises, stirring itself up into a neat tidy little ball of toxic waste. She collapsed into Tony, shutting her eyes as the realization he had been to this place before started to worm its way through.

"You going to be a good girl now?" he said.

She felt her head nod, the pain suddenly and miraculously subsiding. Something warm was rubbing her thigh. She blinked her eyes open to a slim hand with painted nails crawling back and forth across her jeans.

The dance floor was loaded to the brim, all scantily clad leaving little if anything to the imagination. Some wore spandex, while others were in flirty little dresses three sizes too small with their ass checks bursting out. The ones with blouses had them undone to their midsections, their bare breasts bobbing and bouncing to the music. Others were in lingerie, bending over with spread legs to the inner crowd giggling from the ooo's, awes, and touches to their shaven bald parts between their legs. The few that chose to wear a bra, stockings and garters showing off six inches of thigh below their tight little skirts seemed tame when compared to the ones dancing and swaying in nothing but 6-inch high heels.

As the music went on most paired up or made threesomes, dancing close, fondling, kissing, seducing one another, drawing in the crowd. The lights dimmed as the tunes turned slow and sexy. She clamped her eyes shut not wanting to see what she knew would happen next. Pain abruptly shot through her body as all her fingers bent backward.

"Open your eyes ...Watch and learn," he whispered.

She gulped swallowing pain induced saliva, opening her eyes. The steamed setting had stirred to a full boil, engulfing the dancing women and the crowd into the witches' fire. The stage was set for sex. As if on cue they moved, sharing one another as a man and woman might, sliding tongues in and out of wanton lipstick covered mouths. There were deep kisses, caresses in perfumed scented necks, fondled breasts, and bare butts. Some had sank to their knees and were planting kisses with long tongue licks between parted legs, working their painted nails in and out of secret places.

Tony was over the top in arousal. He had long ago undone the clasp on his jeans ripping his fly down, protruding his bulk in the open, fondling and rubbing himself. She could feel little spots of wet on the back of her tee shirt where the tip had hit.

Julie could feel him stroking and bouncing against her. She cast her eyes from the dance floor at once wishing she hadn't as she caught glimpses of the people around her. Many were as Tony, some worse. She was sure the couple two over were having a screw from behind, the woman was positioned in a way that made this all but too obvious. And yet ... as if hypnotized all eyes were fixated on the sluts on the dance floor. She had no other term for them as they were most certainly not ladies of any degree.

The announcer broke in giving invitation for all to join in the dancing on the floor.

Tony dragged her forward.

She planted her feet rooting them to the floor. She was not moving from that spot. He tugged on her giving up easy, trailing one of his fingers across some woman's bare breasts.

"What in the hell is this place?" she said. It was more so a question for herself, than anything.

"It's a swingers party?" Tony whispered back. He trailed his tongue down her cheek and neck, jumping it to the neck of the woman alongside them. She watched in horror as he slithered his tongue deep into the woman's mouth.

Julie jerked her hands twisting and squirming, struggling to free herself. He tightened his grasp, turning her, pushing her hands down toward his bobbing stiff hardness, placing them on top of some other woman's hands that were already well on the way to working him over.

"Since you won't let me fool around behind your back anymore ... I figured this was the answer ... I could fool around in front of your face ... Who knows ... Maybe you'll join in."

Julie's lower jaw separated and dropped hanging there speechless. A passerby seized the opportunity to insert his wet middle finger into her mouth twirling and tickling her tongue with it. He smiled whispering *'Did it taste good?'* It was fresh from Sylvia's wet private innards. He whispered again asking her if she would like more. Julie started to gag, her stomach wheeling and heaving. Vomit rose topping off and pooling in the back of her throat, burning as it slid back down. She tried to spit out his finger lifting it with her tongue moving it toward her lips. He rammed it in further pulling it in and out, in and out smirking and laughing telling her he thought she'd love it.

Julie's entire body started to shake and tremble like she had been plunged headfirst through an ice fishing hole into the lake and left to drown. She wished she could die and be done with it. She didn't even care if her body slithered to this floor and got trampled into pulp in the feeding frenzy going on, or if they used her for whatever. It wouldn't matter. She would be dead and gone. She fastened her eyes shut, waiting and hoping. She heard a moan and opened her eyes hoping it was her last breath fading from her body. It wasn't. She was still, very much alive.

She jostled herself a few inches to the left knocking into the pole set off from the dance floor. She moulded the front of her body to it, clinging without arms and hands. They were still pinned behind her, held in a vice grip with a hand that beared the matching ring to hers. She feared her very soul was about to take wing and fly right on out and through one of the ceiling vents, freeing itself from this hell hole, leaving her alone with nothing to go insane with except what was around her. Her knees started to bang, knocking themselves into the pole. They made a melodious pinging sound, almost a tingling as her flesh bashed off the metal time and time again. She claimed the pole realizing it and her had a lot in common, neither one of them belonged in this place.

She bent her head trying not to look at anything but that soon became no longer a safe haven as people crawled by on their hands and knees slurping and licking at their lips, sucking in dripping white body fluids. This reminded her of one of those scenes out of the bible just before the earthquake or tidal wave hits sweeping them all away. She'd never been much for religion but if prayers could bring on something like that ... Well she was going to be up there preaching on that pulpit and right now.

She took a deep breath, almost puking, the smell of spent sex and heavy musk hung in the air like dense fog. This was worse than anything she could have ever imagined. This was a perverted slime balls haven. Everyone was screwing everybody in every way possible. She heard a coo from Tony over her shoulder. She glanced down to find the woman who had been working him earlier on her knees in front of him bobbing her head back and forth. His free hand was tangled in her hair helping her out.

Julie froze, watching him, horrified, unable to look away just about the time his eyes rolled as he jerked and shook, no doubt in a climax. She unthawed and threw up.

She had to get out of there and now wasn't soon enough. Although the woman was gone, his member was still hanging out of his pants. She seized his bliss, putting one foot on his shin bracing herself, pulling at her hands. He dug his nails deep into the back of her hands. She could feel the flesh tearing. He smiled at her all too knowingly, turning her hand over and placing it over a faceless protruding hard on sticking out from the pack of surrounding bodies. She now knew she had arrived at hell on earth,

Tony moved her hand forcefully back and forth with his as they both surrounded the stiff flesh. She smiled wickedly, eyeing the anonymous female hand that was stroking and stiffening Tony. She leaned over whispering she would rather help hold him for this new woman to play with.

"Now you're talking Baby," he gloated. He let go of her hands.

Within seconds, Julie was standing outside in the twilight air, breathing in and out hard deep breaths, clearing her lungs of all the stench from within. She found a puddle swishing her hands in the dirty water; dirt was cleaner than where they had been forced to be. She wiped her hands on her jeans sitting down on the curb, watching the setting sun.

"Need a ride miss?"

She lowered her eyes meeting the taxi driver's warm glance. He was motioning to his empty cab. "*There is a God*" she thought.

"Yes I do," she said. She hopped in the back seat. "How much is it to Thomasview Crescent?"

"I can give you a flat rate fare. You're pretty far from there." The cabby thought for a minute. "How about thirty bucks, no flag?"

"Just a second I'm not sure I have that much." She unclasped her purse. Tony's wallet fell out onto her lap, fat with twenty's. "Done," she said. She grinned, twirling round the car keys in circles on her index finger. She snuggled back into the seat. She was glad she hadn't died.

An hour later she was home hugging the two boys who had not been picked up from school and had not been taken out for a burger and movie. But all was not lost. They had feasted rather well from the turned off dinner on the stove.

Soon all were bathed and ready for bed, herself included. She had locked all the windows and doors, turned off the answering machine and taken the telephone off the hook as an added measure. *'Can't be too safe these days*,' she thought. *'One never knows who might call after dark.'* It was the very least she could do under the circumstances.

She smiled all the way up the staircase. She took her purse and threw in far up and under the bed, not looking where it landed so there would be no hint of a lie later. If she didn't see it land then how in all honesty would she know where it was. *Yep! ... Worked for her!*

Hours later, she stirred in her sleep at Barkley's barking. Both doors,back and front, had been pounded on for quite a time, but she had not bothered herself with it. A while later she had noticed the garage lights on and had not bothered with that either. Though this time she had smiled. He was out there sleeping with the garbage right where he belonged. He'd always told her payback was a bitch. She laughed hard and long. "Yes it is! ... Asshole!" she said. She rolled over going back to sleep.

Chapter 32

Tony sat on the patio slabs facing the house, his back against the garage door. Julie double-checked the dead bolt making sure it was secure. She did not want any no-goods getting into the house while she was walking the dog. Kind of like the one sitting just off there, behind her.

"Come here boy ... Come see dad." Tony reached for Barkley.

"Don't you dare touch him! He could catch something!" Julie retorted. She wrapped and wound his leash around her hand.

"I've got nothing." He slapped his thigh. "Come on boy ...Don't listen to mom."

"Have you bathed?"

"No ... I can't get in the God damn house, now can I?"

"Like I said, don't you dare touch him. He could catch something." Julie smirked starting down the walk.

"Before you head off, where is my wallet?"

She stopped, wiping off her grin as she turned. She had thought he would want in the house most and foremost.

"Well?" he questioned.

"Well? ... What?" she countered. This was going to be good. She'd been waiting all morning for this.

"Jules!"

"What?"

"What the fuck did you do with my wallet?"

"What wallet?" she asked, nonchalantly.

"Don't play games! ... The fucking wallet I gave you last night!"

"Me? ... Play? ... Games?" She pointed to her chest with her index fingers, drawing out the question. "Well I never!" She drew her lips into her mouth giving him a smug glance. "And ... And ... I don't know anything about your wallet." That was the God's honest truth from her point of view. She did not go through it. She didn't know anything about it.

"Fuck! ... Where's the wallet?" He drew his knees up to his chest resting his arms on them.

"I ... Don't ... Know!" she replied. She had always stuck to the theory never lie when the truth will do. She had closed her eyes when she had thrown it under her bed not looking to see where it landed so technically speaking, she really did not know where it was.

"What do you mean, you don't know?"

"Just what I said! ... I don't know!"

"Okay ... Fine ... Whatever! Can I at least have my car keys?"

"Your car keys? Just when did they become only your car keys?"

"Okay fuck! ... Our car keys! ... Can I have our car keys then?"

"Nope."

"What?"

"Nope!"

"Why the hell not?"

"Cause I don't know where they are either." She could tell he was starting to lose it. But ... this was way too much fun.

"Jules?"

"Yes."

"How is it the black cars keys are our car keys, but the white cars keys are your car keys?"

"Cause the white car is mine, always was mine and still is mine. The black one we bought together which makes the keys ours, not yours, ours." She looked down when she spoke; it was getting harder and harder not to crack a smile.

He hung his head. "Fuck! .... Just give me my fucking keys and I will get out of your hair for the day. Okay?"

"We've already been through this. I don't know where they are." She started off down the walk again.

"How in the hell am I supposed to get to work then? Tell me that one will you?" he called after her.

She ignored him.

"JULES! ... STOP PLAYING FUCKING GAMES!" he yelled. He did not move from his spot.

That made her angry. It was the second time he had said not to play games. She marched back kicking him hard right in the shin.

"Ouch! ... What the hell did you do that for? ... That hurt!" He pulled his jeans up looking at and rubbing his leg.

"I am not the game player here. Asshole! And ... You should be grateful a kick in the leg was all you got. If I could find a way to kill you right now and get away with it I would be sitting in that kitchen with plans!"

"Ah come on. So I made a little mistake last night."

"A little mistake?" she said. Her tone picked up a shrill over cast. "A little mistake!" she mocked. She was full to the brim with hostility. Apparently, his definitions of friends and mistakes sure differed from hers.

"Just give me the fucking keys."

She scowled at him. "You don't listen well. Do you?"

"For fuck's sake. How do I get to fucking work with no wallet, no car?"

She bent over top of him. "I guess the same fucking way you got home last night with no wallet, no car," she whispered.

"Honey ... Come on will you?"

"Fuck off and die Tony!" With all her heart, she truly wished he would just take off somewhere and die. She gathered Barkley and went for a long walk.

Chapter 33

She'd had a long week of the whirling answering machine clicking messages, with the too many 'Hey Baby ... You know I love you honey. You are all that really matters to me. It was a mistake, which got a little out of hand. I was drunk and didn't realize what was going on. I did not know the club was like that,' and everything else in the excuse book volumes one, two, and three.

He had offered her up so many God damn yellow roses she had to buy new yard size garbage bags to put them out in on trash day. Why he kept planting them back every time she chopped them down was beyond her. And the very worst part, he still hadn't died yet. She had told him face to face. She had wished he would. She'd hoped he would. She was starting to doubt he ever would. Someone told her once if you wish it, it can come true. So much for the wishful thinking.

Mixed up in the mess was also the restaurant's grand opening. It was to be soon. Too soon, she thought for the world to partake in Tony's Italian Chinese cuisine. With the extra dabs, added dashes, and pinches of 'I just grabbed my jewels in under my track pants, I just dug my underwear out from my ass crack' and 'I just ran my hands through my greasy hair. And for your surprise of surprises, I did not wash my hands.' The thoughts of the goings on down there made her stomach roll over. She'd had to get her own excuse book down off the shelf several times to get out of going. Two days after tomorrow was the slotted day of days. The opening. '*Heaven help us all!*' She thought to herself.

Chapter 34

"You said you would come for a half hour?" Tony said, offering his hand.

Julie put the book into her lap. "Pardon?" She said, smiling, looking innocent on purpose. She knew why he was there. She knew this was opening day. The restaurant was official within the hour. She got up ignoring his outstretched hand, and walked into the kitchen. "Where's the groceries?" She asked. She scanned the bagless countertops.

"Grocerie's?" He repeated.

"Yes ... Groceries." She stated. "You know. The ones you were to bring home for days now?"

"I forgot."

"You forgot? ... Again?"

"Yeah, I forgot again," he said. He tugged on her hand. "We can eat at the restaurant ... Come on honey! ... Let's go!"

"What are the boys going to eat?"

"Come on! ... We're going to be late!"

"What about the boys?" she asked, again.

"I'll send the driver with something special as soon as we get there. Okay?"

She nodded.

"Come on honey ... I don't want to be late."

If late was never, that still would have been too soon for her. She climbed the stairs, entered the bedroom and changed clothes.

"You ready yet?" He had taken the clock from the kitchen wall and was counting down the minutes.

Julie could hear tapping downstairs on the tile floor. His foot no doubt. She glanced at the time; she had bought herself another thirty minutes. She wrote the boys a note and left with him.

The car ride over was non-stop restaurant expansion plans with a Wok-A-Way number two, three, and four. If Tony had stopped talking long enough to take a breath he might have noticed he had been his sole audience.

They pulled into the plaza and parked right smack dab in front of the gigantic red grand opening sign. He folded his arms across his chest admiring it, beaming no doubt from his great accomplishment. He sat for the longest time then jumped out of the car running into the restaurant like he was being chased by a colony of hornets. Moments later he was back at the passenger door chomping on a chicken-ball offering her a bite freshly pulled from his mouth in afterthought.

"Can you get that Jules?" Tony jerked his head gesturing to the ringing telephone behind the counter.

"Hello?"

"Is this Wok-A-Way?"

"Yes ... But ... But," she stammered. She didn't know what to do or say.

"I want to place an order for delivery. I want two orders of fried rice and ..."

"Okay ... I ... I'll ..." Her mouth suddenly stopping working as she watched tens of people burst through the front door, running towards the counter waving coupons. She threw the telephone down; the customer left ordering to a tiled counter top.

"Tony! ... Tony!" she yelled. "I need help!" She scooted through the hinged door into the kitchen.

Tony looked up from the back. He wiped his hands on his apron looking past her, all at once running, dodging carts and the prep areas like he was on a mission to be first in an obstacle course race. "JULES?" he shouted. "WHAT'S GOING ON? ... WHAT THE HELL DO YOU THINK YOU'RE

DOING COMING BACK HERE? ... TAKE THE ORDERS
FOR CHRISTS SAKE!"

"Take the orders?" she said. She was horrified. She had
been under the impression she was coming to see the opening
for a half-hour or so then going back home, not taking orders.

"What do you think I brought you here for? ... The good
of my health? ... Did you think you were just going to stand
around and look good! ... Fat chance! ... You're here to work!
... You're going to earn your keep from now on! ... Now get to
work!" He slapped a pen and order-pad down in front of her.

'What?' she mouthed. The round wide circle of her
mouth matched her eyes. She could not believe her ears.
"What?" she said. Her voice went raspy as she repeated her
shock aloud.

Tony shoved her bodily towards the counter, lunging at
the telephone receiver lying atop the tiles slamming her into
the wall in the process. He listened for a split second turning
in her direction, banging it hard into the receiver. The order
had hung up. "Way to go! ...You just made me lose my first
customer! ... Get with the God Damn program!" He gave her
a glance that would have not only frozen hell over but the
whole goddamn universe.

He turned, pivoting on his heels to the crowd of people,
shaking his head and putting his hands on his hips,
apologizing for his order girl. She was new and apparently
clueless. He would replace her as soon as he could. But bear
with him for now. He told the crowd they were all going to
get a free dish of their choosing to compensate for any
inconvenience caused. He laughed telling them not to worry;
he would take it out of her wages.

He went into overdrive like the 'Energizer Bunny' on
steroids, criss-crossing back and forth across the counter
taking orders, pushing her out of the way seemingly on
purpose, with each pass. He carried the telephone with him
answering the two lines in between counter orders.

Julie backed herself into the wall feeling the customer's disgusted stares. She looked down. She did not want to meet anyone's eyes. She kicked at an order fallen to the floor with the tip of her runner. Tony had been right in a sideways way; she did not know anything about what she was doing. She bit her lip as that thought drifted back and forth, summing up her entire life right now.

Julie stood motionless behind him staying in the corner where he had shoved her on the last pass. She stared at the tiled floor listening to him tell the customers time and time again what a good for nothing useless wad of a person she was, and how he'd made a mistake in hiring her. She broke into tears as the dust settled with the realization she had just been severely chewed out, chastised, and belittled by the boss she did not know she had.

As the first rush ended, Tony pranced his way over to her kicking up his heels in the *'Hey look at me I own a restaurant. Aren't I great? My shit doesn't stink!'* mode.

He placed an arm around her giving a squeeze that hurt her ribcage while the other stuffed his mouth full of breaded foods. "I thought you did this before? Didn't you?" he asked. He sprayed bits and pieces of batter as he spoke.

She had never ever done anything in her life like this and she knew he knew it. She did not honour him with a response.

He rifled through the orders stapling and placing them in a cardboard box. He shuffled through the papers and menus under the top ledge of the order desk. "Where's the plastic bins and order books I asked you to pick up last week? I don't see them anywhere?" He bent checking under the counters. "WHERE THE CHRIST ARE THEY?" he yelled. "I asked you a fucking question? Where in the fuck are they?"

She ran her tongue over her dried lips.

"What the fuck? ... Can't you hear either? ... I asked you to pick up plastic bins last week. You brought them here a day or so ago. Where'd you put them?" He was on his hands and knees pulling everything off onto the floor, his temper rising as fast as an old die-cast thermometer left lying out in the hot summer sun.

She couldn't do this. He was flinging things off the shelves hitting her in the shins. She reached down taping his shoulder. "It must have been one of your so called FRIENDS you asked." She punctuated friends. "Cause you didn't damn well ask me and ... I ... wasn't here a few days ago!"

He gave her a look that crawled out of hell and was taking her back down with it when it returned. He lifted his eyebrows growing them together, scoffing, letting her know the time frame would be sooner than later.

The front door banged open filling up the front with customers. He popped up from behind the counter like a 'Jack in the box,' smiling away. The smile was a stuck on one, but who was to know?

"Here! I'll show you how to do this." He pulled her by the front of her blouse aiming her at the counter. He went behind her pressing a knee hard into the back of hers making double sure she was getting his point.

He gave a quick spiel to each customer in turn of how brand new she was and that he'd only hired her out of the goodness of his heart. He spoke to her like she was a two-year-old, spitting out slow instructions on how to take an order, write it down, read the menu, and answer the telephone. He made her practice relentlessly real and pretend, chastising and critiquing all the while.

The cook yelled from the back needing help, the orders were piling up. Tony trotted off more important than ever, leaving her in sighing relief.

The second rush over, she lent her wit to doodling. She used the backs of the many receipts that had been made examples of.

"Miss?"

Julie looked up from her stick man wearing a tee shirt that said Tony hanging from a noose.

"Miss," the older man repeated, quietly

"Yes?" She marked in a broken neck, then drew a wooden stake in the left middle of the shirt with blood gushing down onto the ground before putting her pen down. She was hoping it was not another helpful hint or complaint. Tony had taped a sign over her head that read... *'Help me learn. Tell me what to do. I am new.'*

"Miss ... If you don't mind me saying?" He leaned close speaking in a whisper.

She picked the pencil back up drawing another hanging tree, making ready to draw the gentleman. "Yes," she said. She looked up from the paper.

"Miss," he said, again. He spoke just loud enough for her to hear. "I can't help but notice how your boss is treating you. Frankly, you do not deserve this. Any of it. And ... If you want me to say something on your behalf I would be more than happy to." He watched tears bubble into Julie's eyes as she slowly shook her head back and forth in a no.

"Miss," he put his hand over hers. "I know I'm probably out of line, but looking at you ...You don't belong in a place like this." He gave her hand a tender squeeze.

She choked. She was at a loss for words at this man's compassion. And the worst part was, he was so very right.

Tony had noticed the silent exchange at the front counter. He flew through the bat wing doors ripping the order from her hand. He read it off aloud turning to Julie. "One order of combo number two with an extra egg roll. You did not mark paid. Is he paid or not?"

Julie coughed on purpose, blowing her nose and hiding the tears.

"PAID OR NOT?" he boomed.

"Paid," she answered. She placed her hand on top of the man's, closing his fingers over the bills he'd had out to pay.

"Are yo ..." The man stopped mid word thinking better of the question. "Thank you kindly," he said.

"No ... Thank ... You," she replied. She smiled.

Time passed quickly, before she knew it, it was eight p.m. She'd made countless attempts to call home only to have Tony rush her, depressing the telephone lever before the call connected, screaming at her in front of the customers for making personal calls when not on a break. When she'd angrily demanded to know when her break was so she could call, he'd puffed out a strained laugh, playing to the crowds on the opposite side of the counter. "Welcome to the world of fast food! Your break is when you're told you're done for the night!"

She chewed off the skin around the edges of her inner bottom lip watching the clock chalk up another forty minutes. She was worried to death about the boys. She was to be home hours ago. There had been no call from them. There was little if any food at home. Tony had not found the time to cook and send a driver out as promised. They weren't paying customers he'd said. She'd had a terrible feeling in the pit of her stomach that something was not quite right.

As the telephone rang he grabbed it, snatching it up and calling out he had gotten it, assuming she was out of earshot. He had slipped. She stood silent behind him.

"How many God Damn times have I told you tonight to quit calling? ... Your mom is busy working ... She'll call when she has time ... Yes ... I've told her you called ... I don't give a God Damn if you're hungry! ... No you can't have something from here! ... This stuff costs money! ... You got money to pay for it? ... I didn't think so! ... The two of you got broken hands? ... Make a peanut butter sandwich ... Yeah right, there's no bread ... There was some a week ago! ... What did you do with it? ... All you do is want! ... Want! ... Want! ... I'm sick of it!" He slammed the receiver down.

Julie clenched her teeth, the tightrope she had been walking back and forth on all evening snapping. "What the hell do you think you're pulling?"

"What you talking about?" he said. He spoke in a make shift sing-songy voice. He turned to her. He bobbed his head back and forth lifting his chin in and out like a broken *'Pez candy'* dispenser.

"JUST WHO IN THE HELL DO YOU THINK YOU ARE, TREATING THEM LIKE THAT? ... I HEARD YOU!" She poked him in the chest. "I HEARD EVERY GODDAMN WORD!" she shouted.

"Shhh! ... Lower your voice."

"LOWER MY VOICE? ... YOU ARE A GODDAMN ASSHOLE! ... I WANT TO GO HOME! ... TAKE ME HOME!"

"Yeah? ... Is that right? ... I'm not ready to take you home yet! ... We could still get busy ... And, as useless as you are, I may need you .... What do you say to that?"

She plucked her purse from under the counter tucking it under her arm. "Take me home!"

He swung at her purse tearing it away, throwing it to the floor. "I'll take you when I'm fucking good and ready! ... You got that?" He booted it across the floor toppling out its contents.

Julie bent down picking up her things. "THAT'S IT! ... I HAVE HAD ENOUGH! ... I'M OUT OF HERE!" She started for the door.

Tony caught her by the arm, swinging her back around. "Honey," he soothed. "Calm down ... Okay?"

She tried to shake him off. He held fast twisting his grip, grinning when her knees did not buckle in pain. Her anger had been sparked, lit, and fired for way to long. Right at that moment, she couldn't have cared less if he had twisted it off and thrown it in the trashcan. That was what he had been saying all night anyway, she was nothing but trash, trailer trash. She was beyond coping with even the simplest of jobs. He kept putting his finger to his head twirling it round in circles sticking out his tongue making yuck-yuck noises in his throat. *'Yeah right,'* she thought. *'I left a good job with the government so I could move to the city, marry you and start a new life.'* When one got right down to it, none of any of it mattered anymore anyway. The story always changed to fit the circumstances. Whether good or bad, right or wrong. And, speaking of right and wrong, he was always right and she was always wrong. Anything, everything that went wrong was her fault. Hell ... Probably world hunger was her fault too.

She stepped into him. "Calm down? ... Honey calm down? ... How dare you talk to the boys like that!" She lifted her chin defiantly, spitting out her words like poison darts sticking them into his face. "How dare you treat me like you have tonight! ... How damn well dare you!" She wrenched her arm free concealing the pain. It felt like she had torn it loose from the socket.

"Whatever are you talking about?" he questioned. He glanced sideways at the customers filing in through the open door. He took the orders sauntering off into the back.

She followed. "You know damn well what I'm talking about! ... Don't you?"

"Now ... Honey ... I ..."

She cut him off. "Don't now honey me ... You're enough to make someone puke!"

"Now ... Now ... Now ... Look, ... I don't know what you thought you heard but whatever it was it's wrong. Next time you try and overhear my telephone calls listen a bit better, cause if you must know I was talking to a customer. We'd run out of wings and didn't put them in their order and they were upset!"

She pushed him hard, the temper in her cup over flowing. "You're a goddamn asshole! That call was not a customer! You are a lying bastard! I'm going home!"

He poked his head out to the customers, holding up a finger signalling he needed a minute.

She seized the opportunity and was out the door.

He chased her down, stepping in front of her blocking her path. "Honey! ... Cut it out, will you?"

"Cut it out, will you?" she repeated. Tears streamed down her face.

"Come on honey? ... You are making a scene! ... Come back inside. I'll take you home around eleven ... Okay?"

"Nope! ... That's far too late! ... I'm leaving now!"

"Just stay a little while longer ... Please honey? ... We'll have something to eat and I'll take you home .... Okay?"

"No!" She stomped over to the car "Forget it! ... I'm out of here! ...Give me the keys?" she demanded.

He was grinning like a Cheshire cat. "So you," he pointed to her with his index fingers, his grin stretching. "You ... Want the car keys, do you? ... My car keys?" He pointed to his chest. "Let me get this right! ... You ... Want ... My ... Car ... Keys?" He scrunched his mouth up making his lips disappear. "Well ... Maybe I don't know where they are!" He made a loathsome tutting noise shaking his head slowly.

"Give me the keys! ... ASSHOLE!"

"You have no sense of humour at all anymore! ... Come to think of it, I do remember telling you this very thing a while back. Do you remember?"

"Look ... ASSHOLE! ... Just give me the Goddamn keys!"

"Hum ... Be like that then." He reached in his pocket grabbing and jingling the keys, tossing them up into the air, catching them and shoving them down the front of his track pants into his underwear. He pulled the waistband out allowing her to see where they had lodged. "You want them? ... Come get them!" He slowly ran his tongue suggestively over his lips.

"Fuck off asshole! ... I'd rather walk!" She stepped onto the sidewalk.

"It's a pretty bad neighbour-hood!" he yelled. "You could get yourself raped!"

She had caught the wise-ass smug tone of his voice. She mulled quickly over what he had said. She abruptly stopped.

His widening know it all grin became toothy as she turned around walking towards him. He grabbed his jewels inside his pants jiggling them up and down holding out the waistband.

She grabbed onto the top edge pulling it back as far as the elastic would allow, letting it go. It snapped hard against his flesh making him double over.

"I'd rather take my chances with the rapist. He probably hasn't as many miles on him as you have!" she said. She slung her purse over her shoulder and walked home.

Chapter 35

Every light in the house was on, even the outdoor Christmas lights. The house might as well had a giant banner posted in front that read *there's two scared to death boys alone in here, come on in and get them.*

"Mom ... Mom ... How come you were so long?" Caleb and Cory wailed in unison. They bolted wrapping their arms about her middle, all three of them toppling sideways into the front door frame.

"We've been phoning and phoning! ...Why wouldn't Tony let us talk to you?" Cory asked.

Caleb picked up without missing a beat where his brother left off. "He kept saying you were too busy! ... He was so mean mom!"

She looked down at the boy bodies with the ruffled hair and smudges of dirt. She could have answered their questions with the same four words. *How come she was so long? Cause Tony's an asshole! ... Why wouldn't he let them talk to her? Cause Tony's an asshole!*

"He's just ... Just ... An asshole," she said. She had finally said it aloud. There was no other way. He truly was an ass, through and through and a big one! She did not mention the free trip to hell and back she had taken while at the restaurant. She kept that one to herself. She knew nothing in life was ever free which worried her. Common sense commanded that one of these times there would be a return ticket.

She rolled up her sleeve rubbing her arm. Tony's bright red fingerprints had started to fade to pink. Never quite enough to leave bruises.

The police had answered all her questions when she'd stopped in a while back. Questions she never thought in her life she would be sitting down in a police station asking. The answers haunted her still. Tony would have to hurt her bad enough to put her in the hospital or better yet, put one of the boys in the hospital. Then and only then would she ... maybe, be able to do something? Of course, they had said ... It would be her word against his and the burden of proof on her. People really do fall down stairs they had pointed out. *This was such a great country she lived in! ... Just great,* she thought. *'Yep, makes* one *want to run right out and do something good for humanity!'* She grinned stretching her lips flush against her teeth, sticking herself onto her last thought; killing Tony might fit that doing something good for humanity bill. He definitely was a waste of breathing air on this planet.

She opened two tins of tomato soup, fried up scrambled eggs and toasted some bread. She had borrowed the bread and eggs off the next door neighbour on her way home. Toasted scrambled egg sandwiches and tomato soup seemed like a king's feast.

The boys were off to their bath, in bed and fast asleep within the hour leaving her alone with her thoughts. She sat at the kitchen table going over the last few months of her life like it was printed out on cue cards. Her mom getting sicker, her lost job, her husband having affairs, her abortion, the loss of her best friend, her marriage failing, the yellow rosebushes. The more she thought, the more she felt like her whole life had been bundled up into a burlap bag, knotted twice, and thrown into an abandoned well. Where there was no ladder, no rope, no light, no one to hear the screams. She felt so alone. So ... Totally alone.

She took Barkley out for his evening walk, glancing over her shoulder as she locked the door. The night seemed different, as if something had come along and injected it with a squirt of invisible ... She couldn't find the word looking over her shoulder again, peering round the corner of the garage. She buttoned her sweater all the way up as chills shot up her spine standing the little hairs on the back of her neck to attention. *'Don't be silly,'* she thought. She'd already had her daily trip to the twilight zone and back. Walking the dog in the dark was a piece of cake.

She made her feet walk to the end of the driveway stopping dead. The usual late nighters' with the glowing solar yard lights, lit televisions, and homey illuminated interiors were not there. Not a one. The street was dark, this night like something unnatural ... Unnatural ... there was the word she had been looking for earlier ... like something unnatural had come along and slithered house to house flipping all the main breakers off. She could feel her heart pounding in her chest, the beats echoing in her throat. She looked back behind her hearing the grass rustle, swearing her house lights had suddenly blinked.

She stepped out onto the blacktop winding Barkley's leash in half, walking briskly down the street. The wind picked up howling and growling through the treetops, snapping, jumping, following behind her, bending and swaying the tops.

Barkley seemed uneasy, stopping, snarling, and barking at low moving shadows that she pretended not to see out of the corner of her eye. Someone had told her long ago there was more to this world than what could be seen ... And the more to this world seemed to be out full force tonight lurking in and around every house, fence, and bush, scurrying under and through the manicured lawns, keeping in time as they walked. She whirled around running Barkley full out for home.

Julie double latched the front and back doors securely. She turned off the outdoor Christmas lights. While in her bath, she had quite a struggle to convince herself to put out the boy's indoor light show. She found them comforting, though some may have described it as over kill. The overheads, closets, halls, table lamps, even the sewing machine light was on, though the latter did indeed make for a good night light.

She climbed the stairs deciding to work from the top to bottom. The uneasy feeling she had encountered outside trailing itself silently after her, hiding away in the corner as she peered down over the top stair railing.

She left checking out the basement until last, now kicking herself for doing so. If she had done it first it would have been long done. Her body shivered breaking out into a chilled sweat as the uneasy feeling stole around the edges of the carpet winding and attaching itself round her left ankle. She dragged her feet over to the door praying aloud that they had forgotten. They had not missed a single light so far. The law of averages dictated they should at least miss one or two. They were kids. Kids always missed stuff. She hoped this was the one or two.

There were two light switches; One at the bottom of the staircase, and the other at the top left hand side of the lower level. The one at the bottom of the stairs bothered her for a reason she could not explain. To turn it off one had to go all the way down, flick the switch, and then come back up in total blackness. The temperature always seemed like it dropped twenty degrees as soon as the switch flicked off, making you feel like your breath was steaming up into your face like a forgotten kettle left on the stove. The stairs had no backs either, and one's toes always seemed to slip through. There had been times she would swear something had brushed her foot. She gave herself a shake trying to fling the goose bumps off.

The last time Tony had asked her to put something in the basement, she'd spent the better part of two hours trying to make herself go down, only to end up kicking it down the stairs and slamming the door shut too quickly for any meaningful interpretation. She had even rationalized going to the laundry mat because the machines were bigger and held more. Besides, going down in the pitch dark to turn on a light only to turn it off to come back up in blackness seemed ludicrous and a bunch of other words she'd cleverly disguised as a cover up for ... fear.

She breathed in and out, trapping breaths inside, her composure flying off and down the hallway, smashing into the doorframe in its haste to depart. She placed her hand on the knob. It vibrated off, slipping back down and gluing itself to her side. She hunched her shoulders, clenching her teeth trying to stop their noisy chattering. She felt like she was five years old, all at once terribly afraid to open the door scared to death of the bogeyman that lived on the other side. She gave herself another shake that refused to work, flopping her arms at her sides like a dead squid caught up in seaweed. Her palms were sweating so profusely they had beaded.

She lifted her toes rocking back and forth onto her heels until it became full-fledged stomps. She scolded herself aloud. 'Don't be so god damn ridiculous! ... It is a stupid basement! ... A stupid basement like all the other homes on the street! ... They aren't old, where there might be a ghost! ... There aren't any graveyards nearby!" She abruptly found herself wishing she had not thought of those two last things as she suffered an uneasy chill courtesy of the thing wound round her ankle. She pulled the top of her housecoat together returning her thoughts to pre-ghost. *There was nothing different or special about her house! ... And, she had that law of averages thing going too! ... The boys probably hadn't turned on these lights.*

She moved her hand towards the knob, hesitated, then grabbed, turned, and pulled, opening the door, and slamming it shut in one fluid motion. '*Okay ... Okay ... That wasn't so bad? ... Was it?'* She silently asked herself exhaling her held breath in one long stream. '*Now ... Let's try it again ... Shall we? ... With open eyes!'* She firmed her feet, planting them hard into the carpet, stopping them in mid turn from beating it the hell out of there. She counted to twenty with one eye open, then to fifteen with the other eye open. She told herself she was not being ludicrous or absurd, repeating the process; after all, there was no one to testify against her as a witness. Besides, if she ever really needed to explain why, which she would not, she'd pretend she knew nothing about it.

She went back to counting, reefing the door open at three. The lights were on. "GOD DAMN IT!" she screeched. Her voice echoed and bounced wall to wall. She peeped over the edge of the landing number crunching the steps. There were thirteen. Thirteen damn stairs and this was Friday. "Friday the thirteen stairs!" .She said under her breath feeling like the carpet was about to open and swallow her whole. "Why in the hell? ... Is there thirteen stairs?" she asked. This was insane. Here she was a full-grown woman standing at the top of thirteen stairs on a Friday night in her pjs and fussy slippers, terrified to go into a basement and shut two measly light switches off. *'Yeah right,'* she thought. She reached, steadying her knocking knees and searching back behind her. *'Get a grip would you?'* she yelled, silently at herself. She wrapped her arms tightly about her middle.

She swallowed hard, gulping in cool air, waiting for the something to happen when you stood alone at the top of thirteen stairs on a Friday night just before mid-night. There was nothing. She waited on the nothing to run its course. There was still nothing. There was not even a night creek or snap.

She stood silent! ... In the light! ... Inside the house! ... A top thirteen stairs! ... With two light switches at the bottom! ... With no excuse in the world as to why!

She strained, listening for something to give her cause to turn and run. There was nothing ... Nothing but good old honest silence.

The kind they say is calming ... But whoever they were, had obviously never stood at the top of her basement steps.

The air rising was cold. Cold enough she was sure steam was coming off her perspiring palms. Her heart seemed to be suddenly skipping beats, echoing itself into an odd rhythm inside her eardrums. Her temples reverberated, denting in and out, in and out like a dying goldfish flipped out of its bowl onto the table beside its food.

She shuffled herself over to the edge of the landing pointing a toe downward, abruptly withdrawing in retreat. She pushed backward using her arms like oars along the wall, slamming the door shut.

She rubbed her hands together warming them, bawling herself out for being such a yellow-jelly-legged-feathered-chicken-shit. She was letting a set of steps into a basement, thirteen mind you, but still, a set of steps beat her. She lifted her chin smiling at the back of the door with the plan to beat all plans! She was not about to be beaten! All she needed to do was jump down every other stair, run full out, bounce off the wall while flicking off the one switch, pivot round, hit the other, and bolt back up the stairs. She clamped her lips together the top one over the bottom, puffing out her cheeks in pre-victory mode ... It sounded good.

She did not go on from there or ask herself why she was still standing looking at the back of the closed basement door half an hour later. She did not want to and really did not have to. Only crazy people did things like that!

She coughed; the sticky ball fear had lumped itself into pasting and burrowed into the flesh of her throat. She stood humbled before the door, her hands stretched out towards the knob, her entire body shaking in sporadic tremors. Terror had made ready too, sneaking out from under her slippers, concealing itself inside the fuzz, laying in wait until the time was right to jump out and yell ... SURPRIZE!

She inched towards the door, forming both her hands onto the knob, crisscrossing them over top of one another using each to steady the other. She slowly, cautiously, creaked open the door, closing her eyes and straining with ears for anything not right. She shuffled across the landing too frightened to open her eyes, using the sides of the walls as a guide. When the wall ran out on the left side she knew it was time to descend. She concentrated heavily as she went, putting one foot out and down and then the other. The chilled air seemed to drop below the freezing point the further she went. The fear ball in her throat had doubled in size, making her wheeze and choke. Saliva shot out from little holes under her tongue, pooling in her mouth. She spat not able to swallow. It flew onto the next step grouping itself into a neat little oil slick, grinning to beat all hell as it saw the bottom of the slipper approaching. She stopped, her foot frozen mid air, the happy face spit slick close but not close enough.

She had lost count. She couldn't remember how many steps were left. She'd have to open her eyes.

"J ... u ... l ... i ... e," came a gravel filled, low whisper.

Her eyes shot open like a hockey puck fired from center. She swiveled the top half of her body round like a disjointed mannequin looking up the stairs behind her. She had thought she'd heard her name. She felt like she was covered with ice. Her legs seemed like they were firing off little shards as they knocked and clacked against one another.

"J ... u ... l ... i ... e," it whispered.

There it was. She heard and knew. There were only three steps to go, but it didn't matter. Her face as if cast in plaster. Her mouth wide, deep crevices angling out from the corners as it cemented retaining the scream position. But there was no scream. There hadn't been time. Her circuits had unplugged just as it was giving rise, struggling to get past that lump within her throat. Probably no doubt, about the same time the room had circled round and round.

She went down, her lifeless body deflating, slithering, skulking down the remaining steps banging her head off each in turn as she went. She came to rest chest down, her head and neck crooked and tilted into the concrete wall, smushing and contorting her face into something not recognizable as human. Her eyes though open had rolled themselves up into her head. Her right hand bloodied and dripping, dangled loosely from her outstretched arm, the other doubled back out of view, bent underneath her.

The menlo-papered box her hand had made contact with was spattered with fresh deep red Polka-dots. It lay cockeyed, half up on its side against the adjacent wall. The impact had burst it open spewing the contents onto the floor. But it had quickly gathered itself up, trailing down into the lower level leaving barely an ashy footprint in its wake.

Julie lay still. There in body but not in mind; Which was a good thing for her. She needed some time out. It would be quite a spell before she'd begin to stir. And when she did, she'd no doubt scream that scream she'd missed out on earlier. And because she'd be so busy doing that she wouldn't notice much else. But just to make sure, the very least it could do for her was turn the lights off. After all, wasn't that what she'd come down here for?

Chapter 36

"Why in hell is the fucking fridge in the middle of the kitchen?" Tony looked from the fridge to the massive water puddle and back, picking up his feet checking the bottoms of his sneakers.

"Cause it stopped working!" Julie snapped. She had been on her hands and knees since early morning mopping up water.

"What do you mean it stopped working? It was working yesterday!" He opened the door peering inside.

"Well it's not working today!" she countered. She motioned him to hand her the pail beside his foot.

"What did you do to it?" He picked up the cord plugging it back into the wall socket, shaking it when nothing happened.

"I didn't do anything to it."

"Then what's wrong with it?" He fiddled with the plug.

"It's not working! ... It's broken," she said. She rolled her eyes out of exasperation. "We need a new one!"

"I don't think so!"

Julie stopped mopping. "What do you mean you don't think so? ... It is summer! ... We cannot go without a fridge!"

"You got money to buy a new one? ... Well? ... Do you?" he asked.

"No ... But ... We do! ... What the hell is with ..."

He cut her off. "No ... We don't have money! ... I might but ... We certainly don't! ... And I'm sure as fuck not buying a fridge with it!"

"What the hell Tony! ... We can't go without a fridge!" This was a new low even for him.

He threw the cord down into the puddle. "You better haul out the cooler from the garage. Cause I ain't buying one!"

"It's summer! ... We need a fridge!" She felt like adding dumb-ass but resisted.

"Whatever!" He picked up the car keys.

"What are you doing?"

"What do you think? I'm going to work! Someone's got to work around here!"

"Work? ... This is Sunday morning!"

"I'm going to the restaurant." He opened the front door whistling to himself.

"But ... What about the fridge?"

He walked back into the kitchen. "Don't you ever listen? ... Or is that pea brain of yours too small? ... I already told you. You aren't getting a new one! .... Deal with it!"

"Deal with it?" Her voice shrilled. "You're a God damn asshole!"

"So, you keep saying. So, you keep saying. Oh by the way, don't be late for work today like you were yesterday!"

She had been five minutes late, walking for over an hour and a half in the pouring rain. He'd said that it was by accident he'd had both sets of car keys on him. She knew better. "It'll be a cold day in hell before I ever set foot back in there again!"

"Yeah ... Yeah ... Yeah," he retorted. "Just don't be late this time!" He slammed the door.

She watched him leave out the window. She flipped the empty key rack with her finger. She would be God damned if she'd ever show her face there again. She looked at the fridge; the puddle was bigger than ever. She opened the kitchen cupboards taking inventory. They were so close to bare she could not figure out why they did not echo. He had said he didn't eat at home anymore so he wasn't buying any groceries. He had relented slightly telling her he'd give her a bit when they'd had the last knock down drag out argument when she'd tried to sneak food home for the boys. That was three weeks back and she was still waiting. She needed money. Her own money. The light bulb went on. Most people paid for their orders in cash.

She picked up the phone and dialled the restaurant. "I'll be in at 4:00."

Chapter 37

"Don't drive so fast! ... YOU'RE SCARING ME!" Julie yelled.

He did not acknowledge her.

"TONY FOR GOD'S SAKE!" she screamed. "SLOW! ... DOWN!"

"Fuck off! ... Just fuck right off! ... I'm fucking sick of you," he snarled.

Julie came off the seat pitching into him like a rag doll as the car rounded a corner running the red light.

"TONY! ... PLEASE!" She snatched his arm pulling his hand from the steering wheel.

"CUT IT FUCKING OUT!" He knocked her hand off sending her flying into the door side panel elbow first. "I FUCKING SAID I WAS FUCKING TAKING YOU HOME! ... AND I'M TAKING YOU FUCKING HOME!"

"For God's sake!" she pleaded. Tears stampeding down her face into her mouth. "Slow down!" She rubbed at the bright red goose egg rising on her elbow. "Right in the middle of the rush you decide I'm going home? ... Why? ... Tell me why?" She pressed her back tight into the seat; everything outside the window had shape shifted into two long multi-coloured streamers.

"WHY? ... CAUSE I'M FUCKING SICK OF YOU AND ALL YOUR FUCKING PISSY ASSED FUCKING WHINING!"

"What whining?" she asked.

"You fucking bitch me out in front of my customers! You fucking tell everybody you walked in! You make a big fucking deal out of it!" He let go of the steering wheel holding up his fingers making invisible quote marks in the air. "You think you're so fucking special! I am not having that kind of scene again in my restaurant! No way! Not by somebody the likes of you!"

"What the hell are you talking about?" She had no idea where all this was coming from or why. If she didn't know better she'd swear he'd tripped and fallen down a dark set of cellar stairs, knocking his head off, picking up someone else's, sticking it on backwards.

"You fucking know what in hell I'm fucking talking about!"

"No I don't! ... Scene? ... What scene? ... All I said was I did not do badly time-wise walking in. I didn't make any deal of it. What in hell?"

"WHATEVER BITCH!" he yelled. His voice boomed and seemed to reverberate throughout the car. "WE BOTH KNOW WHAT YOU FUCKING MEANT!"

"What on earth is wrong with you? You yell at me in front of everybody for being two minutes late. Two damn lousy minutes! When I had to walk ... Cause, you accidentally took both sets of keys again! I am not some stupid employee in case you have forgotten! ... All I said wa ..."

He cut her off. "JUST SHUT THE FUCK UP! ... YOU DON"T KNOW HOW FUCKING LUCKY YOU FUCKING ARE RIGHT NOW! ... IF I WERE FUCKING YOU, I'D FUCKING SHUT THE FUCK UP WHILE YOUR STILL FUCKING AHEAD!" He gave her a look of sheer unadulterated evil. His eyes sucked in and out of their sockets like they were breathing all on their own. He made slow deliberate wringing gesture with his hands, cocking his head sideways dangling his tongue out the right side of his mouth, pointing to her neck.

She did not say another word.

He pulled into the driveway, the rear tires barely on the road. Julie snapped the door handle back and forth. It wouldn't open.

"You might as well give it up!" Tony said. He spoke quietly like he was tiptoeing through a graveyard at night without a flashlight. "It's locked."

She looked upon his face. He was smiling. Smiling in a way that made make one's skin crawl. And, those eyes, those big black round dead eyes. He resembled one of those sci-fi beings in a horror movie that pop out from behind your back, bite your head off, and slurp your insides out through the opening.

Every bit of air seemed to be sucked from the car. She knocked her chest with her fists not able to breathe. She turned, violently tugging on the door handle wanting out of that car more than she'd ever wanted anything in her life.

"I ... Want ... To ... Talk ... To ... You," he said. His tone was a hairs breath above a whisper.

His tone hit a nerve deep down inside. Her body trembled and shook, registering a four pointer on the Richter scale. She gulped, swallowing down her folded tongue, coughing it back up, gagging. She moved her hands from the door handle, knotting them together in her lap. The cold sweat of her palms leaving wide dark ring marks.

He turned the key shutting off the car, wrapping his right arm in behind the back of her seat. He drummed the headrest with his fingertips, stopping, starting, stopping, and starting.

Her alarms went off, ringing in her ears deafening her as terror froze her solid with the realization there was nowhere in that car out of reach. Her heart shifted into overdrive, pounding and thumping, blowing a piston. It rattled and clanged, making hollow whooshing noises in her chest. Time seemed to stand still.

He moved close. Too close. "Tell me," he began. He smacked his lips making a popping noise. "Tell me ...Why ... You found it," he paused. He did a make shift drum roll on her headrest. "Necessary ... To have a talk ... With my cousin? ... Hum?" He gave the headrest a belt whipping her head forward.

"What ... what ... are ... are ... you talking about?" Her voice shook and rippled up and down like a roller coaster out of control.

Bernie, his cousin, had given her a ride home a few days back. She had been grateful for his kindness, but had kept it to herself. The only way he could have known was if Bernie had mentioned it or someone had seen them. She suspected the latter. Tony had become quite the experienced angler. He seemed to be able to get anything out of anyone, even things that were not there. And yes Bernie and her had talked. But it had not been so much her as him.

Bernie confessed he had lied to Tony telling him something important had come up and he needed to leave. He had said he owed it to her.

He told her many things. Like his feelings of loathing and disgust at witnessing Tony pushing her across the room, throwing her purse at her, opening the cash drawer smacking it into her stomach, stepping on her toes and stomping at her heels making them bleed. He had seen the dried blood stains on her socks many a time. He'd said he had already told Tony off once about it and was advised to mind his own business. He suggested she leave her purse at home. Each and every time she left the front counter Tony ransacked it.

He also told her he'd constantly caught Tony flirting with female customers taking the deliveries himself, re-appearing hours later saying he'd dropped by the house to see if she'd needed anything and was okay. Bernie had asked her if Tony ever did. She had shaken her head no.

Bernie also said Tony had out of control rampages lately before closing. Going over all the bills with a fine-tooth comb, yelling and screaming that he'd put out more than double the orders than were in the delivery trays. He had accused them of pocketing the money. Tony's brother had quit on the spot.

He too was quitting. Doing a favour for family was one thing, but this favour had turned into a nightmare from hell.

He had shared that this coming weekend was going to be his last and he had seriously been thinking of dragging Tony round back into the alley and punching his lights out for starters. He'd also conveyed that if he was her, he would be making plans to get out of there and fast. He had asked her to promise to start and pay herself. He knew Tony was never going to give her one red cent for being there.

She had said she would, but was already way ahead of him. She had been paying herself for quite some time. Not herself so much as her barefoot inside her sock.

"I'm waiting," he announced. He ran his fingers over the back of her neck, stretching his hand lightly around it as if sizing it up.

"Waiting for what?" she asked. Her voice cracked and popped. Her mouth and throat abruptly drier than a desert riverbed in the heat of summer. She untwisted her hands shoving them deep under her thighs. Her pants were so wet she could have over-flowed that dry riverbed's banks herself just by ringing them out.

"JULES!" he screeched. He sucker-punched the back of her headrest pitching her forward into the dash, splitting her forehead open.

He was gunning her down with the safety off. She watched him out the corner of her eye. He was twitching like a murderer watching his prey from outside an open window. He did not resemble anything that was human. She could feel his evil. Feel it inside of him where his soul used to be. She closed her eyes.

He cupped his mouth over her ear. "I FUCKING WANT A FUCKING ANSWER!" he shouted.

She could not remember what she was supposed to be answering. Fear had long since switched to terror circling and vibrating up and down, side to side, shaking the living daylights out of her. She knew her neck was in the noose. She hung her head silently reciting *The Lord's Prayer.*

He grabbed her by the hair jerking her head up. "FUCKING ANSWER ME ... YOU GOD DAMN FUCKING BITCH!"

Her tongue curled, flipping sideways like a thin piece of cardboard. She ceased, her generator kicking on the autopilot just in the nick of time. She had forgotten how to breathe

He shook his head side to side. "I'VE FUCKING HAD ENOUGH OF YOUR FUCKING SHIT FOR ONE FUCKING DAY!" He pulled his hand from her hair ripping it out by the roots. He unlocked the car and got out.

Before her interior auto-dialler could alert her, he was there. Right there. Breathing in her face. Taking in all her air. Leaving her nothing.

He grabbed her by the shoulder sinking his fingernails into her flesh and dragging her from the car. He bent her arms up behind her back twisting them one over top of the other until her legs wobbled in circles like loose rubber bands. Half way down the walk she folded like a spent deck of cards, collapsing onto her knees. He kept on pulling like she was an old sack of potatoes bumping and banging her off the patio slabs.

He turned the lock in the front door, opening it with his shoulder, never once loosening his grip. He kicked the door closed behind them hauling her up to a stand. He grinned, stretching it tight and wide over top of his teeth, growing invisible horns each side of his temples. Here they were together safe and sound, tucked away behind closed doors. He laughed non-stop, dragging her through the house into the living room.

"OKAY BITCH!" he screamed. He bent into her face. The spewed out little oval spit marks landing on her forehead, re-wetting the dried blood and turning it into nice, pretty, pink Polka-dots. "YOU GOT ONE FUCKING LAST FUCKING CHANCE! ... FUCKING ANSWER ME!"

Her body swayed limply back and forth, dangling from twisted bent up arms she could not feel anymore. The pink droplets scooted down her forehead, pinging themselves off onto her cheeks, splatting and smearing, giving her ghost white complexion a hint of color. The skin on her knees was mashed and mangled against her pants. Slivers of fresh sushi-like flesh, burnt and bloodied, poked through slits where the pavement had worn through the fibers.

He looked down at her making a throaty gurgle, spatting out a gooey lump of thick mucus. It landed on target matting and gluing itself into her hair.

A warm wet yellow stream ran down the inside of her thigh, the leftovers drizzling and soaking into the carpeting.

"OKAY CUNT! ... THAT FUCKING WAS YOUR LAST FUCKING CHANCE! ... I FUCKING TOLD YOU! ... I AM THE FUCKING BOSS! ... THE SOONER YOU FUCKING LEARN THIS! ... THE EASIER YOUR FUCKING LIFE WILL FUCKING BECOME! ... I THINK YOU FUCKING NEED SOME FUCKING TIME TO THINK ABOUT THIS! ... DON'T YOU?" He pitched his voice answering aloud for her. "Yes, Tony I think I do need some time ... I'M GLAD YOU AGREE!" He let go of her arms abruptly dropping her onto the floor.

She made a hollow thunk like a frozen pea falling into an empty kitchen sink.

He bent over entangling his one hand in her hair, opening the door to the basement with the other. He grinned showing his dimples, heaving her into the total blackness.

He did not look to see where she landed. He could not have cared less if she'd went down the stairs backward, breaking her neck. He slammed the door shut, locking it, propping up one of the kitchen chairs on an angle under the knob.

She banged off the sidewall tumbling in a heap, almost going over the edge of the landing. She lie still, eyes wide, breathing in harsh cold breaths of air that stung her lungs. It was quite a time until she scrambled to her feet throwing herself forward, hitting the back of the door screaming like a wounded animal to be let out. She screamed and pounded with her fists for what seemed like an eternity. Her voice grew hoarser and hoarser about the same time as her fists fused her fingers all together in a throbbing aching lump. She leaned against the door scratching at it with her nails whimpering, begging, and promising she would be a good girl from now on. She was sorry for all the things she had done. She would never do it again. She slunk against the wall. The bright red streaks on the back of the door running like a finger painting gone all wrong, the darkness swallowing up the source. Darkness was good at keeping secrets.

Tony had sauntered off as soon as he'd put the chair to the door; her screams dulling the further he went. He chuckled whole-heartily locking the front door behind him, hearing nothing but silence. He knew the screams were still alive and well behind that door. It was much too soon for them to have stopped. He made a mental note for future. The house really did have good insulation after all.

He turned to his favourite station turning the tunes up loud and rolling down the window, tapping to the beat as he drove back to the restaurant. *Julie was ... How do you say it? ... Out of control?* He nodded in agreement with his thoughts. She needed a good lesson. He knew she hated that basement, which was why he thought it would be as good a spot as any. Maybe the best. Obedience after all was not taught in a day. He needed to do some teaching and she needed to do some learning. And ... He was going to see to it one way or another. If she had not done some learning by the time he got home, he would leave her there over night. And if over night was not long enough, there was always the next day and the next. That was a good solid chair under the knob. He took a sip of his pop thinking he would let her out sometime soon. When he decided soon was, that is. He laughed so hard tears formed in the corners of his eyes; he did really like this new sport. He wished he had thought of it a long time ago.

Julie slithered down the wall to the floor. She pulled up her knees resting her head; they stung and ached like hell on fire. If this was it for her and what God had mapped out ... so be it. She turned her head sideways squinting into the pitch black. This was so far removed from God and anything holy, it was not even right. It was cold, damp, dark, and something else she could not quite find words for.

She could not see this as her fitting end. She still had children to raise, a dog to feed. She bit at her lip peering round in the blackness. She shook her head back and forth. This place was not a fitting end for anything alive and breathing, man or beast. If this was out of her control and her destiny then ... God damn it, she was going to go out in a blaze of glory. She was going to fight that frigging bastard every step of the way. If it was a fight he wanted, it was a fight he was going to get. Even if ... it was to the death.

She turned hopping along the carpet on her butt; hand outstretched swiping back and forth for the door. Her fingers all at once smashed into it, splaying and slipping sideways in cold slimy goo. The darkness was still keeping its secret.

"J ... U ... L ... I ... E," a gravel filled voice called.

Her breath froze mid exhale leaving a microscopic stream of icicles that hung about the air. Her heart jittered and bounced stalling, pulling out its choke. It rolled over sputtering, re-firing.

Somewhere far deep below the surface of her being, she knew.

"J ... U ... L ... I ... E," it called again.

Julie's mouth formed a perfect 'O' as she opened it and screamed and screamed and screamed. The tribal rhythm already flapping and beating its wings inside her head. Her nostrils flared sucking in a sickening sweet aroma that clung in the back of her throat. She scrambled onto her hands and knees. She didn't need rocket science to tell her, if she was locked in the basement in the pitch dark then ...

She batted for the door with her hands. They missed, connecting with something colder than death. She wrapped her fingers round it frantically pulling herself to a stand. It let loose, thumping down on top of her and taking her back down. She kicked, struggling violently side-to-side, trying to free herself from underneath. It was like a benumbed weight, lifeless, yet duty bound as it stretched across, holding her against her will, for something ... Something by far worse than a Tony could ever be dead or alive. She pushed and jerked her body sideways and up and down freeing herself from it. She righted herself moving her foot sideways, the other tucking itself in underneath, catching and tripping her, sending her back to where she'd started.

"J ... u ... l ... i ... e ... s ... o ... m ... e ... t ... h ... i ... n ... g ... w... r ... o ... n ... g?" it whispered.

Something shuffled across the carpet, escalating the horrid stench.

She became animal like, tearing, striking, kicking, trying to get out from under the heavy thing in the dark. She slid her hands over the length of it. It had a huge clump of something on one end. She right sided it, stabbing the small end into the carpet, swinging herself to a stand.

The bottom stair creaked.

She threw herself up against the door using her body as a battering ram, her mouth screaming silent screams which echoed inside her head jumping ear to ear. She pounded, bouncing her body off the door again and again. The stairs heaving and creaking below as ... Something ... Slowly ... Steadily ... Came.

She backed to the edge of the landing, springing her body forward, tripping, almost going down again. She bent down, feverishly running her hands back and forth over it feeling it one end to the other. She gave off a toothy grin, stretching and stapling her mind in between the outer corners, laughing aloud, reefing the sledgehammer from the floor.

She thrust it at the door, spacing her legs wide apart and swinging it for all she was worth. Time and time again, she reefed, splintering and shattering the wood, turning it into whirling airborne rockets that landed themselves half way across the living room floor. She broke through and was gone, leaving the top stair to echo its heaving creak back onto itself.

Julie ran wildly, zigzagging for the front door, winging the sledgehammer at the garage, fleeing down the front walk. Her heart had jumped into her throat and was beating in drum like rhythms making her breath puff out in wheezes and gasps.

She hit the grass without slowing, slipping and landing face first in yellow rose bushes. She found her voice screaming over and over, pushed herself up, her eyeballs taking involuntary inventory. There were yellow rose bushes everywhere, even up through the cracks in the paved drive.

Her sanity thread snapped. The corners of her mouth turning up in half moons as she wailed hysterically, laughing, snorting, and snickering.

She humped her back placing her hands on the ground four footing wild animal like into the garage, returning moments later uttering an Indian war cry and wielding a machete. She sliced back and forth through the roses like the queen of hearts offing their heads. She hacked, smashed, and obliterated until there was nothing, running off to disappear and reappear with two five-gallon containers of gasoline. She popped the tops shaking and spraying gasoline over the lawn and drive. She threw the empty cans into the heaps of yellow and brown slaughterings, igniting pack after pack of matches until the whoosh bellowed out turning her front yard into a towering inferno.

She stepped into the fire, standing silent, smiling the smile of total complete insanity. Relishing in it. Opening her arms to allow it to filter through her, burying it deep into her core so no one--not even a nightmare--could ever retrieve it.

She stepped back picking up the machete, springing down the street towards the park wielding it over her head, disappearing into the night and becoming part of it.

Chapter 38

"What do you mean, I don't qualify?" Julie asked the woman across the desk in the blue dress.

"Mrs. Porter you do not meet the criteria," the woman said.

"This doesn't make any sense! ... Your telling me, I do not qualify for assistance because I have not left and found a place. But how can I leave and find a place without any money?"

"I'm sorry Mrs. Porter. I don't make the rules," the woman said. She closed the file with Julie's name on the top edge.

"This is bullshit!"

"Mrs. Porter, like I said as soon as you're in your new place come back in."

"So what your really saying is I'm trapped! ... I can't get out without money and you won't give me any till I'm out."

"There is the police. Have you tried? ... You could file a complaint and ..."

Julie cut her off "Yeah right! ... They are about as useless as you are!"

"There are women's shelters."

"They are all full and even if they weren't, they won't let me bring my dog!" Julie snapped back.

"I don't know what more I can tell you. Maybe, some of the pamphlets from the front kiosk could help you!"

"A God Damn pamphlet isn't going to help me much, except to soak up some of the blood when he kills me. I'll get right on that!" Julie said sarcastically.

"I was only trying to help," the woman said. She looked down scanning the paperwork for her next interview.

"You've helped enough! Thanks for nothing!" She left the building muttering under her breath. That sure wasn't what they'd told her on the phone. She'd waited in line all morning for this! This bullshit! If she had known all this was going to be nothing but a huge waste of her time, she could have wasted it somewhere else.

She got in the car dropping her head down on the steering wheel. She was royally screwed. She couldn't stay in her life; she couldn't leave it, either. She banged her head on and off the wheel.

A loud sharp blast rocketed through the air.

"Hey!" the man yelled from his car. He rolled his window all the way down pressing on his horn again. "You going to stay in that spot all damn day or what?"

She studied him using the rear view mirror. He was stopped, not even a foot off her bumper, arms a flapping out his open window.

He yelled again pointing to his watch.

Other cars were slowly circling the overcrowded lot like vultures searching for a meal, which seemed to be sending the man over the top. She could see his mouth opening and closing no doubt cussing her. She figured the next thing he would be doing was urinating on all the corners marking the spot for his.

She turned the key starting the car, edging backwards out of the parking spot pretending not to notice the double shot of middle fingers he was giving her.

She stopped at a corner store and bought a bouquet of fresh flowers deciding to stop by the graveyard on the way home. It had been too long. She so missed her friend. Her life had not been the same since Sherry's death. There was an empty void inside her. She had always been told, when someone dies you never lose them, that they are always within your heart and soul, you carry a piece of them with you where ever you go. *'What a load of crap,'* she thought. When someone dies, they just are not there anymore, plain and simple!

She drove up and down the rows looking for the marker abruptly slamming on the brakes, her eyes almost bailing from their sockets.

"NO! ... NO!" she screamed. "NO! ... OH GOD! ... NO!" Her mouth hung open. There was glistening gold everywhere, even the head marker. The entire grave was covered in yellow rose bushes.

She got out of the car, slamming the door behind her. She rubbed her eyes furiously. They were there, the full blooms gently bobbing in the light breeze. She turned round, facing the car, then back. They were still there. She could smell them. Disbelief, fright, and rage tumbled and pounded up inside her like wet sweaters in a dryer entangling and rolling into a tight ball.

She tromped through the grass, stopping at the grave. "GOD DAMN YOU ALL TO HELL! ... YOU BASTARD!" she screamed, at the top of her lungs. "HOW DARE YOU! ... HOW DARE YOU DO THIS!" She stomped back and forth, back and forth across the length of the grave. "YOU BASTARD! ... YOU ASSHOLE! ... I HATE YOU! ... I HATE YOU! ... I HATE YOU!" She ran in tight circles atop the grave, kicking the bushes, snapping the rose heads. She dropped to her knees wailing and screaming. "YOU THINK YOU'RE SO SMART DON'T YOU? ... DON'T YOU?" She smashed one of the bushes with her fist. "WELL I GOT NEWS FOR YOU! ... YOU'RE NOT AS SMART AS YOU THINK!" she laughed hysterically. She pointed at her chest. "I'M WINNING THIS TIME! ... NOT YOU! ... ME! ... YOU GOT THAT?" she yelled, into the air. "TAKE THIS YOU BASTARD!" She stood back up booting the bushes. "AND THIS! ... AND THIS!"

She smashed at the roses over and over, shredding them. She pulled them out of the ground throwing the spoils up in the air and across graves. She pawed like a dog, rooting, tearing out clumps of earth, reefing the bushes out by the roots. She wiped her bloodied hands on her tee shirt taking in deep breaths scanning the destruction. There couldn't be a single victor standing, not on her watch.

She formed her mouth into a perfect toothy chamber uttering low in-human growls before screaming out another chorus of *'I HATE YOU!'*

She smashed and ground the bushes into the earth like something wickedly possessed at the stroke of mid-night.

The passer by on the sidewalk had long since stopped, her foot hanging mid air poised for the next step. She stared wide-eyed her brow furrowed with disbelief and horror. She stood motionless, as if frozen, mouth open, arm pointing. Her wide eyes as wild as Julie's ... But for very different reasons.

Julie did not notice her audience.

The woman forced her jaw shut with her hand. She cleared her throat, finding her voice. "YOU THERE," she screeched. "STOP THAT! ... STOP THAT RIGHT NOW!" The woman ran over to the iron fence grabbing onto the rails. "THERE'S LAWS TO PROTECT THE DEAD YOU KNOW!"

Julie lifted her head tossing a root back behind her gunning the woman. "NOT IF THEY COME BACK ALIVE, THERE'S NOT," she retorted. She ran her hand across her brow wiping off the rivers of sweat that had been running into her eyes. She left a wide smearing of blood, dirt, grass, and yellow petals across her forehead.

The woman backed from the fence her knees going into sudden convulsions.

Julie looked like the tried and true definition of total out and out insanity.

"I'M ... I'M ... CALLING THE POLICE!" the woman screamed.

Julie offered her a grin that was not at all nice, returning her attention to the bushes.

"I ... I ... MEAN IT!" the woman stammered. She clutched her handbag to her chest unzipping it. "I'M ... I'M ... CALL ... CALLING RIGHT NOW!" She waved her cell phone in the air. "I'M CALLING!"

Julie paid her no mind, lost in the frenzy of unearthing, deep into the realms that defied any logic, other than that which governed total annihilation. "YOU BASTARD! ... YOU GOD DAMN BASTARD!" she screamed. She lifted her head skyward. "I HATE YOU! ... I HATE YOU!"

The woman dialled the police. "Hello? ... Hello? ... Help! ... Help!" she shouted, into the receiver. "There's a crazy woman in the cemetery desecrating a grave! ... No. ... Yes. ... No, I am on the other side of the fence. ... Yes. ... Yes. ... Forest Lawn Cemetery. ... No I don't know which one, but it had beautiful yellow roses on it. ... Yes. ... Yes, please hurry!" The woman threw her phone back in her purse, running back to the fence. "THE POLICE ARE GOING TO BE HERE ANY MINUTE!" she shouted, at Julie's back.

Julie turned squinting at the woman.

The woman kept looking over her shoulder. There was a shrill beep of a siren as a police car pulled a U-turn in the middle of the intersection out front.

Julie had heard. She ran for the car jamming it into reverse backing full out, stopping atop Sherry's grave. She gassed it spinning the tires rocking the car back and forth shoving it from reverse to first and back sending the remainder of the rose bushes airborne out through the fence pelting the woman head to foot with the debris.

Julie watched in the side-view mirror laughing hysterically, giving the tires one last spin. "TAKE THAT YOU BASTARD! ... TAKE THAT!" she shrieked. She tore off down between the graves her rear-view glinting and sparkling from flashing red lights. She crossed the graves at the bottom of the row sending the car propelling through the air. It hit the roadway ripping the right side of the front bumper free.

She sped out the back gate leaving a wake of metal sparks as the police flew through the front. She ditched the car at the mall, parking it way at the back between the delivery trucks. She tore the bumper free throwing it into the ditch, walking off home as lackadaisically as if she'd just been out for a midday stroll.

The house seemed off, almost ominous as she stepped in. Shivers ran up and down her spine. She hunched her shoulders walking into the kitchen, washing off some of the dirt and debris without giving thought to turning on the tap and none the wiser as to why it wasn't coming off. She walked through the dining room into the living room, her body quivering and shaking in the brilliant sunshine. She flicked on all the lights opening the patio door for Barkley to go out into the yard, closing it just before he did.

He woofed loudly, calling her attention. She gave him a quizzical look, and then smiled re-opening the door. "You were just out! ... You want out again?" She patted his head on his way through, shutting the door on her sneaker, catching it and ripping it off, walking away with one sneakered foot and one socked foot.

A stab of cold air hit her square in the middle of her back. She spun round. The basement door was ajar. She raised her arm in slow motion pointing her index finger towards it, staring bug-eyed transfixed, unable to look away as it gave off a slight creek moving a hair's breath. It was like looking at a terrible crash, were everyone was strewn all over the road dead. You didn't want to look--but just had to. And then could not look away.

Her feet rooted themselves to the carpet, her toes curling and anchoring as the door slowly started to open.

Julie took off running wildly through the house heading for the staircase. She didn't notice the dense fog that hung about her feet almost obliterating them from sight. Too bad for her. Maybe if she had the screams leaving her lips would have been more silent in nature.

"N ... o ... w ... n ... o ... w, ... d ... o ... n ... ' ... t ...b ... e ... l ... i ... k ... e ... t ... h ... a ...t!" it said, in a long slow drawl. It popped the door all the way open.

Julie climbed the staircase three at a time. She ran down the hall then back, then down, and then back again.

"J ... u ... l ... i ... e," it called. It dragged its self up the step from the dining room into the living room.

She rushed in and out of the bedrooms, into the bathroom and then back down the hallway. She whirled herself around in circles searching for something, anything she could fit into.

A stair squeaked.

She bolted for the end of the hall. Shoved the linen closet open, picked up the hamper, dumping the laundry, trying to fit herself inside. She fell over on her side, rolling into the bedroom half in half out of the hamper. It was no use. It was too small or she was too big. She squirmed out and along the floor. She used the bathroom doorknob to bring herself to a stand. She spun herself in circles, stopping, catching the wooden credenza out the corner of her eye. She dove for it sliding the door open, wiggling and curling herself up inside into a tight little ball tucking her head in between her knees. She inched the door shut with her elbow. She gagged, jamming her mouth hard into her one leg trying not to vomit from a sickening sweet odour that seemed all at once everywhere.

"Y ... o ... u ... w ... a ... n ... t ... t ... o ... p ...l ... a ... y ... h ... i ... d ... e ... a ... n ... d ...s ...e ... e ... k ... d ... o ... y ... o ... u?" it asked. It was standing at the top of the landing staring at the wisp of tee shirt sticking out the corner of the credenza. "O ... k ... a ... y." It slowly started to move down the hall, drool seeping out from between the gaps in its teeth.

Julie drew breaths in and out through her open mouth. Her head felt light, like it was not there. She closed her eyes, the blackness spinning and whirling like a sideways psychedelic adventure. Total out and out fright had cooled her body temperature allowing paralysis to form and set her. Her eyes glazed and rolled up underneath her shut lids

"C ... o ... m ... e ... o ... u ... t ... c ... o ... m ... e ... o ... u ... t ... w ... h ... e ... r ... e ... e ... v ...e ... r ... y ... o ... u ... a ... r ... e!" it sang. Drool balled from its open mouth splatting the carpeting alongside the credenza, staining it a greenish yellow. It reeked like something that had wound its way up from hell through a sewer in the heat. It forced the slider open a quarter inch sucking Julie's terror up into its nostrils. It bent down slowly working the door.

"JULES? ... JULES!" Tony yelled. He hoofed the front door open. He cupped his hand over his mouth and nose almost tossing his cookies. "Jules? ... You in here?" he muffled. He spoke through his hand. He peered in the kitchen. There was a thick stench in the air like rotting garbage.

Julie didn't move. She was filled to the brim with terror. She could hear doors banging but ...

"WHAT THE FUCK YOU DOING IN THERE?" Tony slid the slider open. He raised his eyebrows wrinkling his forehead in utter amazement. He bent down offering her a hand making his lips disappear. He never would have thought a person could have fit in there. But there she was big as life and twice as real. He stared wide-eyed and speechless watching her crawl her way out and come to a stand, taking in the blood stains, bits of dirt, grass, and the yellow questionable somethings sticking out of her hair. "What the hell have you been up to?" he blurted.

"Nothing," she said. Her response was noticeably half-assed. She tried to clear her throat.

"Nothing?" he questioned. He rubbed his chin back and forth. "You don't look like you've been up to nothing!"

"I ... I ... Just fell that's all." She held on to his arm stretching her legs out, un-cramping them. She peered nervously over his shoulder around the hall, then checked back behind her.

He followed her eyes. "Let me get this straight," he said. He leaned over the railing trying to see what she was looking for. "You've been up to nothing. Fell and then decided to sit in the credenza?"

"Yes ... Yes ... I did," she stammered. She looked back behind her again. Satisfied there was only herself and Tony in the hallway, she un-hunched her shoulders sliding some of the fear to the floor. It landed right beside the drool crawling off under the carpet from the stench. "You have a problem with that?" she added.

He was shaking his head looking at her. *Did he have a problem with that?* he thought. *'N ...O!'* He drew out his silent thought. *Why would he have a problem with that?* He smiled. *This was all absolutely peachy keen. It was a well-known fact that all women crawl into the bottom half of bookcases covered in dirt and blood and whatever else they had on in the middle of an afternoon, at least once in their lives. It was a given.* He did not answer.

"Where's the car ... Jules?" he asked.

"Car? ... What car?"

"Your car?"

"Oh ... That car! ... It's at the mall." Julie walked into the bathroom scrubbing her hands in the sink. The blood, dirt, and grass circled round and round forming itself into a mini hurricane like tunnel in the basin. The saying *'Never lie when the truth will do,'* popped into her head and she suddenly smiled.

"It's at the mall?"

"Yes ... That's what I said."

"Why is your car at the mall?"

"Cause I left it there."

"You left your car at the mall?"

"Yes."

"You're here, but your car's at the mall?"

"Yes."

He was getting nowhere. He knew her car was at the mall. He'd just come from it, courtesy of the police, who had also been asking about her whereabouts over the last two hours. "Do you want to tell me why the police called me at work asking about you?"

"No."

He leaned on the bathroom doorframe. "You didn't happen to be ... Say for instance ... At a cemetery today, were you?" He couldn't wait to hear this one.

She turned to him pointing at her chest. "Me? ... At ... A ..." She punctuated the 'A' drawing it out. "Cemetery?"

"Yes, you ... At a cemetery!" He tapped his foot; this was going to be good.

"No." She looked him straight in the eye. "I was not for instance at a ..." She again drew the out 'A'. "Cemetery today!" If he had asked her if she'd been at Forest Lawn, that would have been different. But 'A' cemetery well ...

"I see," he said. "Jules?"

"Yes."

"Are you all right?"

"No," she replied, flatly.

"I see," he said, again. He didn't talk anymore. There was nothing to say. He had known she was not all right. Far from it actually. It had surfaced after he had locked her in the basement a few weeks back and been going strong ever since. He still wondered how in the hell she'd gotten out of there without breaking down the door and where she'd went off to for the night. She was way more resourceful than he had ever given her credit for. He picked up his keys and headed off down the stairs.

She ran after him. "Wait for me! ... I'm coming in early today!"

He eyed her up and down. "Maybe you should stay home for a few days. You don't look too good."

"I'm okay ... Really," she said.

He reached and flicked a piece of ash off the outer edge of her tee shirt. "Just stay home."

They both watched the piece of ash float to the floor. He glanced at her out the corner of his eye. She was staring open mouthed at it as if it was about to jump up and eat her alive. She beat it past him taking off at a dead run down the walkway.

"WHERE IN HELL ARE YOU FUCKING GOING TO NOW?" he screamed. He ran after her.

"I'M GOING TO MEET THE BOYS AT SCHOOL," she screeched. She didn't look back.

"THEY ... DON'T ... GET ... OUT ... FOR ... HOURS!" he said. He puffed, in short bursts.

"I'LL WAIT," she shot back. She speeded up and hopped a fence, disappearing from sight.

He stopped, doubling over at the end of the street gasping for breath. He had no words. He walked back to the house fetching his keys from the coffee table. The basement door was shut. *'Funny,'* he thought. He could have sworn it was wide open earlier. He shuffled his feet along the carpet as he went up into the dining room rubbing in bits of ash as he went. He had not gotten around to that question yet.

Chapter 39

Julie flew down the stairs in her bathrobe. She turned on the outside lights and opened the front door. The two police officers flashed their badges. A flush of heat rose from her core, settling across her forehead making it instantly bead in a row of sweat. She crossed her wobbling legs, one over the other at the ankle, bracing herself against the doorframe.

She had been afraid of this. And low and behold, there they were, not one but two of them. She had mentally prepared; making ready with all the right answers in the right places a few days back. Just in case, and here was the just in case.

She had practiced in the mirror looking herself dead in the eye. She knew nothing, absolutely nothing from nothing about any graveyard desecration. A friend of hers had borrowed her car that day. And if the person resembled her in any shape or way ... On cue ... She was going to look extremely cute interjecting a little laugh ... Come on now officers, how many women wear jeans, tee shirts and have their hair up in a ponytails? ... Cue again ... To make her lips pucker and disappear, opening her eyes big, batting them just a little, looking innocent.

"How can I help you fine officers?" she asked. She gave them a grand smile.

The tallest one stepped forward holding out a brown menlo coloured envelope. "We were coming up this way, so we thought we'd save you the trouble in getting a permit," he said.

She gulped down the lump in her throat, the edges of her fake smile turning real. She coughed on purpose. "A permit?" she questioned.

The officer opened the package pulling out a bunch of paperwork, a small handgun, two clips, a black gun case, and a set of keys. "This is yours?" He held it up for her to see. It was a thirty-five-auto baby browning with pearl handgrips.

She nodded, holding out her hands.

The other officer flipped his clipboard open, giving her a pen and pointing where to sign. "We've had this for years down at the station. It was in with all your ex-husband's gun paraphernalia when he turned it in to us. When you never showed up to claim it we checked to see if your registration was still valid, which it is by the way, and decided to bring it up to you. This way you didn't need any permits," he explained.

She signed her name on all four pages thanking them for the goodwill gesture. She'd totally forgotten about ever having it.

She gave off a wave watching the cruiser start to pull away. It stopped suddenly back tracking into the drive. The passenger door opened. The tall officer got out rifling through his pockets. He held out his hand palm side down.

"Here," he said. He opened his fingers dropping bullets into hers. "These were in the magazine. I know it is breaking protocol, but they do belong to you. You might as well have them." He tipped the front of his cap, lowering his voice. "One never knows does one?" he said. He gave her a wave out the window as the car with 'Police to serve and protect' written across the back end disappeared into the night.

She closed the door looking at the gun, the gunlock, the case, the magazines, the bullets, and the keys to the lock. She smirked; the lock was almost bigger than the damn gun.

"Yes ... officer," she said. She fiddled with the lock, unlocking it. She filled the magazines, clicking one into place, taking the safety off, loading a bullet into the chamber. She dropped it into her housecoat pocket. "You're absolutely right! ... One never knows does one?"

Chapter 40

"I've had enough of your fucking bullshit!" Tony seethed. He sprayed hot beads of saliva into her face. It burnt and stung, watering her eyes. He backhanded her knocking her into the wall. He grabbed her by an arm forcefully dragging her toward the stairs. "I'm the fucking boss! ... Do what I want, when I want and your life will be fucking easy! ... Go fucking against me and I'll make it a living fucking hell!"

Julie's feet slipped and slid out from under her as he towed. Mid-way up the staircase she bounced sideways, banging off the wall, turning in his grasp. She came down face first slamming her chin and bursting it wide open. He jerked her arm tightening his grip, pulling her up the remaining steps, her forehead banging off each one in turn.

Once at the top he towed her down the hall and into the bedroom leaving a bloody tell all in his wake.

He dropped her like a sack of rotten potatoes beside the bed, dusting her once in the ribs. He peeled a piece of duct tape from the side of his jeans, placing it over her mouth. He fished a length of white rope from his back pocket tying her hands behind her back, crisscrossing her wrists.

He picked her up, heaving her onto the bed. He turned her onto her stomach smacking her in the back of the head, sending her face deep into the mattress. He jerked her pajama bottoms off. He grabbed one leg tying her ankle tightly to the bed frame with another length of rope, forcing her spread eagle as he tied the other ankle.

"NOW YOU BITCH! ... YOU'RE GOING TO GET WHAT'S COMING TO YOU!" he yelled. "YOU DON'T EVER SAY NO TO ME! ... NOT EVER!" he shouted.

He dropped his jeans to the floor, clambered onto the bed, grabbed a fistful of her hair, jerking her head back. "You fucking bitch," he whispered. "You're not so fucking shit hot now! ... Are you mouth-piece?" He gave her head another snap backward cracking and popping her neck. "I didn't fucking think so!" he said. He rammed her face back into the mattress, mounting her.

Julie struggled as he forced himself on her, entering her, ramming her, ripping and tearing her delicate folds of flesh. He pounded her body relentlessly, forging red hot rods of lightening that erupted deep within her body catching on fire, enveloping her in spasms of searing pain. Over and over he lunged, banging into her, battering and mutilating her insides.

She prayed she would die. She did not even come close.

When spent, he collapsed himself on top of her, knocking the wind from her. He dripped with sweat. It soaked into her skin making her stink like him. She struggled for breath, gasping, her nose flattened into the hard mattress. He used her back to lift himself, grinding the heels of his palms into her flesh on purpose. Bright red growing ovals marked his spot as he rolled off her landing himself along side. She could feel him touching and stroking himself, slowly at first, then zealously as he began to stiffen against her hip, coating it with slime.

She whimpered and moaned lifting her chest, collapsing from another onslaught of deep-seated pain. Her entire body felt like it was bleeding from within, about to rupture and blow like a molten volcano in its prime. Her breath laboured and puffed, escaping out her taped over mouth in small shallow whiffs. She sounded like a hurt animal, circling the drainage ditch looking for a place to die.

"Oh you liked that did you bitch?" he asked. His grin was wide and deep. "Is that why you're whimpering and moaning?" He ran his fingers along her backside. "Want more do you?" he whispered. He slid his hands underneath her pelvis lifting her rear-end up. "Here's some more!"

He rammed himself hard into her rectum, grinding full force splitting it open. It fissured, squirting and pumping out bright red blood. "That's a girl!" he cooed. "Coat my nice hard rod so I can fuck the hell out of your ass!" He sat on top of her digging his fingernails into her rump-cheeks, riding her, shoving, driving. He banged hard and inhuman, driving her body forward, causing the ropes to grow taught on her ankles. The fibres protested, turning themselves from brilliant fluffy snow white to deep rich flesh ripping red. He slowed, grabbing his balls and lifting them, withdrawing, expelling his essence over her rump and back. He stood, leaning against the wall and then suddenly spring boarding forward, hoofing her hard between the legs. He smacked her butt leaving a bright red open handprint. He laughed aloud watching the blood sprout from between her legs and the welt rise on her ass.

"Now you know who the fucking boss is! ... Don't you bitch?" He knew she was not about to answer. For one thing she couldn't--duct tape had a way of silencing people. He laughed again. He climbed onto the bed lying beside her, studying her. Her eyes rolled back in her head. There was no sign of life. He waited just in case, tapping a wire coat hanger against his calf. He had always wanted to try it. He had heard it worked wonders.

She lay still, perfectly still, her breath not visible to the naked eye. She lay as she was, ripped and torn, battered and bloodied. Her butt cheek sparkling in the morning sunshine showing off its newly acquired brand.

Tony pulled on his jeans. He rounded the bed, squatting down beside her head, turning it to face him. He stroked the hair from her face. He gave her a rough shake bringing her to. "You know what Jules?" He smiled softly. "That was the best we've ever had! ... Don't you agree?" He lifted her head up and down making her nod yes. "I'm glad you agree," he chuckled. "My ... My ... My ... I must say ... You do look nice!" He gave her an admiring wink. "You know what? ... I think ... I am going to leave you just like this so I can dream about you, until I get back home! ... You didn't have any plans ... Did you?" He made her head nod no. "Good! ... It's all settled then!" He trailed his fingertips up and down her back. "Didn't you say this morning the boys had a birthday party sleep over to go to after school?"

Terror took hold of Julie's eyes overflowing them with air, almost popping them out onto the floor. She moved her head back and forth.

"No?" he asked. "Are you absolutely sure?" He moved close, licking and chewing her ear lobe, grasping her earring between his teeth. He spun it round with his tongue, abruptly jerking his head to the side ripping it out. He spat it onto the floor.

Julie's scream bounced off the duct tape lodging in her throat. She pivoted her shoulders in agony, pain shooting into her temple. Blood oozed into her ear, pooled then trickled down her neck.

He dabbed the tip of his index finger in the blood, finger painting hearts on her neck. "Now ... Lets try that again shall we?"

Her head felt light and woolly, as it spun round and round sending all before her into hazy out of focus ripples.

"Don't keep me waiting! ... You know what happens when you make me wait!" He shook his head making a loud tutting and noise waving his finger back and forth in front of her eyes. "The basement's only two staircases away! ... What goes up, goes down!"

The vomit in her throat bubbled into her mouth, spewing out through her teeth striking the duct tape. It rebounded, gathering under her tongue, overflowing, gagging her as it slipped back into her throat.

"Do ... They ... Have ... A ... Sleep ... Over ... Party?" he asked, very slowly. Too slowly. He grasped her other ear lobe, turning the earring round in his fingertips. He gave her face a hard wallop with his other hand, like a dog offering up a growl before the bite. Or in this case a strike before the rip.

Julie nodded. The left over vomit had coated the inside of her lips, parting them, drying her teeth. She struggled for breath; the inside skin of her lips and teeth all at once seemingly cemented to the tape. Surprising the things, a little wallop could do.

"That's a good girl," he said. He let go of the earring. "See it's not so hard to be a good girl ... Now is it?" He patted her head, got up, and left.

Julie shut her eyes, waiting long after she heard the front door lock and the car leave the drive, to figure out if she was still alive. She was almost positive she had died sometime over the last few hours and gone directly to hell. She could feel her heart beating. It was heavy and laboured, but there. She slowly pricked her eyes open. The red mottled white sheet greeted her, the material sucking in and out of her nostrils drowning her in his repulsive greasy scent. She was definitely alive. Alive and well, duct taped and tied, laying face down spread eagle on a battlefield that used to be a bed.

She turned her head sideways running the tip of her tongue back and forth over the tape, wetting the space between her lips. The tape moved, giving a hair. She swiped her tongue back and forth, frenzied, as if struck with a cattle prod to get a move on. The tape started to yield. When it puckered forming a small bubble, she groped with her tongue, sticking and flipping it against the top edge, curling it inward. She pushed her tongue, inverting the sticky side. She pressed the edge of the tape to the sheet. Repeating the action over, and over, until it caught, stuck and ripped from her face. She opened her mouth, contorting it, puckering her lips taking in long hollow breaths.

She angled her shoulders, lifting one higher. She turned her head, attempting a glimpse at her ankles. She abruptly flopped, doing a face plant into the bedding. It was useless.

She wiggled her hands using her fingers like octopus tentacles groping them blindly over her flesh, sifting for clues. They were crossed; the right over the left, rope double knotted at the top. She fingered the ends. They were short. Too short. She started to flip her hands formulating a sequence, up, down, back, forth, working the rope. She could feel the skin on her wrists changing temperature. Warm, to hot, to burning, to on fire like red-hot coals. As if on a mission, she slid the rope pulling and jerking it, burrowing it into her raw flesh. Tears rolled down her screaming face as little jagged pieces of skin flanked flesh tore loose, all too quickly adding in to the bulk of the cord. The rope seemed hungry, like a starved bloodsucker. It eagerly slurped and sucked at the blood, the overflow dripping and pooling in the small of her back.

Julie fell back into the mattress. She lay quiet drawing on hatred, refuelling. She screeched the mother of all war cries, bringing her chest off the bed, baring her teeth, sliding the rope, working for blood, doubling the puddle in the small of her back. She mashed her lips together, grinding her teeth, dousing her knotted hands splattering everything in a one-foot radius a beautiful hue of ruby red. She pulled, and jerked, and stretched the wet fibres, time and time again. They gave, widening. She slipped her hands out and through.

She folded her arms tucking them under her chest, laying back down on the bed, closing her eyes and smiling a victory grin in sheer agony. She lay motionless mentally coming to grips with the searing waves of pain in her wrists, tucking it away with the rest as it became as commonplace as burning hot apple pie.

She bounced herself on the mattress trying to kneel, flopping back face down. If he had put her on her back she would have been up and long gone. He was more depraved than she had ever given him credit for. *'Evil begets evil,'* she thought.

She glanced up at the blue sky through the window. His words ... *'Till I get back home,'* drilling around in her head. She did not know how long back was and she was not about to be lying there waiting for another brutalizing flight past the pit of hell.

She pulled up her legs one at a time, testing the ropes like a caged animal checking for weaknesses in the bars. There weren't any. They were foolproof and taut. Expertly tied and knotted as any a good maniac could do, to keep what was within it, in.

She pushed the top half of her body up off the bed, using her palms to walk her body backward towards the ropes slackening them. Her legs spread as she went. She bit off a piece of her lip silencing her screams of pain. She suddenly knew what it felt like to be placed on a rack and stretched.

She laid the top half of her body carefully down. Her nostrils flared turning the outer edges dark pink as she drew in and out the smells of sweat, forced sex, and cold wet blood. She grunted, screaming, pulling, snapping, and jerking her legs in frog like movements. She struggled endlessly, grasping onto the bedding as riveting pain rocked her core, surpassing the point called unbearable.

She dropped back onto the bed. She was ... As she was before. Except for the pain. She wrapped her arms tightly about her middle sobbing. He had finally done it. He'd beat her. Won. There was no way out.

"YOU GOD DAMN BASTARD!" she yelled. "I HATE YOU!" She twisted her cramped right foot around in circles trying to free her stiffened rock hard arch from the muscle spasm that had attacked it. The rope pulled taut stopping her dead, one of the loops catching and gluing itsself to the metal frame corner underneath the mattress. She banged her leg up and down. The fibers stretched, popping against the metal edge, fraying and sawing through, making a pinging sound as they started to let loose.

A smile burst from her lips, gleaming and shining, lighting up the room in double rainbows. The pot of gold was almost in her hands. Freedom! She tilted sideways grasping onto her leg, steadying her knee, whipping her foot round and round and then pulling. More and more strands let go. Then, as quickly as this God given miracle had been granted it was taken away.

"NO! ... NO," she screamed. She tugged at her foot. "PLEASE ... NO! ... DO NOT DO THIS TO ME! ... PLEASE! ... PLEASE! ... PLEASE GOD? ... PLEASE HELP ME!" She clasped her hands together searching the ceiling. "I'LL NEVER ASK YOU FOR ANYTHING EVER AGAIN! ... PLEASE! ... PLEASE!" she pleaded.

She threw herself forward, ripping and clawing over to the edge of the bed begging, screaming for God's help. She had never asked for anything before. She grunted, kicking her one leg up towards her. The room all at once swimming in dizzy, lazy circles. She rocked her foot back and forth, sawing the rope through her flesh. The blood shot out as if on cue, like a mock eruption on a timer. Dark, red-black oozed down from her ankle, blanketing her foot, separating as it trickled in between each of her toes and then down to the floor.

She formed her fingers into the edge of the bed, turning her knuckles as white as her clenched teeth. She pulled, ripping her flesh, rolling and twisting it into the rope. The rope tightened as it stretched letting go with odd eerie snaps, like the devil himself had a hold of the other end and wasn't about to give it up as long as she still lived and breathed.

The rope snapped without warning, hitting against the frame in a hollow thud like a dog snarling through bared teeth into a length of pipe. Her knee flew into her neck, flipping her eyeballs up into her head. She gasped, huffing out yells in sheer utter agony. She clutched her leg, instantly out grinning any would be Satan after a good days reap of soul taking.

She did not stop to thank God, the prayers leaving her head as fast as they'd come into it. She brought her leg up underneath her whirling round, spattering the flowered wallpaper with blood, leaning over and untying her other ankle.

She dropped, arms outstretched angel fashion, flopping onto the bed on her back. She smiled. She never before realized how wonderful it felt to lie on one's back.

She lay still, silent, without thought. Her chest heaved, drawing and expelling breath after breath. There was nothing left inside. Her eyes closed of their own accord, giving and offering her up to the restless realms of sleep that waited off in the shadows. She dreamed, screaming and running through a brand new set of nightmares that she did not remember when she awoke.

Hours later, she examined her battered body, naked from the waist down, ripped and bruised, and smeared in blood. She could not figure out why she was still alive. She stroked her ankles folding the stiff blood soaked skin back into place. She chewed on the insides of her cheeks thinking of the husband that had dragged her up the stairs by her arm, brutally raping her not once, but twice. He had gone at her like a rabid animal. He needed to be netted, his head cut off and dissected.

She looked upside down out the window. It was dark. Very dark. She blinked catching the tail end of a banner on the inside of her eyelids, later was going to be soon a coming. She lunged at the phone. Husband or not, she wasn't going to let him get away with this. This was so far over the line; it was in the next country.

She dialled 911.

"911 emergency," a male voice said. "Constable Hutchings spe ..."

Julie cut him off. "HELP! ... HELP!" she blurted. "You've got to help me!" She broke down, crying hysterically.

"Okay ma'am. Calm down. What is the problem?"

"I've been raped!" Julie sobbed.

"What's your location ma'am?"

Julie could not remember her address. "I'm at home! ... I'm at home!" she blurted.

"Do you know who the perpetrator was?"

"My husband!" she wailed.

"Do you wish to file a formal complaint ma'am?"

"YES!" Julie shouted.

"Just a minute ma'am. I will be right with you. Okay?"

"Okay," Julie replied. The telephone clicked on hold, then off again.

It was a different male voice. "This is Constable Jenkins from the rape unit. Are you Julie Porter of 1497 Thomasview Crescent?"

"YES! ... YES! ... Yes I am! ... I want my husband arrested! ... I want ..."

The officer cut her off. "Just a minute ma'am." The telephone clicked on hold again.

"Ma'am?" A female voice asked.

Julie nodded yes.

"Ma'am? ... This is Constable Williams ... You still there ma'am?"

"Yes," Julie replied. She lost some of her zest. She could not figure out why she was being shuffled around.

"Your husband is Tony Porter?"

"YES! ... YES!" Julie piped. "Yes he is! ... And I want him charged with rape! .... He raped me!"

"Are you sure ma'am?" the female voice said.

Julie's jaw dropped open drying her tongue in place. She couldn't have heard right. She could have sworn, the officer just asked if she was sure she had been raped. "Pardon?" she asked. "I don't think I heard you right."

"Are you sure you were raped ma'am?" the female officer repeated.

Julie's eyes rimmed, widening in horror. How on earth could she not be sure of such a thing? "What ... What ... Do ... Do ... You mean? ... Am ... Am I sure? ... Of course ... I ... I am sure!" she stuttered. She made a fist with her free hand, rapidly letting it in and out, grabbing the bedding scrunching it between her fingers.

"Ma'am? ... Julie?"

"What on earth are you ..."

The female constable cut in. "It's just ma'am ... Your husband was in here a few hours ago. Also, a couple days back. And ma'am, these are his words not mine. He said he wanted to give us a head's up on the off chance you phoned today ... In case you tried to pull something, like saying you were raped, and wanting him charged. He said you were into rough sex lately and that the two of you had a bit of a tiff this morning. And he was afraid you would call in to us, claiming rape to get back at him. He'd said you yelled at him, threatening this out the window as he was leaving."

Julie's jaw fell off and hit the floor. "Say ... Say that again would you?"

"Your husband, Tony Porter was in our station this morning, informing us about the situation in case you called in claiming rape. That the two of you had an argument and you had threatened him and ..."

Julie cut her off. "He ... He ... Wh ... What?"

"Ma'am, your husband was in today advising you both partake in very rough sex. That you'd had an argument. You were known to be very spiteful. You might be calling claiming rape to get back at him. Ma'am ... He was also here for over three hours last week."

"Go on," Julie said.

"Last week, he'd come in asking for our help and advice. He said he did not know what to do anymore. You were acting really, strange lately. He was scared you were going

305

completely off the deep end. He expressed concern that you might hurt yourself or someone else. He was wondering what he could do about it before it became too late."

"OH MY GOD!" she cried. She started to sob. "OH MY GOOD ... GOD! ... THINGS?" she asked. Her voice shrilled "WHAT THINGS?"

"He'd said, the neighbour's cat had been killed, mutilated in fact, in their rose bushes. I think he said yellow ones. And that you hated yellow roses and the cat. The day the cat had been killed was the very same you had come home with rose petals, leaves, mud and blood all over your person with no viable explanation. He'd gone on to say he'd caught you stealing money from your own restaurant numerous times, the till never added up. You made up stories to his cousin that he was abusive to you. You often locked yourself in the basement or outside in the rain pretending it was by him. On top of that, he had informed us the neighbours had witnessed you running down the street late at night into the park waving a machete over your head. And these are but only a few things ma'am."

Julie bent her head sobbing uncontrollably.

"Ma'am?" The police officer lowered her voice "If I were you, I might be thinking of packing myself a bag and checking into the local hospital for observation before he finishes getting the papers drawn up to commit you. He had them with him when he was in here."

"But ...But," Julie stammered. She was devoid of any other word.

"Did you wish to proceed with the charges ma'am? ... Ma'am?" The officer shook her head. Tony Porter had been right. His wife was a total out and out basket case.

Julie dropped the receiver. She reached behind the night table ripping the telephone line from the wall. She could not believe this. This was total insanity. Worse ... If there was such a thing.

She sat on the edge of the bed in dumb-founded horror. *'How could he do this? How could he?'* she asked herself silently. And, he had gone to such lengths. She could not have ever gotten close to any of this even on somebody else's bad day. He had become so good at being outright evil. He was even out there in broad daylight ... Spinning off to the police and they were buying it, hook, line, and sinker. She started to weep. She didn't want to know him anymore. She didn't want to know who he was, or what he was. She wanted him to die. He did not deserve to be in this world. This planet was not made to hold such things as him.

She slid down off the bed landing on her butt, suddenly reminded of her deep seeded wounds as they reared their heads sending her into instant agony. She slowly crawled on her hands and knees into the bathroom. Her entire body ripped, torn, and bloodied, aching from the inside out.

She drew a hot bubble bath. She hung her arms in the water until her wrists stopped stinging. She climbed in one foot at a time, seeking the same results, finally submerging her body. She tilted her head back soaking and soothing away the stink of Tony upon her and in her. She put her head under, blowing air through her nostrils clearing away any hangers-on.

She was dead inside. There were no more tears. There was no more anything. There was nothing, but a shallow grave with no marker. Any trace of feelings, the tainted love, had packed its bags and left around the same time as the repeated non-bruising beatings had started. The rape had just flattened out that last shovel full of dirt on the grave. The one she had needed to be able to hate him with as much passion as she had once loved him.

She sat in the tub gently running water over herself, making sure her skin squeaked with a clean that is found only after one is made to feel dirty. She let the water out and refilled the bath. Her inner body parts ached and burnt, stinging like they had been doused with gasoline and lit on fire. Her mind reeled back into the nightmare she had just somehow lived through.

She had wished for death this past afternoon. More times then she cared to admit. But, death would have been the easy way out. He would have had to pay for that one. Or maybe not. After her telephone call to the police, she was almost sure he would be able wiggle out of that too. She was willing to bet her last red cent, he would be able to come up with all kinds of scenarios on how she had accidentally killed herself. (By ... His ... Hand ...) Rough sex? She wondered if he was already setting the stage.

She looked at the water. Ribbons of red whirled from between her legs, her wrists, and her ankles, turning the water a nice baby pink. She shook her head, disgusted with herself. What on earth had she become? A nothing? Something disposable? Never to be seen or heard again? She did not know who she was anymore. Nor, could she remember who she used to be. The person named 'Julie' had ceased to exist. She had been reduced to a form of sub-human, totally dependent on a creature. Doing as he said when he said. Jumping when he said. Tiptoeing around on eggshells. Afraid of her own shadow. Fearing punishment of no food, being locked up, or in, or out, or ... Whatever else he dreamed up in the ways no one could find out or see. She wished she'd never ever laid eyes on Tony.

She changed the bed, ripping the bedding from it and throwing it in the trash. She dressed fully and then put on her bathrobe tying the belt in place. She sank her hands deep into her pockets, all at once smiling, and then laughing out loud.

She turned off all the lights in the house, climbed into bed, and waited. Waited ... For her prince charming from hell to come home.

It was not long before she heard the car pull into the drive and the front door bang shut. Her laugh returned.

Tony climbed the stairs four at a time. He threw off his clothes as he went. He'd been thinking of her all day and was more than aroused. He had beat himself off on the way home in the car, not being able to contain himself. Power and total domination was a newfound thrill. His erection throbbed within his hand. He could barely wait to get at her again. He liked this new sport so much that he had decided to put an ad in the paper advertising for other like-minded men. He was going to offer her up for the taking, say five hundred, and see where it went from there. He was going to inform her this was to be her new job.

He pranced into the bedroom naked. His member fully erect, bouncing up and down. She was fast asleep in bed. Not on it. In it. Anger skyrocketed melting his erection. "FUCK JULES," he screamed. He ripped the bedding from her, hoping she was as he had left her, naked from the waist down, smelling like a whoring slut.

He stood dumb founded. She lay on her side, wrapped in a bathrobe, sleeping as sound as all get out. "You bitch. You fucking wreck everything," he said. He bent over making a hissing noise into her ear.

She did not budge.

He studied her, not feeling like smacking her out or locking her up. Something new was needed. All that smacking round was getting old hat. It did not do it for him anymore. It took too much control not to leave a bruise. He clomped off downstairs into the kitchen making himself something to eat.

He sat in the armchair at the end of the bed. In the dark, slurping and scoffing down his food, grinning away to himself while rolling over ideas to fix her up.

Julie did not move a muscle. She lay in wait on her side, for the thing, in the chair, in the dark, to make his move. He ate with his hands totally engrossed, sucking, burping, and farting. He more so resembled something that was born of darkness than anything human. But then, she already knew this--All too well. She expected his head to start and rotate round as he sprayed out pea soup. He did not, at least not that she heard.

The sound of the plate thudding to the floor told her all she needed.

He crawled into bed, snuggling, putting his arm around her like everything was perfectly fine. Everything was so far removed from perfectly fine it was not even right for either of them to be together in that bed.

She waited for the signs. His breathing to slow, the lip smacking, the uncontrolled farting to tell her he was nearing sleep.

She moved his arm. She rolled facing him. She slowly, carefully, reached under her pillow dragging out the thirty-five auto. She slammed the cool metal into his temple pulling back the hammer.

His eyes almost blew from their sockets.

"Tony," she whispered.

His entire body was rigid.

She smiled. "Do I have your attention?" she asked.

He nodded. The whites of his eyes ripe and round, almost glowing.

"Good," she said. "I thought I might." She pivoted the gun barrel back and forth digging it into his temple. She grinned, showing off a toothy smile as a spurt of urine shot from between his legs wetting the sheets.

"Tony." She paused, waiting for another nod. "If you even so much as think of touching me again. I'll kill you! ... You got that?" She was cooler than a cucumber.

He nodded again.

She held the gun to his temple driving home her point. No additional words needed. She rolled onto her back, placing her right hand and the gun on her chest.

"You ... You ..." He coughed clearing his throat, trying to get a grip on himself. "You wou ... wouldn't ... wou ..." He cleared his throat again. "You wouldn't wou ... would you?" he asked.

She did not respond.

"You ... You're ... just...bluffing ... You ... wouldn ..." he stammered. "You ... You wouldn't do somet ..."

She fired into the wall just above his head.

He soaked the bed with urine.

"No?" She jumped in between his legs facing him, drawing up both her knees resting the gun atop and aiming it dead center of his forehead. "Are you sure?" she asked. She put her finger on the trigger.

Saliva ran from the outer corners of his mouth down onto his chin.

For the first time in a long time she laughed. She laughed so hard she cried. *'It's a funny thing,'* she thought. *'How quick one can turn the tables with the right instrument.'*

Humpty Dumpty

Humpty Dumpty
Sat on a wall
Humpty Dumpty
Had a great fall
All the King's horses
And ...
All the king's men
Couldn't put Humpty Dumpty
Back together again.

Chapter 41

Sometimes you don't choose ....
If you live in hell,
You just do whatever it takes to survive.

"MOM! ... MOM! ... HELP!" Cory screamed.

Julie threw the dishcloth, taking off in a dead run. She scrambled for the stairs, grabbing hold of the banister.

"MOM!" Cory screeched. "MOM! MOM!" His voice was shrill and panicky. Something was wrong.

She flung herself up the staircase. Her slippers barely grazing every third stair as she bounded and leaped. The screams and sounds from above mixing and collapsing around her.

"MOM! ... HELP ... ME! ... M ... O ... M!" Cory wailed. His voice pitched and hollowed like it was being sucked from his mouth into the ceiling. It seemed to gather in a heap, blasting back through banging and pinging into the drywall.

Her nerves were all ready on edge. She had been hearing the strangest of things on and off all day. Odd-ball things, like the kind that made one's skin goose bump and the hair on the back of your neck stand. She had given herself quite a few shakes, yet still felt unsettled. The sounds were like nothing she had ever heard before. It was as if something had come alive and crawled off out of sight, taking up residence in all the cracks and corners of the house, possessing it.

She had run dry of excuses with the last glance over her shoulder. The wind was all she had left. Her stomach had long since flipped, turning sideways, burning holes in its self, sending scorching embers up and down her windpipe making it difficult to catch or hold a breath. It knew something was not quite right. Not right at all. That was number one on her top ten list of things she did not want to know. If she knew, then all the excuses would have to be thrown out the window along with the wind. And she was not opening a window for love or money. Not this day.

She had been telling herself that people did not get scared in their own homes. It just did not happen. Noises, or no noises no matter how strange. It just did not happen. All the lights were on in the daylight because they looked nice. The doors were locked and bolted because one couldn't be too careful these days. That was all there was to it. It was plain and simple. Besides, it was just the wind.

The wind had done it all. Everything. The wind had blown the locked basement door open. Brought yellow roses and left them on the front stoop. It had banged and thudded on the backside of the doors. It had made shuffling noises in the empty rooms. It had left footprint marks on the carpeting.

The boys had been hearing the wind all day too.

Wind was a powerful force. All one had to do was watch television and there would always be something wrong, somewhere in the world because of the wind. Even the low-pitched inhuman growls they had all heard at dinner through the floor vent in the kitchen, was the wind. It had whisked through the basement window distorting something, somehow.

It did not matter there was no basement window. All that mattered was the explanation. It had taken a lot of pounding to get that square piece into that round hole. But, she had been determined. She had slammed it over, and over again in long hard, wilful blows until it fit. Everything always fits if one pounds it long enough. She knew this first hand, courtesy of Tony.

She stood breathless at the top of the stairs, her hands finding her hips. She shook her head smiling ear to ear. She had been drawn and ready. Lips parted, tongue braced to spit the words, *It's just the wind, again,* but this time there was no need. Before her was a boy body with two arms and two legs, wearing the invisible nametag on his shirt of *'Caleb.'* She burst out, roaring in laughter.

Caleb had his back to her. Feet braced and squared at the base of the door, arms extended with both hands on the knob, leaning back into it for all he was worth.

"MOM! ... MOM! ... HELP! ... YOU OUT THERE MOM?" Cory beat his fists into the back of his bedroom door.

Julie wiped the smile from her lips, leaving it in her eyes. She cleared her throat on purpose alerting her number one son that his mother was a mere couple steps behind.

Caleb hunched his shoulders. He released the knob slowly tucking his hands into his pockets. He started to turn. It seemed like it took longer than forever. She cocked her head, suddenly mesmerized, watching, waiting, wondering what he was up to with the slow motion antics.

He brought his body round first, keeping his face pinned on the bedroom door. He changed his stance, lifting the balls of his feet from the carpeted floor. He slowly pivoted his head, stopping and starting in jerks.

"Come on Caleb! ... That's about enough! ... I ... I ..." Her words froze, blanketing her tongue in a white frosty film. Her blood thickened into dark syrup, clogging, stopping her heart before it could skip a beat. Her limbs fossilized. She swayed back and forth like a bent lightening rod in the throes of a fiendish thunderstorm.

Caleb lips were pulled and raised in a diabolical sneer. He tilted his head lifting his chin, flexing the corners of his mouth, stretching and expanding the skin until it cracked like cheap plaster, exposing decayed black teeth too massive for his mouth. The tips were broken and jagged. They hooked, plunging into the flesh under his bottom lip. A thick pea green mucus oozed out from beneath each. It dripped in wad like beads, staining and clinging to his flesh like snot from a bad cold. It stank and reeked like something crawling with maggots.

Julie stepped back becoming part of the banister. Her mouth hung, half hinged like an old broken gate, seized in place from too many winters.

Caleb rounded his lips, reverberating them in a hollow laugh, the wrinkled blue-gray skin of his face splitting and rupturing. Thick baked on rubber flakes peeled away landing and sticking to his tee shirt. Snarled, crusty vein coils popped themselves out through the cracks. They hung about in clumps, like a mass of worms. The ends pulsated as if alive, opening and closing like they were sniffing for blood.

His round amber eyes were blood streaked and bulged from the sockets like something had taken them from somewhere else and jammed them in. His face was elongated and distorted as if he'd been buried alive, dug back up, frozen, then thrown outside in the open air to rot.

He shot his head back, wheezing, blowing out a protracted ribbon of dark gray mist. It fouled the air whirling and thickening into a jellified floating mass. It hovered above his head reeling round and round forming its self into a single ring.

The wooden railing creaked and groaned from the force of her weight as she pushed into it. She watched in horror as the swirling streamer collapsed, turning inside out, shooting down, striking, and smacking the floor in front of her slippers, encompassing them. It made little puffing sounds as it wrapped round her ankles, then legs, expanding, as it progressed up her length.

Her hands twisted like coiled serpents around the banister, cementing her in place. Terror spawned, growing inside her like a massive tumour, filling her to the brim. Her breathing shallow and then still, as if she had been suddenly freeze-dried. She stared straight ahead with non-blinking eyes into the gray matter as it swirled, engulfing her, paralyzing her like a malformed caterpillar about to meet death within its cocoon. The substance wound and wove building, layering, and drawing in tighter and tighter.

She felt as if she was suddenly no more ... Gone. Even her mind was gone, running off over to the edge, crawling through and under the rows of razor sharp barbed wire that protected the jagged boundaries of existence. She'd watched as it turned and laughed at her, then rolled down the backside of a hill landing upside down against a yellow sign with an arrow that read 'insanity this way'. She followed it, her bare feet skipping along the damp cobblestones unaware that something, born out of darkness silently, steadily, crawled and slithered after her. It was planning on introducing her to insanity, first hand.

"MOM! ... MOM! ... HELP!"

Julie closed her eyes.

The thing behind her tripped and fell, dropping over the bank and landing on its back in the ditch.

"MOM! ... HELP! ... ME!" Cory's screams echoed inside her head like a bunch of lit firecrackers setting off in an old barren house.

She struggled, fighting, trapped between the realms of sanity and insanity as the screams and yells faded in and out of her consciousness. The gray substance swirled and twirled, sucking in and out of her lungs as the contest ran on, tying as it reached halftime.

The thing clawed through the mud heaving itself back onto the pathway.

Cory screamed banging and kicking the door.

She was in the place where heaven and hell collided. Where, all time ceased to exist. Where, angels and demons co-existed alike. She had to get out. She had to breathe. Her heart would restart if she breathed.

"MOM!" Cory screeched. "MOM! ... PLEASE HELP ME!"

Julie struggled, battling herself. Trying to disband the infantry that surrounded and protected her, summoned from the demon survival handbook she had scrawled with crayons from under her bed as a child. Loud drums beat and wailed, echoing, knocking, and tapping out that age-old primitive rhythm. The one, she once knew all too well. Her survival book opened, turning to page one.

Demons came in all shapes and sizes. Hers was a fat over stuffed cartoon man with a black blot for a head. But ... If one squinted at him, he looked like family. And ... If one, turned on the light he looked like a father. Her father. The father who placed a yellow rose on her pillow so she would know to expect him later that night. But what does a child of six expect at night? Certainly not a bedtime story of a heavy sweating body on top of hers, poking a scorching ram-rod deep into all her secret places; Smothering her mouth with wide rough hands, muffling her cries and screams of pain. Whispering into her ear, instilling the terror of ages if she ever told, as it grunted and groaned, pounding relentlessly at her little body filling it up with gobby whitish liquid that seeped out later, staining her sheets.

'This is what little girls are for,' he told her. *'This is why fathers have daughters,'* he said. She could remember the smell like it was yesterday. The stink of his sweaty shit stained ass cheeks. The smoke riddled saliva upon her bubble gum scented skin. The mix as putrid as the gray enveloping her. Her eyes shot open.

The thing directly behind swiped, clawing at empty air as the ground shook beneath its feet, opening, swallowing it whole. Shooting it down into the darkness of its birthplace.

"MOM! ... HELP ME MOM!" Cory's screams darted in through a slit in the mass. The gray started to shake and convulse. Pieces shattered and fell knocking her handbook to the floor. Bright light skipped through bringing whips of fresh air, tumbling and whirling the mass side to side.

"M ... O ... M!" Cory's scream drilled its self into a heat missile landing on target, blowing a gaping hole dead center of the gray.

318

Julie heard. And remembered. She let go of the banister shoving herself forward, propelling her body like a human sling-shot through the tattered matter. She landed with a heavy thud up against Caleb planting him backwards into the door, sandwiching him like a cheap ham and Swiss.

The matter whiffed and puffed, dissipating quicker than a lightning strike. Just like it was never, really there in the first place.

"Mom we were ... Pla ... Playing and he got stuck." Caleb said, in small bursts. He peeled himself out from under her like a piece of heated up plastic wrap, shrunken and half-melted into the food. He shook his hands and feet.

"MOM? ... MOM? ... ARE YOU OUT THERE?" Cory yelled.

Julie's eyes were wider than pie plates. Her entire body trembled, wobbling her knees in circles. She stretched out her arm putting her hand to the wall, steadying herself. She could not remember anything. She looked from Caleb, to the door, back to Caleb.

"Come on Mom! ...Let's get him out!" Caleb said.

"Get him out?" she asked.

"MOM! ... HE'S STUCK IN THERE!" Caleb yelled. He yanked and pulled on the doorknob. "Don't you remember?"

She gave her head a shake ungluing her wide-eyed stare. "Yes ... Hon ... Of course I do." She fibbed. She didn't remember. She didn't even remember coming upstairs. She pulled and twisted at the doorknob. It was stuck fast as Caleb had said. She put her foot into it reefing the knob. It didn't budge.

"He ran in to get a game and the door slammed shut." Caleb did not take his eyes from the door. "Do you think it was the wind again mom?"

"The wind?" Julie asked. 'Well maybe,' she thought. "If the window was open," she said matter-of-factly. She tugged and yanked at the doorknob again.

"Caleb ..." Julie motioned to the banister. "You back up and then run as fast as you can jumping at the door. I will turn the knob and shove at the same time. Okay?"

Caleb nodded, backing, making himself ready.

"On three," Julie instructed. "One! ... Two! ... Three!"

Caleb rushed the door, bouncing off, tangling up in her legs, bringing them both down.

"Just wait here. I'll be right back."

"Where you going mom?" Caleb questioned. He put his mouth against the door reporting the play by plays to his brother.

"TO GET THE SLEDGE HAMMER!" Julie yelled, behind her. She bounded down the stairs running into the garage.

The sledgehammer slid from Julie's hands like greased lightning, bouncing as it hit the floor. Cory's bedroom door was open. All the bedroom doors were open. Open, just like the space containing the bodies of her sons. Open. Not occupied. There was no Caleb, no Cory, no nothing. Just an uncanny deafening silence, like the white noise piped into an office building, put there on purpose to cover up the some-things no one wanted known.

Julie stared at the open doors. Her mouth hung, huffing out breaths she swore she could see. She went up on her tiptoes rocking back and forth onto her heels. She rubbed her eyes. The doors seemed to be looming towards her, watching, waiting. She rubbed her eyes again. It was as though something had swooped through, swallowing everything in its path up whole.

She cautiously studied each doorway. It was like adding two and two on a haunted chalk board and getting seven in a mirror that all of a sudden materialized out of nowhere in front of her face.

She backtracked. She had run downstairs from the hallway with the closed bedroom doors. She had booked it to the garage, retrieved the sledge to break down a bedroom door. A stuck shut bedroom door. The door with a son on each side. Not even a minute later she'd ran back up the stairs. She suddenly felt like *'Alice in Wonderland* ' on bad mushrooms. Nothing seemed right. Nothing made any sense. Her mind picked up the blackboard scrawling in bright yellow chalk ... 'Closed doors, sons, noise. Open doors, no sons, silence. She held it to the mirror. A large number seven appeared with two little red smiling happy faces tucked in neatly underneath.

Julie stood dumb-founded. Her mouth a huge gaping hole, eyeballs whipping furiously back and forth, door to door. She all at once stopped dead, snapping her teeth together. All the doors were open in the same manner right down to the one tenth of an inch. It was like looking at a picture of the 'Royal Palace' window blinds. All, the same. Always, had to be the same.

She slowly started to creep down the hall forcing her eyes into each room. She felt as if something was trailing her, matching her footsteps, stopping when she stopped, stealing out of sight each time she turned to glance over her shoulder. She would have sworn on a bible that she could hear something--Something shuffling along behind her. She ran back to the landing.

She sank to the floor, her limbs bending in ways they were not meant to. She gazed straight ahead into Cory's empty bedroom. She flopped her head back, all at once squinting from the bright overhead lights. She kicked her feet out from under her like a starved fish hitting the bait, scrambling to a stand, instantaneously remembering why all the lights were on.

Cold air seemed to hiss and coil, shooting out from everywhere, surrounding her as if she was suddenly under attack. She shook head to foot, jarring sideways and knocking into the railing. Her flesh chilled and goose bumped like she had been sitting cross-legged for hours in the throes of a blizzard wearing nothing but a swimsuit. She grabbed onto the wood of the banister, her hand slipping off and slapping into her thigh. The wood felt wet and gooey like it had been gobbed over with slime.

She doubled herself in half, blowing and gulping in breaths that seemed robbed of oxygen. Her head spun making the air seem like it was waving and forming whitecaps. She clung onto the backs of her knees with her hands, shoving and forcing her toothpick-like legs to take step after step down the length of the hall.

Another bout of cold shivers hit, zoning in on her shoulder blades, digging and biting. She let go of her legs about facing, racing back the three feet she had come.

She gave herself a shake, like a dog coming into the house from a cold pelting rainstorm. "This is silly," she said. "I am not scared." Her thoughts sling shot around in her head as she relived the past few minutes frame by frame in the deafening silence. "Yes I am," she whispered. She twisted her hands together wringing out her palms.

She shot a look over each shoulder glancing up and down the hall. Her breath echoed in her eardrums making it sound off key and hollow, like it was coming from somebody directly behind her. She jumped sideways. Her legs started to shake, knocking her knees together. They seemed to bang and thump, clacking almost rhythmically, like a drum beat. She jumped again. The hair on her arms rose and stood, pricking right through and out the other side of her robe. Her tongue felt like heavy rubber. She peered up and down the hall shooting another look over her shoulder. She started to hum.

Something inside the wall rustled. Julie's eyes bulged like hot water slopped on a dry sponge. She bolted. All of a sudden finding herself four feet from where she had been standing. Something snapped behind her. Her legs rubberized, swaying her weight back and forth like a rowboat caught up in a tide. She couldn't move.

An earth-shattering crack rocked the hallway, reverberating and bouncing back and forth, echoing down the staircase in a high-pitched squeal. The wall exploded. Erupting like a detonated landmine, spewing, hurling bite size particles of debris through the air in a thunderclap that collapsed and folded back into itself, shaking and rattling the ceiling and walls. A stench steamed and funnelled, clinging to the underside of the dust-laden particles.

Julie's ears popped and rang. She was blanketed in white. Her eyes stung and burned. She instinctually shut them rubbing with the heel of her palms.

Hands snapped from the hole like a cyclone ripping a house from its foundation. They snatched her throat, whipping her backwards, slapping her into the wall and knocking the wind from her. Snarled fingers closed on her neck, anchoring twisted razor sharp nails deep in her flesh, digging, rupturing, and slashing, like she was a fish about to be flayed alive for dinner. Blood sprouted, streaming down her neck. She opened her mouth, screaming a silent scream, smashing her tongue into the back of her bottom teeth. Her feet left the floor as it hauled and dragged her body up the wall.

"J ... U ... L ... I ...E," the gravel filled voice cooed. "A ... T ... L ... A ... S ... T ... W... E ... M ... E ... E ... T ...A ... G ... A ... I ... N."

It bent its head flipping the point of its black tongue on and off her neck just under her ear, like a snake taste testing its meal. It smiled a toxic grin she could not see, puking out thick green mucus from between its decayed fang-like teeth. It snuggled its face dog like into the nape of her neck, all at once biting down hard, shearing off a strip of her skin.

She found her voice and screamed and screamed and screamed.

It threw its head back, tilting up its blood soaked chin, chewing with its mouth open, dropping miniature pieces of her own flesh into her hair. It gulped, swallowing, smacking its lips in a puck sound, running its tongue back and forth scooping up her blood from its face.

"I can't decide," it whispered against her ear. "Should I eat you up all at once, or take it slow and easy, piece by piece?" It gurgled, and then laughed the laughter of death. "Or," it paused rolling its black tongue back and forth in her red blood. "Or," it continued. "Should I take back what is rightly mine?" It growled wolf like baring its teeth.

Julie's screams shrilled, lapsing into high-pitched non-stop squeaks. She bent her knees slamming the soles of her slippers into the wall, lifting off, and kicking wildly, bouncing her body side to side. She clawed her fingernails up its forearms peeling the rotten flesh off in layers.

It smiled, amused. "You ... Want ... To ... Play ... Do ... You?" it said.

Julie opened and closed her mouth in screams she could not hear.

It bent its head burrowing into the other side of her neck, clamping its fangs deep into her flesh, sucking and sniffing up the rich ripe red juices, leaving vampire like punctures. It licked at the holes smearing them with a green mucus overlay. It snapped its fangs into a flab of skin jerking its head sideways, tearing off a huge band of flesh. It made a popping whishing noise as it ripped free. Her neck bubbled and hissed in wet warmth. It chewed slow and deliberate, relishing and savouring her flavour. But there was more. Lots more. It grinned.

Julie twisted her body, banging her feet and hands against the wall moving herself up and down. Her hand brushed over a hard bump in her robe pocket. Without thought her fingers dug and grasped. She threw her hands over her head firing the thirty-five-auto upside down-- Unloading two rounds.

There was a horrendous sound, kind of like a balloon full of water smacking down onto the top of a car roof.

She dropped like dead weight to the floor.

She looked up. It was an unimaginable horror. Her mouth went through the motions of a shriek. The wall and ceiling were spattered and clumped in chunks, of what looked like hairy stewing beef doused over in blood red gravy. Its upper body protruded from the wall cavity like someone had rammed it through headfirst from the opposite side. It was slumped over to one edge, head down, arms dangling. The few tuffs of hair that remained saturated with a thick black blood that dripped profusely off the bridge of its nose. Two black-red rivers raged and surged down its face from its forehead, where the bullets had entered and blown clear through its skull.

She watched as its fingers twitched, curling slowly in and out. She felt nothing. Its lips parted as its lungs made a leaden whiff noise the word 'm ... o ... m ... m ... y,' in a little boy voice, escaping through its mouth as it stilled and started to grow cold.

The room faded in and out, flipping back and forth from light to dark, dark to light. Julie's heart stopped beating. Her eyes blew from their sockets. Cory lie dead, his upper body protruding from the hole where the thing had been. He was slumped to one side; his little arms dangling free and loose. The top of his head was blown off. The walls and the ceiling spattered and clustered with brown hair chunks, off white bone fragments, gray mushy worm like goo, and deep red blood like syrup.

Her mouth opened in guttural scream after scream, like an animal being tortured to death. The red syrup started to run down the walls and drip from the ceiling.

"C ... O ... R ... Y!" Julie screamed. "NO...NO..." She smashed her chest with her fists. "NO," she wailed. She got up on her hands and knees crawling over to the wall. She pulled herself to a stand lunging at her dead little boy, wrapping her arms around him. She grabbed and jerked at his body, pulling and tugging. She could not pry him loose.

She lovingly stroked his face, wiping the blood from his eyes. She cuddled him close spitting saliva onto her hand and combing what was left of his hair through her fingers, trying to arrange it. She slumped against the blood soaked wall crying, screaming, and howling. Her voice echoed through the empty house changing in tone and pitch as if mocking her. She clung to her dead son, her throat swollen with screams. She held his hand in hers rubbing it back and forth on her cheek whispering to him, telling him how much she loved him. She stared up at the ceiling and walls stretching out that frayed tightrope she had been walking back and forth on, for far too long. Pulling it taut, snapping it, scattering her sanity into a million pieces.

Julie was no more.

She smiled looking at her son, giving new meaning to the phrase, 'The lights are on but nobody's home.' She jumped and bounced up at the walls, scooping up chunks of hair and bone and brain, collecting it in her hands, giggling and laughing to herself like she was on an 'Easter' egg hunt.

"Cor," she said. She opened her cupped hands in front of his face. "Look what I got. Mommy's going to fix you all up. You will see honey. Everything's going to be all right." She carefully sorted through the pieces placing them gently back into his head, patting them in place with her hands.

She waited. Nothing happened. She slumped onto the floor, stretching out and rolling her body down the hall, first one way and then the other, figuring these kind of things could take a bit of time. If need be she would fetch an extension cord in a while and plug him in. It worked with the battery charger. It would work with him.

She snaked her way over to the wall, bumping her butt up tight against it. She chuckled to herself, putting her legs vertical like two walking sticks, laying her back flat.

The wall above her feet suddenly moaned and squealed like someone clawing fingernails across a blackboard. The plaster made an enormous popping noise, all at once blowing. Erupting and spitting, huffing out white expulsion in every direction. It swept inside her mouth clinging to her tongue, turning her saliva into thick cement like paste. She choked and sputtered, her airways all at once shrinking, narrowing, clogging. Her body stilled as the massive dust storm settled, concealing her one end to the other in a silken white veil of death.

Hands ejected like lightening, grabbing, twisting, stealing round both her ankles, anchoring and embedding scalpel sharp claws deep through her flesh. The tip of one poked right through and out the other side of her ankle playing a gory game of peek-a-boo, 'Now you see me ... Now you don't,' as it drew in and out. Blood geysers bubbled, spurted, shooting up and then down. She lifted from the floor.

She hung upside down, gagging, coughing up miniature marshmallow like morsels. She opened her mouth, gasping, hauling in laboured breaths. Her head swam in dizzy circles. She vomited. It slid from her upper lip, setting up camp in her ears.

Her bathrobe had folded neatly in half, doubling over, obscuring her vision. She squirmed, flopping her elbows, groping blindly with entangled hands. Her heart thundered inside her head deafening her. Her robe clung onto her face, staying up close and personal, as if mulling over the pros and cons of suffocating her.

"You ... Didn't ... Think ... You ... Were ... Going ... To ... Get ... Away ... That ... Easy?" It drawled out the words injecting a southern accent. "N ... O ... W ... D ... I ... D ... Y ... O ... U?" it shouted.

It heaved her up the wall, hand over fist, slashing her as it went. Turning her into fresh as it comes pulped mincemeat.

It stopped when it reached her knees, flaring its nostrils, sniffing and snuffing like one of the three little pigs about to dine on roast beef. It opened its mouth, tonguing her flesh fly-like. Thick droplets of pea green slime gobbed and cemented into her skin, splattering and burning holes like battery acid.

"Hum ... I can smell tasty treats!" it said. It smacked its lips. "That's a good girl." It rolled its tongue propelling it through its lips, whipping it side to side. "Such a good girl ... That's it! ... Keep-A-coming ... So ...you can get ate all up!" It howled and squealed, drooling and smacking its lips together like it could not wait to get at her.

She could hear it. She could hear each and every word. But, that was all she was left to. Hearing words. Words, that held no meaning. She was far past the other side of no return. She burst into a hysterical bout of laughter as it resumed pulling her upwards.

Rancid goo seeped from the corners of its mouth, steaming as it hit the air, rupturing and peeling its skin. Pus riddled, grape-like bulbs popped, bursting open, spattering blood-black muck over the sides of its face. It drew its tongue in and out of its mouth swiping the tip back and forth across the crotch of her pajama bottoms.

It shifted her, grasping her ankles in one hand, turning the other palm side up, inserting its index finger claw up through the center of her robe, slicing it in two. It held its middle finger to her face. "Would you like one or," it paused unfolding it's index finger, placing it adjacent. "Or ...Two?" it said.

There was no answer.

It did not figure on one. It gave her a swift jerk, dipped its face between her legs sinking in its fangs, biting down hard, turning her baby pink pj's a dark deep red. "Hum ... Going to have good eating treats tonight," it said.

The microscopic particle of sanity that had tucked and hidden its self away in case of emergency picked up the axe and swung it at the glass, breaking it, diving in head first. It tunnelled deep inside her core, striking and sparking at her electrodes. They hummed, then fired, fusing into one solid mass releasing the code. The one and the only. Old as time itself. 'Kill or be Killed!'

Her eyes glowed; ringing with florescent blue light that spawned the fear of death. She jabbed, tearing at the robe releasing and freeing her arms and hands. She swiped at the floor, cool air whiffed through her outstretched fingers. She humped up her back, bracing her palms into the flat of the wall, slamming her thighs together in a loud thunderclap that ground its head jarring it loose.

It drew back its blood soaked face. Its half-cocked amusement glinting across its amber eyes. It grinned stretching its lips back from its ragged teeth. It pulled the bottom edge of her pajamas taut, biting down and through, whipping its head back and forth, slashing the material open, exposing more and more bare leg as it went.

She bucked against the wall, smashing her hands against it like lift off levers.

"It won't hurt ... After awhile," it whispered. It moved the material from between her legs, opening its carnivorous mouth wide and full, gorging its tongue with blood, rolling and folding it over into a stiff dagger sharp suction tube.

Julie all at once stilled, lying like a limp dishrag, free and easy within its grasp.

"What a good little girl ... That's more like it," it said.

She walked her fingertips across her chest running them back and forth over the edge of her upside down pocket, making them all at once disappear. She lifted her head, bringing her back off the wall, snapping and baring her teeth, sitting herself vertical, stretching out her arms. She fired the thirty-five into its face.

It made a dull heavy whoosh, like a tire suddenly going flat.

She dropped to the floor.

She did not look up. She did not need to. The river of blackish red streaming down the wall was all the verification required.

She pushed her body with her toes, slithering on her stomach like a snake into the bathroom, locking the door.

She did not look back. She did not even pass go and collect her 'Two Hundred Dollars.'

Too Bad ...

If she had ... She would have been privy, through the pride of ownership program, to the matching set of macabre bookends. Both her sons lay dead. Projecting from giant size holes in the hall walls. Barely four feet apart. Their flesh torn and thrashed, pieces of their hides embedded in the tattered raw plaster edges. One was slumped to the right, the other to the left. Their small arms dangled free and loose, blood dripping from every fingertip, pooling in the carpeting like watered down red mud cakes. The only major difference ... The smallest was missing the top of his head, the biggest his face. The words inexplicably horrid would not have even come close to doing it justice.

She curled up inside the bathtub tucking herself into a small neat little ball. She pivoted back and forth like a plastic toy rocking horse. She sang 'Bram's' lullaby softly to herself. She thought about sucking her thumb, and then did.

Something scratched and scuffed at the door. She popped her thumb from her mouth. It scratched again. She crawled from the tub to the floor, laying out flat on her stomach, eye balling the crack between the floor and wood. Four furry feet pranced and danced back and forth. Two feet disappeared leaving two to carry on the waltz. The back of the door thumped. She grinned. Someone's dog wanted in. She opened the door. Shutting and locking it, getting back inside the tub. She tapped her fingers, motioning for the dog to come and join her. It did.

She drew up her knees, wrapping her arms around, resting her chin, beaming at the dog. It reminded her of one she'd once had. She dipped her head rolling her eyes across the I.D. tag dangling from its collar. "Barkley," she whispered. She grinned. It even had the same name.

She reached out her hand. It growled. She tried again. It showed teeth. She brought her feet up under her, coming to a stand. It uttered a low moaning growl, bristling its hackles. She backed. It stepped forward.

Her back was flush against the tiles. She had nowhere to go.

"Come ... On ... Now ... Doggy," she said softly. "I won't hurt you." The dog sought her eyes and glared. It did not move so much as a muscle, as if waiting for something.

She glued herself to the tiled wall. It pulled its lips from its teeth. Her eyes widened. It looked as if it was grinning at her. It took a step forward. Its eyes whirled like a kaleidoscope, stopping on blood streaked amber. All the hair on its body raised, standing erect like summoned to attention. It more so resembled a mutated form of porcupine than dog.

Horror rippled across her brow as it opened its mouth, which suddenly looked like a wide, deep, dark, endless cavern. It spewed out a yipping rumble that grew into thunderous proportions, filling the air-space between them, binding them together with the stench of decaying road kill laying along a curb on the turn pike to hell.

She stiffened, freezing.

It backed, then hunched. Its right hind paw knocked the cold water tap, turning it on as it sprang forward, jumping, and hurdling through the air. Gunning straight for her. It flew as if weightless, landing on her chest. She smashed at it knocking it into the tub. It slid, flipping onto its side losing its footing on the wet enamel. It rolled gaining its feet, lunging, springing, into the air, connecting to target. Its canines sank deep into her throat.

She criss-crossed her arms clamping her hands onto her wrists, rapidly jerking up, batting it off. She wrapped her hands around her neck. Blood spurted in little bursts from between her fingers staining her hands beet red. Her head spun. Her legs shook and wobbled. She bashed against the wall, her body collapsing to sit on the tub edge. She wound a bath towel around her neck knotting it in place.

It lurched again, hitting her full force. She went down. It climbed on top of her, lifting its head and blowing out long eerie sounding howls as if in undisputed victory. Greenish drool seeped from the corners of its black rimmed mouth, splashing as it landed. Adding a whimsical touch of green slime dollops to the abstract white and blood red towel wound round her neck.

She raised her knees banging them hard against it, knocking it from her torso into her face. She kicked her feet up under its backside booting it up and over, hurling it off her.

She struggled to her feet.

It circled closing in, attacking, tearing, and ripping at her legs. She grabbed the towel rack, folding her arms through, holding herself upright.

It backed, and then sprang. She dipped into a crouch, ducking her head down between her knees. It flew over top, smashing into the back wall. It sprang again. She fumbled with her pocket grasping the thirty-five, tilting it straight up, firing once, catching its chest dead center. It thudded down on top of her, dropping like a stone. Its head slammed off the side of the tub, splitting open, knocking one eye free from its socket. She dumped the thing off her, shoving it far up the other end of the tub, unknowingly blocking the drain. The water bubbled and foamed, collecting in little waves and swirls, bouncing the eyeball back and forth. The frigid waters turned a soft sultry pink, then a deep wine red as the dog-like thing bled out.

She sat in the tub. In the cold blood stained water with the floating eyeball bath bead. Devoid of all thought. The lights in her eyes dull and frayed. She hung her head.

The bathroom door thunder-clapped; Reverberating in earth shattering quakes and snaps as it scattered to pieces. The hinges contorted and bent, crying out in high-pitched squeals as they ripped free, twisting and turning into malformed metal ribbons. They slung shot, bouncing and pinging, hitting the tiled floor, up-ending in the corners.

She gasped, her chest heaving, struggling to breathe. The knotted towel was torn from her neck and replaced by fingers that wrapped and dug, closing off her throat. She hung upright, her feet swinging blindly back and forth in the air. Its face ... Its hideous ruptured face, in hers, taunting, mocking in a way indefinable in words.

She opened her mouth huffing and panting, hurdling screams encased in little red bubbles through the air.

"You've played so hard to get," it said. "It could have been so much simpler ... Don't you think?" It turned her round in its hands, examining her. "No matter ... I got you now. Or, what is left of you, I should say." It laughed aloud, widening its round amber eyes sucking them out and in.

Her voice shrilled and stopped. Her mouth gaping and silent as if plaster cast in place. Her chest lifted and shook, rattling like a tin can kicked across pavement. Blood coated and streamed down the inside walls of her throat, forging ahead into her lungs. Her face paled, turning a ghastly ghost gray, almost identical in colour to the wide bands within her hair. Her brow etched into deep furrows, laying insanity and horror on top of one another like good bedfellows. She was like a mixed bag of tricks with no bag.

It held her at arm's length.

Her eyes pivoted back and forth not seeing, rolling up inside her head and staying.

"Now, now there," it said. "Daddy will make it all better. Just like Daddy used too." It gave her a shake.

Her head flopped to one side, bouncing on her neck as if nodding.

Her right hand sneaked out from her pocket. She whirled the thirty-five through the air like an expert baton twirler, right siding it, firing it off just under its chin. Its bottom jaw spattered the wall.

She did not drop.

It contorted its face, writhing, twisting, and turning what was left of its upper jaw. It belted out a laugh that hissed and gurgled up through its nostrils. It shifted her to one hand, swiping the wall with the other, gathering up the jello like blue-gray lumps and blackish muck, gobbling, shovelling, and tucking it against the roof of its mouth. The goop wiggled shaking up and down, side to side, stretching and expanding like warmed up 'play dough' drawing out and reforming a bottom jaw. It worked its mouth snapping and popping it, like it had been seized and in need of oiling. It drew its lips taut showing off its fangs, offering her up the omen of things to come.

It made a scoffing noise deep in its throat. "I'm growing tired of this crap!" It stretched out its free arm, growing it, tripling the length, curving and wrapping it round and round her chest, tightening and squeezing until two of her ribs cried out with loud crisp snaps. "Snap! ... Crackle! ... Pop," it hissed.

Her breath whiffed in short bursts.

It smacked its lips together. "I was mulling over going easy on you," it said. It pushed its lips out, then sucked them back, pushed them out, then smacked them together. "While you were still alive, that is." It opened its mouth, darting its tongue back and forth over its chin. "But ... My precious little girly ... Now I don't know." It slipped its hand between her legs stroking her with its fingers. "Dessert before the main course?" It opened its mouth wide, making a sucking popping sound, slapping and flipping its tongue off and on the roof of its mouth.

She screamed and screamed and screamed. They were full and long and shrill, the kind that pitched on forever. Her life flashed and played possum, reflecting back at her through the pair of round blood tainted amber eyes before her. She screamed again. And again and again.

It squeezed her throat off, ramming her feet down into the tub, forcing her to turn, pushing her head down, bending her over.

Her hands splashed down into the water, knocking together as they hit hard at the bottom of the tub. Blood sprouted and poured from her nostrils. Her lungs drew and sucked back air, all at once inflating.

"That's' a good little girl. Bend over nice. Just, like daddy taught you." It ripped her pajama bottoms free. They floated down into the frigid water, drifting back and forth on the surface, all at once sinking like a rock. "You can never win with me, little girl. I told you that when I first started doing you, at six. And I'll tell you that now. You cannot win. You're mine. You always were. You always will be." It hissed, growling and wailing, howling and chanting like a demonic entity about to sacrifice the lamb in front of the unholy one.

She giggled a little girl's laughter, shifting her weight, spreading her legs wide, propping her butt tight into it. She wiggled back and forth, lifting one hand from the water, pressing the other flat to the tub base.

It grabbed her hips, ripping, tearing, and clawing her flesh into ribbons, bending at the knee, preparing to mount and reap its' just desserts.

She rammed the thirty-five into her temple. "No ... I win," she said triumphantly. She pulled the trigger.

Tony popped the driver's door open, leaving the car running. He sauntered along the stone walkway towards the front door, throwing his half-eaten chicken ball in under the pine shrubbery. He turned the knob. It was locked.

"GOD DAMN IT!" he howled. He punched the front door with his fist. He yanked the keys from the ignition, retraced his steps, stopping at the garage and peering in through the window. He unlocked the front door and stepped in.

The house was still, silent. Silence like the type one found in old abandoned houses. He strolled through the bottom of the house returning to the base of the stairs. He grabbed onto the banister post swaying his body back and forth.

"JULES!" he screamed. "JULES?" he questioned." JULES!" he bellowed.

There was not even a pin-drop.

He swung himself around in a semicircle, bumping up onto the first stair step. He cupped his hands into a make shift blow horn. "YOU GOD DAMN FUCKING BITCH! ... ANSWER ME WHEN I FUCKING CALL YOU! ... ANSWER ME, YOU FUCKING GOOD FOR NOTHING CUNT! ... I, FUCKING KNOW YOU'RE HERE! ... I'D CUT THE FUCKING CRAP IF I WERE YOU! ... I KNOW YOU'RE FUCKING HERE YOU WHORE! ... YOUR FUCKING CAR IS IN THE GARAGE AND THE KID'S BIKES ARE ALL OVER THE DRIVE! ... AGAIN! ... QUIT WITH THE FUCKING BULLSHIT GAMES! ... I WANT TO TALK TO YOU!" He strained, listening.

There was nothing.

"WHATEVER THEN, JULES! ... JUST FUCK OFF AND DIE!"

He slammed the door behind him, sauntering back towards the car. "God damn fucking good for nothing whoring bitch," he muttered." I fucking wonder, what fucking damn fucking excuse she'll fucking use this fucking time?" He mimicked her pitching his voice, ruffling his shoulders, swaying his hips girl like, holding up his one hand flipping it daintily to and fro from his wrist. "I didn't hear you ... or ... I was upstairs ... or ... I was in the tub." He backed out of the drive, pointing the car into the beautiful crimson red sunset.

The kitchen light fixture had long been dripping. Soon it would let go crashing down to the floor, leaving a gaping hole in the ceiling where the coloured frigid water could whirlpool and transcend into a rampaging torrent, thundering down into the kitchen, splashing, churning, and up ending all in its path, coating all a beautiful crimson red too.

Epilogue

Approximately one in three women is a victim of domestic abuse.

With abuse, living inside a nightmare is a daily occurrence. Only when one is able to look back does the realization of how unbelievably scary it was, set in. And this ... In itself ... is more terrifying than anything, to realize that this kind of life was commonplace.

May each day that passes find more women looking back at the terror than are still living with it.

A note from the author

When all is said and done...

The one thing we will always have to hold on to is our memories.

May yours be full of joy.

Sincerely

Ina Louise Jackson

THE DREAM

[An excerpt from The Peep Show by Ina Louise Jackson.
Fall 2013]

It is what you do not hear that matters...

"What do you see?" Its three voices blended as one, female, male, and male all distinctive, yet together, raspy, inhuman, terrifying in an indefinable way.

His gaze lifted from the back of the recliner where it sat, its head and shoulders miles above the pillowed leather headrest, dwarfing it.

His eyes drew across the window. Nothing but total complete blackness, no streetlights, no illuminated houses, nothing. Even the dim room lighting offered up nothing. No reflections in the glass, no outline, no form, no profile of what sat in the chair. He wanted to step forward, come closer but unadulterated fright had frozen his limbs, rendering him but a darkened gray statue figure of the night.

"What do you see?" it asked again.

Once more, his eyes traced the windowpane. "Nothing," he muttered.

It laughed hysterically.

"What is your name?" he asked the tone of his voice two octaves higher than it should have been. He tried to clear his throat, failing, croaking like a frog.

"Name, name, name ... They're all the same ... Plain Jane ... What's in a name?" It responded brashly.

"What is your name?" he asked again.

"Ching-chang, walla-walla bing-bang," it sang smugly.

"Tell me your name."

"Banana fana fo fana, fee fi mo manna ... N ... a ... n ... a" it answered quickly.

"What is your name?"

"Paddy cake ... Paddy cake ... Bakers man ... Make me a cake as fast as you can."

It all of a sudden raised its right hand, pointing the index finger, swaying its shoulders. Babies began crying, soft and gentle. It raised its left arm, suddenly dipping its head up and down as if signalling to begin. All at once the tempo of the whimpers picked up. Others joined newborns, older babies, young children, and older children. It flicked its wrists back and forth extending the index fingers as if conducting an orchestra as the sobs intensified, strengthened, turned to screams.

His breaths came harder, faster.

In an instant the screams halted. And it was there. Right there in front of his face. Hunkered down. Its massive, orb like, black onyx eyes staring right through him.

Warm urine spread out in a butterfly pattern across his crotch.

"What is your name?" it asked mockingly. It cackled like a hyena. "Colton; it's time to wake up now," it whispered.

The Peep Show by Ina Louise Jackson. Coming Fall 2013.

www.pinelakebooks.ca

www.pinelakebooks.org